REASON TO STAY

THE MCINTOSH RIDGE SERIES

DENISE DEMARCO

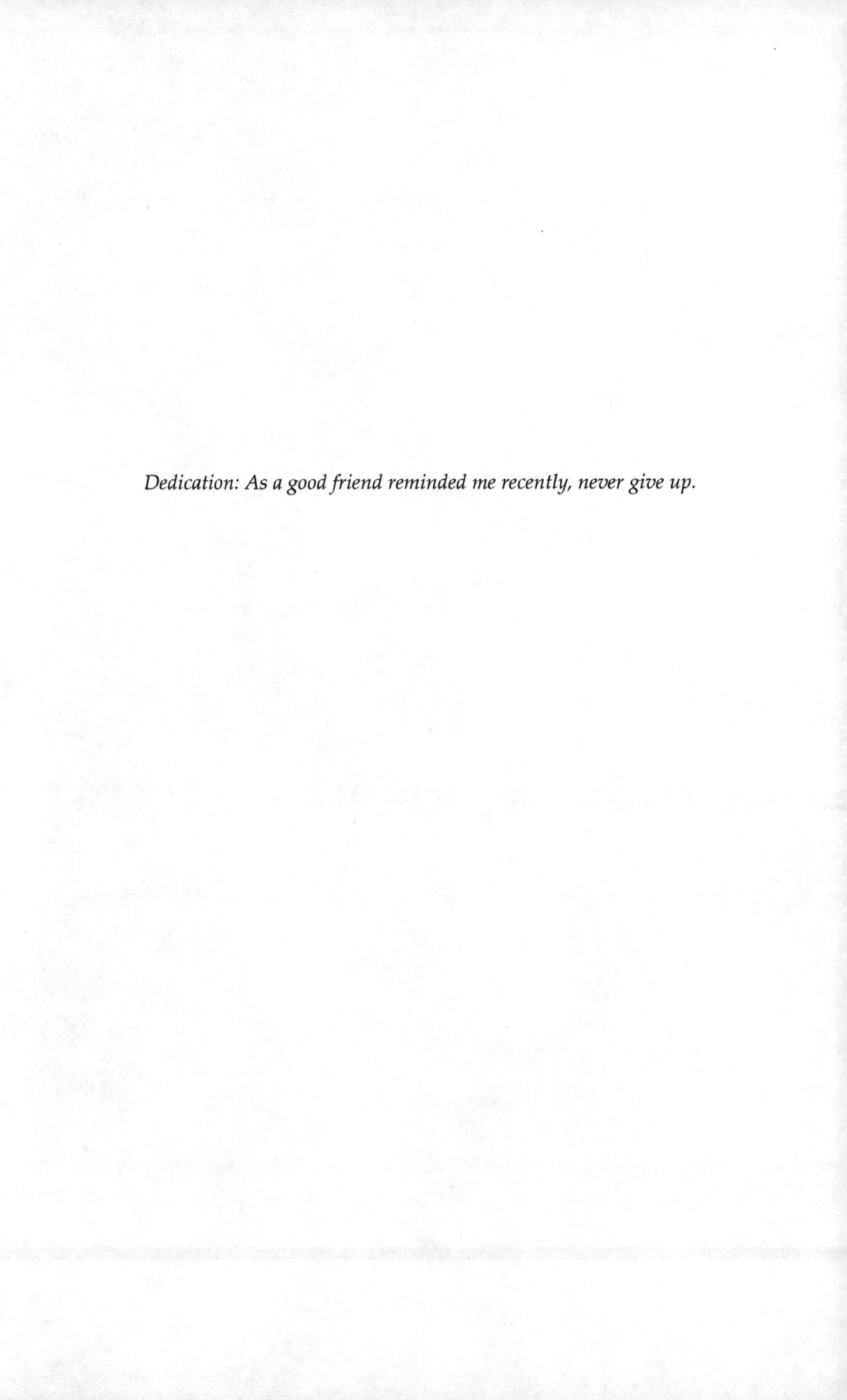

Dedication: As a good friend reminded me recently, never give up.

CHAPTER 1
REBECCA

"COME ON, Rebecca, don't be that way." Kyle's voice is wheedling, almost whiny, which isn't going to gain him any traction with me. It's bad enough I have to deal with him here in the store. There's no way I'm voluntarily getting together with him outside the store. It would feel great to tell him that, but as a businesswoman, it's not a good move.

I settle for pointing out the obvious. "The store's busy today, and I don't have time to talk."

Kyle Mulvaney is nothing if not oblivious to rejection; rather than graciously accepting my refusal of his invitation to dinner, he doubles down. "Dinner can include after-dinner drinks and even breakfast in the morning, if you play your cards right."

In case I didn't understand his insinuation, he leers at me in a disgustingly obvious way. It would be comical if it wasn't so gross.

A tension headache keeps building behind my eyes. Why do so many men persist in thinking women want their uninvited attentions? Owning a business requires me to behave professionally at my workplace, including displaying polite smiles and courteous behavior almost all the time.

That doesn't include tolerating harassment. Not that skimpy clothing justifies harassment, but I don't wear that *just in case*. Yes, when the weather is hot, I sometimes wear shorts and T-shirts or tank tops, but nothing inappropriate. My place of work is a hardware store, for heaven's sake. I can't very well tromp around in pencil skirts, delicate blouses, and high heels. Usually, I wear a Spencer Hardware branded polo or T-shirt and jeans when working. Oh, and an- oh-so-stylish blue carpenter's apron tied around my hips. The malfunctioning central air conditioning unit has me wearing shorts in the store today, but needs must and all that. Even now, it's not like I have on Daisy Dukes and a bikini top.

I take a (hopefully) calming breath and mentally count to five. During the pause, I remind myself that I'm still relatively new at being the owner and operator of the family business. Even though I've spent years and years of my life working for the company in some way or another, the full responsibility is a heavy one and is now planted directly on my shoulders. It's my birthright and a privilege, but it's also a lot of pressure.

It doesn't take an expensive education to know that it isn't good business to alienate another business owner. No matter my personal feelings about Kyle, the fact remains that he's part-owner of several good-sized apartment complexes in the area. Apartment complexes that consistently require supplies my business can and does provide.

I try to ratchet down the tension between Kyle and me. I manage to keep some of my exasperation out of my voice – but not all of it. At this point, Kyle Mulvaney isn't treating me like a professional – like a business owner – so why am I so worried about acting like a perfect one? We don't have to be friends, just cordial enough to conduct business.

"Look, Kyle, I appreciate your business. I do. But that doesn't mean we're going on a date at any time of day this weekend, or next weekend, or any weekend. Like I said, thanks for the invitation, but no."

"I also want to get your opinions about restoring the new development instead of just renovating it."

I can't stop myself from hesitating because of that statement's allure. "Restoring it to what, exactly?"

"I don't know, exactly," Kyle admits. "A couple of the buildings have some old stuff in them. If you have a look, you can probably figure it out."

Knowing Kyle, he isn't giving any details because he's making it up. He must know I'm interested in restoration and wants my attention.

Be professional.

"I'm sure it's not going to be difficult to figure it out. Check your deed and property inspection paperwork to see when it was built, and that's probably enough to tell you what you want to know."

"Maybe." He sidles closer to me again. "But after I find that out, I need to know what's involved in restoring it."

"If you decide you want to do any type of restoration, you'll need an architect to render plans," I take several steps away from him, restoring the distance he'd cut – that's the only restoration I am willing to participate in that has to do with Kyle. "You might simply want to use paint colors and finishes reminiscent of the era you want to recapture."

Kyle looks way too pleased with himself. "Excellent. You can guide me about that."

"I'm not taking on any new projects. Sorry." *Definitely not sorry.*

Instead of waiting for him to reply or comment, I raise my voice and call over to Dave who's restocking small bottles of adhesives on the other side of the archway that leads into the main part of the store. "Dave, take over the register. I need to check on something."

"Sure, boss. You got it," Dave responds. He's young and easy-going, but he handles the register like a pro after six months working in the store.

"Thanks," I ignore Kyle, who is *still* standing on the other side of the counter like he is waiting for me to say something else to him. Biting my tongue against telling him off, I turn on my heel and walk calmly to the end of the counter where the door marked EMPLOYEES provides an entrance to the warehouse. I push through it, and simultaneously unclip the small radio from my belt. With the button on the side of the unit pressed down, I notify the staff. "I'll be in the warehouse if anyone needs me."

Behind me, I hear Kyle raising his voice even more to try and catch my attention. "Hey, we didn't set a time for our date!"

The door closes behind me and silences him. It's not like I think he's going to come through it, but I turn the lock anyway because it feels like I'm saying "so there", which is probably petty, but still satisfying. My work boots make a thudding sound on the concrete floor, because I'm stomping.

What can I say? It feels good.

At least the temperature in the warehouse is cooler than in the store. The part the HVAC guy needs so he can fix the cooling system is on backorder, but it's finally due to arrive in the next few days. Hopefully I won't melt by then. It didn't make sense to figure out where to install through-the-wall air conditioners or how to ventilate standing units when the problem would be resolved in a reasonable length of time.

Too bad the weather is being so unreasonably hot.

"Great timing," Mike comments as he hoists another box onto the top of the stack he already built. "The lumber delivery is confirmed for tomorrow."

"That's one good thing today."

I hear how grouchy I still sound, but I still don't care, although now the lack of concern is for a different reason. Mike is one of the very few people in front of whom I can comfortably grumble. I've known him most of my life, since we first met in Miss Cooperman's third-grade classroom. He's worked at least part-time for Spencer's Hardware since he was old enough to have a job. It surprises me that he still works here, even only part -time again, when he has a profitable graphic design business. He insists he has to do something that doesn't involve sitting all the time. It seems to me he could get a standing desk and solve that problem... but what do I know? And anyway, it's good to have a friend in the store whenever he works.

It took years to make my parents understand that there would never be anything romantic between me and Mike. Ours is a solid friendship but there is no *spark*. Life would have been easier if there had been even a tiny flicker of *something* between us , but an experimental kiss a few months before high school graduation confirmed for us both that we're always going to live in one another's friend zones.

"Want to share?" Mike asks, looking away from me and continuing to stack inventory.

"Not particularly."

I pull the clipboard off its hook on the wall near him. Clipboards and lists, I understand. Most men, I really do *not* understand. "I look okay, I guess, but I'm not Helen of Troy or some other great beauty. My business does well, but it's not some billion dollar Empire. And no is no." There's no mirror nearby to check, but I feel my own scowl scrunch my face. "The whole pushy guys thing is ridiculous and annoying."

I don't bother adding that the unwelcome attention can also be embarrassing, uncomfortable, and frustrating at times. It isn't that I don't enjoy some witty banter or flirtation. But there is definitely a difference between that and harassment.

It'd be nice if more guys understood that.

My mouth starts sharing details without permission from my brain. "Kyle again. And this time he tacked on an ask about period-accurate work on the project his company has going near the border with Eagle's Landing."

"Since when does he do extra detail work like that?"

Mike's voice drips sarcasm. "From what I know, his company builds simple and straight to the point, minimal bells and whistles."

Mike's skepticism is weirdly satisfying, probably because it validates my own. I knew I wasn't being a petty bitch after all. "Right? My thoughts exactly. He doesn't put extra effort into things. He does finishes barely good enough to be one step above cheap. Flash but no substance. Just like him."

CHAPTER 2
SAM

I BET the old man would've claimed he did me a favor by waiting until I had my twenty years in before he finally did the world a favor and dropped dead. For those two decades, the missions gave me peace and purpose. Some people thought being a SEAL was the polar opposite of a peaceful career, but to me, it made perfect sense.

I'm not looking to get all philosophical and shit, but my purpose was to "train for war and fight to win" and "defend those who are unable to defend themselves." Fulfilling that purpose the best I possibly could gave me a calm focus unlike anything else. There was no peace, calm, or purpose to be found at Hidden Haven.

Just about the first thing I did when I arrived at the property was knock down the interlocking H's on the posts marking the entrance to the driveway. The only thing ever hidden there, at least during the lifetime of my *father*, were abuse and suffering, and the place was only a haven for misery.

McIntosh Ridge wasn't a big city where people simply got lost in the shuffle. No. It was a small town where people just chose to ignore that which wasn't comfortable to deal with. So what if a woman and her child paid the price.

Bottom line was I didn't train relentlessly, and beyond all reasonable expectations, for a small-town existence that was the very definition of ordinary. It was boring. Brain-numbing. Total bullshit. My destiny is on foreign shores, across turbulent waters, and accomplished by stealth in the dark of night. I accepted a job at a private security firm on Long Island that at least had some appeal; they even dealt with international clients of all types, which potentially put those foreign shores in my operational sphere again.

And then the lawyer tracked me down.

Now here I stand, trapped in McIntosh Ridge, a painfully ordinary town in upstate New York, waiting in line like a dumbass to buy nails and wood and other supplies to fix the roof, too many walls, and a host of other problems. All under the blazing sun. I'm not stationed in the sandbox anymore, but I'm still sweating like an animal.

I probably look as grim as I feel, and it doesn't matter, because there's no escaping the truth of it. There's no escaping this personal mission, either. Not in good conscience. I couldn't save my mother from Parker, but I can save her property from his worthless relatives. I can defy him even now that the old man is dead. That'd piss him off. I couldn't stop the derisive sound that comes out like a snort. The guy in front of me glanced over his shoulder quickly, then swiveled his head back to the front just as fast.

Yeah, mind your own business.

Some other guy further back in the line muttered to himself in discontent, obviously annoyed. I get it. Standing here feels like such a waste of time, but I have to get things done on the property so I can leave the house and the town, again. Do what I have to do with it and escape, that's the goal. Even the darkest parts of the world are a better fit for me than the Ridge.

It's as hot in the store as it is outside. Sweat runs down the back of my neck and under my shirt. What kind of crappy hardware store has broken air conditioning, and a ceiling fan so poorly hung that it clangs and scrapes every third rotation? The floor tiles are scuffed and chipped, peeling in places. The ceiling is stained. The display racks in my field of vision look old. But the shelves are well-stocked. Inventory doesn't appear to be old, which indicates that business was good. I rotate my head and neck to release some tension and remind myself that the issues in this store aren't my problem to solve. If the guy who owns the place wants it to be a ramshackle sweatbox, it's his choice.

Some guys don't take pride in anything.

The guy in front of me moves up a few steps, and I watch as he shoves a new extension cord and some other electrical-looking item under his left arm. The customer then uses both hands to smooth down hair that wasn't messed up. In fact, from head to toe, the guy is dressed like he's going on a date or something, not picking up stuff at the hardware store. He must've squeezed in this errand on his way to somewhere else.

Realization dawns as I look ahead to the man ahead of that guy in line. A long-sleeved dress shirt and tie? What kind of fool wears that to the hardware store in this heat? I started looking up and down the line with increased interest. Usually, I'm very observant of my surroundings. For two decades, my life frequently depended on my powers of observation. Today, I've been so lost in my own head, I didn't notice that everybody in line is a man and every damn one of them was dressed way too well for a quick run to the hardware store. The good men of McIntosh Ridge are a strange bunch. This town is more boring than I originally thought if going to the hardware store is an event requiring careful clothing selection.

The line moves forward again, more this time. Just past

the two customers in front of me, the path of the line turns right and is hidden by other aisles of merchandise. The guy in the long-sleeved shirt moves forward around the corner. He lifts his chin and grins widely as he walks out of sight.

A small sign dangling from the ceiling is in the shape of an arrow pointing in that direction: PAY HERE. To the left of the main aisle, a small convex mirror is mounted on a short bracket that extends from the ceiling; it provides a blurred reflection of the very end of the line, but not what leads beyond.

I look down at my dirty boots and focus my senses, particularly my hearing. I tune out the clunking of the ceiling fan and the general sounds of the store around me, concentrating on sound to my right and in front of me. I hear a man speaking and a woman laughing.

The guy directly in front of me is staring straight ahead, shifting his weight from foot to foot. Who the hell gets nervous in a hardware store? Suddenly, the other customer rushes toward the register, clearly excited that it's his turn.

I take the man's spot at the front of the line, and immediately it all makes sense. Slightly petite and much more than slightly curvaceous, perfect sense. The woman behind the payment counter is the kind of beautiful that makes you do a doubletake, and then probably sneak another look after that. Delicate features, big golden-brown eyes, and full lips tinted a dark pink color. Or is that their natural color?

Her well-worn denim shorts are definitely worn well, with a dark blue and white bandana threaded through the belt loops. Her blue tank top has a round neck, not too low but low enough to highlight impressive cleavage. Long, wavy hair in shades of honeyed blonde is drawn up in a ponytail positioned high at the top of her head. She's nodding in agreement with something the customer directly in front of her is saying as she turns around and climbs a track-mounted ladder to reach a high shelf on the wall behind the counter.

The sway of her hair draws my attention to the bandana wrapped around the base of her ponytail, then the end of her ponytail pulls my attention to a third bandana. Lucky number three is jammed in the pocket adorning the right side of her heart-shaped ass.

With a small box under one arm, the woman holds on with the other hand as she climbs back down. I can't help but notice how perfectly her legs are proportioned for her height and wonder how tightly she could wrap them around me.

It's clearly been too long since I've been with a woman if I'm fantasizing about a stranger.

Still admiring her legs, I notice she's wearing small Timberland boots and has replaced the standard brown laces with bright blue ones. Something about that is appealing, and I don't know why. Maybe it's because she's not just doing what she has to for her job; she's owning it.

The lovely cashier rings up the other guy's stuff, smiling politely. But her body language indicates she is trying to hurry him up and move on to the next customer. She then raises her voice to interrupt the man, "Boyd, there's such a big line today. Come back another time, and maybe it'll be less busy, and we can talk more."

Boyd obediently picks his bag up off the counter. "Why don't we go out to—"

Poor Boyd never even gets a chance to finish his sentence before she leans around him and signals to me. "Next!"

CHAPTER 3
REBECCA

BOYD ISN'T CREEPY like Kyle, but he also doesn't spark even a flicker of interest within me. I'm not interested in so much as a completely platonic conversation with the man outside the parameters of business or a passing "Hello" on the street. He seems like a good guy, but he isn't a guy who appeals to *me*. Instead, he's that slightly goofy guy you don't mind having as a friend, but that's absolutely, positively, all he's ever going to be. Boyd is the type of guy the "friend zone" was invented for. I keep nicely letting him know that I'm not interested, but he persistently tries to change my mind.

Not happening, Boyd.

Now the next guy in line, the one I just waved over... well, I doubt any woman anywhere *ever* friend-zoned him. I'm not shallow. Really, I'm not. I know looks aren't every-thing, and everyone has their own preferences. There's a cover for every pot and all that. But still ...

Dusty jeans cling to his muscular thighs and long legs. The edges of the sleeves of his blue T- shirt strain around his biceps. Broad shoulders, narrow hips, muscles that look sculpted from life and the elements, not only hours spent in a gym—he looks positively delicious. I don't want to be caught staring, so I force my gaze up to his face, and it would be easy to get caught staring again.

I think I know pretty much everybody in the area, at least on sight, and I've never seen this man before. He first caught my eye on the security camera screen, and since he'd been in my actual line of sight, I've been having trouble not staring. Since I hate being objectified in any way, it's embarrassing to recognize that I'm doing it to someone else.

And I'm doing it again, right now.

Not cool, Rebecca.

He's handsome in a way that makes me think of ads for rugged outerwear or men's aftershave. Well, maybe not that because it had obviously been a couple of days since he last shaved. The stubble accentuates the sharp angles of his face and makes his strong jaw even more defined. His hair is dark, clipped short on the sides, but longer on top and slightly tousled, like he (or some lucky woman) had run their fingers through it. Over his ears and at his temples, the hair is ever so slightly laced with silver, and somehow, that makes him even hotter. His eyes are an unusual light gray, and the way they catch the light make me catch my breath. Very fine lines at the outer corners of those eyes speak of a man who spends a lot of time in the elements.

A slow, creeping awareness makes itself known as it coiled low in my core, like a beast getting ready to strike. The aching heat is unexpected, but definitely not unwelcome. Is the man a new homeowner in the area or a renter? If he'd bought a house or farm property, I probably would've heard about it already. The McIntosh Ridge gossip tree is extremely efficient.

I refuse to allow myself to daydream when I'm working in the store, not that there's ever much free time for that. But I notice he's looking at me expectantly. Like he's waiting for something. And then my brain slams into gear – I haven't actually *said* anything except to call him to the counter. I clear my throat and ask, as coolly as I can manage, "Did you find everything you want?"

There. That sounded good. Relaxed and calm.

The stranger puts several boxes of roofing nails on the counter and answers me in a deep voice that totally fits his man-candy appearance. "I need supplies to fix a roof and some interior walls. I've got some of what I need, but not everything."

"I'm sure we have what you need. We have a full warehouse behind this building."

I wish he'd say he needs some of *me*.

Doesn't that sound like the start of a bad porno?

I smother my own laugh at the thought.

Another completely unrelated thought pops into my mind. How does this guy smell so good during this heat wave—like crisp soap, cool mint, and clean man—when most everyone else who's come through the store during the heat wave have been various degrees of rank?

I mentally yank myself back from that line of thought and take a form from a supply bin under the counter. "What supplies do you need? Do you have measurements or quantities?"

"Here's my list."

He pulls a folded piece of paper out of his back pocket and hands it to me. The motion makes his fingers curve under my hand, and his thumb brushes over mine as he pulls his hand back. Plenty of people have handed me things and never once did I feel the strange sensation that runs up my arm when this stranger does it. It's like a mild electric shock.

I know I am probably looking at him strangely, but I don't say anything about it because that would definitely be weird. Right?

His list is written in precise pencil strokes. (I do appreciate a neat and thorough list!) He needs a 6-foot fiberglass ladder and a 16-foot wooden one, a half-dozen pieces of sheetrock, some waterproof underlayment, an array of two-by-fours, and a bunch of other things.

"Not a house roof then." I remark to fill the silence. He is most likely quick-patching some outbuilding.

"Affirmative."

It doesn't seem like he is going to add to that, but then he does. "I'm doing some quick, urgent repairs, but I might be interested in a more authentic renovation. Not perfectly authentic materials, but–"

"Replicating the feel of the original," I finish for him.

"Yes. Do you know of anyone local who consults about that kind of thing?"

"Can't say that I do."

I quickly start to fill out the order form but of course, Mike overhears at least that part of the conversation and sticks his uninvited two cents in. "Rebecca, you know all about that kind of thing. Maybe you could consult?"

Yes, I know a heck of a lot about authentic restoration and renovation. It's a specialty I want to add to Spencer Hardware and Lumber. I've taken every course I could find about the subjects, gotten every certification I could, and spent more than a year after college studying hands-on with a top tier restoration team in the Washington DC / Virginia area.

It helped me cope with the Josiah aftermath. And I've kept up with changes and developments in that industry. It's something that endlessly fascinates me, and I'm determined to make part of my future. I already set up a separate LLC for that business. But I'm not ready to actually *do* it yet.

Two years ago I was ready… then Dad announced his plan to retire in two years, so he and Mom could pursue their long-delayed dreams of traveling across America and doing all the things they never got to do because he spent the last 50 years of his life devoted to the store. They are in their mid-

60s, they *should* be reaping the fruits of their labors or whatever it's called, and since the business is such a successful one, they can afford to do whatever they want to do.

It's not like they forced me to step into his shoes. I chose this.

Dad said he was fine with bringing on a general manager to oversee the whole operation, or even with selling the business entirely. I'm the one who turned a thumbs down on those and other options. *My* decision.

The affinity, the appreciation I have for old buildings and preserving or re-creating their original character, well, that also applies to the family business.

"No, unfortunately, I can't right now, Spencer Hardware and all it entails require all my attention." I offer the stranger what I hope is an apologetic smile. "I don't know of anyone locally right now, but I can provide a name or two to you of regional experts, if that would be helpful to you."

"I'll think about it."

I finish writing up his order form and ring it up. "The waterproof underlay will be here sometime tomorrow or the day after that. We can drop it off to you Friday around 5:00 if you give me your address. We can deliver everything all at once so you don't have to wait to load up out back today."

"Or I can take what you have now and come back when it comes in to pick up the underlay."

"Sure. If you don't mind waiting in line."

One of his eyebrows lifts in surprise. "Is there always a line like today?"

"Not always, but more often than you'd think." I spin the form around to face him on the counter, then use the tip of the pencil to indicate the total and the section where he should write his name and address.

He produces a slim wallet from his back pocket and extracts a credit card. "What's the total with the delivery charge?"

A glance at the credit card reveals his name –Sam Miller. It suits him. A look at the address he wrote on the form couldn't have surprised me more. It's near my own house.

"Happy to tell you, Mr. Miller, that we can deliver to that address free of charge. Isn't that Ronald Parker's place? Wasn't it, I mean?" I know Mr. Parker died a month or so ago.

"Yes."

I desperately want to ask questions about who Mr. Miller is, exactly, and what is he doing at Ron Parker's place, but it's none of my business. I can almost hear my father's voice in the back of my mind lecturing me: *Rebecca, this is a hardware store, not a social club.*

I shake that off quickly. The thing I need in this moment is the echo of a parental voice in my ear while my lady parts are clamoring for attention from the man standing across the counter. Right behind that thought, I decide that I'm going to be the one making his delivery.

CHAPTER 4
SAM

WHEN I LEAVE the hardware store, and it's unexpectedly intriguing owner, I don't bother moving my truck from its parking place on the street out front. Instead, I walk two blocks down to where Golden Key Realty is located in a Victorian-style home on the corner immediately past the end of the primary business district.

The entrance to the business is situated on the main thoroughfare, marked by a freestanding sign bearing the name of the business and what appears to be a Golden Delicious apple. I never paid much attention to the house when I was young and lived in McIntosh Ridge.

The house is a beautiful structure with intricate architectural detailing and gorgeous plantings that are thriving despite the summer heat. The main house at Hidden Haven could probably look this good or even better. I go around the corner to check out the rest of the façade visible from the streets. Another entrance on the side street I assume is private because a small sign there points people to the other door. Returning to the business entrance, I do as the door placard instructs – ring the bell and walk right in.

Inside is a decently sized room with a reception desk near

the door and a trio of desks beyond it. Across from the reception desk, six waiting room chairs are clustered near a coffee table that has decorating magazines in a semicircle upon it. A middle-aged woman sits in one of those chairs, scrolling through something on her phone. She looks up at me, smiles, then continues to watch me although she pretends to return her focus to the mobile device in her hands. My brain automatically assesses and catalogs her-- not a threat, just an interested bystander. Probably a local, to whom newcomers are always interesting.

"Welcome." A tall, sandy-haired man emerges from an open doorway and greets me. "I'm Mitchell Carruthers, a broker-owner here. What can I do for you today?"

He extends his hand, and I reciprocate. Carruthers meets my gaze directly as we clasp hands, both gestures conveying something about the man.

"Sam Miller."

Carruthers nods toward the woman who is avidly watching the interaction between the broker and me.

"Your other visitor was here before me," I tell him. I'm not sure if the woman is as a client, customer, or something else. Not that it really matters.

"That's quite all right, I've already spoken to Mrs. Ahearn." Carruthers gives a small smile to the woman in question. "She's waiting for my sister, the other broker-owner here."

Well, then.

"I'm Sam Miller. I have property in the Ridge that I could use assistance with. I'm aware there are other realtors in the general area, but I wanted to come here first, figuring you know the area best. It's a complicated situation, but I'm hoping you can handle it."

Or that since you're the most local, you'd have the most patience to deal with the situation, but close enough.

"I'll certainly do my best to help you if you decide you

want to work with me. Do you have time to sit down with me now?"

"Yes."

"Excellent, let's go into my office." Carruthers turns his attention to the woman in the waiting room, who has completely given up any attempt to act at all disinterested in what's going on in front of her. "Mrs. Ahearn, as I said before, I'm sorry Angelina was delayed. At this point she should be here very soon."

"Oh, that's quite all right, I hope you and Mr. Miller have a good get- to- know- you meeting." She bats her thickly lacquered eyelashes at me. "Welcome to MacIntosh Ridge, Mr. Miller!"

I don't bother informing her that I'm no newcomer. I don't want to waste time, and I'm not in the mood to be chatty. As if I'm ever in that kind of mood. I settle for, "Thanks," and leave it at that.

Carruthers leads the way back further into his private office. A short hallway with several other doors within it opens up into a slightly larger one. The first door is closed, the inscription on its nameplate –*Angelina Carruthers*.

He continues on to the next office door. "Make yourself comfortable, Mr. Miller."

"Call me Sam." I choose one of the leather chairs facing the desk. It isn't grandiose or ostentatious, but even I can recognize the quality of the furniture.

"Will do." Carruthers moves behind the desk and takes his place in the high-back chair on the other side. "Basics first." Picking up a pen, he holds it poised over a printed form on his desk. Some kind of intake or new client data sheet, no doubt. "We can start with basic info. Address of the property?"

The man takes notes manually, instead of typing directly into a computerized form or database. Interesting. Carruthers is surprisingly good at reading people because he says, "I prefer the old school way, of taking notes."

Carruthers looks younger than me, so using the phrase "old school" seems strange, but I say, "I understand." Trying to get more comfortable, I cross one ankle over the other knee and provide the address.

As he writes it down, Carruthers muses out loud, "That's Ronald Parker's place, isn't it?"

McIntosh Ridge projects the aura of a small town, but it actually encompasses a fairly large area so I'm impressed that the man recognizes the address.

"Yes."

"I'm not being nosy, but I need to know your connection to the property. Roughly at least. Are you a family member, a beneficiary of the estate, or an administrator or executor with authority to sell?"

"Family member. I'm Parker's son." I decide to answer what's probably the next question before it's asked. "I legally changed my last name some twenty years ago."

Carruthers jots more notes. "I'll need verification from the attorney handling the estate." He looks up and meets my eyes. "Nothing to do with the different last name; I would need that no matter what your name is or who you are. A lot of people try to skirt the law in estate situations."

It makes sense, and I appreciate the explanation. From my own dealings with terrible people over the course of my career, I don't doubt that all. "I'm sure they do." I pause, then add, "There are stipulations to my inheritance of the property."

Carruthers leans back in his chair. "Okay?"

Damn it. Much as I hate talking about Parker, if I'm going to do business with Carruthers, I need to. "Ronald Parker wasn't a good father. He wasn't a good man to anyone." Least of all to his wife, but I'm not going to go there. "I enlisted as soon as I could after my mother died, and never came back to the Ridge." Carruthers raises his eyebrows, and I answer the silent question. "Twenty years and a few months."

Drumming my fingers on one arm of the chair, I aim for transparency. "When Parker's attorney contacted me, I told him I didn't want anything from the old man. He then informed me I would have to sign paperwork declining the inheritance, and that it would instead pass to Parker's nephew."

And I can't let *that* happen. Not if I can prevent it. Elliott Parker is six years older than me. The few times I encountered him, both as a boy and as a teenager, I instinctively disliked Ronald's sister's son. Using professional investigative contacts I've acquired over the course of my military career, I checked more than once on what my first cousin was up to, and the result was never anything good. Petty crimes, minor fraud, bad debts... Never anything earth shattering, but the only thing consistent in Elliott's life was his ability to make bad decisions.

When the lawyer informed me about what would happen if I declined my inheritance, a vehement "not happening" snapped out of me. That property had been handed down in Helen Miller's family for at least 100 years, and there was no way I'd let Elliott Parker benefit from it.

"According to the terms of the will, I have to hold onto the property for six months per year that I was away from the Ridge."

I've tried to find a way around the manipulative stipulation—and so far I've failed.

In his next comment, Carruthers reveals some depth of knowledge of the New York State real estate law. "So, the property is held by a Trust?"

"Yes." I scrub a hand across my prickly jaw. "I'm told that there is nothing I can do to break it, either."

I demanded that of Parker's attorney immediately upon learning what Parker had done. I don't know if Parker had devised the terms of his manipulative bequest entirely on his own, or told his lawyer what he wanted to accomplish and had the man tell him how it could be made reality. The details of how it came about were ultimately irrelevant. To keep my mother's property out of the greedy hands of Parker's family, I need to work within the damnable framework within which I have been trapped.

The central air conditioning unit is humming unobtrusively as not much more than background noise in the otherwise quiet room. Carruthers waits a beat, then two, as if to see if I have anything to add. The realtor continues, "The properties in the area where this address is located are usually large. Anything on it besides the house?"

"There's a one-bedroom cottage, a barn with four horse stalls and a loft, a chicken coop, a large shed and a smaller one, a dog run, a pair of completely empty outbuildings, all on some 30 acres of property. Parker started to cut back on farming the sections used for that a long time ago, before I even left."

Carruthers scribbles more notes rapidly as I go through my own mental list. He looks up again and asks, "How would you describe the condition of the main house?"

"Run down." I shake my head. "Everything on the property is run down."

Carruthers again leans back in his chair and studies me. "What exactly do you want to do with the property?"

"It has to remain my permanent address," I tell him.

At least temporarily, I add silently. I don't know what I want to do with it permanently. I can't live in the main house, with its memories and endless reminders of too many things I don't need to be reminded about every day. The cottage is better, but also full of sad shadows.

Out loud, I continue, "That doesn't mean I have to live in the main house." I flex my fingers on ends of the armrests and share my intentions. "When I'm local, I'll live in the cottage that's on the property, and I'll entertain offers to rent the rest." I've got no intention of actually living in McIntosh Ridge. In all my Navy years, I barely spent any time at the "permanent" addresses I had at any given time.

"Have you considered subdividing the property?" is Carruthers' question. "Sell off at least part of it?"

I had thought about that and discarded the idea. Better to keep the property intact until I know what I am ultimately going to do with it. I can eventually have my mother's cottage relocated to one edge of the property and keep that. I want to sell the rest. The main house can be torn down and rebuilt, but it seems like there's architectural value to it that might benefit from restoration instead. My mother would definitely appreciate that.

To accomplish that, I have to deal with my own mental shit, and I'm not sure it's worth it. I've had to handle enough mental fallout from my military service; why voluntarily add to all of it? I don't see how that will benefit me or impact my future.

Unaware of my internal conversation, Carruthers goes on, "Do you intend to rent it 'as is'?"

"I'm making some improvements to the main house, cottage, and barn." I uncross my arms and flex my fingers on the armrests of the chair. "Probably nowhere near a full renovation or anything like that, but enough to improve its appeal."

"Probably?" he echoes. "Does that mean you might conduct a full restoration of some kind?"

Kudos to him for catching that careless slip. I should gloss over it, but I'm not dishonest and don't feel comfortable doing that. "I'm no expert in the subject, at all, but there's a lot of original detailing in the house, early 20th century stuff, that might be worth restoring."

"You know, there are always buyers who will pay a premium for those qualities," Carruthers says, and I can almost see the thoughts whirring through his mind. "Where are you staying while you're here? Are you on your property?"

I nod. "In the cottage." I'm not going to bother explaining that it'd been my mother's small escape from the reality of her life with Parker. "I've started doing some of the work myself."

His eyebrows lift in surprise. "The restoration work?"

"No, I'm starting with the other buildings. Figure I'll bring someone in to check on what can be done with the main house."

"I can check my files and call you with a couple of names of people who consult on that. Or text you with the info," Carruthers offers.

"I'd appreciate that." In his line of work, it makes sense the guy has resources.

Carruthers pauses again and taps the back of his pen on the desktop. "Rebecca Spencer from Spencer Hardware knows a lot about that kind of thing. She's certified, in fact. We were speaking about it recently..." He trails off with a small smile like he's remembering the conversation with more than professional courtesy. For no reason at all, it's irritating.

"I've met her. I'll have to stop in there again and ask about it." I don't bother telling him she already shot me down about it; none of his business.

"I could speak to her for you –"

Now it's my turn to cut him off. "I have to stop in there right now so I'll take care of it."

The sound of female voices drift into the broker's office, too indistinct for us to hear the conversation.

"Okay." Carruthers drops his pen on the desk and leans back in his chair. "I'll pull together some comparative reports with other properties that have been rented or sold in the area in the last few years, and also those that are on the market now. None of them will be identical to yours, of course – they never are. But comparative reports give us and potential buyers a place to start."

"Makes sense." I shift in the chair just enough to indicate I'm done with this meeting.

He speaks more quickly. "I'd like to look at the property more closely. Take a few pictures. When's generally a good time for me to come by?" Carruthers asks. "Or we can make a specific appointment."

"No particular day or time. I want to get a plan together, just shoot me a call first. I'll make sure to be there." The faster Carruthers can work out lease agreements for all or part of the property, the faster I can get out of town for a while. I'll need a property manager, but the rent will cover that expense. I'll be a mostly absentee landlord for a decade and then sell it. Maybe along the way I'll find a good tenant who wants to "lease to own" or something like that.

"I expect to be at the property every day working on what needs to be done, except when I'm getting supplies or doing errands." I stand up. "Like I said, give me a call before you come out."

Carruthers stands as well. "Of course."

It wasn't necessary, but he walked with me out to the door. The woman in the waiting room was gone, and there was no sign of anyone else.

Carruthers extends his hand. "Good to meet you, Sam. I hope we'll be doing business together."

"Likewise." I shake his hand, already considering possible ways to persuade Rebecca Spencer to have a look at my potential renovation project.

CHAPTER 5
REBECCA

KYLE IS ALREADY GETTING on my nerves this morning, and his behavior has graduated from borderline harassment and launched into straight-up creeper territory.

"Look, Kyle, I told you enough times today – I'm not interested in having lunch, dinner, drinks, breakfast, or anything else with you." I hold up a hand to forestall his next comment. "No coffee, tea, dessert, or whatever else you're going to say."

"Is there a problem here, honey?" A strong arm slides around my waist at the same time the baritone voice asks the question. I immediately recognize the voice, the aura, and *the scent* that accompanies all of it. The prickling hairs on the back of my neck a couple of minutes ago should have warned me Sam Miller was nearby.

I don't really know the man, but right now I couldn't be happier to see him.

"No, no problem . . ." I start to say, then stumble over my own words.

What do I call him, what do I call him? My mind settles on the obvious, "It's okay, Sam. Kyle and I finished our discussion."

Instead of taking the opening presented in which to make his exit, Kyle puffs up like a demented rooster looking to defend his part of the yard.

"Who are you?" Kyle demands, like I'm some juicy worm another rooster is about to steal right out from under him.

Sam says nothing for a moment, so I open my mouth to answer for him, but he beats me to it.

"I'm the man with Rebecca; that's all you need to know."

I'm too stunned to comment on that immediately, but Sam is turning me toward him while he pulled me closer and my brain hurries to reformulate the words I've been planning in my head to direct them at *him* instead of Kyle. All words vanish like a proverbial puff of smoke at Sam's declaration when his mouth crashes down over mine. It starts off as a close-mouthed, practically platonic kiss, but then it quickly morphs into something *more*.

My rational brain starts off shocked by the touch of his mouth on mine, but my feral , lady -lizard brain is all on-board with this new plan and is already directing my lips, tongue, and teeth to kiss him back. My hands eagerly get in on the action, the right one tangling in the short strands of hair at the back of his neck and the right one gripping his shirt like I need to hold on. And I might, because my heart is pounding and my knees are trembling, and that might mean I'm having some kind of medical episode or something.

Sam's mouth is hot, talented, and skillfully melting my brain. His body is generating heat of its own, not just because of the sculpted muscles I feel beneath his soft shirt, but because heat from his body is pulsating through the cloth, searing my fingertips. Everything else around me blurs into static, nothing more than meaningless white noise.

Until he draws back slightly, enough to whisper, "He's gone."

Who's gone? Gone where? My kiss-addled brain poses

both questions but my still tingling lips don't manage them exactly. "What?"

Sam releases me completely and steps back. The air between us is startlingly cold. "Your overly aggressive whatever he is."

Kyle was overly aggressive but he never kissed me, so doesn't that make Sam the overly aggressive one?

Except if Kyle had tried that I'd have slapped him, or punched him, or something like that. Since the kissing bandit was Sam, though, I'm still standing by the paint mixer machine where Kyle had cornered me. I'm fighting the urge to grab onto Sam with both hands and kiss him this time.

Get yourself together!

A quick look around shows Sam was right about Kyle, who's nowhere in sight.

I say the next first thing I can think of. "Thank you."

And realize that might sound like I'm thanking him for the kiss, which I definitely enjoyed. What I *should* thank him for was effectively putting an end to Kyle's relentless harassment.

Even though it'll probably cause a new stream of town gossip.

Even though I'm making myself a little nutty now with my own mental pinball routine.

"Sam, I meant to say I appreciate your help, even if it wasn't necessary. I had the situation under control."

Mercifully, he doesn't challenge me on any of that, just stares at me in silence.

I continue. "I'm surprised to see you back here so soon?" The words are technically phrased as a statement, but I definitely ask it as a question.

Sam's own mouth is still slightly reddened from that powerhouse kiss he laid on me, but he answers readily, as if it's days in the past and not barely three minutes. "I wanted to ask if you'd reconsider looking at the house I'm considering renovating with an eye toward preserving its original style."

I automatically start to tell him again that I'm not doing work like that yet, but he interrupts me. "Rebecca, I heard what you said earlier, and I respect that. But more than one person has now told me that you're on this type of thing, and before I start hunting down someone to handle or guide a restoration type renovation, I want to know if it's worth doing that, or if I should just modernize everything and be done with it. I don't mind paying more than your usual rate; it's worth it to me to not have to find someone else to consult."

There is a huge difference in time and cost between the two options in front of him. There are a few experts in the general vicinity, but getting on someone's schedule could easily take months. Since I'm not actively working in the field, I can do it almost anytime.

And now I kind of owe him, don't I?

It's like he reads my mind because Sam says, "Don't factor in what went on here just now, Rebecca. That was because the jerk was harassing you. It doesn't have any bearing on this conversation." He runs a big hand through his already messed up hair (messed up by my own fingers, if I dare acknowledge that) and looks almost embarrassed. Almost, but not quite. His next words and the steady way his eyes continue to connect with mine make sure I understand that's the case. "The way I kissed you without asking or something was probably also harassing you, but I'm not apologizing."

An announcement comes over the store speaker system, not that I could tell you what the announcement was about. It's like those old, classic Charlie Brown cartoons where all adults sound like *mwah, mwah, mwah* and don't make any sense at all.

A customer rounds the corner into the section where Sam

and I are still standing and that finally snaps my brain back into business mode.

"I'll be making the delivery to your property Friday late afternoon or right after close, I believe, because the water-proof underlay is due in that day. I'll check out the matter then, if that works for you?"

His eyes have also tracked to the third person now in the aisle, looking at outdoor paint options. Sam says, "Thanks again." Then he's gone. Barely a minute later I hear the distant tingling of the bell over the front door and know it's announcing his departure.

CHAPTER 6
SAM

"HELLO?" There is no breeze to carry the sound, but I still hear a woman's voice call out in an unnaturally high tone. "Hello? Is anyone here?"

With my forearm, I wipe across my forehead to clear some sweat there, noticing too late that there is dirt all over my arm – some of which has undoubtedly been transferred to my face.

The unknown owner of the voice moves closer to directly below where I've been working on the roof. "Hello? I'm looking for the owner."

She isn't giving up and going away. I maneuver around into position to drop a booted foot onto the ladder. The voice of a younger female adds to the intrusion into my day. "Maybe he's not home."

"His truck is here, Sadie." The first woman speaks more quietly this time, but her voice still carries clearly. Closer this time. "Oh!" She finally spots me.

The younger woman echoes the word in a much different tone of voice. "Oh, my."

"Can I help you ladies?" I didn't bother turning my head until both feet are on the ground. I take an extra second to try and smooth the scowl that's definitely on my face; I can be polite.

When I face my unexpected visitors, both are staring at me. Immediately, I recognize the older woman from the waiting room Golden Key Realty. She's carrying some kind of casserole dish with padded handles and a lid that is strapped into place by what looks like miniature bungee cords. To her left and a step behind is the early-twenty something woman with a pie in her hands. Both women are blonde and blue-eyed, and the similarity in their features declares them mother and daughter.

"We heard the new owner was here, and we wanted to welcome you to McIntosh Ridge." The mother-looking one (I never forget things, how did I forget her name?) smiles so widely it looks painful, but she keeps talking. "I'm Marisol Ahearn and this is my daughter, Sadie." She looks around for the girl, who can't be older than twenty.

Mrs. Ahearn doesn't mention having seen me at the real estate office. Does she think I didn't notice her there, or that I forgot being introduced to her? I didn't see her when Mitchell Carruthers walked me out; she'd been somewhere with Angelina Carruthers. It was obvious she'd overheard at least some things that gave her my direction, or the woman had gotten information out of the Carruthers' sister.

Sadie takes a few steps forward until she stands closer to me than her mother does. Whereas Marisol Ahearn is wearing a modest, blue blouse and color coordinated pants, both tailored to fit perfectly, her daughter wears a short, strapless yellow dress that was probably expensive but barely contain her breasts. The Western style boots on her feet are tooled with an elaborate floral design. Gold jewelry at her ears, wrists, and throat reflect the sunshine. She's a pretty girl, but trying way too hard – unlike Rebecca, whose beauty requires no embellishments at all to outshine Sadie Ahearn.

Neither of my uninvited visitors seem like the type to

cook for a new neighbor, but I don't want to make snap judgments like that. Doing so is a habit I need to break. Or at least lessen.

Sadie tilts her head and makes her shoulder-length bob sway in a practiced move. "I made a pie for you. Apple, of course." She winks at me. "I see you take great care of your body, but I hope you enjoy a little something sweet sometimes."

Her eyes rove over me again, and I become acutely aware that I'm not wearing a shirt. Two hours ago I dropped it down to the ground without concern about where it landed, and I'm not about to look for it right now with this audience present.

Mrs Ahearn prompts me, "I didn't catch your name, Mr...."

Is there something really wrong with this woman?

Does she truly not remember being introduced to me by Mitchell Carruthers?

Or is this some charade for her daughter's sake?

I don't know, and I don't really care. But it's simpler to go along with her game and get done with them more quickly instead of confronting her, because no matter what she says, I still won't really care.

"Sam Miller." I feel in the blank because even I won't be rude enough not to in the current situation, with her daughter present. "I appreciate the kindness, ladies, but I wasn't expecting visitors so..." It's my turn to utilize an unfinished sentence as I show them my dirty hands. "You can leave them in the shade on the porch for now." I force what I hope looks like a smile. "Thanks for the food."

Mrs. Ahearn makes a show of looking around "Is your wife anywhere around? We'd love to meet her."

"No wife."

"Your girlfriend then?"

I'm not about to tell them I've got no girlfriend, either. It's none of their damn business, so I ignore her question.

"I don't want to be rude, ladies, but I've got adhesive drying out in the sun, and I have to get back to it." None of that is true, but I'm confident they won't know that.

"Of course," Mrs. Ahearn says. "I totally understand. We'll just be on our way so you can get back to your adhesive in time. We don't live far from you so we'll leave a number in case you need anything at all." She nudges her daughter. "Right, Sadie?"

"Absolutely right," Sadie agrees. She favors me with a bright smile. "I'd be more than happy to show you around town."

I make what I hope is a noncommittal sound and turn my back on them to return to the ladder. "Thanks again."

Their eyes are on me as I climb up the ladder. I crouch a bit past the roofline and out of their sight for several minutes before I hear them return to the front of the property. I yank the claw-back hammer from my toolbelt and get back to pulling nails.

———

A cloud of dust kicking up announces the arrival of a red pickup truck driving up the winding driveway fast, heading for the house. It has to be the delivery from the hardware store because I'm not expecting anyone else. Not that I'd been expecting Marisol and Sadie Simeone that morning. I'm not in Macintosh Ridge to socialize with people and make friends. After I finish fixing up the house and property enough to rent it out, I'll be washing my hands of the place.

When I circle the front of the main house, as soon as I get closer and the dust starts to settle, I see Rebecca Spencer. I smile despite myself. I've thought about her – and our kiss – more than once since leaving the store.

The driver-side door swings open, and Rebecca scrambles down onto the high running board. I'm in time and in position to get a good view of her heart-shaped ass in black denim shorts today when she turns slightly to slam the door shut.

"Mr. Miller! I mean, Sam. You're in my bed!" she calls out cheerfully. A flush rises on her face, probably because she realized how that sounded. "Your *order* is in my truck bed."

"I liked the first option better." I stop a few feet in front of her. "Do me a favor, though, and don't mention that. I won't be in McIntosh Ridge for long, and I'd rather not fight with anybody while I'm looking for tenants or a buyer." I keep it simple because there's no point belaboring the complicated details of my inheritance.

I take pride in my self-control, but I still struggle to keep my gaze respectful because my private parts are having all kinds of dirty, disrespectful ideas about this woman's bountiful rack today. Now that I know how her mouth tastes, how she feels in my arms, well, I have to keep my libido under control.

"No boss, no husband, no person, so I guess you've got no worries. At least about that." She laughed, then added, "I figured you knew that, otherwise you wouldn't have done what you did at the store the other day."

She's right, of course, but I decide to not dwell on that and instead confirm, "It's *your* store then?"

"Sure is." She nods, hands on those great hips, then goes on, "I'm not trying to pry, but what's your connection with the property?"

"I'm going to be renting it out. Most of it, at least. Met with the broker this week." I liked Mitchell Carruthers thus far, but still had surprisingly conflicted emotions about signing on the dotted line to officially put the property on the market, even as a rental. No way I'm analyzing that right now.

I avoid it by answering her other question. "I inherited this place."

"Really? I'd heard Parker left it to his son."

"He did."

It's obvious she wants to ask more questions and I'm glad she doesn't. Instead, she shifts gears. "Where do you want things unloaded? We can start with the sheet rock."

"Everything can be left here, in front of the house. I'll take it from here."

"Dumping things isn't the same as making a delivery." Rebecca curls those hands on her hips into small fists. "Not an acceptable answer."

My eyes narrow, and I feel one corner of my mouth twitch. I'm not going to laugh at how she looks all feisty about whatever ruffled her feathers. "I'm the customer, and that's what I want."

"You expect me to believe you want to single-handedly put everything where it belongs? If I was a man, you'd let me do my job."

As I take in Rebecca's fierce glare and indignant tone of voice, I continue fighting a smile. She isn't wrong. I decide to go with honesty – something that almost always serves me well. "I know I could insist, but I'd like you to stay a little longer, so please suit yourself."

It's her turn to smile. "Then where do you want everything?"

Gesturing toward the ramshackle barn barely visible behind me and the main house, I explained. "Some things go into the old barn structure, other items into the house. I put a few of the supplies I brought home from your store into the cottage near the main house."

I step past her and lean in to grab two containers of spackle off the flatbed. "I can explain in more detail as we work."

"Got it." Rebecca drops the steel-plate tailgate on the truck.

She climbs into the truck bed with an ease that told me she's done it countless times before. During my years in the Navy, I've seen plenty of extremely capable, hard-working women. Objectively, some of them were as beautiful as Rebecca Spencer. But I never looked at any of them that way; they were professional colleagues, and that was all.

Not for the first time, I try to mentally catalog Rebecca in the same way and fail completely.

This isn't the Navy. She isn't my colleague. Yes, she is a professional in her industry, and I respect that, but it isn't a barrier to silently appreciating her assets. And I am appreciating every glimpse as she disappears again into the barn with another box of supplies in her arms.

CHAPTER 7
REBECCA

I PUT another box of supplies on a small folding table Sam has situated maybe a yard past the front wall of the barn. That's pretty much the last of the load I brought with me, so I finally take a minute to look around a bit.

I note some visible rot around the barn doors, the kind that comes from years of exposure to the stressors of the weather. Further into the dim interior, a sagging joist dips over the rear door, and rotten floorboards sink slightly on the ground beneath my feet. The air is musty and stale, even though I can't see any remnants of old hay or forgotten feed. It isn't like I'm formally examining the structure; those are all easily observed, as are a half dozen other things.

"It looks like you've got plenty of work ahead of you to rehab this building," I comment.

"The goal isn't necessarily to make it all perfect. Shooting for safe and usable." Sam walks outside and probably heads back to my work truck for the last of the supplies.

I follow him, but since it's clear he isn't particularly interested in my observations about the barn, I don't waste my breath replying.

Sam sets down the two heavy panels of sheet rock he was

carrying, leaning them against old-fashioned hitching post that decorated the front yard area of the cottage.

The small house is separated from the larger one by maybe 150 feet to the side and another hundred feet to the to the back. Whereas the exterior of the main house was a traditional, Queen Ann style complete with wonderful architectural features, the cottage exterior is simple. From the outside alone, I can see that the main house was gorgeous although run down. The cottage, however, has nice shingles, window boxes, and a front door with a stained glass inset. It would benefit from a fresh coat of paint, but otherwise the exterior is in decent shape.

It doesn't exactly fit with the rest of the property. Although the window boxes attached to the pair of front windows are empty, the grounds immediately surrounding the cottage have been trimmed and the weeds pulled.

Sam reaches past me and opens the door. It swings open silently, indicating well- oiled hinges.

I can't help but notice the surprising smell inside the cottage; despite the run -down appearance of basically every-thing I've seen here, the cottage smells fresh and lemon-scented. Maybe soap and furniture polish? There's a space inside with a sitting area and attached kitchen, then a hallway leading away from them. It probably leads to a bedroom and bathroom.

Sam walks a few steps past me to the battered refrigerator and opens it. "I've got bottles of iced tea and beer."

"I'm driving, so I'll take an iced tea."

He twists the top off one and passed it to me, then helps himself to a beer.

Silent swallows fill minute. He gestures toward the table to invite me to sit, but I shake my head and instead rest my hip against the counter.

"Have you owned the hardware store for a long time?"

Sam sounds genuinely curious, not like he's making a desperate attempt at polite conversation.

"It was started by my grandfather, expanded by my father. When my parents retired, responsibility shifted to me." I know he has questions, but he's being polite enough not to ask them outright "It's complicated."

"I remember the hardware store being there when I was growing up here, but never paid attention to the name," he admits.

"It probably wasn't interesting to a kid."

Sam makes a noncommittal, kind of a grunt, deep in his chest. I can't even guess what he is thinking because his expression is remarkably blank.

He finally says, "I imagine it's a lot of work."

"It is. I grew up in that store, though. I worked there stocking shelves when I was a kid, behind the register when I was old enough to count change." I shrug. "When I graduated college, it was natural to come back and be involved."

He gestures toward me with his beer. "Tell me if I'm being nosy, asking too many questions."

"No, it's fine." Another sip from the bottle in my hand is only intended to wet my throat, not give me some false sense of courage. Right? "What do you want to know?"

Sam braces his feet a little further apart. "What did you study in college? Did you go away to school?"

"Business, of course, since we had a family business. With a marketing minor. And yes, I went away. Not far, just to Washington, DC."

He raises an eyebrow at me, inviting me to share more about school.

"George Washington University," I clarify.

"Tough school. You probably had plenty of job opportunities after that."

"I only looked a little," I admit. "I knew I was going to come back here, so there wasn't much point."

"But you still went to a prestigious school, even if you planned to come back to the Ridge."

"My parents insisted I go away to school." I can't help but shift in place, uncomfortable with the subject. I hardly knew this man, why am I sharing so much? And why does he care? I feel like pacing, but don't want to do that in front of him, so I change my mind about sitting down and tug an oval-back wooden chair away from the table enough to slide onto it.

Sam follows my lead and sits across from me at the square oak table. Instead of asking a follow-up question about why her parents "insisted" she go away to school, Sam comments, "That couldn't have been very long ago."

I can't stop my laugh. "You must think I'm younger than I am."

Sam smirks. "Even a rough and ready Navy man knows not to ask a woman her age."

"Well, I brought it up, so I think you can assume it's a safe topic. I'm almost 32."

"Evidently, I'm bad at judging women's ages. I'd have guessed 26."

No way is he being honest about that, but I think his motives are good; he's trying to pay me a compliment. He has no way of knowing that my own age doesn't bother me at all. I'm stronger than I was in my 20s – both physically and emotionally.

Life will do that to you.

Before I can wander down the ugliest part of Memory Lane – my college years – I change the subject and ask pointedly, "Since you brought it up, and how old are you?"

"38." He raises those eyebrows again. "Decrepit."

"Is that how you feel or are you asking my opinion?" I counter.

"Definitely not how I feel." He sort of smirks again, but it's more like an actual smile this time. "I'm wondering what you think of that number?"

"It's a good number."

It's not like I'm exaggerating about that at all. The more I look at Sam, the more I want to look at him. He isn't good-looking in a classically handsome way, but he's attractive in an attention-grabbing, heart-pounding, catch-your-breath kind of way.

Before he can respond, I ask another question. "How long have you been back in town?"

"Not long. Why?"

"I'm wondering if word has gotten out about you. Eligible bachelors are always a hot commodity here."

"Unfortunately, yeah, I was wondering why anyone cares about me being here? Are you saying it's because I'm single?" He sounds incredulous. "Is there a shortage of single men in the area?"

"If only! I'd be hassled less if so, but no, any woman in need of one could just hang around the hardware store." This time it's my turn to snicker. "Maybe I could stock them in aisle three."

"I did notice an abundance of enthusiastic male customers when I was there."

"Enthusiastic," I repeat. "That's a very tactful way to put it, Sam."

An idea is crystallizing in my mind, and it has my own heart rate speeding up. On the surface of it, it may sound corny, but it could help us both – in more ways than one.

Maybe I should've had that beer.

CHAPTER 8
SAM

I'M NOT a man who speaks without thinking, and I don't speak about anything personal with people – except, on rare occasions, with my closest brothers-in-arms, so I don't know why I tell Rebecca, "I inherited this place from Parker. I'm his son, technically, but we didn't have an actual relationship."

For the moment at least, it's the closest I've come to sharing the fact that Parker was an abusive drunkard who never hesitated to verbally and otherwise attack his wife and only child. The only thing Parker and I ever shared was mutual animosity.

Rebecca looks thoughtful as she considers my words. "Just because somebody happens to *technically* be family doesn't mean we have to get along with them," she said. "I have a good relationship with my parents, but even so, we don't always get along; for a few years, we barely spoke to one another." She laughs, but it's clearly without humor. "You can imagine how lovely that is when you worked together almost every day." Rebecca's focus doesn't waver from me. "I have friends who are like family to me, who have no contact with their biological families. Human dynamics are complicated and frequently suck."

"Nicely said. Wise as well as beautiful." I toast her with the longneck bottle in my hand.

"I have plenty of experience with unfortunate family situations."

"Some things no hardware can fix."

"Exactly." She toasts me back with her iced tea bottle.

Rebecca Spencer intrigues me. She also makes me feel something I haven't experienced in a long time. Nervous. She's sexy as fuck, yeah, but that wouldn't cause the unfamiliar twist in my gut.

I haven't been nervous around a woman in a long time; it's been twenty-one years since I lost my virginity in Carrie Conway's basement rec room when we were supposed to be watching a movie. She was eighteen, a year older than me, and she had more experience than I did. I remember being nervous as hell, incredibly grateful, and determined to be respectful toward her. All these years later, and I'm no longer nervous with women, but I'm still appreciative when a woman shares her body with me, and always respectful of women no matter what happens or doesn't happen between us.

My father was horrible, but my mother tried her best to raise me right.

Sitting there, across from Rebecca, I'm feeling the familiar but unfamiliar vibration in the air between them was a moment distinctly unto itself. I have been physically attracted to many women in my lifetime, but it never felt like this. In my career, whenever I sensed danger, I got a very specific feeling in my gut and on the back of my neck. A particular kind of excitement. The feeling flooding my senses at that moment were an intoxicating blend of arousal and excitement.

What do I do about it?

Rarely do I need to think twice before I act. My training, hell, my whole life has taught me to be decisive in all things.

But Rebecca isn't a random woman I met in a bar or some other miscellaneous place, both of us looking for a good time, or at least glad to have stumbled upon one. McIntosh Ridge is a small town, and Rebecca Spencer is a respectable business owner. I was born in the Ridge, but I haven't been here in decades and am only passing through. Yeah, I have to be an occasional presence here sometimes, for a while, but the timing was going to be sporadic at best.

It wouldn't be right for me to make a move. Would it?

Rebecca is capable and confident. Those qualities, combined with her effortless beauty, are incredibly attractive. Sexy, sure, but more than that. I can't remember the last time any woman captured my interest so thoroughly. Even watching her pick at the label on the iced tea bottle is enticing – her neat, short nails with their ruby-red polish stroke up and down, making pathways through the condensation and leading my mind into dangerous areas.

If the business she owns is successful, that's probably another reason money-focused men sniff around her.

I'm watching Rebecca closely enough to see the moment she squares her already tightly held shoulders and takes a deep breath. Like she's fortifying herself for something. "I have a proposition for you."

Immediately the reptilian part of my brain skittered down a pathway of sensual propositions I would love to hear from her, starting with "kiss me" and ending up with me buried between her tanned thighs. For hours. Maybe for days.

Rebecca sits up even straighter in her chair. She drops her hands into her lap and meets my gaze with renewed intensity. "Local women and their unmarried daughters are going to pursue you because you're single, own a large piece of property, and look like *that*." She gestured vaguely toward me. "It doesn't matter that what's on your property is a mess; everything here can be fixed up."

Rebecca brings her hands up again and places them flat on

the table to the sides of her drink. "It doesn't matter that you intend to move from here or that you may have other plans. They are still going to focus on you."

A shrug is my response to her declarations. "They can focus on me all they want. I still won't be interested."

Rebecca curls the fingers of her right hand around the damp bottle in front of her. "I'm not interested in the guys who hit on me, either, but that doesn't stop most of them."

Leaning toward her across the table top, I keep my voice at an even pitch. "They have a problem understanding that no means no?" The increased tension in my jaw makes my voice rougher than I intended it to be. "While I'm here, I'd be happy to explain that to anyone who needs a lesson so they get it loud and clear. In technicolor."

Her cheeks flush rosy pink and don't know if it's from embarrassment or arousal. Rebecca clears her throat and answers me like my concern was for myself, not her. "You might be able to get that message across without getting yourself arrested or scaring away potential buyers, or wasting your valuable time, and at the same time protect yourself from your own overly enthusiastic pursuers." Her tone makes it clear she doubts I can accomplish that without the negatives I want to avoid. "I understand you don't need anyone handling that for you, but it could quickly get annoying and distracting. Right?"

The groundwork she's building is crystal clear. "So you're suggesting a mutually beneficial deterrence system? A way to keep our enemies at bay?"

"I don't know I'd go so far as to call them enemies, but… yes."

Well, I hadn't been wrong about where I thought she was heading with her preliminary words. But I'm still surprised.

It makes sense to gather more intel.

I casually stretch out my legs and cross my booted ankles. "Tell me more about how you see this playing out."

Rebecca swallows more of her iced tea, then rubs her hands on her legs or her shorts – from across the table, I can't see which.

She starts speaking quickly, like she's trying to get the words out before I can interrupt and shut her down. "I'm thinking we can date. Pretend to date, while you're here. Exclusively. It'll get women to leave you alone, and men to steer clear of me.If anything changes for either of us, simply just stage a break-up. Easy peasy. But that probably won't happen while you're here because no one will bother either of us because they'll think, you know, that we're together."

When she finally takes a breath, I ask, "If people are so interested in your personal business, will people want to know that we break up?" I gesture toward her. "In your scenario."

"Oh, people will absolutely want to know." Rebecca is the one who shrugs this time. "I'm sure it'll be easy to come up with a reason. We'll figure it out at the time. We can do it so neither of us looks bad."

I open my mouth to reply and Rebecca holds up a hand to stop me. "Before you say anything, I'm *also* willing to assess the restoration possibilities of the main house for you. I prefer you keep my involvement kind of quiet though because I'm truly not starting that business yet. Yes, I'm qualified, and have both training and experience, but for personal reasons I'm not ready to do that yet."

Well, I hadn't expected that. At least, not right now.

Why isn't she interested in starting up "that" business? I'd like to know, but it's clearly something that's a problem for her, so I'm not going to put her on the spot and ask; it's none of my business.

I answer honestly, I answer honestly, "Much as I appreciate the offer, I don't want you to have to do something you don't want to. I'm gonna pass."

"If I wasn't willing to do the job, I wouldn't offer."

"Be that as it may," I say with exaggerated civility, "I know you've got a lot to handle with the hardware store and all, and I'm sure you have good reasons for not doing the restoration thing, so we can just leave it at that."

Now Rebecca looks pissed off. Her words prove it. "I say what I mean and I mean what I say. I said I will look at the main house from a restoration standpoint, and I *will* give you a full and thorough report about its potential and what your steps would have to be if it's feasible to restore it."

It *would* be a big help to me if she is willing to do that. Still...

Rebecca leans forward, looking very pleased with herself. "Hear me out because I thought it through and it actually all fits together. I'll do this for you and make sure a few people hear about it, and *they will know* that I'm doing it because we're dating. It gives me local experience for when I'm ready to launch that part of my business, and it removes me from being anyone's dating target. It gets you the information you need for your work here, and it removes you from being targeted by local women." Her smile is genuine, and beautiful, even if it's almost smug. "Win – win."

My instinct is to immediately dismiss her idea. It sounds like some kind of chick flick movie plot.

Rebecca remains perfectly still, and the atmosphere around us is now fraught with tension, her happy smugness already gone. I choose my words carefully.

"I want to make sure you understand something; I'm going to be tied to this property in one way or another for a long time. Faking a relationship, especially when I'm not going to be here much, could be tricky. It could prevent you from meeting and connecting with someone for a real relationship."

For all my skill and experience at reading body language and micro- expressions, it's tough to get an accurate assessment of what she's thinking when she asks, "How long would *you* want this ruse to continue?"

"Truthfully, I haven't thought about that," Rebecca admits. "I didn't realize you'd be in McIntosh Ridge for long. I thought you were selling and moving, and that was it." Again, she shrugs. "It's fine by me, though. We could fake breakup anytime, and I can use the aftermath of that for a good while."

My gut instinct is screaming at me that going along with Rebecca's plan is a big mistake. I know better than to ignore my instincts, but she's looking at me with so much damn hope in her beautiful eyes that my mouth defies those instincts (and all logic, too), and I tell her, "Okay."

I'm an idiot.

CHAPTER 9
REBECCA

I'M shocked Sam isn't doing whatever he can to sell the property quickly if that's his goal. From our limited interactions through his business with the hardware store, I already thought he couldn't wait to be permanently done with McIntosh Ridge.

Having his plan confirmed is good news.

Really, it is.

I don't understand the intense attraction I'm feeling for this man. It makes no sense. After all, I'm not some sheltered, naïve miss. I've been around plenty of men in my life, from academic types to tradesmen, from farmers to ski instructors, from lawyers to landscapers.

It's not some military mystique thing, either. Sam isn't even the first military man to come into my life. One of my friends, Xander, is a Navy veteran now. Colton, one of the bartenders at Braeburn Tavern, is a military veteran, I don't know which branch he served in. Then there's Thomas and Bryce, both of them Army veterans. Good guys but no spark between me and either of them.

Sam, though?

Being close to him sets off fireworks within me so bright

I'm surprised we both can't see them cartwheeling into the air and screaming their way joyously across the sky.

A failed relationship with Sam could leave a woman shattered and unwilling to try again for a really long time, like my relationship with Josiah during my last two years of college. His betrayal had been so complete – so thorough – it'd taken years to move past it. I wondered more than once if I ever truly moved past it. It's not that I have any lingering feelings for Josiah; I haven't for a real long time. With the clarity of hindsight, I knew that I loved the idea him more than I ever actually loved *him*. But I've never trusted a romantic interest in my life again, and I probably never will.

Luckily, I'm not proposing a real relationship with Sam.

Sam is going to be traveling a lot, apparently, and he's not looking to settle down. Not settle down as in with me, but as *in one place*. It's truly only going to be pretend for him. He doesn't have hidden motives. The fear that he wants my business – my hardware store – and not me, is silly; what would a world-traveled man want with a small town business? Nothing.

I don't need details to know he's kept company with plenty of women in who knows how many places in the world. I'm sure I'm not anything special by comparison. But I can keep intrusions into his life at a minimum while he's in McIntosh Ridge, and maybe we can share something at least slightly more than a hook-up.

If he's even interested.

"You don't need to make a decision right now." As the words leave my mouth, I jump up out of the chair, making it skitter backward on the scuffed tile floor. "If you it's something you want to try, we can hammer out the details."

I really thought my idea was a good one, but now I'm overwhelmed by the need to make a hasty exit. With the empty bottle clutched in my hand, I hurry to the kitchen sink and rinse it out. I hear him following close behind me.

Sam's deep voice rumbles over my shoulder. "I'm intrigued by your proposition, Rebecca."

My next words pop out of my mouth before I can second-guess them, and my heart rate is picking up at the possibility he might agree. "We could have dinner and talk about this some more. You probably don't know the best places to eat in the area yet. They might have changed since you left. How about dinner tomorrow night?"

Sam doesn't answer right away. I turn to face him, wanting to see his face. There was surprise there, and maybe interest, and if I am not mistaken, some heat, too. But maybe I am imagining that last part because of the heat I'm feeling.

He finally speaks, voice thoughtful. "I would like that. Very much."

Now I feel strangely… awkward, and take a step to the side, intending to put my iced tea bottle in the bright blue recycling bin.

"Great. Okay, then." I raise the bottle slightly like I'm signaling my intention. "I'll be done at the store by 5 o'clock tomorrow. Is 6:30 okay for you?" With a flick of the wrist, I send the bottle tumbling into the recycling bin where it clanks against the other bottles and cans already there.

"Sounds good."

"I have your number from your order form."

Time to escape the awkwardness I created, so I hurry toward the door. "I'll text you to figure out logistics." Something makes me stop with one hand on the doorknob and look over my shoulder at him. "Okay?"

Sam has an amused expression on his handsome face, which I didn't expect. He nods and says "Okay."

My face is warm with the heat of embarrassment when I yank open the door and rush outside. I don't stop until I'm in my truck. I press both hands to my hot face.

"Smooth, Rebecca. So smooth." I grumble. "Not."

The truck starts with a rumble, and I check my mirrors

before putting it in drive. One of them shows Sam leaning against the fence in front of the cottage, arms crossed, eyes focused on me.

I can't pretend I don't see him. That would make me look even more ridiculous, instead, I lift my hand in acknowledgment and wiggle my fingers in some sort of pathetic waving motion.

Another glance in the side mirror shows that Sam is gone from view. At the same time, a cloud of dust heading for the house caught my attention. I carefully turned the delivery truck around and got a better look at the incoming car. It's a bright yellow import, the color beaming through the kicked up dirt like a beacon. The car is instantly recognizable.

Donna-Marie Donner.

What is she doing here? I punch forward slightly and to the right, pretending to look for something in the glove compartment. Behind my sunglasses, my eyes stay on the other woman. I don't know Donna-Marie well, but what I do know, I don't particularly like. Too loud, too flashy, too determined to be the center of attention. She also went out of her way to interfere in a new relationship my friend Tara had last year, and it was ugly, to say the least. Fortunately, Donna-Marie and her three-inch fingernails never frequented the hardware store.

Donna-Marie steps out of her car and makes a big production of smoothing her skirt over her hips and checking her off-the-shoulder blouse. She flings open the back door of her car and leans in, then stands back up with a covered dish in her hands. With a hip, she shuts the door and then tries to brush off her bright orange skirt with one hand; the driveway dust easily transfers from the car's paint job to her painted on clothes. With the disgruntled expression, Donna-Marie heads for the front entrance of the house.

I don't know if I'm more disgusted at her antics, the fact that she's here, or at myself for hanging around. I throw the truck into gear. Sam is either going to be delighted or dismayed by his unexpected visitor. No way was he expecting Donna-Marie, or he would have told her he wasn't in the main house.

Well, if it's a happy surprise for him he'll be canceling our dinner plans. It'd be disappointing, but I'll figure out something else to do tonight. No big deal. Not at all.

CHAPTER 10
SAM

THE SOUND of my boots disturbing the gravel path on the side of the barn is louder than it should be, and I'm not going to analyze why. Just like I'm not analyzing why I agreed to her ridiculous plan.

Yes, I'm attracted to her. What heterosexual male with a pulse wouldn't be?

During that too short conversation I confirmed for myself that she isn't simply beautiful and sexy; she's also intelligent, has a sense of humor, and is surprisingly bold. Engaging in a "fake relationship" was something that happened in the movies, not in real life.

There's no downside for me. I'm not going to live in McIntosh Ridge. She knows I'm not looking for a real relationship and don't want to settle down with a wife and kids. Spending time with Rebecca certainly wouldn't be a hardship. I've got nothing to lose.

When I followed her toward the front of the property where her truck was parked, I got treated to another display of her unnecessary embarrassment. She is clearly a strong and capable businesswoman, and forthright. The blush on her face was unexpected.

Yes, Rebecca keeps surprising me. And maybe the biggest shocker of all was that I don't dislike surprises when they have to do with her.

After tossing my beer bottle in the recycling bin, I grab the blue bag that lines it will and take that plus two of the garbage bags out the door. The trash receptacles are on the side of the main house, and I haven't bothered moving one closer to the cottage. I won't be living on the premises for long, but maybe I should move it temporarily to make things easier.

As I round the corner of the back of the house I hear a woman's voice muttering in obvious agitation, punctuated by more than one f-bomb. The cursing doesn't bother me; women have every right to pepper their language whenever they want to. But the woman also sounds upset, and that does concern me.

The woman in question is trying to pull her shoe out of mud he'd created when he ran the hose to clean off paintbrushes and other supplies that needed rinsing before they could be used again or put away until tomorrow. There's a covered dish in her hands and an angry scowl on her face.

Careful to not actually touch her hand, I take the dish from her. "Let me help you."

She's visibly startled. She obviously hadn't noticed my approach. Her expression changes immediately, her scowl replaced by a serene mask.

"Thank you so much!" The woman shifts more of her weight to the foot that's on firmer ground. "I seem to have gotten myself stuck, and I didn't want to drop the apple cake I baked for you."

She halfheartedly wiggles her mud-covered foot again, like she's trying to free it. The woman gazes up at me with wide eyes and manages to toss her shoulder-length hair back without losing her balance. "Could you help me free myself?"

Her comment is said like it's a question, but it clearly isn't.

She could pull harder, or pull her foot out of the shoe. And why is she tromping about private property in high-heeled shoes like she's at a dance club? It doesn't take a lot of smarts to recognize she's angling for attention.

She's playing a game and trying to make me her savior or some nonsense like that.

I ought to walk away and leave her to deal with it herself, but the quickest way to get rid of her is to free her and send her off the property. I put the covered cake plate on the grass, then crouch as close as I can get to her without kneeling in the worst of the muddy mess. I wanted to get some more work done before I get ready for dinner, and I don't need mud-cake denim drying out and stiffening up on me if I can avoid it.

"I'm Donna-Marie Donner," she said.

What the... Her parents named her what sounded like Donna Donna? Don't know if Marie was attached to her first name or was her middle name, but hopefully she uses it all the time. "Sam Miller." I pause to ask a question. "Do you have any physical injuries or conditions I should know about right now?"

"What? No, I didn't hurt myself if that's what you mean."

Mission go. I give her a heads up. "Pulling you out on three."

Donna-Marie reaches toward me. "What if I lose my balance? Maybe you should pick me up –"

"One, two, three." I ignore her words, tug firmly, and her shoe pops free of the mud.

Donna-Marie hops awkwardly but manages to maintain her balance. She flutters her eyelashes at me like a character in a bad movie. "That was a perfect Hallmark movie meet-cute!" The woman actually sighs at me like she's overwhelmed by … something. "The only thing that would've made it better was if you'd swept me up into your arms."

I shudder at the thought of what her response would have

been to that but ignore her comment entirely. "Thanks for stopping by."

"Oh. I thought we could enjoy a slice of cake together."

I almost feel bad at the sight of her crestfallen expression – *almost* being the operative word. I know her name now, but I've got no idea who she is beyond that, or why she'd taken it upon herself to show up here uninvited. It's a nice welcome to the neighborhood gesture, I guess. I've been polite, *and* I helped her get out of the mud that she should have easily seen before she planted her foot in it.

I shoot a glance at my watch. Yeah, I've got to get going doubletime.

"I've got an appointment to get to, but thanks again for this," I say, bending over to scoop up the cake plate. The lid was a solid white plastic so I can't see inside, but it smells good. Not that I would say that at the moment and be caught up in more conversation.

No way I'm walking her back to her vehicle, and giving her the opportunity to start a conversation again. I turn around and start back the way I came from. I hear her muttering and moving about, probably deciding what to do with that mud-caked shoe. When I get to the end of the house I look over my shoulder. Donna-Marie is clutching both of her shoes in her hands and hurrying toward the front of the house.

I consider following to make sure she drives away, but immediately decide against it. Why would she linger?

With the cake holder balanced on one hand, I check my phone again, looking to see if Rebecca texted. All I find is our exchange from twenty minutes ago:

REBECCA: Is 6:30 still good?

SAM: Yes

REBECCA: How does Italian sound?

SAM: Sounds good

REBECCA: Okay. Let's meet at Tony's Pizzeria. 418 Suncrest Rd.

SAM: See you there

Inside the cottage, I deposit the cake plate on the counter next to the pie dropped off by the Blanchard women. Why were strangers showing up uninvited? How the heck does anyone know I'm here? One visit to town yesterday, that's been the sum total of my inroads into the community. I sure as hell hadn't worn a sign around my neck announcing my identity and location.

Head shaking, I catch myself muttering about it, then cringe because it reminded me of Donna-Marie doing the same thing when I discovered her trespassing. *Trespassing?* God, now I'm sounding like that asshole Parker.

Shoving that thought away, I replace the liners in the garbage pail and recycling bin before heading the bathroom. The cottage bathroom is too small to be called comfortable, but it's more than enough for my needs, and a lot better than what was available during my naval career. Today, after spending all day working on the barn, I'm drenched in sweat and hungry. A cool shower takes care of the first issue, and dinner with Rebecca well take care of the other.

CHAPTER 11
SAM

I DRY off then drape the towel over the shower door to so it can dry. Naked, I stride the into the bedroom. Blue jeans, a short-sleeved, dark blue T-shirt, and my cleanest pair of boots are easy choices.

As I thread my leather belt through the loops on my jeans, I spare a look at my reflection in the mirror hanging on the wall behind the single dresser. Should I shave? I discard the thought as quickly as it came. Rebecca's dinner invitation was unexpected, and appreciated, but pizza doesn't require a shave any more than it requires a suit and tie. I already washed off the sweat, brushed my teeth, and used mouthwash –that was enough personal grooming for this evening.

When I leave the cottage, I close the door behind me with a snap and lock it. I'm confident McIntosh Ridge isn't a hotbed of crime, but that doesn't mean I'll be careless. A lack of insurgents doesn't mean there's a lack of troublemakers.

Once in my truck, I search for the restaurant on my phone, then put the address into the GPS. Hidden Haven is on the outskirts of town, so I gave myself more than enough time to get to the business district where Spencer Hardware, Golden Key Realty, and a bunch of other businesses are located.

Growing up, I rarely ventured into town. When I was a small kid, sometimes my mother took me with her to the grocery store or Farmer's Market. Those are vague memories that hover on the edge of vanishing. My middle school and high school memories are a lot more vivid and a lot uglier.

I flex the palms of my hands against the steering wheel. The days of not being in control of my life are long gone. Even during the decades when the Navy had de facto control over my day-to-day existence, giving it that authority over me was a choice and decision *I* made. I signed the enlistment papers of my own free well. Eagerly signed them.

I don't regret it.

Downtown McIntosh Ridge is picture-perfect. There's enough variation that it doesn't look cookie-cutter in design. But the Chamber of Commerce or the town board or whoever made the rules made sure the buildings and the storefronts complement each other.

I brought some supplies with me when I drove into the Ridge, knowing there would be things in need of repair. It shouldn't have been a surprise that everything was worse than I expected especially given the lawyer's warning.

The office of the old man's lawyer, Herb Lefferts, is in a bigger town more than an hour's drive away from McIntosh Ridge. When Lefferts told me the details about the strings tied to my inheritance, it wasn't entirely unexpected. I knew there'd be something twisted about it. After all, manipulative, underhanded behavior was typical of Ronald Parker when he was alive, so why would anything he left behind be any different?

When the lawyer went over the details with me and asked if I had questions it was easy to see how uncomfortable he was. It looked like he'd rather have been almost anywhere else when he said, "I or someone from my firm will have to verify your residence at the property at least a few times each year." As Lefferts handed over the legal paperwork and the keys, he also gave me a heads up. "I met with your father at Hidden Haven once a couple of years ago, Mr. Miller. I'd be remiss if I didn't warn you that it needs work."

"It needed work when I joined the Navy, so that doesn't surprise me."

Lefferts offered a handshake goodbye. "All right, then. If you need anything else from me, including references for any businesses whose services you might want to hire to do the renovation work, let me know. I'll do what I can. My assistant has lists of those types of companies."

I didn't mind shaking Lefferts' hand. I even appreciated that the lawyer had been quick but thorough. It wasn't the lawyer's fault his client was despicable. "I've got your contact info. Thanks again."

The meeting had been short because there wasn't much to discuss. Parker died with practically nothing in the bank, no life insurance, and no assets besides the property that was in my mother's family for generations.

Before I let that train of thought run away with me to places I don't want to go, I refocus on the here and now. Turn off the GPS. The town is small enough that I don't really need it.

Bronze-toned streetlamps each bear a small plaque with the name of the town and a flat, pewter -colored apple with a stem and decorative leaf on top. The carving manages to be slightly more elegant than kitschy. Very slightly.

I make mental note of businesses lining the street as I slowly drive past, consciously obeying the speed limit. Gala Bridal and Formal Wear. The Evercrisp Diner. Caitlin's Confectionery. Village Candles. The Bungalow. Braeburn Tavern.

I don't fail to notice that most of them have apples of some kind worked into their logos, or that several of the names include mentions of apple varieties.

A pale golden-colored sign with Golden Key Realty

emblazoned on it in black glossy script catches my eye. It's mounted on a slim post outside a large house on a corner in town, across from the entrance to one of the public parking fields. I've got to contact that realtor soon and consult with them about Hidden Haven. Maybe the broker can get a decent lease executed before I complete the repairs. I plan to make only the bare minimum repairs anyway, and some people might prefer to rent a fixer-upper and pay a reduced rate. Unless, that is, Rebecca does the restoration prospects of the main house and I go that route....

Between Baxter's Department Store and McIntosh Memories, my destination comes into view. Tony's Pizzeria is brightly lit and from what I can see through the plate glass windows, it's crowded. I'd been to this pizza place a couple times back in high school. From what I remember, it was simpler then. It currently looks like a full-service restaurant, not just a simple pizzeria.

I guide my truck into a right turn at the corner, following the arrows on a sign for parking. There are open parking spaces in the metered lots behind the stores, so it only takes a minute to part and exit the truck.

McIntosh Ridge gives off nostalgic vibes, but it's parking game is contemporary. I make mental note of the parking spot number. I don't bother to download the app suggested by the posted instructions; I'm not going to be in the area long enough to bother with that. Instead, I approach the machine at the entrance to the parking field. Keying in my spot number and deciding how long to pay for takes a minute. I don't even know what time the restaurant closes. I make a decision and swipe my credit card to pay. The terminal spits out a receipt, and I slip it into my shirt pocket with my phone.

I'm on a personal mission with no backup and a desired outcome that feels vaguely like it's not so well-defined as it was last week.

A glance at my watch for a time check and it coincides with the sound of my stomach protesting my failure to bother with lunch.

It's 6:21.

I'm not late for dinner.

CHAPTER 12
REBECCA

BEFORE YOU PASS through the front door of Tony's Pizzeria, the delicious fragrance of vine-ripened tomatoes, fresh cheeses, and aromatic spices in the coal-fired pizza oven embrace you and your taste buds. While you're distracted by that, it coaxes you over the threshold. A staple of downtown McIntosh Ridge, Tony's is more than a good place to grab a slice or a whole pie. The glass case and the counter staff working behind it showcased the fresh pizza, calzones, garlic knots and more.

I wave to Anthony, who is busy ringing up customers at the end of the counter nearest the door. Without missing a beat in what he's doing, he gives me a chin lift and calls out a greeting. "Good to see you, Rebecca!"

Anthony's grandfather is Tony, *the* Tony who'd established the restaurant in his own name. Anthony's father is Tony Junior, known just as Junior. Anthony III prefers the full version of their name. It's a good way to separate them in conversation – if you ever spoke about two or more of them in one conversation. Which I don't think I ever have, but still…

The place is crowded, but I know where I'm going, and

carefully weave my way between the white melamine tables and toward the back section of the restaurant. In the more decorated rear area, two of the walls have murals of the Italian countryside and stereotypical accents like grapevines and statuary. The seats in the "restaurant" portion of the restaurant are lined with black tufted backs and headed red seats. A slim bronze sign welcomes patrons to PLEASE SEAT YOURSELF.

The dining room is crowded, and there are only two available tables. I choose the booth in the very last row and toss my pocketbook onto one of the bench seats before I slide onto th e other one.

What if Sam doesn't show?

He'd already be a terrible fake boyfriend if he stands me up on our first outing.

A quick pinch of the skin on my own wrist puts the brakes on what could become a flood of negative thoughts. It's a technique I learned years ago to snap myself out of negative thinking. I hardly utilize it anymore, but it works when I need to do it. And I might need it more frequently again if an agreement between Sam and I happens. That's still a big If.

Sam and I didn't agree about anything yet. And if he doesn't show up tonight, it pretty much tells me his answer is a resounding No. Maybe Sam decided he doesn't want to discuss it and made other plans. But he doesn't seem like the type of person who'd shy away from telling me that, face to face.

"Hey, Rebecca!" My friend Natalie's cheerful voice effectively pulls me out of my own thoughts. Natalie puts a glass of ice water on the table. "Do you want a menu or to hear the specials?"

I try to sound casual. "I'm meeting someone here, Nat, so two menus, please. Could you tell us the specials when he gets here?"

Natalie drops her order pad and pencil into the wide

pocket of her waist apron. Her pale blue eyes are focused on my face like truth-seeking missiles. *"Who?"*

We've been friends since middle school, through our respective college years, and for all the time after that. I wanted to avoid the diner and its dinner crowd that was certain to include at least a couple of busybodies, but I stupidly hadn't thought about the likelihood of Natalie working the dinner shift here.

"The guy who is working on some repairs at Ron Parker's place." I don't want to reveal anything about Sam's personal business, especially since there seems to be in something painful about it for him.

"I haven't heard about anything going on out there." Natalie's surprise at the information is understandable. Gossip and town news seemed to spread around McIntosh Ridge at the speed of light. "Who is he?"

"Like I said, he's the guy who is working on Ron Parker's place." Being cagey with my friend is an uncomfortable thing, but I don't want to add fuel to the gossip train, either. It will chug right along without me unnecessarily fanning the flames.

An increase in the buzz of conversation at the front of the restaurant snags my attention and sure enough, I spot Sam coming toward me. I notice more than one head turn in his direction. Some customers twist around so much it's ridiculous.

The low-key flutter of anticipation I have been feeling bursts into a wave of excitement. I grab the edge of the table to keep myself from jumping up to greet him with an entirely inappropriate display.

"Hey, Sam, I'm glad you made it." There, that was friendly but mature.

"I hope I haven't kept you waiting," Sam says.

Natalie is still standing at the end of the table, now blocking Sam from sitting down.

"Hi, I'm Natalie." She darts a glance at me and introduces herself to him while steppin all g to the side so Sam can join me in the booth. She smoothly transitions into server mode. "I'll come back with another glass of water and your menus."

Natalie takes a few steps away and stops to check on the customers at the next table. I can feel her eyes on me but fight the urge to look in her direction because Sam slides into the booth across from me. Refusing to be ignored, Natalie waves an arm over her head to make sure she gets my attention.

I allow my eyes to flicker toward her. Natalie mouths, "Oh, my God." She melodramatically fans herself with her order pad and waggles her eyebrows.

I can't completely stop the laugh that bubbles up inside me because of Natalie's antics. Sam's facial expression is quizzical, but he doesn't comment on my little outburst. I really hope he didn't see any of Natalie's reactions.

Grateful for that, I don't try to explain it away. Instead, I say, "I'm glad you came."

He moves in a bit further towards the center of the bench seat. "Did you think I'd make plans with you and not show up?"

I cringe because that's definitely how my comment sounded. "No, not at all. I didn't mean it that way. Let me rephrase. I'm glad you're here."

Natalie appears tableside again. She sets a tumbler of ice water in front of Sam, and with a flourish, she hands each of us a menu in a leatherette cover. "Today's specials are inside the front cover. I'll be back in a few minutes."

Even though I know the menu pretty much by heart, I take a couple of moments to read over the short list of specials before flipping through the laminated pages of the main menu. I feel incredibly awkward, that itchy in your own skin kind of uneasiness, because I can't stop wondering if Sam is thinking about my suggestion that we pretend to be in a relationship. I'm not seeing the menu anymore, I'm casting about in my mind for something to say. Finally, I settle on making a comment about the food. "I've never eaten anything here that wasn't delicious."

Sparkling conversation, Rebecca.

Sam looks up from perusing the menu. "Good to know."

I lower my eyes to the menu again. I don't want to do a typically female thing and order a salad. God knows– and so do my hips – that I love carbs. And I don't want to wrestle with spaghetti, linguine, or cappellini in front of this man. Nothing with a lot of garlic, either. It isn't really a date, but maybe it is. Kind of?

Sam closes his menu and slides it towards the end of the table. He picks up his water glass and jostles it slightly to move the ice cubes around before he drinks. "This place smells good. That's always a good sign."

I put my menu on top of his. "The way it smells makes me even hungrier."

Natalie returns with a full bread basket, its contents fragrant despite the white cloth draped over it. She positions the basket in the center of the table alongside a ceramic butter dish it, then makes eye contact with me, then Sam, then me again.

"Are you ready to order or do you need more time?"

Sam gestured at me, "After you."

It takes less than three minutes for my Chicken Marsala and his Chicken Parmesan to be duly noted on Natalie's order pad. Thankfully she stays in business mode and simply slips away to place our orders, after reassuring us she'll be back soon.

I restart the conversation with Sam by asking something innocuous. "Is anything in town at all the way you remembered it?"

"I've only been in town a couple of times since I've been back, and I don't have many memories of it from when I was a teenager." Sam flicks open the cloth over the bread basket. "I can't make fair comparisons."

He pushes the basket an inch or two in my direction. "I haven't looked too closely, but at least a few of the stores and the layout seem familiar."

Everything looks good, and I eye a slice of fresh focaccia bread, but the salads are usually right out so I wait. "A handful of businesses have been here for generations, but there are also some that are pretty new. Village Candles is four or five years old. Caitlin's Confections is maybe three years old."

"I recognized the Appleton Farmer's Market, the Empire Country Store, and the diner." Sam smears butter on a sourdough dinner roll. Both the role and the butter knife look tiny in his hands. "I remember this place. It was smaller, though."

"Tony's son, Anthony, redesigned the interior to make a nicer dining area." My over the shoulder thumb gesture is meant to encompass everything. "When the card store next to this place closed, Anthony took it over and added on a party room and small events space."

Sam settles more deeply against the padded back of the booth. "Smart idea if there is the business for it."

"There always seems to be something going on in the area, and this place is a fixture in town, so I figure there is." I take another sip of my water. "McIntosh Ridge isn't a big city, but it's also not a tiny nowhere town."

"I guess it's a matter of perspective." Sam briefly toys with his butter knife, then abruptly stops. He moves his hand away from it and flexes his fingertips against the tabletop. "Seems like a lot of things around here have been around a long time." While he's talking, Sam's eyes briefly scan the room. "Generational businesses, like yours."

A restaurant food runner appears with our pre-dinner salads on a tray. The young man, who looks like he's a teenager, offers us freshly ground pepper and grated

Parmesan as enhancers for the mixed greens. He deposits a silver caddy between us with different salad dressings, and then disappears from the tableside. After Sam and I fix our salads to our liking, conversation resumes.

"Well, it's not like this is the only thing I've ever known," I feel compelled to point out. "I'm not a world traveler like you must be, but I spent four years living in Washington, D. C. I've been places."

He raises an eyebrow at me. "Places."

Is this his way of asking me to tell him more?

"I've been to California, Virginia, Illinois, Florida, Maine. The Bahamas."

"Those sound like vacation spots."

It's my turn to smirk. "They certainly are. But I also did a two-month internship in California, and another in Illinois." I spear a cherry tomato on my salad fork. "Where have you traveled?" Given his career, I know it might be a long list.

Sam takes his time chewing the bites already in his mouth. "I can't answer that; it's usually confidential information."

I should have thought about that when I asked my question.

"Sorry." After two more bites of my salad, I joke. "I guess if you tell me, you have to kill me."

"Something like that. Seriously though, you could probably figure out at least some of hotspots I've been sent to. That will have to be enough."

It strikes me as odd that someone with enough wanderlust to choose a career that requires so much travel didn't then also travel for leisure purposes.

"You haven't done any traveling outside of work?" I ask.

"Nothing significant." Sam uses the side of his fork to break off a piece of his chicken. "Visits to the homes of a few different guys on my Team, things like that."

Conversation fades as another young man stops by our table and collects the salad plates. Natalie is on his heels to offer drink refills and assurances that the entrées will be out shortly. Before she, too, disappears again into the background, Natalie makes kissy faces at me while barely out of Sam's field of vision.

I have to pretend not to notice her at all. Instead, I ask Sam another question. "I know you said you're not sticking around here. Where are you heading next?"

"I have a job waiting for me in private security, as soon as I get things wrapped up here."

I can't help but notice that he doesn't say *where* the job is located, and I don't ask. Needing something to do with my hands, I finally take the slice of fresh focaccia bread from the breadbasket, "They don't mind waiting?"

Sam mirrors my actions and reaches for another roll from the breadbasket. "It's an independent contractor sort of situation."

I'm curious about what type of job it is, but I don't want to be nosy. There are enough nosy people in the Ridge without me joining their ranks. But I can't help myself.

"Can you tell me what your new job is?"

Sam's mouth quirks up on one side like he's trying to not laugh. "No, not exactly."

I can't resist prodding him. "And you don't want to say what it is, exactly?"

Sam finishes chewing the bread in his mouth and swallows. "Not so much I don't want to, as I can't. I'll be fulfilling assignments for the company, and I won't know what they are ahead of time."

I'm not stupid; I understand what he isn't saying. Whatever the job is will utilize skills from his military years. It's possibly or probably dangerous and confidential.

Natalie's return with our dinner dishes stops the conversation. My friend efficiently serves the main courses and clears away the salad plates. "You've got salt, pepper, and grated cheese on the table," Natalie reminds us. She picks up the nearly empty breadbasket. "Would you like a fresh bread basket? Or anything else to drink?"

Sam politely gestures to me with one hand, inviting me to reply first. His hands capture my attention again. They are big, with long fingers and neatly trimmed nails. I know he was working at his property all day, and he must've spent some time focused on scrubbing them clean before meeting me for dinner. His are capable hands. I can easily envision them doing all kinds of tough military-ish stuff during his career and the rough renovation work he's doing now. And I can't help but wonder how it would feel if he touched me with those hands... Not just to shake hands, but *touched* me...

Time to wrench my wayward thoughts away from that tangent. "I'm good, Nat."

All Sam murmurs his agreement, and Natalie hurries away to attend to her other tables.

I don't believe in lying to people, especially not to myself. The one time I ignored the truth that was in my face, I definitely lived to regret it. That isn't a road I plan to travel again.

Sam is extremely attractive in a lot of ways. I'm honest with myself enough to admit he probably doesn't find *me* attractive. Yes, some local guys think I'm appealing, but they aren't worldly like this man, and he isn't going to be tempted by the fact that I have a successful local business.

I can't believe I'm sitting here hoping I'm wrong.

CHAPTER 13

SAM

NATALIE RECOMMENDED Italian cheesecake after the dishes were cleared away. Rebecca was enthusiastic, and I like that she isn't a woman who thinks ordering dessert is unladylike or something. My own sweet tooth is a powerful one, although I usually control it. Most of my life, excellent desserts haven't been an option.

There is minimal conversation over cake, although we both lingered over the coffee. Natalie returned to our table.

"Nat, can you give me the check please?"

Natalie's gaze shoots to me and then back to Rebecca. "It's already taken care of."

"What do you mean?" I hear the confusion in Rebecca's voice. She continues, "I don't understand."

Her gaze ricochets between me and her friend. Irritation takes over when she says, "You paid the bill before we finished."

"He also left a generous tip," Natalie volunteers as she drops a handful of individually packaged dinner mints on the table. "Have a great night. Both of you."

"You went to the men's room one time." Rebecca sighs.

"We weren't done eating, so how did you know what the bill would be?"

"I found out what the total was at that moment and told Natalie to add double what dessert would probably be for both of us, rounded up, and added a tip." It's my turn to shrug. "Simple."

"I don't mind if a man asks me on a date, and on that date wants to buy dinner," she says. "But *I* invited *you* out for dinner. I should've paid."

I wasn't trying to demean her or something; I wanted to buy dinner after she had a challenging day. The very short time I've known her has been long enough for me to recognize she is independent and probably has to be tough all the time.

It's Italian food, not a flex of the patriarchy.

"I'm not a caveman," I assure her. "Even if I've been told I act like one sometimes."

Rebecca half smiles at that.

"I was trying to show my appreciation," I add.

"For what? You paid regular prices for the supplies you purchased."

"For the dinner invitation. For the good conversation." I shrug again, an attempt to lessen the significance of my next words. "For your company."

Rebecca looks pleased and a little embarrassed, but not unhappy. She rests an elbow on the table and her chin on her hand. "Not a caveman, but maybe caveman adjacent?"

I hold my hands up in mock surrender. "I can't argue with that assessment."

Her smile is a fuller one this time. "Want to walk off some of this good food? Orchard Park is down the block. We could walk there." She pauses and repeats again. "If you want?"

I slide out of the booth. "Good idea."

Both the back and front of the restaurant are even busier than they'd been when I arrived. Multiple heads turn in our direction. A couple of people in the more casual part of the place call out greetings to her. She acknowledges a couple of them with little waves and calls out greetings in turn, but doesn't hesitate or deviate on her mission to get out the front door and back onto the street.

Although by this time it's past 8 o'clock at night, the air is still heavy with the heat of the day. The contrast between it with the air-conditioned restaurant is dramatic.

I take up a position on Rebecca's left flank, so I'll be closer to the street. We fall into a relaxed pace as we walk to the park.

"Orchard Park," I muse. "I remember a Patterson Park, but not Orchard Park."

"It's the same park. More than a decade ago, the Town Council and the Chamber of Commerce started naming more things after apple varieties. Some of the merchants already had apple-ish names, like Braeburn Tavern and Appleton Farmer's Market."

"And others were all willing to change?"

"Some did, some didn't. Spencer Hardware, for example. We've had the same name since the store was started by my grandparents, and my father wouldn't change it." Rebecca seems lost in thought for a moment before she continues.

"McIntosh Ridge town administrators didn't want to keep businesses from opening here or staying here, though, so they raised money to have decorative signs for every business with different apple insignias. New street signs for downtown with the McIntosh Ridge design on one end of them, and a bunch of other touches to create an ambience."

"I haven't been paying close attention, but I noticed some of those things." Force of habit has me continually scanning our surroundings. I nod toward a place we are passing. "They were creative about it."

The storefront sign announced its name as *It's Paw-some*!

The accompanying image is a rendering of a large, fluffy dog with an apple balanced on its shaggy head.

"Yes. Molly McBride owns that business, and she used her own dog *as* the model." Rebecca looks back over her shoulder. "The photo shoot was actually held in my backyard. The owner of McIntosh Memories Photography is another friend of mine."

"The owner of the dog business is also a friend of yours?"

"For a long time. Molly was a year behind me in school."

At the street corner, Rebecca pushes the *Walk* button on the yellow post on our side of the intersection. She is wearing a small handbag that drapes across her body on a long strap, the pouch portion resting on one lushly curved hip. Her fingers fiddle with first the toggle clasp that kept the flap of the bag closed, and then the edges of the flap itself. To my eyes Rebecca doesn't look anxious; is she a little agitated because she's excited?

Of course, my eyes are experienced at assessing people up to no good, like criminals, terrorists, and other "bad guys," not sexy single women. So maybe I'm wrong.

But I don't believe I am.

I put my hand on the base of Rebecca's back when we cross the street, and I'm glad it's so warm that she isn't buried under layers of fabric. We continue walking in comfortable silence. At least it's comfortable to me.

There are sounds all around us– distant voices, car doors opening and closing, a vehicle with a loud exhaust pipe, someone singing along with a Kelly Clarkson song. Orchard Park is a block past where I parked at the municipal lot. Well-placed light posts illuminate the entrance to the small park.

"I'm surprised it's so well lit," I comment. Surprised, but glad.

"I think it was either that or figure out a way to lock up the entrances." Rebecca zips her thin jacket. "Then they would have to keep teenagers out, which would mean more police coverage. There were plenty of town hall forums about it."

"So they left it alone?" By silent agreement we slow our pace on the paved walkway and I reluctantly drop my hand from her back. A combination of retro-style lampposts are strategically placed around, but the lighting doesn't compete with the glow from the waning moon or the blanket of stars that spreads out above us.

"Enough people walk through here and use the benches or sprawl on the grass that there wasn't enough support for the motion made at town council for closing it or making it all accessible after sundown." She points at one of those benches. "Want to sit?"

"Sure." I gesture for her to sit first and then join her. It's an average sort of park bench and our shoulders touch. I am already acutely aware of her scent – a unique combination of vanilla, wildflowers, and something uniquely Rebecca.

Our conversation earlier reinforced my observations that Rebecca is well-known in the community.

I ask, "Is there anyone in town that you *don't* know?"

Rebecca tilts her head back and raises her face to the moon, closing her eyes. "A lot of people come through the hardware store for one reason or another. Multiply that by the years I've been working there, and I encounter a lot of people." She pauses for a second. "Probably three quarters of those people are men." Rebecca opens her eyes although she doesn't look at me. "I also overhear tons of talk about all kinds of things, including stuff I wish I hadn't heard."

It sounds like she has to be on guard too much of the time.

I try to let her know I understand without going over-board. "I can imagine how much you get hit on."

I feel her arm and shoulder shift against mine. "It's a lot. It doesn't have to do with me as a person so much as the fact that I'm *there*. I think being around tools some guys feel like they can behave like whatever they think manly is." Finally, she turns her head to look at me. "I don't know if I explained that well?"

"I understand." I understand, all right. A lot of men are sexist jackasses, and they step over the line with Rebecca. She grew up in the store, and it's her birthright, and she's making light of their bullshit, probably to help her cope with it.

She's interested in having a pretend boyfriend to scare off the jackasses and creeps.

I prefer being direct and dealing with things head on, but I'm sure it isn't the right time to press Rebecca further on the subject. If we are going to do this, I'll have better opportunities to bring it up.

Companionable silence continues again for several minutes. I think back to what I overheard the first time I met Rebecca at the hardware store.

"Is that what happened with Boyd?" I ask before I think better of it.

"You know Boyd?" Rebecca turns all the way toward me, and I look down at her, watching her mouth as she continues. "That was the day you were in the store, and I was at the register." She settles back against the wood and wrought iron bench again. "Boyd is harmless. Sweet, even. Just not my type."

"What *is* your type?" I'm curious to hear what she's going to say. Not for myself, of course, but out of natural curiosity.

Out of my peripheral vision I see her lean her head back over the top edge of the bench again and return her gaze to the star-spangled sky. "Honestly, I don't know anymore."

"Sounds like there was a time when you did know."

"I thought I knew." Rebecca speaks slowly, like she's choosing her words carefully. She pauses. At least I initially think it's a pause, but then she stays silent.

I decide to change the subject; I've learned a lot about her reasons for wanting the playacting she suggested. "Your idea about staging a relationship is a good one."

Rebecca twists toward me again, more this time, her left knee hiking up onto the bench and her right foot scuffing forward to keep her balance. The expression on her beautiful face reflects both surprise and excitement. She grabs my arm. "Does that mean you'll do it?"

"You made some valid points," I say.

Her smile widens. "Who hit on you? Somebody did, right?"

How the hell does she know that?

I hedge, which isn't like me at all. "I wouldn't necessarily call it that." This feels awkward. I know how to handle female attention, even the unwanted kind. "But I don't have time interruptions."

"Sure." Rebecca She hasn't removed her small hand with its delicate, pink-polished fingernails from where it rests above my elbow.

"We should formulate a plan."

"For what?" she asks.

"For making people buy the story we're going to sell," I point out. "You told me you haven't dated much for a good length of time. Why are people going to think you suddenly decided to get involved with someone?"

"I wasn't sure you'd agree with the idea, so I didn't really think about all the details."

I should probably wait to mention this, but I don't. "Have you thought about the fact that there's going to have to be PDA?"

Rebecca's eyes drop to where her hand has been gripping my arm, and she releases me. She's still smiling, but it's changed to one that's sexy instead of surprised. "You want truth or what I think I should say?"

"Always the truth. I get that we'll be lying to other people, but this isn't going to work if there isn't truth between us."

She nods vigorously. "Absolutely."

"Hit me with it, then."

"I'm good with PDA." Even in the dim light, I see her face flush with embarrassment. "I'm not saying I'm good at it, just that I'm good *with* it, as in its happening. Between us." She gestures awkwardly between herself and me. "You and me."

My response to that is, "Good to know."

I brush her hair off her shoulder and she shivers. I don't think it's from the night air. I play with her hair, allowing the silky strands to caress my skin, to curl around my fingers. Rebecca exhales a breathy sigh, and I ease my thumb to her cheek, stroking a light line across her jaw. I adjust my position so my other hand moves to her waist.

I don't mince words. "We should make sure we are believable. I want to kiss you."

Neither does she. "Good, because I want you to kiss me."

My grip instinctively tightens on her waist, like I'm worried she'll vanish into the night if I let go. This kiss is meant to merely be a test of our chemistry, a taste of what we'll need to do to sell our story. A trial run of sorts. The equivalent to running mission scenarios.

I don't believe me, either.

We're so close already, less than a second later my eyes are closed, and I'm brushing my lips against hers. A bolt of pleasure sparks down my spine as I finally taste her —lip gloss, a hint of chocolate from dessert, and sweetness that has nothing at all to do with the cake we enjoyed; it's pure Rebecca.

Sugar and sunshine, even amidst the darkness that's settled around us.

I explore her lips with gentle sweeps of mine, feel her hands sliding up my chest, over my shirt yet her touch still burning hotly into my skin. My thumb is still on her jaw, and I shift my hand so I'm cradling her soft cheek instead. Then I'm threading my hand into her hair, again appreciating the way the loose curls caress my fingers as we kiss.

Rebecca doesn't really relax and let me take the lead. No. She is a full partner in the kiss, in the melding of our mouths, the slow, deliberate tangling of our tongues. I hear my own pulse beating in my ears, punctuated by her little moans and throaty purrs that find refuge in my mouth.

We break contact once or twice to realign our heads and drink in enough air to continue whatever's happening between us right now. I manage to find enough self-control to really end the kiss. I pull back enough to fully breathe and clear my head. It's difficult partlybecause Rebecca is practically in my lap… and damn, I like it. I like it a lot.

Since when does a kiss affect me so much? Hot on the heels of that thought, I say something to show I haven't been taken unawares. "So PDA is not a problem, then."

Rebecca's voice is husky enough to tell me she's not unaffected, though all she says is, "Nope, we're good."

Rebecca is undeniably beautiful, but with on her face at that moment… she is nothing short of stunning. Her breath mixes with my own, hot and ragged. In the moonlight, our eyes lock . Hers are wide. Startled . It's a moment suspended in time, like when a landing craft is caught at the top of a rogue wave, no landing spot in sight.

It's almost too real. Too much.

Evidently Rebecca feels the same, because she says, "I better be getting back. I've got an early delivery coming in tomorrow."

I don't ask why someone else can't accept whatever the shipment is. I don't tell her that her participation and response to our kiss is making me think of staying right here and kissing her for hours. Instead, in light of her last comments, I give her another reason we can pump the brakes right now. "Sure. I've got patch to set and a dozen things to fix tomorrow."

CHAPTER 14
REBECCA

"SIX BOXES. THREE BOXES. ONE CARTON." I'm muttering my counts under my breath as I make notes on the top form of the stack on the clipboard within reach. "Quarter-inch, three boxes. Half-inch, four boxes."

Working on inventory is keeping my mind off Sam, especially off thoughts of kissing Sam. No, I'm not thinking about kissing that man; I'm just thinking about how I'm not thinking about it. The thought doesn't count when it's in that context. As long as I don't think about how his body felt under my hands, or how the hair at the nape of his neck felt between my fingers, or how his mouth tasted, or how he smelled so good in a way that lingered long after I left him in town.

Nope, I'm not thinking about any of that.

If I keep the business on the path for modernization at the pace I have set for it, (which I will), then by next year Spencer Hardware will be fully digitized and inventory will be handled much more efficiently.

After I returned from that year I "took off" after college, I managed to convince Dad it was time to modernize the family business by using Excel spreadsheets and barcoding.

To this day, I think he gave in because he was afraid I'd leave again if he didn't let me modernize things more. Those were major changes for him, but he couldn't deny the improvements it all made in accuracy of our record-keeping. Even so, physical counts are necessary twice a year. And even with my store supervisors helping, the process is time-consuming and brain numbing. Necessary, but…

"Rebecca, sorry to bother you." The woman's voice is familiar, but nevertheless startles me. I look up and Lilac Woodfield is standing in the aisle, a sheepish expression on her face.

"No bother!" I hurry to reassure her. "It's good to see you, Lilac. How are you?"

"Pretty good." She nods toward the shelves behind me. "Sorry to interrupt, I just need a picture hanging kit for the shop."

I shove the stack of boxes further down the aisle to clear the space in front of the display Lilac needs to access. "Lightweight, medium, or heavyweight?"

She wrinkles her nose in thought. "You mean what I'm hanging?"

"Yes. Sorry, I should've said that."

"It's for picture frames showing collages of wedding dress styles, and stuff like that. Medium, I guess, to be on the safe side."

"We have a kit that includes light and medium." It only takes a second to find the right box on the shelf. I hand it to Lilac. "Check that out. The weight limits are on there."

Lilac turns it over in her hands. "This looks like it will work. Thanks so much." She gives me an assessing look. "Do you know what you're wearing for the AppleFest Ball? Because if you want something new, I unboxed some great options yesterday."

"I haven't even thought about it, yet." Which is a total lie.

I know that AppleFest is in a couple of months; Spencer

Hardware is always involved in some way. The three -day celebration of many things that make McIntosh Ridge wonderful is a big deal around here. The annual event officially kicks off with a street fair that highlights the great shopping to be found in town and offers a fun, carnival-like atmosphere for the whole family. It's a town party.

Weather permitting, there is a casual, Friday evening welcome party and bonfire. During the day Saturday are niche store events and things that feature the farms and growers that are so important to the Ridge. On Saturday night, we have the AppleFest Ball, a surprisingly fancy dinner, dance, and silent auction that raises money for special town projects, and supposedly proves that although the area has plenty of rustic charm, it's still chic. Then Sunday, the focus returns to family-friendly special events and experiences throughout the entire area. Hopefully when visitors leave on Sunday evening, they take with them fond memories that they want to revisit in person again and again.

"I know you'll be there representing Spencer Hardware, and you'll want to look good." Lilac arches a delicate eyebrow at me. "Right?"

Lilac is right, even though I'm reluctant to admit it. "I have to be there."

She isn't done making her point. "You don't want to look like Tool-Time Barbie or Lumberjack Lucy."

"Who the heck is Lumberjack Lucy?"

"I have no idea but it sounds fitting!" Lilac exclaims, then wonders, "Is there actually a Tool-Time Barbie?"

"No clue. She's a doctor, an astronaut, a veterinarian, and who knows how many other things. Why not?" If there is such a thing, wouldn't I know about it?

Lilac has already bounced back to her point. "Well, then, you need to figure out what you're going to wear, and that's what I was meaning to say ; if you need or want something new, we just got in some great options."

I mentally flip through the clothing hanging in my closet. Practical, serviceable, practical, sturdy, casual. The couple of "fancy" options I have are five or more years out of date. My parents always went to the AppleFest Ball; it was just the kind of social thing they loved. Maybe I can get them to come back to town and go to the Ball ?

"You have to go, Rebecca," Lilac says quietly. She looks around furtively, checking for potential eavesdroppers, I think. "This is *your* business, and you can't sub them in for you because you don't want to go." She hesitates. "You can do that if you want to, I guess…"

"No, you're right." It'd be simpler if she wasn't, but she is. "I'm going to need something new," I admit.

I can tell she's trying to not look smug, even though she's not succeeding. "Well, if you want to check out what we have at Gala, come in when I'm working. I'll try to make it as painless as possible." Lilac hesitates. "Are you going to attend on your own? If you want a date, but don't want to give some guy false hope, I can find out if my brother is free that night."

Lilac's brother, Forest, is two years older than me; I've known him since middle school when we were friendly enough to sometimes acknowledge each other in the halls, but we were never in overlapping friend groups. If I had no other options, Forest could have been a good choice – but I *do* have another option.

This is probably a good time to mention Sam. I lean toward Lilac conspiratorially. "It's a good suggestion, and thanks for it. But I've kind of been seeing someone…" I allow my voice to trail off and give her what I hope is a meaningful look.

"Shut up! Since when, and who, and why didn't I know about this?" Lilac practically bounces in place with excitement.

Am I so pathetic that this is such big news?

"It's very, very new." I wasn't prepared to share anything

about the new arrangement yet, but I don't have a choice now, do I? "He's new in town, and it's all happened so fast, I think we are both still surprised. I think."

"New in town." Lilac zeros in on that part of my awkward explanation. "The guy at Hidden Haven? Is it him? Are you talking about him?"

"Yes. You know about him?"

"He's who you had dinner with at Tony's, right?" Lilac keeps talking, "I heard he's hot and mysterious and sexy and a little grouchy and hot."

"You said hot twice," I point out. "I think he's too old to be described that way."

Lilac waves a hand in dismissal. "Even silver foxes are hot these days. They can be any age. Is that what he is, a silver fox?"

"No, not really." He is simply a man who looks good, feels good, smells good, and tastes good. Oh my God, why am I thinking about all this again? "None of this is the point."

"Whatever you call it, I heard he's more than *fine*." Enthusiasm is practically vibrating off of her. "Good on you for snagging him quick!"

I try to slow the runaway train of Lilac's enthusiasm. "He's not even sure how long it will be before he has to... go."

Sam and I haven't discussed all that much about what the story is about that. I understand he has to be in McIntosh Ridge periodically, but he has no intention of living here more than necessary. Truth be told, I'm not even sure Sam has a precise plan about that.

"If everything goes well, maybe he won't *go* at all," Lilac ventures, watching me closely.

I also don't have an answer for that, at least not one I'm willing to give. I definitely don't think Sam is the type of man who will change his plans because he wants to date some random store owner, especially not in a town he wants to leave.

From the little bit I know, Sam's life in McIntosh Ridge was so miserable he can't stand the thought of living here again. He's tolerating it because there's an end date of sorts, even if he doesn't know exactly what that date is yet.

That entire situation is something else we should probably talk about. Or maybe it's none of my business as long as the guys around here back off because they believe I'm unavailable.

Instead of giving Lilac a definitive answer, I fall back on the two words people use to describe relationships that they didn't know how to describe. I look her straight in the eye because it's a completely honest statement. "It's complicated."

Isn't that actually the understatement of the year?

CHAPTER 15

REBECCA

FRIDAY NIGHT, after a long day of inventory, instead of relaxing to music or sharing good conversation, I'm listening to a repetitive series of hideous, jarring noises. The growling and grumbling coming from the washing machine is getting louder and louder, and I still didn't know what's causing the ruckus. I cleaned the machine thoroughly and examined what I could with the manual in hand. I have the advantage of owning just about every possible tool to make it easier, and whatever I don't own, I can get. But the washer is still making terrible noises as it works its way through fill, agitate, rinse, spin, and repeat.

From somewhere near the storage shelves built into the basement, my phone starts ringing. I push up from where I'm kneeling by the malfunctioning machine and its ominous racket. Hopefully Tara is the caller; I could use a break, and maybe I can convince her to join me for a drink, a snack, or anything else that removes me from this basement. As I grab the phone my eyes zero in on another familiar caller ID. I grimace, and immediately felt guilty.

I force a smile on my face to help force myself to sound cheerful. "Hi, Mom."

"Hi, sweetheart," my mother says. "I've got Dad on the line with me."

My dad's voice booms across the line, as warm as always and slightly too loud, like it tended to be when he was here in the house. "How are you doing, Rebecca?"

"I'm good, Dad. Are you both staying out of trouble?"

My father laughs. "What's the point of retirement if not to get in trouble?"

"Fair enough," I agree. "Any plans to get in trouble this weekend?"

Mom speaks up again. "We're laying low tonight. In the morning your dad has an early tee time, and I am meeting Phyllis and Eileen for brunch."

Dad grumbles, but I can tell he doesn't mean it. "They think I don't know that brunch is code for breakfast with booze and a shopping chaser."

"Paul, that's not nice!" Mom scolds him, but there is an undercurrent of laughter beneath the words.

I also hear the smile in my father's voice as he tells me, "You notice she didn't say I'm wrong. Right Rebecca?"

"I'm more interested in finding out who you had dinner with at Tony's." Mom doesn't try to hide the excitement in her voice. "I understand he's a very good-looking man."

"How do you know about that?" I'm genuinely shocked at how quickly my mother found out about that. "Are you still linked into the McIntosh Magpies?"

"That's really not nice, Rebecca," Mom chides me. "You make it sound like we are a bunch of gossips."

I have to laugh at that. "You guys *do* gossip!"

Like in any stereotypical small town, local news in McIntosh Ridge spread faster than wildfire and with just as much intensity. It was as maddening now as it had been when she was a kid, and news of her most recent misadventure with Tara had made it home before she did.

"We share news, information, and opinions. That's not gossip."

"I still can't believe you all group text." I shake my head although my busybody parents can't see me. "Mrs. Murphy struggles to open an umbrella; how does she manage to text?"

"Sometimes it's tricky for her," Mom admits. Never let it be said that Arlene Spencer isn't a loyal friend. "But she sticks with it."

"And it's funny when she gets frustrated with the phone keyboard." My dad chuckles. "I liked when she wrote that the mayor pooped into the school board meeting."

"Paul, be nice."

"I am being nice, Arlene. I didn't talk about how she wrote that Chief Kershaw thoughtfully provided his naked, candied nuts for the summer bake sale."

I can't stop the indelicate snort that escaped me at that, so I don't hear all of my mother's response.

"–and we all make mistakes sometimes." Mom is truly empathetic.

"That's true." I have to agree with her. God knows, I've certainly made plenty of my own mistakes.

Dad throws in his two cents again. "The Facebook group page is really entertaining. I don't know why you don't check it out. I have told you before, it's a good way to keep on top of things that might benefit the business."

"Don't start talking about business yet, Paul," Mom warns. "I want to know who you had dinner with. I understand he's someone new in town?"

The McIntosh Magpies were *incredibly* efficient.

Recognizing that it's a losing battle, I give in. "He bought supplies at the store to do some work on a property he inherited in McIntosh Ridge. He's going to sell it and move on. End of story."

"So why did you have dinner with him? Does he have a

name? What property did he inherit?" My mother's questions were delivered quickly, one right after the other.

She directs a question at my father, "Who died recently, Paul?"

Mom doesn't give him a chance to answer before she replied to her own question. "Susan McNally. Bonnie Bauer. Ronald Parker. Patrick Goldsmith." She pauses and I can picture her head tilted to the side as she thinks it through. "It had to be Bonnie Bauer or Ronald Parker. Ronald Parker, that's it, right?"

I don't even want to know how Mom deduced that so quickly. I simply say, "That's right."

"His son left home right around when he turned 18. I heard he joined the military." Mom makes a humming sound that signals she is mulling something over. "The Navy, I think."

"He was a good kid," Dad says. "I sponsored the uniforms for the high school baseball team even back then, and we went to the games all the time. Sam Parker was a great pitcher. There were major league scouts interested in him. *That* level of great."

I can easily imagine a young Sam excelling at athletics. "He didn't try to go pro?"

Her father's voice had gone quiet, which probably meant he was thinking more about the subject, or that he was thinking about something completely unrelated to it. Not that it mattered anyway, not really, but I'm interested in anything having to do with Sam Miller--or Sam Parker--including the reason he changed his name.

My eyes drift toward the tools scattered on the floor in front of the washing machine. Since I wasn't able to fix the problem, I'll have to call the appliance repair company based in the next town.

My mother's voice finally broke the silence instead of my father's. "Rebecca, I'm sure Dad wants to know about the store, so I'm going to hang up and figure out what I'm wearing tomorrow."

I'm surprised she's ending her part of the conversation, but why quibble about it?

"Okay, Mom. I love you," I tell her.

"I love you, too," Mom says. "Paul, don't chew her ear off about business."

Then she clicked off.

Dad resumes talking as if he hadn't gone completely silent in the middle of our conversation. Do I let that go? Answer his questions, or ask one of my own? Right now, the only questions I have are about high school Sam. I don't really want to open that subject up again and invite questions I don't want to answer, do I? Just because Mom isn't on the call right now doesn't mean she isn't close enough to hear what Dad says, and if it's about something that piques her interest…

I decide to focus on the business questions, and simultaneously start picking up the tools and putting them away.

"Business is good, no significant issues with anything." I slide the toolbox into its space on its shell. "Spencer's is sponsoring the high school baseball team and the community athletics program that covers K-12. We're also sponsoring some of the supplies for the community adult recreation program."

I can hear approval in his voice. "If the costs aren't too high, those sound like good exposure for us."

"The numbers work. It gets our name consistently in front of the community in a positive way. We also have a billboard display planned for the fall festival." I pin the phone between my shoulder and ear so I have both hands free. "I have staff to work at the booth, but I don't have to give details to the planning committee until two weeks from now."

"Excellent, Rebecca. Now tell me, what were you working on with tools?"

Just What the devil…

I start up the stairs to the first floor. My father doesn't miss much. Deciding what to say, I clear my throat and repeat his last word. "Tools?"

"Your toolbox makes a distinct sound."

I picture his distinctly paternal expression that must've been on his face when he said that and roll my eyes.

"Don't roll your eyes at me, young lady." I know he's trying to be funny, but the echoes of his attempts to be stern with me during my mostly happy childhood come through. For all their somewhat meddlesome ways, my parents really are the best. They are the primary reason Spencer Hardware is so important to me – it's always been important to *them*. Not that I don't enjoy the business, because I do, but it doesn't matter as much to *me* as me carrying on the family legacy matters to *them*.

"Sorry, Dad." I shut the basement door, glad last week I finally found time to oil the hinges. Even though I own a hardware and building supplies business, fixes around my own home are always getting away from me. I grew up hearing my father grumble about that same exact thing more times than I can remember, but never understood it as well as I do now.

My phone buzzes in my hand and the screen flashes with and incoming call. Tara. Awesome. At this point I could use that respite more than before.

"Dad, can I call you back? It's Tara, and I have to pick up. I'm sorry."

I know he'll understand; when we were growing up, my best friend always had one crisis after another, and we spent plenty of nights on the phone for hours or sleeping over at each other's houses.

"It's okay, go. Tell her we said hi. Love you, Rebecca."

"Love you too, Dad."

I end the call and click into the other one just in time to prevent it from bouncing to voicemail. "Hey, Tara."

Tara wastes no time on pleasantries. "You had dinner at Tony's with a hot guy?"

"My parents asked me about that, so why am I surprised that *you* know?" It was another reminder about the perils of living in a small town, as if the conversation with her parents and with Lilac weren't enough.

"I heard about it from three different people," Tara tells me. "My bigger question is, why didn't I hear it from you? And are you really dating this guy now?"

"There's nothing to hear." I put the call on speaker and set the phone down on the kitchen counter. "I've got to wash my hands."

Over the sound of the water in the sink Tara says, "I can wait."

I don't say anything as I dry my hands on a kitchen towel and hang it on the oven door handle. "How was your day? Wasn't your mom working at the store today?"

"I wish she'd agreed to come in Mondays or Tuesdays when it's quieter, and I could take the day off completely. Now stop changing the subject."

"Ahh, it all makes sense now," I tease. "You want to imagine something interesting or exciting in my life to distract yourself from your co-owner."

"No, I'm just nosy. We've been friends forever and a day; you already know that about me." I hear liquid pouring quickly followed by crackling sounds on Tara's side of the line. "Rebecca, I refilled my glass and opened a new bag of potato chips. Talk."

I stall. "Cheddar and sour cream?"

"Of course." Tara crunches down loudly on her snack. "Stop stalling."

"Tell you what, I'm dealing with some household issues

right now, and I've got inventory clogging my brain. How about we get together tomorrow night in person?"

"How do I know you're not stalling again?" Tara asks suspiciously– although she knows I always end up telling her everything.

"I might stall," I remind her. "But don't I always tell you what's going on?"

"Eventually." Tara chides me gently, "Sometimes it takes years for you to do it."

I know she's right, and my protest is weak. "That was different."

Finding out Josiah was thinking about the next co-ed to cheat on me with while I was thinking about engagement rings… it crushed me. It was all I could do to get through that semester at college.

I couldn't handle returning to the safety of McIntosh Ridge right after graduation which was always the original plan.

The Grand Plan. Stay in McIntosh Ridge after college and take over the family business someday. I believed Josiah when he said that he'd be happy with me here. I'm still not sure who was the bigger idiot – him for lying or me for believing his lies.

Because of him, when the time came, I couldn't cope with the idea of returning home and having people ask about my boyfriend, or my ex-boyfriend when they found out it was over. I was lucky to snag a job/internship opportunity with a company in Virginia that specialized in restoring old buildings to their original glory. Since my interest was genuine, it was a good way to lose myself in something that wasn't self-destructive.

And it kept my family and friends at bay while I sorted myself out.

"I promise," I tell Tara with absolute sincerity. She's my ride-or- die. She's the friend who helped me pick up the last shattered pieces of my heart and self-esteem when I finally shared the details with her, nearly two years after Josiah's betrayal.

"Deal," Tara readily agrees this time. "I'll text you tomorrow."

SAM

I HEAR the driveway gravel kicking up and then a vehicle engine slowing down until it comes to a stop by the main house. Sounds like a car, not a truck. That's confirmed when a car door opens and then slams shut a moment later.

I stay very still on the roof. I know the visitor isn't an enemy combatant, but I don't have time or patience to deal with another uninvited female visitor. Three of them two days ago, a pair of them yesterday, and two more individual visitors thus far today. What the hell was it around here that has me in the crosshairs of single women and their mothers?

Before I have eyes on the unwanted intrusion, a man's voice calls out. "Hello in the house. Xander Baxter, looking for Sam Miller."

The voice isn't familiar but the name – the last name – is vaguely familiar, like I have heard or seen it before. I stand and carefully move toward the roofline. "That's me. What's your business with me?"

"Good to meet you." The sandy-haired man tilting his head back to look up at me sports familiar sunglasses and a wristwatch that, from a distance at least, also looks like my own. With the sun at my back, and my overwatch position on the roof, the tactical advantage is mine.

"We know some of the same people. Welcome back to the Ridge." Baxter takes off his sunglasses and slips them into his shirt pocket. "I can come up there and give you a hand," he offers. "My family owns the department store in town, but don't hold that against me."

"I'm coming down." I grab my T-shirt off the roof where I discarded it a couple hours ago, the crumpled fabric now hot from the sun. I jam the hammer I'm holding into the toolbelt buckled around my hips and yank the shirt over my head. I'll come up later to finish the patching.

Climbing down the ladder takes only a few seconds. When my boots hit the ground I turn to face my visitor. The guy is of a similar height as me, with brown eyes and a solid, muscular build.

Baxter extends a hand to go along with his movie star smile. "Good to meet you. Ethan at Infinite Security gave me a heads up that you'd be in town for a while." He maintains steady eye contact. "I thought I would come say hello."

I shake his hand warily. "How do you know Ethan?"

The name Ethan I recognize, but I don't *know* him. I don't know any of the guys at the security company well. Why would someone I only met once or twice bother mentioning me to someone else? I can believe Baxter was military, but I need details before I'll bother finding out why the man wants to talk to me. Whatever it is, I'm not interested.

This impromptu visit is another interruption, and the steady stream of those is getting ridiculous. Bad enough there is more work to do than I anticipated.

Baxter braces his feet hip-width apart and crosses his arms over his chest. It could be either a combative or a defensive position, but the energy I get from him is calm. "We spent six years on the same team."

The reference to Navy Seal Teams is vague, which it

should be given the situation. Or the guy could be a cagey pretender. I was at Infinite headquarters for barely a week and barely met Ethan while I was there.

Baxter continues, "I doubt comparing Navy ink is going to be enough confirmation for you, so when you call Dax or Mason, tell them Uncle Cal said thanks again for the upgraded security system."

I pull my phone from a pocket in my cargo pants and quickly have Dax Mead's private number pulled out of my contacts and have the director of Infinite Security on the line.

"Sam. How's it going in McIntosh Ridge?"

Confident Baxter isn't a threat, I tilt my head back to look up at the cloudless sky. "It's going," I reply. "I'm making good progress."

"Are you heading back here soon, then?"

"There's still a lot to get done." I shift my gaze and while I continue the conversation, I look at my visitor. "I've got someone here with me who says he knows you. Xander Baxter."

"So he did reach out to you," Dax says. "Ethan said he might."

I don't get to know what the newcomer wants, but what I ask Dax is, "Can you give me a description of him?"

"I only met him a couple of times, but Baxter served with Ethan for years. He facilitated a connection for us with his uncle, to get the man's cooperation with security on a case involving Liam's wife." Dax tells me. "Tall and blonde. Decent-looking guy. My wife commented on it."

"Thanks, Dax." I know my job is potentially on the line when I tell him, "Back to your earlier question. I'm going to be stuck here at least a few more weeks." I frown. "Could be more than a few."

I can hear the shrug in Dax' voice. "Door's always open," Dax reminds me and ends the call.

I drop my phone back in my pocket and lift my chin

toward Baxter. Referring to the phone call, I say, "I hope you understand."

It doesn't really matter to me what he thought about me checking out the truth in his words, but since there's a connection with Infinite, I can be polite.

"Not a problem. Due diligence and all." Baxter moves his hands to his hips. "Any chance you're ready to take a break? Burgers or whatever you're in the mood for are on me. A welcome to the neighborhood lunch or whatever."

"If you want something, you don't need to feed me. Whatever it is, expect a no in response because I need to get done and gone."

"It'd be embarrassing to beg you to come with me, but I'm starving and didn't think to eat before I showed up here." Baxter grimaces. "But if I show up anywhere alone in town somebody will want to make conversation, and I'm not interested in that."

I'm skeptical. "But you're okay making conversation with a total stranger, Baxter?"

"Absolutely," Baxter agrees, then adds, "Call me Xander."

I don't understand the guy's logic ... but also, I do. People in the area seem extremely "friendly", and maybe that's not just because I'm new around here. Well, at least newly returned to the area if not exactly *new*.

The thought of grabbing a meal somewhere sounds nice, especially if I can avoid running into one of the women who'd dropped off food for me.

"Okay. Give me a few minutes to change my shirt and clean up."

CHAPTER 17

SAM

THIRTY MINUTES LATER, I pull my truck next to Xander's in a gravel lot on the opposite end from the downtown business district. We passed several different warehouses and industrial- looking buildings along the route here. It looked like just about everything was closed, probably because it's Saturday, but this parking lot is full.

The wooden and metal sign hanging to one side at the entrance of the lot proclaims the establishment is The BBQ Pit. The sign is unnecessary, though, because the smell of barbecue announces it better than any sign ever could.

Side-by-side we approach the log cabin style structure where other patrons are congregating. Customers are sitting at long picnic tables on both sides of the squat building, and open windows reveal more tables inside.

Xander jerks his head toward where the handwritten menu boards are hanging on the wooden building itself. "The restaurants in town are all good, but this place is great."

From the way people are digging into the food piled on their plates, I have no reason to doubt him. The line moves fast. A staffer at window one takes the orders, someone at window two takes the money, and a person at window three hands over the food. The system keeps the line moving.

The dark-haired woman who takes Xander's order is friendly. "Your usual?"

"Please." Xander agrees and asks. "What are the pies today?"

"Apple, apple cranberry, and lemon meringue."

Xander says decisively, "I'll take a slice each of apple and lemon meringue."

He moves over and I take his place. I order a classic two meats and three sides plus apple pie and the house-made iced tea/lemonade blend.

When we are seated across from each other at one of the picnic tables, we start eating right away. It isn't until I'm more than halfway finished that I speak.

"Want to tell me why you showed up looking for me today?" I spear another forkful of brisket. "I'm figuring you've got a reason."

"You don't believe I simply wanted to take a fellow veteran to lunch today?" Xander sinks his teeth into a square of fresh-baked cornbread.

My reply is succinct. "No."

"Fair enough." My lunch companion wipes barbecue sauce off his fingers and drops the dirty paper napkin on his empty plate. "There's a veterans group here, meets every week for an hour or so. Sometimes at the library, sometimes in the back room at the Tavern. Sometimes other places." Xander is serious now, no sign of the easy-going guy of a few minutes ago. "I get that you're not staying in the Ridge permanently. But until you leave, could you join us once a week for the meetings?"

I shift on the wood picnic bench. "Look, man, I'm sure it's a worthwhile thing and all, but meetings aren't really my –"

"There's a guy who comes every week and doesn't say much. I can tell he's seen or done some shit. Probably both."

I don't comment, but I also don't mask my thought. *Ditto.*

Xander takes a long draw of his drink and then continues. "I'm no psychologist or psychiatrist or therapist or whatever, but I do know that in a group setting, the addition of the new person can inspire new developments." He half shrugs. "Maybe you being there will do that. Maybe it won't. Still a good thing to try, right?"

In the midst of other people's conversations and punctuated by the hum of light traffic, silence reigns at the table. I'm not sure I believe that maybe helping out a fellow veteran really is the only reason Xander showed up today, but as much as I'm focused on finishing what needs doing so I can be gone from McIntosh Ridge, it would be more bearable if there's something else to do sometimes. Besides spend time with Rebecca. This place is only an intermittent deployment in my life, so that "something else" shouldn't be *someone* else. Definitely not the way it would need to be for that someone else to be Rebecca Spencer – the only woman to snag my interest for far too long.

Having a few local acquaintances wasn't a bad idea. Maybe a couple of guys I could shoot pool with, throw some darts, watch a game of something on TV. Give myself a mental break from the constant physical labor and the weight of ugly memories.

I grab a plastic fork and pull my slice of pie in front of me. "Sounds good."

How My

CHAPTER 18
REBECCA

AFTER DEALING with yet another upsetting encounter with Kyle in my store, Sam's sudden appearance is nothing short of a godsend. I feel bad that because I was startled, I spun around and spilled coffee on him.

When I apologized profusely and he asked why I was rattled, I probably shouldn't have mentioned Kyle's name. But I did.

Sam doesn't try to minimize his irritation. "Why won't that guy take no for an answer?"

"He wants me to evaluate some new acquisition of his with an eye toward restoring it to its former glory. I told him no I can't."

I'm relieved that Sam's all in on this with me (like showing up at the store to surprise me the way a good boyfriend would), but now my brain needs to focus on something actionable.

I point at Sam's dove gray shirt, now with its still spreading coffee stain. "By the time you get that home and wash it, it's going to be hard to get clean."

He doesn't even look down at it again. "It's a T-shirt, Rebecca."

"It's a quality T-shirt," I protest. He's right, it's just a T-shirt, but it's not a cheap one, and I need something else to think about right now. He saved me from Kyle, the least I can do is save him from… wearing a coffee splattered shirt?

Not equivalent, but at least it's something.

I whirl around and rush to a set of shelves along the side wall of the stockroom we are standing in. "I've got T-shirts and polo shirts here, all sizes. I'm sure I have yours."

"How do you know what size I wear?" Sam asks, sounding unmistakably amused.

I crouch down, peering at the labels on some plastic storage bins. "You're an athletic guy. More than a large." I twist part-way around, surveying him. "How tall are you exactly? 6 foot one? 6 foot?"

Not that it matters, I don't think it has much of an effect on shirt size. Does it?

I snap my gaze back to the bins, looking for extra-large shirts of any kind. "Bingo!" I shout, way too loudly.

"I'm six-two, actually, if you want to know," he says, walking closer to me. "Whatever you find is fine. Keeping this one on until I get back to my place is fine, too."

I ignore what he says because right now I'm focusing on nothing but the task I set for myself. Standing up, I toss the new shirt to him.

I don't know what I thought would happen next. Maybe that he'd retreat into a dark corner, or duck behind some of the shelving units. Maybe go behind any boxes stacked neatly across the opposite end of the space.

That he'd at the very least turn around.

I sure as heck didn't expect that he'd put a hand behind his head and in one smooth motion grab the back collar of his shirt and pull the whole thing up and over his head. It's a smooth move that takes the longest single second in history.

The breadth of his chest.

The dusting of hair over it.

That hair marking a happy trail down, down, down, and then his abs…

Good Lord. Sam has abs for days. For years.

All of it gloriously, evenly tanned.

He must take off his shirts all the time when he's working outside at Hidden Haven. It's a sight I've never been lucky enough to see.

Why is it so hot in the storeroom? Did the air conditioning break again?

I feel like my mouth is salivating, but my throat is dry. I need water.As he grabs the shirt and moves to put it on, I get a real look at the tattoo I've only seen an edge of under his shirt sleeves. It's a lion rendered in shades of black and gray, the masterful execution of the design making it look like it could leap off Sam's arm.

The dark blue fabric of a Spencer Hardware polo shirt falls into place and obscures the glorious masculine landscape and its lion tattoo from view. It's like an elbow to my side and snaps me out of my gaze. I force my eyes up and Sam's staring at me, something that looked suspiciously like humor tugging up the right side of his mouth.

"Something wrong, Rebecca?" He asks, I can hear the laugh he's trying to smother. "You're looking at me … strangely."

Now I know I'm blushing. Am I that completely transparent? Obviously, yes, I am.

Embarrassment heats my skin. I'm more than embarrassed. I get so annoyed when I catch men ogling me, and I just did the same exact thing to Sam.

I can't lie to myself; I'm a total hypocrite.

Best thing to do? Stick my head in the proverbial sand and act like I don't have a clue what he's talking about. Maybe it's not the *best* thing to do, but it's what I'm going to do.

"Looks good," I say, brushing nonexistent dust off my hands and onto the legs of my jeans.

That he did. "Yes." I nod so enthusiastically I might look unhinged. "I'm stoked you're willing to do this."

Sam is definitely fighting to not laugh at me, probably because I sound like one of the stock boys, but that doesn't matter. What matters is that I can kiss relationship pressure goodbye, and if I handle it right, it'll be a long farewell.

"There's enough upside for me that I'd be stupid to say no." When he crosses his arms over his chest, biceps bulging and straining the fabric there, it's all I can do to focus on his words. "I'm thinking you want to keep the detailsprivate and not discuss them here."

He's right about that. Loud voices from the warehouse are filtering forward to our ears, and I hear the beeping of some truck's back-up warning system at the loading dock. This is definitely not the place for a personal discussion, and I was crazy to get physical with Sam in any part of the store.

"You are absolutely right," I say a little too loudly. My mind scrambles for a plan. "How about breakfast tomorrow, somewhere public. We can talk details on the way."

The door from the store swings open into the stockroom and both of our heads swivel in that direction. Mike stands in the doorway, backlit by the store lights.

"Sorry to interrupt, Rebecca, but Mr. Burroughs has questions about his plumbing special order and Trevor is off today."

"I'll be right there. I had to get Sam a new shirt because I accidentally dumped coffee on the one he was wearing when —" I stop my over talking about the incident Mike was front and center for and repeat, "I'll be right there."

"Okay." Mike makes a gesture that's somewhere in between doffing an imaginary hat and saluting me, then escapes back into the store.

With my owner/manager hat firmly in place again, I take two sideways steps toward the door myself. "I'll text you to set up a time and place for tomorrow morning, if that works for you?"

Sam scoops his discarded T-shirt up off the floor. "Okay."

I hear him behind me when I pull open the entrance to the store. Mr. Burroughs is leaning against the custom orders counter that runs perpendicular to check out. Without looking at Sam again, I hurry over to Burroughs, though my attention is split enough that I hear Sam and Mike say goodbye. .

CHAPTER 19
SAM

THE EVERCRISP DINER is an eclectic mix of classic Americana and modern touches – although the retro aspects are simple interpretations of the perceived past and not particularly authentic. The front windows are already painted with autumn scenes, some of which are so realistic they are almost three-dimensional.

As Rebecca warned me, the restaurant is crowded. Some people stand in clusters on the sidewalk outside, and others wait in a designated area in an alcove near the glass front doors. Everyone is talking, and I don't know who is coming and who is going.

The mouth-watering aroma of burgers and bacon on the grill-top enhance the smells of other favorites, and they all make themselves known before I even open the door. The hostesses and wait staff are wearing pastel uniforms with matching aprons, the effect startling juxtaposed with modern haircuts and the occasional tattoo.

"Hi, Rebecca, everyone else who's waiting needs more tables for bigger groups, so if you see a two-top or two seats at the counter, you can grab whichever you want." The speaker, a woman who can't be older than 19 or 20, smiles at us both and answers the phone that's balanced on the narrow podium in front of her.

"Come on." Rebecca grabs two menus from a pocket built into the side of the podium. She hurries toward a table wedged against one side wall of the restaurant, in an area where multiple small tables are positioned.

I pull out a chair for her before taking my own. "I haven't seen many two-seater tables in restaurants here unless they were being used to fill in available small space."

"Yes," she agrees and passes me a menu. "I think places usually set bigger tables for two people, but the diner is always crowded so I guess it works better for them to have space-saving options. Especially since there's always some-body here alone or with just one other person."

I flip through the ample offerings covering meals typical for all times of day. Rebecca said we were going out for break-fast, so I make my decision and set the menu aside. Her menu is on the table, her fingers occasionally turning the pages. As soon as she closes it, I reach out and snag one of her hands again.

It startles her, because Rebecca squeaks like a mouse. "Oh!"

I raise an eyebrow. "Holding hands makes sense, doesn't it? We walked into the restaurant holding hands."

"Yes, of course," she says, and adjusts her hand to nestle it more comfortably within my own. Rebecca lowers her voice, even though the place is noisy enough with conversations, dishware clinking, and background music playing, that no one will hear her even if they try. "Now you understand why I wanted to –"

I interrupt. "Great choice for breakfast, darling." I wink at her. "You certainly brought out my appetite."

Before Rebecca can manage a response to my abrupt conversational turn, the server I saw approaching our table is speaking to us. I'm sure the young woman with the pixie haircut overheard me, like I intended her to. She says brightly, "Good morning! Hi Rebecca!"

According to the white oval name tag pinned to her shoulder, the server's name is Charlotte. She's an older woman who studies me with curiosity she doesn't try to hide. "Good morning to you, young man."

"Sam Miller," I answer her unspoken question.

Rebecca jumps in. "Lottie, this is Sam. He owns Hidden Haven." She stops there and her eyes flash to me, her expression easy to read; she isn't sure how much to reveal about me and my situation.

Lottie gives both of us another huge smile. "I know who he is, Rebecca. It's very good to see you here, Sam. Do you still like pancakes?"

She takes an order pad and short pencil out of her frilled yellow apron. "I'm figuring pancakes, scrambled eggs, and bacon for Sam. What do you drink these days?" She arches a white eyebrow at me.

I'm trying to remember the servers who worked here the last couple of times I was in here, a rare treat the last year of high school. "Coffee, please, and water."

The smile I give her is genuine. This woman has been working here for so long, clearly, and she somehow remembers *me*?

"What can I get you today? Waffles and fruit? Oatmeal?"

Overa minute time span, , as we receive and enjoy our breakfast, no than three people stop by our table to greet Rebecca, make small talk, and get introduced to me.

I enjoy breakfast more than I thought I would. I honestly like Rebecca. But the few times I've been interested in a woman for more than a casual good time, I wasn't the charming Romeo-type. I'm not a liar or a cheater, don't drink to excess, or do drugs. I control my temper and never let *it* control me. I like to have a laugh and a good time, but it isn't ever like this. Natural and easy, but never boring. A feeling of camaraderie with her right alongside urgently wanting to ravish her.

Damn, since when do you even think words like "ravish"?

Rebecca sips at her second cup of tea and then smiles at me over the rim. "Not too bad?"

"Not bad at all."

I leave Lottie a gratuity bigger than the total on the check and we make our retreat.

I need to get my thoughts back on an even keel. Remember why I'm doing this fake thing with her. She gets what she gets out of it, and I get guidance on the restoration project, and freedom from single women in the area who want but I don't, And maybe we both get some mutually desired with each other.

I decide to bring the restoration project into focus right now. "You want to go back to the property and make some assessments?" It's not really a question but I'm polite like that.

CHAPTER 20

REBECCA

THE DRIVE from the diner out to Hidden Haven was heavy with silence. Sam beat the awkwardness back with music, tuning the radio into some local station playing classic rock. Not her favorite, but not bad, either.

Now, walking through the small cottage on Sam's property, I'm trying to focus on the tasks at hand. Better to do that instead of focusing on more nerve-racking things.

There are renovation supplies piled neatly in one corner of the main area in the cottage, but the patchwork on the walls has already been completed.

I assess the wall I remember being in the worst condition within this building when I made the first delivery. "You already did a good amount of work."

"There's still a lot to get done. I'm keeping a good pace."

I hear what he doesn't say – that he isn't wasting time and plans be done and as soon as possible. Yes, he'll be coming back a few times a year, but those times will also be as quick as possible. And yes, I hear all that in his last five words.

Sam points out the prep work he'd done in the hallway and the bathroom. There are two closed doors in the hall, and I refrain from asking where they lead. I don't want to see his bedroom. I'm already wondering if any women in the area saw it before Sam and I struck our agreement.

The thought makes me unreasonably agitated. I mean, I don't know Sam well and don't have any claim on him before our agreement. Even that agreement isn't something he's bound by, is it? I had a supposedly monogamous relationship with Josiah and he'd stomped that into the dust.

Can I really expect Sam to keep up his side of the bargain and his word to me?

I think I can. I want to. Obviously, Sam isn't Josiah; the former Navy SEAL and the self-absorbed college student couldn't be more different from one another. But still…

I'm not going to think about Sam kissing someone else, or making another woman feel the way he made me feel when *we* kissed. And the thought of him doing more than that with someone in the area, someone I might know, that I probably *do* know, well I'm definitely not going to think about it. At least not any more.

This is supposed to be casual fun, and I'm going to remember that. I absolutely will.

Thoughts of Sam's kisses, and his flexing muscles when he changed his shirt at my store, and the way his ridiculously *manly* scent floods this small space – it's making me a little crazy.

I have to get out of the confines of the cottage.

"Let's look at the main house." I say as brightly as I can, moving toward the door instead of toward the bedroom.

Sam is crouched by the building supplies, and he straightens up. "You have time for that today?" he asks, jaw flexing.

We've looked at the outbuildings already, and I got the feeling he's been stalling about looking at the big house with me. But it's the most important part, and I can't stay in here, where he's been living. Sleeping.

"I have time."

I hear him follow me out the door and along the narrow path that winds around the cottage, leading to the main house. Of course I looked at it the couple of times I've been here, but I never actually studied it because each time I've been with Sam or distracted by him.

Now, I allow myself the opportunity to really look at the core of Hidden Haven, and it's simultaneously sad and exciting. Sad because it's been allowed to fall into such disrepair, and exciting because I can envision what a full restoration could accomplish. If the bones are good, and Sam is willing and able to spend some significant money on it.

He stays silent as I walk around the three-story structure. From the ground, I can see there are some gaps in the gutters, and exterior weather damage. Those things will take time and materials to breathe life into them again, but hopefully that's about it for outside repairs.

I tell Sam that, and add, "I can't assess the roof from here, so I'm not speaking about that yet."

"Understood."

On the way back around to the front door, I ask, "Have you noticed any rot or mold inside? Ceiling stains?"

The few steps up to the front porch are uneven now, and the wide porch creaks slightly when we make our way to the front door. I look at Sam, and he's looking at the breadth of the sheltering overhang.

"I didn't think I missed checking out anything inside or out," he says. "Found some rot, no mold. Some discolored ceiling areas on the first floor, not upstairs. I knew if the ceiling was leaking, it might need to be taken down to the studs."

The front door is solid and heavy, even though the finish is also weatherbeaten because there is no storm door shielding it. Sam holds it open for me to step inside. A staircase hugs the right wall in front of us, leading up to the second floor and a gallery type of layout.

Some people might be put off by the musty smell that clings to the inside of the main house, or the dingy wall coverings. Not me.

"We've got to look over whatever we can of the structure beneath the plaster." I walk beneath the arched doorway that leads into what was clearly a formal dining room. "If there is water damage, or any bug infestation damage, we will need to take it down to the wooden frame before we can fix and restore anything."

Sam acknowledges my words with a grunt. I'm getting fluent in that Neanderthal language of his, and don't take offense.

He's mostly silent while I explore the rest of the first floor, and the second. Even though time and lack of care haven't been kind to the house, I can clearly see it was once beautiful. I bet it was built for a large family because the rooms are generously sized.

There are two staircases in this old house, the second one off the kitchen. The third floor is made up of several small rooms, and an attic storage space.

"I bet this was used as some kind of quarters for house staff, originally," I think out loud. "In the early 1900s, it wouldn't have been uncommon for a relatively well-off family to have one or two staff members."

Sam stands in the narrow hallway outside the small room as I'm studying the walls. Another grunt to tell me he heard me is his only response. Not that I'm looking for one.

I take a moment to look out the narrow window, and the excellent view at the rear of the property. Flat, farm land gave way to a dip and then small rise, and then more land that gently slopes away from the house and other buildings. Different types of fencing outline different parts of the property, and I shudder to think of what condition they might be in, given the poor condition of the house.

Not your problem, I remind myself.

I make a few more notes in my phone, then exit the room and edge past Sam in the hall. He doesn't move at all to make it easier for me to pass.

Not that I really want him to, but it would've made it easier for me to try and ignore his overwhelming Sam-ness.

His space dominating size.

And the heat radiating from him, like he's internalized some kind of furnace.

And his intoxicating scent; how does he always smell so good?

And the crazy force field of whatever it is that overwhelms me whenever he's around.

"I better be going," I declare. "I'll work up a renovation action plan for you." Without waiting for any comment from Sam, I head down the steep stairs. "I've got a lot to get done today."

"You said you weren't working today," Sam reminds me, sounding amused, which makes no sense.

Why did I tell him that when we spoke about getting breakfast today?

I round the post that marks the end of the upper staircase and start on the next one. "I'm not working in the store, but I have things to do at home. I'm going to work on my ideas about your project, and I might get a head start on the list of what I need to do this week."

Finally back in the kitchen, I pause to give Sam a tight smile. "A businesswoman's work is never done."

Sam makes yet another inarticulate sound that could signal agreement, understanding, or even that he is making fun of me. I don't know which it is and I am not sure I want to. He follows me through the living room area where the shifting afternoon sunlight casts golden patterns on the dirty floors.

We are almost to the front door when he commands "Wait."

I can't help it, I freeze with my hand on the doorknob.

"I want to take you out on our next non-date," Sam says. "We are both benefiting from this arrangement, so it's only fair that I set up some of the necessary outings. Would tonight or tomorrow evening be better?"

I'm momentarily taken aback by his offer. He's been really good about this idea of mine, but I never thought he'd make time to *plan* something to further our ruse.

I want to give him a list of ideas for things we could do, but I think better of it because wouldn't that kind of interfere with the reason he just gave me?

Get over yourself, Rebecca. The man planned military missions for years, he can plan a non-date.

I simply pick one of the choices offered. "Tomorrow."

He's right behind me, so close he's almost touching me but not quite.

"I'll pick you up at 6 o'clock tomorrow." Sam speaks more quietly. "From the store or from your house?"

My heartbeat is so loud in the silent house, I wonder if he can hear it. "My house."

"See you then."

It's like his words release me from some kind of suspended animation and I grab for the door handle. I don't hesitate and I still don't look back, even when I think I hear him laugh behind me.

CHAPTER 21
SAM

ON SUNDAY, I'm on my way from the cottage to my truck to pick up Rebecca, and I detour into the main house. I was going to check on how the patchwork in the barn was drying and curing, but I have an urge to check on the house.

I can walk stealthily in my boots, but I don't right now. I make a point of stomping up the three steps to the porch, and across the depth of it to the front door. When I open the door, I shove it in and then slam it behind me. The noise echoes loudly through the mostly empty first floor.

"Too loud, Parker?" I snarl at the ghost of my father.

He always wanted quiet. Demanded it. Some of my earliest memories are of him loudly shouting at me to shut up when I was a young kid, too young even for school yet. My mother would hush me constantly whenever Parker was home, trying to make things perfect for him. It wasn't that she wanted him happy so much as she wanted me safe from his nasty mouth and his violent outbursts. Yeah, I'm sure she wanted to spare herself the fallout of his fury, too, but I vividly remember how many times – too many times –she put herself in his path to intercept his rage.

I was too young, too small, too weak to protect her.

When I was finally big enough and old enough and strong enough to stand up to the piece of shit, she was ill. Parker still went after her, but he had to go through me then, and that sucked the fun out of it for him.

Then Mom died.

I left, killed time until I could enlist. That grew into a career that enabled me to kill scumbags who terrorized and terrified innocent people.

All the while, I kept my promise to Mom and didn't kill Parker.

"I should have, you son of a bitch." My hissed words echo loudly in the room where he liked to guzzle cheap booze and terrorize us. "I should have tortured you until you begged me to kill you."

I turn my back on that space and drift into the meeting room. I close my eyes and I can see Mom putting a home-made chocolate birthday cake on the table in front of me, candles lit and glowing between blue frosting flowers. For my birthday, she let me have cake before dinner, before Parker came home and whatever the hell of the day would be broke loose.

Mom always had some kind of birthday gift for me. A special meal, or a special outing, or maybe even both. My favorite was a small, stuffed lion, the inspiration for the tattoo on my arm. I cherished that toy for years until Parker punished me for something by throwing it into the trash, right in front of me, laughing while I cried. What kind of psycho enjoys making his child cry?

I shake off the ugly memories and resume my circuit around the first floor. I'm not in here to make peace with my past. How can I make peace with a father who hated me and hated my mother? What kind of person hates his wife when she's a kind-hearted and gentle soul if ever there was one? I can't make peace with the memory of a man who would backhand a helpless child and punch a wife who was a foot shorter and more than 100 pounds lighter than him. Nope. Maybe some people could, but I can't. I shouldn't have come in here before taking Rebecca out, but I need to be able to work in these rooms, with other people, to restore them to something that would make my mother happy. Mixed in with the crappy memories of Parker are good memories of Mom telling me about *her* life growing up at Hidden Haven.

I slam the door shut behind me as another fuck you to Parker.

When I text Rebecca for her address, she sends back a pin drop. She hadn't been exaggerating when she told me she lives nearby. I meant to spend 15 minutes in the main house. Somehow I let myself get mired in memories for nearly twice that time. Now I'm on the wrong side of the speed limit to pick her up on time.

Her house is dark red shingle with white trim, decorated with empty window boxes and a flagstones front path. I wonder if she recently added them and hasn't had time to fill them, or if she's preparing to plant something different from whatever filled them. It's not until I get closer to the house that I can see the planters definitely aren't new.

Before my foot hits the first step, the front door opens inward and then she's pushing open the storm door. "I'm ready."

Rebecca pauses in front of the now closed doors and makes a big gesture at herself. "You didn't tell me where we're going. Is this okay?"

Her legs are clad in dark wash denim, her neatly tucked in blouse is white, and so are her flat, slip on shoes. There is a jacket folded over her arm, and she raises that arm to draw attention to it. "I might need this if we go to a movie or restaurant with air conditioning"

I know she wants to know where we are going. That's why I'm not going to tell her. From the short time I've known her, I already know she likes to be aware of and in control of everything. I'm sure that is necessary as far as her business goes, and her personal life, too.

"Good idea," I say, and change the subject slightly. "Did you accomplish what you wanted to yesterday?"

Her snug jeans don't slow her down at all when I open the passenger side door. She tosses in her jacket, steps up onto the running board, and climbs into the seat, all before I can offer to help.

She starts speaking as soon as I get in the other side and start the truck. "There are a lot of things around my house that need repairs. Mostly small things, but stuff my father never got around to doing before my parents moved."

"A lot of things?" I repeat her words back to her, but as a question, hoping she'll elaborate.

"Sometimes it feels that way, but not in the grand scheme of things." She looks out her window, watching the neighborhood pass by more quickly now that I can pick up speed. I have guided us to the county road that leads northwest of Macintosh Ridge.

Her next words have nothing to do with my question. She asks one of her own. "Mind if I turn on the radio?"

"Go right ahead."

We are both silent as she spends several minutes looking for something that catches her interest. I make a suggestion. "Want to hook up your own tunes?"

She seems inordinately surprised by my invitation. "That's nice of you, but I can probably find something."

A few seconds later she finds an old song by Queen. "Is this okay?"

"Fine by me." Who doesn't like the classics?

"Bohemian Rhapsody" is a long song, somewhere around six minutes. In my peripheral vision I can see her mouthing the words sometimes, and even tapping her head back on the seat during one particular section.

It's definitely a catchy song, which is one reason it's still well-known and played 50 years after it came out. For me, some of the lyrics hit… differently than they would for most people.

When the song fades away Rebecca shuts off the radio. "Where are we going?"

I'm impressed she managed to wait so long to ask. Should I tell her or let her figure it out for herself? She's lived in the area almost her entire life. It's not like it's going to be hard to predict once we get closer.

"You don't like surprises?"

"Not particularly." She returned her gaze to the passing scenery. I let the quiet sit while I navigate the curves of this part of the road. We are almost to Eagle Landing when she speaks again. "Most surprises we encounter as adults are bad ones."

There's not a trace of humor or anything light in her voice.

I am not typically a big fan of surprises, either. I endured a lot bad ones in my life, just like she evidently had. As an adult *and* as a child; the adult ones during my time in the military, the childhood ones, all related to Parker.

Thinking about it, I have to say something. "I think you will like this one. I get the feeling you have to plan and do everything in your business and personal life, and I wanted to plan and do something for you. I promise, if you don't like it, we'll do something else." Rebecca thinks about that for a minute before she says, "Okay. I'm going to trust you on this because I believe your reasoning is really kind." Her tone shifts into a teasing one. "As long as you mean it, that we can do something else if this non-date is a non-starter."

"Absolutely," I confirm. I feel like I just won a small battle in a war I hadn't known I was fighting.

Eagle Landing isn't that far away from the Ridge, less than an hour's drive, but it has things McIntosh Ridge doesn't. There's a psychedelic 60s-themed burger place, a three screen movie theater, a restaurant that only serves breakfast foods, and a bowling alley. There are other stores, of course, but those are the ones I thought about when I agreed to Rebecca's dating plan.

Parker's lawyer is a couple of towns further away, and I've stopped in Eagle Landing on my way to and from his office when I wanted to do quick errands without necessarily running into McIntosh Ridge locals. Of course they come into the other local towns as well, but it cuts down the odds.

Silence takes its place in the vehicle with us again, but it's not uncomfortable this time. And this time Rebecca doesn't reach for the radio. The hum of the wheels on the asphalt becomes our soundtrack until we passed the *Welcome to Eagle Landing* sign and I slow down.

Rebecca doesn't say anything or looked particularly interested until I put on my turn signal. "This is the destination?" Now she's looking around. "We are not going through the town?"

"Nope," I say and make a right turn at the corner that leads to the bowling alley. It's on the street that runs parallel to the main shopping strip, but a few blocks further in.

"Are we going bowling?" she asks, and I'm not sure if she is happy or horrified.

I know she's not a snob and her nails are short so she's not worried about breaking one. Maybe she's bad at it?

"Bowling isn't so bad." The bowling alley has a good-sized parking lot and I start looking for a place to put the truck. "You don't have to be good at it to have a good time."

I am scanning the lot so I don't see her eye roll, but I hear it. "I didn't say it was bad. I am just surprised you picked something out of the Ridge."

A spot at the end of the third row is empty, and I waste no time claiming it. I shut the engine and give her all my attention.

"There is a good chance somebody from the Ridge will see us here anyway, because it's the closest bowling alley. If not in here, then walking down the street, or getting food afterward." It's my turn to feel like I want to roll my eyes. If I actually did that, which I don't. Much.

I would have preferred us to eat first, but when I called the alley yesterday to try and reserve a lane for tonight, everything later was already booked up. The woman who answered the phone explained more than I wanted to know about weeknight bowling leagues.

Rebecca glances at the building. "It's been years since I did this."

"Then it's high time you did it again." I open my door and challenge her. "Come on, Rebecca. Be a good sport."

This time I see the eye roll when she joins me at the rear of my truck. I feel her startle when I take her hand while we are walking to the entrance.

"Relax, Rebecca. Holding hands isn't even PDA."

She huffs at me. "What is with you and that expression, anyway?"

"What do you mean? You think I'm not cool enough to know the expression?"

"I won't even bring up the fact that *cool* isn't *cool* anymore, but yes."

I open the surprisingly heavy front door, and the loud sounds of probably every alley everywhere greet us. To make sure she hears me, I have to raise my voice slightly when I answer her.

"I'm very familiar with the term and the abbreviation for it. The military is strictly against displays like that."

As soon as we step inside, I'm instantly reminded that I forgot to tell Rebecca we are here during Black Light Bowling, something management apparently does to bring in people when business might normally be slow. The black lights catch the white stitching on her jeans, her sandals light up like beacons, and her shirt glows bright as a spotlight. The effect is instantaneous, and so is the snicker I can't stifle.

"What's so funny?"

"I meant to tell you about the lighting situation here today, but now I'm glad I didn't."

Rebecca's answering laugh is big and bold. It echoes through every corner of my soul, and makes me realize how empty I've been feeling. That's a sobering realization that slams the brakes on my laughter.

I jerk my head toward the counter and focus on getting us a lane. The place is loud, but not exactly busy. The first 20 or so lanes nearest the door are occupied, but the rest are empty, their overhead screens flashing colorful promotions for the bowling alley and concession stands.

I request a lane toward the far end of the place, and the teenage girl behind the register rings me up. She's bubbly and flirtatious, and I suspect that's her normal demeanor. The guy who hands me the two pairs of bowling shoes I rented looks about is thrilled to be there as he would be in a dentist's chair.

"How do you know my size?" Rebecca asks when she accepts the pair I hand over.

"I guessed."

I put my free hand on the base of her back to guide her to our lane, and wrestle with my own desire to tease her, joke with her, get her to laugh again. The woman is unarmed, has no military training, and somehow sent me reeling with nothing but her laugh.

She's dangerous.

CHAPTER 22

REBECCA

I HAVEN'T BEEN BOWLING in a long while – not since the last time Tara coaxed me into coming here. When was that? Maybe two winters ago? But putting our names into the electronic scoring system is easy. It'd be embarrassing if I couldn't figure it out, because some of the lanes we walked past were occupied by actual children, and I saw a boy who couldn't be older than 10 setting it up for him and his companions.

My skin tingles in that way it does when Sam is near. The effect was so distracting on the drive here that I could barely focus on conversation. His arm brushes mind when he moves past with the bowling ball he picked from the racks. I watched him heft one after another, his forearms and biceps flexing and releasing again and again until I fled to our lane in self-preservation.

I can totally handle this.

"I'm up first," I inform him.

"Sure. Ladies first. Always." The way he says it… I don't know, it sounds like he's insinuating something that has nothing to do with the game. At least not with bowling.

I correct him. "Alphabetical order."

Because everyone knows that's fairer. The truth though, is I just want to go first.

"Do you want to warm up?" Sam asks. "Get a feel for the lanes?"

"Do *you* want to warm up?" I counter. "When was the last time you hit the lanes?"

"I'm sure you know frequency of play isn't the only reason to warm up, Rebecca. Lanes are always going to be different because of the boards themselves, the oil on them, the variables."

I smirk at his seriousness. "This isn't the Pro Bowlers Tour, Sam. It's supposed to be a date."

"Oh, it's definitely a date." He smirks right back at me. "I haven't been on one for a while, but this qualifies."

There's a lot of answers I can make to that, but they are all mostly flirty, and it feels dangerous to go there because this isn't a date, it's very specifically a non-date. Given how attractive he is, I can't risk blurring that line too much. I settle for saying nothing but, "Hmmm" and leave it at that.

I pop up from my plastic chair and brush past him to grab my neon pink ball, which also glows in the dark alley. I heft the ball and line up one arrow to the right of center, like that's going to make a difference. My bowling "routine" comes back to me like I did this yesterday.

I bend my knees a little bit, rock back a few times, and try to tune out the Aerosmith song blasting through the sound system. When I hurl the ball down the lane, it feels great. It's almost a gutter ball, riding the sharp edge of the lane for a long moment while Steven Tyler shrieks in the background. The ball veers back onto the polished hardwood and clips two of the pins, sending them backwards into two more.

My enthusiastic fist pump punctuates the whoop of excitement I don't try to contain. When I finish out my frame, however, I get the gutter ball I avoided the first throw.

Sam is surprisingly graceful on his approach and

smoothly throws his first ball, muscling down most of the pins. He finishes his frame by getting the spare.

In his clean, worn-in jeans and a long-sleeved cotton shirt, Sam looks good. Too good. Even the bright red and blue bowling shoes with the glowing 14 on the backs of them can't take away from the sexy eye candy he is.

It doesn't escape my notice that the three young women who recently settled in on the set of lanes to our right are checking him out. Except I have the right to ogle his ass and they don't. It shouldn't irritate me the way it does.

"Rebecca?" The way Sam says my name gets my attention.

"Yes?"

Sam doesn't try to hide the smile that plays at the corners of his mouth in the way I've become familiar with. "You're up."

I stand up and grab my ball from its resting place at the top of the ball return. "Are you sure you don't want me to get you the bumper guards?" After our first frame, my smack talk is totally unjustified, but I don't care.

Sam doesn't call me out on it, just says, "It's not like this is a tournament or something," He sits in one of the seats that puts his back to the lane with the women watching him so closely. "Have at it."

I glance again at that trio of women and smile widely at Sam. I sashay closer to him and lean over slightly, "Good luck kiss?"

He puts a hand behind my head to pull me closer and kisses me like he'd been in my bed only an hour ago and can't wait to get back in it again.

When Sam removes his hand and I stand up straight, I stumble back a half step, lips tingling and knees a little weak. Not even hiding his smile this time, Sam nods toward the polished lanes. "Go on with it, sweetheart."

I hesitate a second, trying to decide what to say, then give up on that and turn to take my turn. I feel his big hand swat my ass.

The shock of it makes me stop in my tracks and spin halfway back around. Our closest audience is watching with wide eyes, and Sam is looking entirely too pleased with himself. Or maybe with our kiss. Both of those things are curiously satisfying.

I don't want to examine why.

But this is the best time I've ever had at a bowling alley.

CHAPTER 23
SAM

THE RESTAURANT I chose ahead of time for dinner is almost as loud as the bowling alley. I don't consider myself old, but a juicy burger and perfect French fries aren't enough to make it less irritating.

"Headache?" Rebecca asks before she takes another bite of her own big burger. It's impressive how she manages to chow down without looking one bit less gorgeous than she usually does. Even after a long day, and nearly 90 minutes treading the boards at the bowling lanes, she still looks great taking down an impressive burger platter.

"Not yet, but I'm getting there," I tell her. "After Black Light bowling, I should have picked a quieter spot to eat."

She chooses a long french fry and drags it through the splotch of ketchup on the corner of her plate. "It probably seemed like they were a good match –the bowling and the 60s diner."

I can't deny that she's right; that's what I thought. "Yep, on the surface I thought they were.

Rebecca finishes her latest bite of burger. "You haven't been here before, so it's an understandable mistake."

Now it's my turn to swallow before I can speak. "The food's good so it's not a complete mistake."

"No argument there," she agrees.

I pull a few more paper napkins from the old-fashioned dispenser at the inside edge of the table and present them to Rebecca, then snag a few for myself. We simultaneously clean the telltale signs of our feast from our respective fingers.

After I drop my used napkin on the table, Rebecca grabs both my hands and turns them over. "I didn't think of this before, but your calluses must have improved your grip on the bowling ball. Unfair advantage!"

I extricate my hands and counter her move, then examine Rebecca's own palms. There are tiny calluses on her right hand. I gently brush a finger over them. "You had a little traction of your own, then."

Rebecca's posture stiffens, and she raises her chin, her brilliant eyes flashing at me. "I'm not ashamed of a few calluses. I work hard and that just happens sometimes."

"Why would you think you should be ashamed of a few rough spots?" As soon as I say the words, I already know the answer. "What fool told you that? Kyle? Someone else?"

"They aren't wrong." Rebecca says, her word choice telling me she's heard comments like that from multiple people. "It doesn't bother me."

There's no way I'm pointing out that her response to thinking I was criticizing her is proof that it does, absolutely, bother her. A lot. Instead, I focus on a different truth

"Humor me, let me tell you what I think. The fact that you're a smart, capable, confident woman who doesn't let her beauty get in the way of her success, well, that's sexy as fuck." I leaned closer across the table. "So only an asshole is going to consider those calluses as anything other than more proof that you're the real deal."

I'm great at reading people, but I can't identify her expression with certainty. Shocked? Pleased? Happy? Embarrassed? From the size of her pupils, maybe turned on?

A server in bellbottoms and a wildly patterned shirt stops at our table to ask if he can bring us anything else, then drops off our check after we decline dessert. With everything we ate from the bowling alley concessions, it's a wonder we had room for what we already ate here.

After I leave cash on the table for the bill, Rebecca and I emerge from the front door onto the street. The temperature dropped while we were enjoying our food, which and the air feels good. Rebecca pulls on her jacket on our way to my truck. I slide my arm around her waist in a move I never had the urge to do with a woman before. That's a small observation I stash in a corner of my mind to examine later.

The drive back to McIntosh Ridge is a comfortably quiet one. Rebecca clicks on the radio like she did on the way to Eagles Landing, but this time she doesn't ask first. She chooses a different radio station now, one playing easy listening ballads . It's long past nightfall when we get back to the outskirts of the Ridge. I pull up to Rebecca's house and shut the engine.

Rebecca puts a hand on the door, then darts a glance at me. She doesn't lean into me or anything, but she also doesn't make a move to actually open the door. "Tonight was really good, Sam. I had fun."

"You don't have to sound so surprised."

"I'm not surprised, it's just that…" Her voice trails off into silence.

I try to finish her thought. "You're surprised that you're surprised."

Her right hand falls back onto her lap as she turns to me with a correction. "No. Don't say it like I was expecting something crappy, or to have a terrible time. That's not it at all."

Her eyes search my own. "I wasn't expecting you *to get me* so well."

That's not a comment I expected her to make, that's for sure. "What *did* you expect, then?"

"I don't know," Rebecca admits, shaking her head, her hair falling into her eyes.

I let her words sit where they land in the space between us. Three words that say a hell of a lot more than their three syllables. Three words that cause her lips move in ways that lead me to think of putting my mouth on hers, nipping and licking and making it mine again.

The air around us has a pulse. I feel it, and I'm sure she does, too. It's like we are sitting in a bubble made of sexual tension and it could pop at any second.

Right now, this night can go a few different ways, and it's tempting to wait for Rebecca to decide our path. But I don't want to do that. I don't want to put the weight of that decision on her. Maybe I don't want to give her that control, but I'm not examining that thought now, either.

I rip my attention away from the temptation that is Rebecca's mouth and snap open my door. The outside air rushes in, blanketing me with reason.

There's a purpose to Rebecca and I spending time together, having these non-dates, and it's not what my dick thinks it is. Hopes it is.

Nope.

I'm going to be her shield from male attention for a while and give her plausible deniability against relationships for however long she wants to stretch it after we publicly call it quits. She's going to guide my restoration of Hidden Haven. A simple exchange of services, maybe with some benefits thrown in occasionally, if and when we are ready for that.

Simple stuff.

I focus on that bogus story and stride around the back of the truck, taking advantage of the extra few seconds to get the situation in my pants under control. I've never led around by my dick and I'm not going to start now.

Rebecca has her door open by the time I get to it, which means she purposely hurried. She doesn't meet my eyes, just wiggles into position and hops down from the truck, pointedly ignoring my helping hand.

"Good night. Thanks again," she says brightly and pushes past me on her way to the front door. My intention was to walk her to the door, kiss her good night, then get my ass home and deal with what I know will be the lingering effects of that kiss. Looks like her intention was different from mine.

I follow Rebecca and in two seconds she's at the front door, keys in hand. My feet stop at the base of the front porch steps, and I watch as she unlocks the door and ducks inside.

"Good night, Sam," she calls out loud enough for me to hear her through the door.

There's not much for me to do except answer, "Good night, Rebecca."

———

Loud banging – knocking, really – wakes me up from a dead sleep. Well, as close as I get to such a thing. I don't have regular nightmares anymore, but I don't typically sleep "well" either. At least not what would be considered well by most people's standards, I think.

My phone screen shows me it's 3:02 in the morning.

I'm already pulling on sweatpants when the noise starts up again. I don't bother with the pistol I keep in my bedside drawer; no one here to rob me would bother knocking.

The place is small enough I'm at the door less than two minutes after I opened my eyes, ready to verbally blast the source of my rude awakening. "What the hell –"

The words die in my mouth, smothered by Rebecca's much more delectable mouth on mine.

She's here, on my doorstep, hands clutching my bare biceps, pulling me down so she can reach my lips with her own. My shock evaporates, replaced by my always present hunger for her taking center stage. My mind gives thanks for this unpredictable, unexpected woman. Still kissing her back, I pull her all the way over the threshold and slam the door shut. I immediately have her back pressed against the wooden surface. Her response is to crawl one of her legs around mine. Her enthusiasm is as intoxicating as everything else about her.

Before this goes any further, I press my hand against the door near her head. I have to slow this down. "Wait, Rebecca."

Where she's still pressed against me, I feel her body tense, but she doesn't retreat. Her plush lips move to the side of my mouth, then trace my jawline and skim down my neck. Warm breath caresses my skin. "Do you really want to talk right now?"

"Yes." I cradle her cheek in the palm of my left hand. "What is this?"

"This?" Rebecca nips my ear. "Or this?" She slides a hand up and along my abdomen.

"Yes. This, and that, and everything." I'm trying to reconcile her earlier speedy retreat into her house with her behavior here and now. This is more in keeping with who I thought she was, but I need some clarity.

Rebecca rests her forehead on my chest. "I'm sorry for how I acted when you brought me home."

"I get that you apparently changed your mind. But before I can enjoy the change, you have to fill me in."

I won't do anything more with her if she can't explain her about-face. I know she's been through some shit, and no way am I going to add to it. I have enough on my conscience without adding something avoidable to the list. Especially something that might somehow hurt her.

She's not saying anything more, so I step back and try to think of what will defuse the situation. "Want a drink?" is all I come up with.

"No, thanks."

"I need one," I tell her and head for my refrigerator. Looks like I'm going to have the beer I didn't have when I got back here earlier. Rebecca watches me pop the top and gulp down a long swig. I'm not much of a drinker, one or two beers is where I cut myself off, but the cold brew feels good going down. I lower my hand and lightly tap the cold bottle against my sweats.

"I was embarrassed. When you dropped me off, I mean."

"Why?"

She blushes, like she wasn't trying to climb me like a jungle gym a few minutes ago. "I told you it's been a while, Sam, and I wanted to, with you, but wasn't sure if you wanted to come up with me, or just with any woman."

Well, that burns. That's what she thinks of me, huh?

I force myself to bring up the bottle again, not because I want more but because I want to give myself a few seconds to decide how to handle this. Rationally.

She doesn't know much about me. Not about *me*, the man as opposed to the guy who appeared back in McIntosh Ridge after decades away. I lean back against the kitchen counter and cross one arm over my middle, use the other to lightly tap the beer bottle against it.

"I'm not understanding why you showed up here unannounced, in the middle of the night," I direct a smirk at her, "and molest me."

Her discomfort vanishes immediately. "I did not molest you!"

No, she didn't, but now she's distracted from her embarrassment. "No, no you didn't," I agree. "I'm teasing," I add, because I'd rather she think of it that way then start flushing again. Truth be told, I did kinda like the blushing, but not when I found out the reason for it.

Rebecca copies the basics of my stance, but her posture is rigid, her arms tightly folded across her chest. It doesn't take body language training to see she's doing it to mentally protect herself.

"Look, I would be a liar if I didn't tell you I enjoyed your greeting." The proof of that understatement still hasn't gone all the way down, and since I'm wearing unstructured pants, I know she can see it. "Maybe we should give ourselves a mutual…" I pause, and note the way her eyes widen as she wonders what "mutual" activity I'm about to suggest. I bet it's not the one I go with. "…rain check."

She repeats the words. "Rain check?"

The situation would be funny if I wasn't also depriving myself of what she came here for. The knowledge that my idea is the better course of action right now is little comfort.

"Think about it, Rebecca. Between the project here, and us being busy with our non-date social activities –" Doesn't that sound stupid, but I can't think of a better way to describe her dating plan without sounding sarcastic. "We'll be spending a lot more time together, right?"

"Yes." Rebecca agrees.

"I don't want things to get weird for you." Yeah, I'm protecting her feelings and emotions, but I'm also protecting myself from something… I'm just not sure what that is, exactly.

She doesn't look convinced that what I'm saying is right.

Me neither, sweetheart.

I continue the offensive charge; hopefully not offensive to her, at all, but my thoughts run in military terms. It is what it is.

"It's obvious there's a mutual … thing here, between us," that sounds better than saying we want to fuck like animals, doesn't it? "We can take more time to go easy with each other."

Her lips, puffy from our kisses, are pressed together and squished up a little on one side as she thinks about what I said. Rebecca is wearing the same clothes as before, her curvy hip jutting out the side in her thinking stance, stiff nipples making themselves known through that white shirt. Obviously, it's not glowing in black light now, but she's still radiant. She's so fucking hot standing there, the guys in my unit would mock me forever about telling her we should wait.

The Jiminy Cricket part of my conscience that won't die, chirps again. *It's the right thing to do.*

"You're right, Sam, I guess." Rebecca finally says. "I'm sorry I woke you."

CHAPTER 24

REBECCA

"WHAT DO YOU MEAN, you attacked him?" Tara is at her store, so her shriek startles me.

"What do you mean, what do I mean?" I hiss. I'm in the hardware store, and there's no way I'm raising my voice, not about this.

"Attacked him like some kind of demon, or like a sex-starved maniac?"

She's talking way too loud for a peaceful candle shop. If I didn't hear the easy listening music she prefers for the overhead speakers in her store, I would be sure she's at home.

"I know you are working. How can you be so loud right now?" My words sound like an accusation, but I'm self-aware enough to understand why. I mean, it's not fair she has privacy to raise her voice right now and I have to keep a lid on mine, when I'm the one freaking out.

"I'm the only one here right now, that's why." Tara goes right back to her question but reframes it. "Oh my God, tell me you attacked him like a demonic, sex-starved maniac! And that you were naked so he didn't misunderstand."

"Do you even hear yourself?" I pin the phone more tightly

between my ear and shoulder and make a halfhearted attempt to organize some of the papers on my desk.

Tara is laughing when she says, "Of course I do."

There's a clatter of something and then the music at Village Candles gets louder. Then she moves the phone closer to her music system and *Ride*, a Chase Rice song from several years ago, blasts its sultry sounds my way.

She can't see me, but I cringe and hide my face behind my hand. "I hope a couple of church ladies walk in there right now. And your mother."

"Did he make you feel his loving, get you weak all in your knees?" Tara chokes out her approximation of a line in the chorus, laughing so hard I can hardly understand her.

"I'm going to… do something to you; I don't even know what." I can't help it, she's got me laughing along with her now.

"I know it won't be whatever he did to you," she wheezes out.

One of us has to settle this down, and I think it's up to me. "Do you still want to get together?"

At least she has her laughter under control again when she answers me, "We'll have to reschedule."

I don't hear the rest of what she says because now I'm remembering all the details about Sam's suggestion about a rain check on our steamy encounter. It made sense when he explained it, and I got kind of hung up on him saying we have mutual attraction.

Tara has lowered the volume of the music but I hear another sultry song playing in the store. "Maybe I'll re-create that display of sensual scent candles I had out in February," she muses. "I'll give you a couple free for inspiring me."

"Thanks." I lean my head back on the cushion I strapped to the chair for that purpose. Why get rid of a beautiful old desk chair because it doesn't have a head cushion? "I still have the ones I bought in February."

"Candles are for burning," she chides me. "You don't have to ration them. Your best friend owns a candle store, Rebecca." She knows what my response will be and cuts me off before I can say it. "And don't tell me they smell just as good without being lit, because –"

It's my turn to interrupt. "Everything is better when it's lit."

"That's right. Even friends. So when are we going out to get lit?"

I'm surprised she's letting the conversation about my earlier comment go so easily. "I don't know. Things are crazy here."

"When are they not?"

I hate to admit it, but she's right. Things *are* always crazy here. Even with two full-time office employees, a solid roster of managers and other staff, I *always* feel the weight of this place pressing down squarely on my head. And my shoulders. And my back. After nearly two full years of it, it's like I'm developing a hump there.

It could be a whole new marketing approach: "Come on down to Spencer Hardware and to see the hunchback. *The Hunchback of McIntosh Ridge.*" We can make figurines of me to sell at McIntosh Gifts. Maybe small stuffed ones. Raffle off a big one at the fundraiser next month.

I wonder if Lilac has something at Gala Formals to fit me and my hump.

"What are you laughing about like that?" Tara demands to know. "You're cackling like the wicked witch in Snow White."

Was I laughing? I have no time to spend laughing.

I have work to do. Work to plan. All the things involved in running a business. I have people depending on me for their paychecks, for supplies to build and repair their homes and businesses, for answers to problems they have no idea how to handle. I have parents whose early retirement is counting on me to make their ongoing business shares sufficient to pad their retirement income and savings. I have grandparents in the cemetery across from the ridge that gave the town its name, monitoring me, making sure I keep their legacy intact.

Okay, maybe that last part is a little dramatic, but it's how I feel.

I don't say any of that. Instead, I go with, "The wicked witch is in *The Wizard of Oz*. You're probably thinking about the wicked stepmother in *Snow White*."

"The wicked stepmother was in *Cinderella*," Tara claps back. "Don't come at me about fairytales. I know my fairytales."

I rub my fingertips against my forehead, in a halfhearted attempt to soothe myself. "You're right."

Indistinct voices in conversation somewhere beyond my office door grab my attention. I straighten up in my chair and try to look like the serious businesswoman I like to think I am.

"I'm sorry, T, I've got to go."

She starts to object but I press the red button on my phone screen and end the call as Sondra opens the door.

CHAPTER 25
SAM

I'M NOT A PARTICULARLY poetic guy, but I can see the apple orchard is beautiful in the kind of way that reaches into your soul and quiets it. I'm definitely not poetic enough to explain why Rebecca also has that effect on me.

But I *do* recognize both of those things as being facts.

When Rebecca texted me yesterday to coordinate this outing with her, I thought the idea was trite. McIntosh Ridge and the surrounding area are well known for apple orchards. Damn, half the businesses and locations have apple puns or other references in their names.

We barely got here in time to do whatever we are here to do. I am armed with the apple wrangling pole and she's carrying a bushel basket. I never did this before, even when I lived here. When I tell her as much, Rebecca gives me a side eyed glance. "Teenage Sam didn't want to chase the girls through the apple trees?"

"Teenage Sam wanted to get the hell out of town."

She tilts her head to the side, studying me. "Wanderlust over regular lust?"

My laugh sounds more like a snort. "I had plenty of both." I still do.

Rebecca, in her floaty dress, with sunshine highlighting the different shades in her hair, is a living, breathing reminder of the second part. I can't stop thinking about how good she would look with her hands pressed against the bark of a tree, that dress flipped up over her sweet ass, me between her thighs.

Or sprawled on the thick grass, arms around my neck, me between her thighs.

Yeah, there's a pattern there.

There are location markers throughout the orchard, and occasional signs explaining facts about the varietals growing. Some are like street signs, others look like mile markers on the highways. Some of the trees have empty crates beneath them, which I assume are for people to use for gathering apples. The one we brought from the tram stop is similar, only slightly rounded. I don't know why we had to carry one with us when they are also scattered around, but I suppose it doesn't make much difference.

Looks like this segment of the orchard is populated mostly by McIntosh apple trees. Seems fitting.

"The McIntosh are one of my favorite apples," Rebecca remarks. "I like that they aren't too tart, and not too sweet, and the flesh is a little soft, and almost always juicy."

I'm some kind of twisted creep, because now my mind is comparing her to that description of a fucking apple. She's looking at me over her shoulder and it dawns on me that she's waiting for an answer to something. "Sorry, I didn't catch the last thing you said?"

"Do you have a favorite apple? We could see if they grow it here."

I don't want to tell her that I didn't eat apples for years because they reminded me of this town, because it makes me sound like a head case. I also don't want to tell her that I don't know one type of apple from the next. Well, except for green ones and the Golden Delicious ones, and that's only because of color.

Nope. Instead I steal her answer. "McIntosh are always good."

Without warning, Rebecca stops in the midst of a row of trees that look like all the other ones we passed. I'm glad I have an excellent sense of direction, or even with the assorted signs, a person could get turned about the way out.

"This looks good." Rebecca rises to her tiptoes, reaches up and grasps an apple from a low branch. With a twist of her wrist she plucks it and drops it into the basket. She looks at me expectantly.

I understand how to use the apple picking pole. You bring it up under the piece of fruit, twist, and the target drops into the attached bag. It's a simple device.

I get to work, starting to methodically make my way around the tree she chose, using the pole to capture one apple after another, stopping after every two or three to pass my catch to Rebecca. She quickly transfers them to the basket.

"You're doing great, Sam, just keep making sure you try to pick good ones." The praise is ridiculous; I'm popping apples off a tree, not saving lives or fighting for freedom or doing anything of any importance. It's equally ridiculous how her words spark a warm feeling in my chest. Something that feels like pride.

About apple picking.

My return to McIntosh Ridge is messing me up more than I expected.

While I'm collecting more fruit, she's also plucking apples from lower branches.

We finish collecting fruit from this tree and she picks another one. The air is cool, the sun drifting its way toward what seems bound to be a glorious sunset. I've seen sunsets around the world, and I am still always impressed by them. Sunset and sunrise, the cornerstones of life.

"We are going to have to call it quits, I think," she says, her voice sounding… regretful?

I pass her the last couple of apples I snagged. "Yeah."

I insist on taking the basket from her because it's heavy now, piled with apples fresh from the trees. "I can also carry the basket and the pole."

Rebecca frowns at me. "You seriously think I can't carry an apple picking pole? I've been doing it as long as I can remember."

"Of course you can do it. But I'm here, and you don't need to."

She tosses her hands up in the air. "So I should skip along and whistle or something while you carry the basket and the pole?"

"Works for me."

Rebecca rolls her eyes at my words. "I don't know if you're trying to piss me off or just enjoying that you are."

I have to ask. "Why would you think I'd ever intentionally piss you off?"

"I don't know. I'm just trying to figure you out."

"I'm not that complex, Becca." Suddenly this playful give-and-take feels important. "I'm not playing any games. I don't have hidden motives or some secret agenda, beyond what you and I agreed to between us."

This conversation is uncomfortable for me because it's so personal, but I try to make sure my sincerity shows, that it isn't clouded by my need to bury the past. I haven't told her everything about my life, about my past, but she doesn't need to know those things. She just needs to know I'm not the asshole who lied to her and treated her like shit.

The sky is still sliding into dusk. Distantly, I hear someone ringing bells that probably signal visitors to come in from the orchard. I hear voices, and know people are hastening to obey. But I'm not moving until Rebecca understands that what I'm saying is true.

Her eyes lock on my face. "We have to leave."

"They can wait." I'm not moving until I know she understands.

"We'll miss the last tram out of the fields."

"Then I'll carry both you and the apples."

I see she's trying not to smile. "What about the pole?"

"Fuck the pole," I growl. "Do you understand what I'm telling you, Becca?"

Her gaze flicks downward. "Put down the apples, Sam."

"Why?" I ask, because her request makes no sense. What does me holding the apples have to do with this conversation?

Rebecca slowly repeats the words as if I am a nitwit. "Put. Down. The. Apples."

I don't know what she's getting at, but I do it anyway. She moves swiftly, using one foot to shove one of the overturned crates near the base of the tree closer to me.

"What are you . . . "

She steps up on the crate and plants her hands on my shoulders. "I understand."

Then she brings her lips to mine. She doesn't hesitate to take control over our embrace. And it is *ours* because I'm all in.

This woman fits in my arms like no other ever has. I don't want to think about why that is, I just want to enjoy it. Which I do, right up until a loud voice is speaking almost directly behind me. "The orchard is closing, guys, you have to leave."

I can't believe I let someone get the drop on me, but here we are.

Becca drops her forehead to my chest. First I think she's crying but a muffled laugh quickly tells me her shoulders aren't shaking with upset at all.

"We're going," I tell the guy without turning around. I need to make sure Becca is ready to face whoever that is before I stop shielding her from his eyes. She herself takes that worry away. "Sorry, Trent. It's my fault."

"That you, Rebecca?" Now it's the guys turn to laugh. "You're the last person I'd expect to find in an orchard clinch. I'd say take your time, but it's an insurance thing. You know how it is."

I maintain a steadying hand on one of hers as Rebecca steps down from the wooden crate. She pushes a hand through her hair and smiles at the orchard guy in the dimming light. "Indeed I do. Business insurance is no joke." She gestures between the interloper and me. "Sam, this is Trent Delmar. Trent, this is Sam Miller."

Trent is an inch or two shorter than me with a solid build that tells me the guy works plenty of hours at a physical job; you don't get that kind of result with weights alone. The guy's also got a friendly enough demeanor when he extends a hand. "Nice to meet you, Sam."

"Same, Trent." I'm used to working in the dark, and even without night vision goggles I can see he's what would be considered a good-looking guy. He's also around Rebecca's age. She helpfully provides more data. "Trent and I went to school together."

I'm figuring she means elementary or high school. Was he a high school sweetheart? Not that it matters. But I eye him more speculatively.

"Leave the pole, guys," Trent says. "The last shuttle of the day is at the stop now. If you miss it, wait there, and I'll give you a lift in the golf cart on my way back."

"Thanks, Trent," Rebecca says too brightly and then to me, "Come on, Sam. Maybe we can make it."

Damn right, we are going to make that tram if there's any chance at all. We do, and she doesn't mention helpful Trent again at all – not when I pay for the apples, and not on the drive back to my place where she left her car.

When she suggests coming inside to divvy up our bounty,

I'm stupidly enthusiastic. For all I care, she can have all the apples, but it's as good an excuse as any for her to come inside. Her body language isn't saying anything in particular to me, and I wish I could see inside her head to what she's thinking.

I'm thinking about that kiss between the apple trees. On the drive back, that kiss was mostly what I thought about. I know it's pathetic but that's the truth.

As soon as we get inside, it's like the floodgates open and words start flowing from Rebecca in a steady stream of consciousness-type barrage. "I don't remember if I already told you that Delmar Farms is my favorite of the local orchards. You saw why, right? It's got the petting zoo, the crafts barn, the bakery stand, and all the fruit trees laid out in such easy to navigate sections." As she's talking, her hands are busily grouping the apples on the counter according to size or something else she's got in mind. "Most of the U-pick orchards offer some kind of transportation assistance, at least for the field furthest from the entrance."

Now Rebecca is wiping down the inside of the already clean sink and running some water into it. "Trent and his brothers run the place. He's a good guy, intensely focused on the business, though. I can certainly understand that." She's putting some of the apples in the bathtub she created for them and interrupts her own monologue to ask me, "I don't suppose you have any fruit and vegetable wash?"

She talks quickly and before I can answer her question, she answers herself. "Of course you don't, I think most people don't. Not that we really *need* it, because Delmar is an organic farm so we don't have to worry about pesticides. I just like to be able to wash out any little bugs hiding under the leaves or stems or anywhere." Cute isn't a word that's used to describe adults. It especially wouldn't be used to describe a strong, independent businesswoman like Rebecca.

But damn if she isn't cute standing there in her pretty dress, hands in the sink, carefully bathing a load of red apples.

Moving slowly so she can stop me if she wants to, I step into the zone of personal space. I set my hands on her hips and bring my mouth close to her ear. Her hands stop moving in the sink, the sound of water swishing around the apples stops. I breathe in the scent of her skin, of sunshine and the outdoors, of fading floral notes from her soap or body wash. Her breath hitches.

"Becca."

Her whisper is almost too quiet to hear. But I hear it. "I like when you call me that."

"I do, too."

Neither of us says anything else as I press my lips to the delicate area below her ear. Her pulse hammers erratically against my lips. Rebecca tilts her head to the side to give me better access to her skin. My groan is matched by hers, and I can't help but do it again.

CHAPTER 26
REBECCA

SAM USES his hands on my hips to spin me toward him, and the desire burning in his eyes overwhelms me. I can almost hear the flames ignite between us.

I don't know what it is about the man, but *something* about Sam makes my breath come faster, and my pulse pound harder. It gives me a feeling of anticipation like being at the top peak of a rollercoaster, breathlessly waiting for the plunge. It is exciting and frightening at the same time. I can't bring myself to stop it – not that I want to.

He kisses me slowly at first, like we have all the time in the world. His lips move against mine, testing, tasting, then teasing. The kisses we've shared before were like a drizzle compared to the storm of passion that explodes between us.

Sam tastes faintly of apple cider from the orchard and cool mint, the two blending perfectly with the unique flavor of him. He tastes *right*, and I feel my own appreciative sigh.

I curve my left hand around the column of his neck, holding on tight, holding him to me, feeling my pulse throb in my own neck and between my legs. My right hand wanders from his muscled shoulder down his bulging bicep, up again, over and down to his sculpted chest.

I'm not a woman who ever hooks up with a man I hardly know. I've never done it even once in my life. It's not that I'm a prude or anything remotely along those lines, but I prefer a man to be in my life a bit before I welcome him into my body. That itself is an intimacy I never shared with somebody I wasn't in a relationship with at the time. Sam and I talked about PDA, but this is way more than that.

Since the long-ago breakup with Josiah, my dating life, by choice, has been sporadic at best. I joke about it with Tara. With most people I act like I'm unaware that the days I'm primarily at the register are the days more men tend to come in –sometimes for ridiculous reasons. Usually it's harmless. Sometimes it's funny. Other times, it's harassment or very close to it.

At the moment though, I simply want to get closer to Sam without examining the reason. Pressing against his chest, I savor the friction of my lace bra against my suddenly stiff nipples. His hand slips down the back of my sundress until his fingers spread across my lower back. His thumb rubs circles on the skin of my lower back.

"God knows I don't want to stop kissing you, but I have to say this…" Sam touches his forehead to mine, one hand still caressing my back, the other gently running up and down my side. "Are you sure this is what you want, Becca?" He pulled back enough to look me in the eye. "I'm not staying in McIntosh Ridge, and this fake thing we are doing has its reasons, but none of them are to build some kind of relationship between us. Honesty is important to me, so I want to be sure I'm not misleading you or anything."

I know he's making the point again that he is not staying, not really.

Well, I'm not a relationship person, either. Even people who love you leave, for one reason or another. Whether they betray you and dump you, or leap into early retirement in another state, the end result is the same. You end up having to figure it out on your own and survive on your own. No thanks. At least with Sam, he gets something, I get something, and we both get something hot.

If he didn't already know I want him, the husky note in my voice gives me away when I tell him, "I want you."

Again, I wonder how terrible his life here had been that, decades later, he still can't tolerate the thought of staying. Not that I'm in any position to pass judgment; it isn't like I completely moved past the pain from my own life, probably muchsimpler than what his suffering involved.

I arch into him, steadying myself with my hands curled around the sides of his neck. "It was my idea, Sam. I'm not looking for forever, not looking for a fairytale, not looking for something that doesn't exist in real life." My lips move along the side of his jaw, like he did to mine moments ago. "I'm just looking for the benefits we talked about." I nip at his earlobe. "A private display of affection."

Sam groans, the sound rough like it's torn from some-where deep within him. My words must have been enough because he picks me up and carries me to his bedroom. He shoulders on the light switch, carries me to the bed, and sets me down beside it.

Clothes and hesitation shed, condoms on the nightstand, anticipation and desire fill the moment until I can barely breathe. I try not to feel embarrassed about the imperfections of my body when he stares at me, his hair wildly tousled from my fingers, his gray eyes turbulent with hunger, his lips reddened from kissing mine. I take my time appreciating the sculpted lines of his upper body; this is absolutely the time and place to revel in the male perfection of him.

The noise I make at the full-on view of his shaft is mortify-ing; part whimper, part hungry, and part awestruck, it all adds up to desperate desire.

"Incredible," he murmurs, hands tracing my curves up and down, back and forth, gently caressing and occasionally pinching with sharpness that heightens everything. I'm so into the warmth of his skin, the magic of his touch, I barely notice when Sam maneuvers us both onto the bed. The only thing hotter than his talented hands and fingers on my body is the way his breath wafts across everywhere his eyes go first.

"You are incredible," Sam whispers. "Incredible."

I catch my breath, and Sam sits back enough to grip his impressive cock, his gaze still touching me even as he shields himself with a condom. Sam braces himself on top of me, one arm behind my head, the other hand stroking my cheek, then my collarbone, my breast, my rib cage. I appreciate that he's not rushing this, but my anticipation has morphed into urgency. I reach between us and guide him to my entrance. The slickness between my thighs is more than ready to ease his way.

Moment by moment, inch by inch, he pushes inside me, and I arch up again to draw him in. It seems like he's trying to hold still, maybe thinking he'll let me get used to his size, but I desperately need to feel him moving within me. I slide my hands up his muscled arms, over the lion tattoo and his strong shoulders, want to tug him down and feel him all over me. Sam pushes one hand beneath me and pulls me up against him. I wrap my legs around his waist and he thrusts deeper, harder. Faster. The sound and scent of sex fills the air, simultaneously primitive and divine.

Time passes slowly and too quickly, I can't hold back any longer. The spasms of my release seem to trigger Sam's, because his rhythm falters and he mutters a curse into my neck.

We collapse in a breathless tangle of limbs and satisfaction.

The room is quiet now, those erotic sounds of passion replaced by our roughened breathing, which gradually smooths out into a relaxed, synchronized pattern. Sam reaches out and pulls me against him. I go willingly into his arms, my head finding a natural resting place on his chest.

"Damn," he finally says several minutes later, and moves like he's going to sit up. "I don't want to get sweat on you."

My laugh isn't elegant but it's honest. "Sex sweat doesn't count."

He laughs as he settles back against the pillows, helping me reposition more comfortably. "Is sex sweat a thing, and is that true?"

"I don't know if it's an official thing, but it should be. Right? I don't know." Me and my big mouth keep veering into embarrassing territory. "It's not something I've ever experienced before, so I don't know."

Sam drops a kiss on my head and starts gently stroking my back. "Give me a minute. I've got to take care of the condom and I'll be right back."

Sam slides out of the bed and disappears into the hallway. I clutch the sheets more tightly around me. Now that I'm alone, the unsettling thoughts in my head get louder and take center stage.

That felt like more than simple sex. I'm not the most experienced woman in the world, but I've had a simple hook-up (or three) over the years, and it was never like this. It's not just that the sex was good (it was phenomenal!), It's something I'm struggling to define.

This feels *right*. I feel like Sam has been missing in my life, which is ridiculous, because I don't need a man to complete me… that's a concept society feeds little girls from the time we are old enough to understand stories. I am a modern, educated, independent woman and I don't need anyone to validate me or complete me or me or anything like that.

I'm just experiencing post-sex endorphins or some of the biochemistry effects, and once they pass, I'll be thinking clearly again.

CHAPTER 27
REBECCA

HEART POUNDING FRANTICALLY, I disentangle myself from Sam a millimeter at a time. The chill that strikes me everywhere that my skin loses contact with his is more than skin deep. Sam murmurs something unintelligible, and I lean in to kiss his back with its stark graphic ink.

Sam's discarded shirt is on the floor near my feet, where it landed last night. I know he's watching as I pull it over my head, letting the soft fabric drop into place. I can't help but look over my shoulder. His hair is tousled, his eyes sleepy but focused on me.

I hurry to speak before he can. "I'm going to the bathroom, Sam. Why don't you go back to sleep. It's early, but nature calls." I say the middle part as a statement, not a question, hoping he will listen and cooperate. He probably thinks I'm blushing because I'm talking about needing to pee, but that's not it at all.

His deep voice is deliciously morning-rough. "Do you need anything?"

A flurry of answers flit through my mind.

No, nothing.

Yes, everything.

Freedom.

Love.

None of the above.

All of the above.

Instead of saying any of them or anything at all, I manage a small smile, shake my head and leave the room, easing the door shut behind me.

I stand in the bathroom for way too long, (though in hindsight it probably was no more than five minutes from when I closed the bedroom door). I relieve myself, because after I mentioned it, that call of nature became real. I automatically wash my hands. There's no way to avoid seeing my reflection in the mirror above the sink.

The woman in the mirror shows me everything. Bed hair and sex hair combine in a tangled mess around my face, which is a little flushed but bright eyed and sort of… radiant? I guess it's true, orgasms can be a beauty tool –at least ones delivered by someone else, because the self-service variety never made me look like this.

No one ever made me feel like this before. Sexually, of course, but it's somehow more than that. Whatever it is feels… important, and scary, too, because I wasn't expecting to feel anything except physically relaxed. Not this.

I turn on the cold water to shock myself out of these thoughts. It doesn't work.

I can't stop thinking about how even last night, when Sam's desire for me was obvious, I had no doubts. It was more than him making sure I was giving full consent– which I definitely was. No, Sam was being careful of me for me. That itself was sexy as hell.

The mirror shows me that I'm running my hands up and down and over the fabric of Sam's shirt that I'm wearing. It makes me feel almost giddy, like I'm wearing the quarterback's varsity jacket, or dating a big man on campus in.

That last one I actually did, of course, so I can make a fair comparison. Except being with Josiah never felt this good.

When that thought barrels into me, my physical response is instantaneous; I clutch my abdomen and fold over like someone punched me.

What have I done?

When things ended with Josiah, it wrecked me. And I'm already well on my way to feeling more for Sam than I ever felt for Josiah.

This is a door I never should've opened.

I should've taken one of the outs Sam gave me. I should have pulled up my big girl panties and kept them on, realizing that all the things he brought to the table were too much for my long-denied, romantic heart.

Sam isn't the Beast in the castle on the hill, or Prince Charming, or any other fairytale hero. He's not the male main character in a rom-com or a romantic suspense novel, a legend or myth or anything but who and what he is – a man who survived a crappy childhood and left McIntosh Ridge, who's only here to deal with his inheritance, and then plans to be on his way. Yeah, he'll be back as required by whatever stuff his father's will requires, but he's not staying. He couldn't have made that more clear. And I really didn't care. I wasn't lying about that.

But now it feels different. I'm feeling things I have no business feeling.

I ask myself a different version of the same question; What the hell am I going to do about what I did last night?

My clothes are scattered around Sam's room. If I get them, no way he's not waking up if he fell back to sleep, or if stayed awake, I'm going to have to talk to him. I can't do it right now.

I kicked off my shoes when we came in the cottage door last night, I remember that. Another quick look in the mirror reassures me this shirt is long enough to be a short dress. Has a morning-after walk of shame ever been so embarrassing?

As quietly as possible, I open the bathroom door. I have to get out of this place – not just the bathroom, but the cottage, the whole of Hidden Haven. The little house is so quiet, I hear the hum of the refrigerator and not much else. I am a few steps from the front door when the scent of apples catches my attention.

On the counter in the kitchenette area, all the apples we picked yesterday are piled up in the sink where I left them overnight to dry. It doesn't feel right to leave them like that, jumbled together like they don't matter. I'm not thinking rationally about the fact that apples don't have feelings that will get hurt, or about my need to get out of here. No, I detour over to the pile of fruit.

My focus doesn't stray from the red gems in my hands as I start lining the apples up in rows along the countertop. They are mostly dry, which is helpful, because I'm not taking the time to wipe them off. I take the last two apples with me as I flee the house and quietly shut the door behind me. Thank God Sam didn't have an alarm on the door.

Anyone watching me maneuver my car out from where it's parked or make my exit at a snail's pace to try and minimize the gravel noise, would probably think I'm crazy.

And right now, I feel crazy. I look in my rearview mirror a few times, half expecting to see Sam chasing after me. I'm relieved and disappointed when that doesn't happen. When I get to my own property, I pull all the way up the driveway. It's not likely anyone will see me, but I don't want to risk not just taking whatever precaution I can.

I catch a glimpse of myself in the etched mirror my mother hung in the front hallway when I was nine and I cringe again. Everything looks as bad as what I saw in the mirror at Sam's place, made worse by time spent mentally beating myself up.

In the thready light of dawn, when I grabbed my purse

from where I tossed it when Sam ushered me into the cottage the night before, everything felt wrong. The nondescript handbag is my own property, but tucking it under my arm, shoving apples into it, and slithering out the door made me feel like a thief. I glare at the offending object where it lay on the little table under the mirror. Now it's stuffed with the apples I swiped. *See, thief.*

I have to figure out what I'm going to do about all of this. *Not the thief part, that's just a metaphor. Or is it a simile?* First step, shower and change clothes. My cheeks pop up when I blow out a weary breath. *I drove home in a stolen shirt.*

And I'm not done cleaning the front part of the house yet. Cleaning is a good way to wash, wipe, mop, and vacuum away the stress caused by lots of things, like guilt and frustration. Guilt is one reason why I'm not a one-night stand, hook-up, happy-go-lucky person. So, Sam isn't a one-night stand, not technically, but it sure feels kind of the same, I imagine, as that would feel because he's not going to stay in McIntosh Ridge. He's made his intention to leave very clear, right from the start.

It's not that things won't work out between us; there's no us, and never will be.

Which is precisely what I want.

I just need to remember that.

I must've been too long without sex… or even male attention that I welcomed… and let whatever natural endorphins or hormones or something like that temporarily mess with my reasoning and cloud my judgment.

"This house isn't big, Rebecca," I scold myself. "Clean yourself up, then clean the house up, and get your thinking in order, too."

I take a speedy shower in the hottest water I can tolerate. No lingering with lotions and potions, hair removal or anything that could remotely be considered beautifying myself. This is a shower for functionality. It's not for noticing love bites and whisker burn, or for remembering how it felt when a certain someone did certain things to certain parts of me. It's not for that at all.

choose clean, comfortable, non-sexy clothing. I'm going to clean and think practical thoughts. Lightweight sweats are perfect for cleaning.

I'm nearly 31 now. I'm not overly emotional. Not anymore.

In one hand I hold the long cord of the vacuum up and out of the way so I can pivot around the end of the coffee table and move behind the comfy couch that was my first furniture purchase when I took over the family home. The couch is sky-blue and piled high with throw pillows, and a far cry from my parents' brown color palette.

When the carpet is so clean it looks like it was just installed, I stop stalling before I vacuum a hole right through it. I prep myself to make the call. "You're a grown woman, Rebecca. Call him, tell him you freaked out for a few minutes. And you shouldn't have."

A surge of determination has me stopping the vacuum and abandoning it in the middle of the room. I hurry back into the kitchen and scoop my phone off the table. The second it's in my hand it rings. Tara. "Hey, can I call you back?"

"You've been dodging me since yesterday, and you expect me to believe you'll call me back?" Tara joked, but I hear the seriousness behind the veil of humor.

She's right. "Okay, I'm sorry, what's going on?"

"It's my brother again…" Tara's voice trails off, and I sit down heavily on one of the kitchen chairs. Tara's younger brother has a history of making bad decisions, frequently fueled by alcohol -driven temper and frustration.

Her emergency trumps mine. "Do you want to come over? Or have me come by you?"

"I think I need to go out and shake it off for a while, you

know? Pretend to be an only child for a few hours at least."
Tara makes a half-hearted attempt at a laugh.

"Whatever is best for you right now is fine by me," I
assure her. "Where do you feel like going? A movie? To shoot
pool?" I try to think of options. "Are you hungry? We can go
to one of the restaurants in Eagle Landing or Crosby Corners?
Maybe in Middletown?"

Trouble with Tara's brother isn't a new thing, but it's been
a while since she specified him as the source of a need for a
night out. She's the eldest of three siblings, and the one who's
always shouldered the most responsibility since their father
died years ago. Her brother Rhett seems determined to never
grow up, bouncing from job to job and scrape to scrape. Her
sister, Melanie, well, she's a whole different source of stress
for Tara. Her mother co-owns Tara's candle business – an
unhappy consequence of the investment she made when Tara
was getting the business off the ground. Growing up, I often
wished I wasn't an only child, but I don't envy Tara's family
situation one bit.

I shove my own problems and worries aside. I might be a
little too glad to do it, but I also want to be there for Tara.
"Whatever you want to do, I'm there."

I'll make things right with Sam tomorrow.

CHAPTER 28
SAM

WAKING up alone wasn't what I expected the morning after what happened here last night. The light filtering through the thin window coverings tells me it's still before dawn, and Rebecca isn't in my bed. When I heard – and felt – her leave the bed, I opened my eyes to see what she was doing. Rebecca was already by the door, wrapped in the shirt she pulled off me the night before, her hair rumpled from bed sport and sleep.

She anticipated my question. "I'm going to the bathroom, Sam." Her voice was soft. "Why don't you go back to sleep?"

"Do you need anything?" I matched her tone.

Rebecca shook her head and opened the door. I watched her pull it closed behind her and lay back down to wait for her. My body must have been uncharacteristically relaxed from our passionate pursuits the night before, so I shouldn't be surprised I woke up again and the light pouring into the room is much brighter.

I jump out of bed and step into my boxer briefs from yesterday that are on the floor where I shucked them last night. It takes less than two minutes to confirm Rebecca is gone.

No note anywhere – the cottage isn't big, and I look. I even look on the windshield of my damn truck. No text sent to my phone, no voicemail. The woman snuck out like a ninja in the night.

I go back to the bedroom. First order of business now is a shower to wash the scent of her, and of us, off my skin. I don't linger.

I'm too annoyed.

If Rebecca wasn't sure about being with me last night, she could have said so. I myself pumped the brakes a few times, talked about how we had time to get to know each other more. Hell, she could have put a stop to things at any moment and I would have instantly obeyed.

I scrub shampoo through my hair, replacing the feeling of her fingers in the strands with the reminder of my own. I made it very clear to her, multiple times during our acquaintance, I don't like liars. That's why I was so hesitant about her fake relationship fairytale. Yeah, I'm not telling her everything about my past, but she knows that. It's not a lie that some things are private me.

I rinse one more time then shut the water off. Not paying attention when I step out of the shower, I almost wipe out on the slippery tile. Whoever chose these tiles for the bathroom floor was an idiot. At the sink, I swipe the palm of my hand over the fog mirror. Since I have not dried my hands yet, it doesn't do much to clear the moisture there. Not that it matters; I know what I look like, and I don't need to see the jumble of emotions I'm feeling reflected there.

There are clean towels on the wall rack and I grabbed one to dry off. Too bad I can't wipe away my thoughts as easily as the water droplets.

Some lies benefit a greater good. That's why I could deal with them when related to mission ops. That's why I could see the benefit Rebecca would gain from this plan. Sure, I benefit from the restoration guidance, but I could get that somewhere else pretty easily. Outside of those things, between us, I need honesty. It doesn't take a genius to figure out that a pretend relationship could bring up feelings that the situation is real, even though it isn't. Kind of like a twisted version of Stockholm Syndrome where a captive falls in love with their keeper, or a victim falls for their victimizer.

That means I can't very well lie to myself, can I? It would be hypocritical. Foolish, too.

I'm not simply surprised that she is gone; I'm also surprised that it hurts.

How pathetic is that? At least it confirms that the honesty requirement and not lying to myself are absolute rules.

Next order of business is to strip the bed. All the bedding is going into the washing machine stat. Rebecca's scent better come out of it all or I'm not going to be able to reuse those sheets until it does. I ball everything up and leaned over to sniff the mattress like a weirdo. I must still smell her because the sheets are nearby, but just in case I'll hit the mattress with Lysol or something.

It's stupid to spend any more time thinking about this. Rebecca and I spent some good hours together. Then we fucked – more than once, thank you – and that was great. Since when do I care about what happens after?

Thankfully, I left the washing machine empty yesterday, so I have the bedding stuffed in, detergent added, and machine started quickly. I've got a lot of shit to do today. I'm behind my self-imposed schedule because I spent so much time with Rebecca yesterday.

I leave the machine to do its job and go back in the kitchenette.

My mind snaps back to questioning when I started caring so much about what happens after sex. I'm never not polite to a partner afterward. That means I don't sneak out. I say goodbye and take my leave, or walk her to the door, or to the car. Didn't I deserve that much from Rebecca? She left nothing behind except the scent of her on my sheets.

What are you, Miller, a 16 -year-old girl who got ditched at the school dance? I hear that jibe in the voice of a scary ass drill instructor I did thousands of push-ups for in the Navy. If he was here and could hear my internal monologue, he'd mock me and give me endless drills to burn that nonsense right out of me.

I stand in front of the kitchen counter where a formation of clean apples are lined up in neat rows along the counter. Rebecca didn't take time to say goodbye, let me know she was leaving, but she took time to assemble the apples like some kind of shiny red Battalion.

I need coffee to get my head on straight and deal with what needs to be done. I can skip breakfast, but coffee would be good. Here or in town?

Here. I don't need to risk running into Rebecca when I'm aggravated like this, or encountering townspeople who might have questions about me and Rebecca. I'm not in the mood to fake anything.

I fill the coffee machine reservoir and slot in a pod grabbed from the open box in an upper cabinet. Mindlessly, I shove my mug under the spout and complete the process when the ready light comes on. I brace my hands on the counter and stare blankly at the machine while it hisses and gurgles.

I picture my to do list in my head because I don't want to look at my phone. Objectively, I know my reaction to Rebecca sneaking out doesn't make sense. Morning-after conversations could be awkward under the best of circumstances, and by ducking out she spared us both. Our strange relationship situation wouldn't have made it any easier.

The coffee cycle finishes and I get on with the day. The forecast is calling for rain so I planned accordingly. Some things I don't want to do in dampness, but this rough work will be okay. Thoughts of Rebecca tucked firmly away, I get busy.

Three hours later or so, when I hear tires outside, my shoulders tense. I'm not expecting anyone. It better not be a random woman dropping by with smiles and food containing ulterior motives as added ingredients.

Maybe it's Rebecca? Not likely. I roll my shoulders and stay focused. I can hear a vehicle door being opened and then slammed shut.

The grass and gravel entryway to the barn doesn't provide footsteps sounds the way hard surfaces do, but I hear rustling that tells me whoever was in the vehicle is on approach. The sliding doors are both open, airing out the musty interior and the pungent smells of spackle and paint.

The overcast sun behind my visitor shrouds the man in shadow until he moves further into the space. It doesn't matter because the sound of his car engine told me. Xander takes off his baseball cap, runs a hand through his hair, and replaces it. No greeting, he asks, "What's the plan for this space?"

"Same as the plan for everything else. Sell it or lease it." I go back to hammering the last hinge pin into the tack room door I hung this morning. "Why are you here? What do you want?"

Xander barks out a laugh. "You're Mr. Personality this morning."

I'm only half kidding when I point out, "You don't know me well enough to say that."

"No," Xander agrees. "But I'm guessing you're not always an asshole to people who stop by."

I pull the door open and then let it swing closed, testing and re-testing my work. "People don't exactly stop by. And I am not being an asshole, either. I just have a lot to get done and don't believe in wasting time."

Finished with the door, I turn to face Xander directly. Not

like I am going to tell him, a guy I barely know, that my -
pretend girlfriend snuck out of my bed that morning and I'm
irrationally irritated because of it. Automatically, my mind
starts to analyze the situation again; we are not really in a
romantic relationship, so what is my problem? I'm not in the
mood to talk, so I stand there for barely 15 seconds then walk
across the floor to one of the old horse stalls, where I busy
myself assessing the condition of the wood. The act is as
phony as Rebecca's girlfriend status. And the word "girlfriend" itself is ridiculous for someone my age to use.

Xander clears his throat. "I can see you're busy, but a few
of us are getting together at Braeburn tonight at eight o'clock.
Casual, burgers and beer kind of thing." The guy coughs, but
it sounds suspiciously like he is covering a laugh. "If you can
take a break then and tear yourself away from all this, you
could kick back for couple of hours."

I stop pretending to examine something that doesn't
require any attention at all, because I thoroughly examined it
the first few days I was here. I shake my head, irritated at
myself. Is this my automatic default now? Faking things?

I turn around and give Xander my full attention, like I
should have when he first showed up. "Who is the 'us' you're
talking about?"

"A few of the guys in the veterans group I told you about.
It's not some official meeting or anything. Some of us are
friends and get together because, why not?" Xander shifts his
weight back and then forward slightly in his polished loafers.
"It's also not unusual to run into other friends and acquaintances at the Braeburn."

"Not a lot of local options, huh?" I only noticed a couple
of bar-type places when I was in town, but I wasn't actively
looking for them, either.

"Only a few, otherwise you have to drive into one of the
neighboring towns. Except for couple of exceptions for
specialty places, none of them are better than what we've got

here." Xander shrugs a shoulder. "Like I said, tonight's a casual thing. Braeburn is more than good."

The "No" is on the tip of my tongue when I stop it. I'm probably going to have a beer or two alone in the cottage, anyway. The men I'll meet tonight are not my personal brothers-in-arms who'd pepper me with questions or tease me mercilessly about anything and everything. But they could be decent company while I have a drink or two and relax a little before putting in another long day tomorrow.

I'm not going to get drunk, but I know that drinking alone to kill time isn't a great idea. During my military career, I saw too many guys drown their sorrows, their boredom, and their feelings too often and end up with drinking problems on top of it all. Same way I won't drink hard liquor like Parker did, I'm careful not to go too far down that potentially rocky path.

"I'll see you there," I tell him. Xander doesn't try to mask his surprise, just reaches out for a clap to my shoulder. "Great." He gestures vaguely to the area where we're standing. "I'll leave you to it."

I can't believe he came here for that. "You could have saved yourself a stop and texted."

"Nah." Xander stops and it's his turn to face me directly. "You would have texted me back a No and gone on with your day." He raps his knuckles on the door frame. "See you later."

I stare at the open doorway for too long. The guy called me out on my shit in a direct but low-key way. He wasn't wrong, either. I absolutely would have refused if he invited me over text. I would have said no even if he'd called.

I start cleaning up the materials I used in here today. Tomorrow, I've got plans to work on the big shed where ATVs can be kept. Surprisingly, it doesn't need much, and I can bang out the punch list for that in a day or two, tops.

Rebecca hasn't contacted me today. Not that it really matters, but if anyone asks about her tonight, I hope our stories still match up.

Meeting up with Xander and his friends could be a good distraction. I'm wasting entirely too much time thinking about things like what's going on with Rebecca, instead of what I need to do for myself and the reason I am in Macintosh Ridge.

The barn doors make a solid, satisfying sound when I close them. I don't know if the future owners or tenants will have horses, but this barn will be ready if they do. Hands in my pockets, I take my time walking back to the cottage.

I can't think of one damn thing I could have – or should have – done differently with Rebecca. Except maybe I shouldn't have crossed that line with her at all.

No, I admonish myself, *not going there*. I'm handling my issues, doing something to help Rebecca with hers, and that's enough. I don't need to get pulled further into her drama and her life. Once I finish restoring or renovating this place, I'm out of here. The woman did me a favor.

I was honest and straightforward. Respectful. No pressure. Gave her every opportunity to change her mind. Repeatedly. If Rebecca regrets what we shared, I can't do anything about it now. I scoff even though there's no one to hear me.

CHAPTER 29
REBECCA

MY PHONE BUZZES on the kitchen table, sounding like an angry insect. I instinctively take a step toward it then stop myself mid-motion.

What is the point in looking at it? It's probably Tara again, since I haven't called or texted her back after the last batch of messages she sent. It definitely isn't Sam.

But if it *is* Sam, I'm not going to answer. And if it *isn't* him, I'm not going to be disappointed, even though I have no right to expect it will be him. Screwing around with your fake boyfriend doesn't make the connection any less fake. It just makes it complicated.

I spray some non-toxic furniture polish on a clean cloth and scrub at the kitchen table. I thought it had that power, right? That was the whole point of the fake dating thing, right?

And since I am one of the people involved in the scheme, I am immune to it. I have no right to feel hurt or disappointed, then, do I?

The cloth flies out of my hand and its momentum carries it to the floor. Hands on hips, I inhale deeply through my nose and exhale through my mouth. Then I do it again, and then one more time.

Every now and then I get the bright idea to reduce stress through yoga. Even though my friend Amberly is a wonderful yoga instructor, the only thing I manage to keep practicing are the breathing exercises.

The steam swirling in my head today hasn't been helping anyone, least of all me. The source of the fog? The way I left Sam's place in the dark of night was sneaky and rude. I knew that, even as I did it.

Waking up with my cheek pressed to his bare chest, the fingers on my left hand splayed through the dusting of hair there, my entire body suffused with the heat of him… my rapidly awakening mind flooded with live-action memories of all that passed between us in the hours since we came together at the front door… and came together again, in his bed.

It wasn't like we mindlessly decided to have sex – or had definitively agreed to *not* have sex. We calmly and rationally discussed PDAs (and more), some of that kind in public where lust driven urges needed to be kept under control.

No, he had to talk to me with his rumbly voice, sexy forearms and honest words, all unfair because honesty packs a one-two punch that are both catnip and kryptonite to me.

I didn't have a chance against all that.

Who would?

CHAPTER 30

SAM

THE OUTSIDE of Braeburn Tavern is as picturesque as a visitor might hope to find in this town. The wide front windows aren't simply clear panes. No, they are bow windows boasting seasonal decorations that fit with the Tavern vibe. In one, a table for two is set with beer mugs and plates I suppose signify food customers can order inside.

Above the door, a black metal sign announces the name of the place above an artistic rendering of an apple. A Braeburn apple? I have no clue, and I don't care, either. The official kickoff of the fall season isn't for a couple of weeks, and though the days are still between warm and hot, the nights are already getting cooler. The currently dropping temperature makes the warmth to be had inside the Tavern especially inviting.

The door hasn't fully closed behind me when I feel a buzz of awareness stir the fine hairs on the back of my neck. I look around, taking in the distressed brick walls with their wood accents, and the wide plank flooring. There is a mix of booths, freestanding tables, and hightop tables, plus the glossy wooden bar that dominates one long side of the place. Over the sounds of music and customer conversations, I hear my name. "Miller!"

Xander approaches from further down the bar, three pint glasses balanced in his hands "Great timing. Take one."

Am I that tuned into this potential new friend already? So much so that I sense when he's in the same space as me? No fuckin' way.

"You work here?" I say it in jest, but who knows, maybe he does.

"Nah." He jerks his chin towards the glasses in his hands. "Just grabbed a round. Nothing fancy. Coors draft."

I take the glass that looks most precariously balanced. "Thanks."

A waitress balancing a tray laden with someone's order eases past us keeping her heavy burden balanced. "Excuse me, guys."

We both turn slightly to give her as much space as we can.

"I'm glad you made it," Xander tells me.

There isn't much to say to that, so I lift my chin in acknowledgment and leave it at that.

"The guys got here over the last twenty minutes or so. They just grabbed one table to use as a base."

The place is crowded, more so than I originally thought. I follow Xander to a hightop table not far from the bar where four other guys are spread out. There are nachos and some other bar foods on the small tabletop, things that don't require a fork. He passes a glass to one of the guys and makes quick introductions. "Sam Miller, these are Luke, Ryan, Carson, and Donovan."

Each man acknowledges me when he says their name. I mentally categorize them.

I make eye contact with each man as they are introduced. Tall, lean Luke gives a chin lift and doesn't bother hiding the fact that he's assessing me. Redheaded Ryan offered a friendly "Hi" and waves with his beer. His smile doesn't reach his eyes.

Carson, aviator sunglasses hooked on his shirt collar, offers an easy going "Hey." Sandy-haired Donovan speaks in a distinct Southern drawl, "Nice meetin' ya." It's a regional accent rather than more state specific, and I can't use it to figure out where the man is originally from, but it isn't McIntosh Ridge.

I offer an all-encompassing, "Good to meet you."

"There's one more technically in our group here tonight," Xander says, indicating a dark-haired man working behind the bar. "That's Beckett. Someone called in sick, so he's working tonight."

I don't know if that means Beckett works here, or he owns the place, but I don't ask. All I say to that is, "Gotcha."

I don't know if these guys are all part of the veterans' group Xander mentioned, or if one or more are the "others" he'd spoken of.

The guys in front of me all look to be in their 20s and 30s, though age doesn't mean anything regarding service. I signed up as a teenager and look at me now.

Luke raises his beer to his lips, and I glimpse shadowed stars in a row on his forearm. I suspect those stars mean the same as the ones I have; they signify servicemembers who didn't survive. There were a lot of stars in that row; I hope I'm wrong about their meaning.

"We're going to grab another table if one opens up," Xander tells me. "You want to order something to eat from the bar, or wait for Nora?"

"Nora?" That's not a name I've heard here before.

"The server," he explains. "She's here somewhere."

I saw her when we were by the bar, and the woman was clearly slammed with customers and orders. "I'll check out the bar menu."

Ryan and Donovan are laughing about something. Carson

and Luke are talking quietly with one another. If Carson's rigid stance and Luke's narrowed eyes were any indication, it's an intense talk. I'm not going to push my way into either conversation, so I take another sip of beer.

I wasn't particularly hungry when I got here, but now I've been inhaling enticing fried food aromas for a while, I could eat. Might as well.

The bartender Xander called Beckett is pouring shots for a group of guys whose faces remind me of new recruits; they look barely legal to drink. The other bartender, a young woman with an asymmetrical haircut and a nose ring, (and who looks barely legal speech all herself), eyes me like a pro at her job. "You have a drink. Do you need a menu or a shot?"

She is tall and has striking features, plus a physique easy to appreciate in her Braeburn Tavern T-shirt, tight pants, and black boots. Above the name of the bar, a small tag proclaims her name is Chrissy. Her smile is friendly not flirty, and I'm glad.

"Menu."

"Here you go." A laminated menu is dropped in front of me. "Shout out when you're ready."

"Actually, I'm ready now. Burger and fries, please. That's it." I noticed several burgers being consumed on my way to and from Xander's table and noticed how good they looked.

"Okay. Hamburger, cheeseburger, Braeburn burger, or Tavern burger? "

I ask a question before I can think better of it. "What are the last two?"

Someone slides a Heineken bottle across the bar to her and requests another. The bartender tosses the empty green bottle somewhere behind the bar and it clinks against other discarded empties. Chrissy keeps talking the whole time. "The Braeburn has a sautéed apple slice on it. The Tavern has bacon." She swiftly produces another Heineken and plops it down in front of her, twirling a bottle opener tied to her apron before she peels off the bottlecap.

I can't help but repeat, "A sautéed apple slice?"

"It usually a Braeburn apple slice, but sometimes it's another kind. I make no promises."

"Is there a difference? When you put it on the burger?"

She leans over the bar a little and lowers her voice. "Not to me because I won't eat a Braeburn burger, but some people love it."

"Really?" Sounds disgusting to me.

"I don't like to yuck anyone's yum, but not for me." She shrugs.

"A cheeseburger, please. Medium rare."

"American cheese okay?"

"Yes."

"You're Sam, right?"

That is unexpected.

"I am," I confirm. "I know we haven't met before."

Blue eyes twinkling, she shrugs. "I'm Chrissy. McIntosh Ridge is a small-town, you know." Chrissy leans in toward me again. "Maybe you know this, but I'm guessing you don't yet. Rebecca is here." Her gaze flickers toward the opposite side of the place from where I briefly stood with Xander's friends. "I'm not trying to stick my nose in your business, but I figured if you knew she was here, you'd have gone over to her."

"Of course," I murmur, scanning the area Chrissy indicated. "Thanks."

"I'll have someone find you with your burger," she tells me helpfully.

I'm already moving toward the area she indicated, so I raise a hand over my shoulder in thanks.

A heavyset man in the rear corner of the tavern moves aside when I indicate I need to pass him, and beyond a grouping of potted plants, Rebecca's burnished blonde hair beckons me. It taunts me, a beacon of loveliness in the dim light, and sparks a flash memory of the silken strands rippling across my pillows, my sheets, barely 24 hours ago.

Before she ducked out on me.

My jaw tightens.

Rebecca's back is to the room. So maybe she doesn't know I'm here either.

I can't see her face or get a good look at her companion, but I can see they are engaged in an intense discussion, both leaning across the table between them. Is the other woman Rebecca's friend, Tara? Or somebody else? Not that it really matters.

I take a sip of the beer I still hold. I could go about my own business with Xander and the others and see what, if anything, might happen with Rebecca. Or I can act like a good boyfriend would – reveal myself and greet her.

My eyes remain focused on the hair flowing down her head and her back. It's swaying this way and that like it's dancing to a rhythm only she can hear.

Target acquired.

My irritation at her disappearing act remains. Yet I would be lying to myself if I said I wasn't glad to see her here. At least I don't have to say it out loud.

One corner of my mouth lists in a wry smile I can't quell. *This* explains the unsettled feeling I got as soon as I walked into the Tavern.

CHAPTER 31
REBECCA

"WHAT DO YOU MEAN, he's heading this way?" I hiss, leaning across the table so I can keep my voice down and Tara can still hear me. Then I shrink back against the padded booth as if I can magically melt into it and hide. "Are you sure?"

"What do you mean?" Tara whispers back. "I know what he looks like from the picture you showed me, and he's heading this way."

"You said he was going to Xander's table." I can hear it sounds like I'm accusing her of something, which is ridiculous, but at the moment I don't care. Isn't the whole situation ridiculous?

"He was." Tara sounds defensive but has the nerve to look amused. "Then he went to the bar and talked to Chrysanthemum, then went toward Xander's table but continued past it and now he's heading this way." Her detailed description was delivered in a barrage, and her amusement blossomed into a full-on grin.

Questions and answers race through my mind at breakneck speed.

Did Sam ask Chrissy about me? No, that doesn't track

with what I know about him. Would Lilac's sister sell me out and tell Sam where I'm sitting? No, why would she? She doesn't know him, or about him and me.

Does Sam know Chrissy outside this place? She's gorgeous and friendly and gorgeous... Nope, not going there.

None of that matters so much as my urgent need to flee. Which I can't do, because everyone thinks we are dating. Not only can't I run, I need to be dating-level warm and friendly. (At least the warm won't be a problem, because I already feel the heat in my face that tells me I'm blushing.)

. My eyes dart around like I'm going to find a hitherto unknown portal so I can escape to another dimension. Or at least to outside.

"You said you need to talk to him," Tara reasons, "so why are you freaking out?"

Yes, Tara is definitely amused. I'll deal with that later. First, I have to figure out what to do about what I thought was a pending confrontation with Sam that is about to become a here and now thing.

"I'm not freaking out," I declare, although I am. Kind of. "I'm just not prepared to see him right now."

"What do you have to prepare? You look great." Tara has the audacity to wink. "The sex must have been even better than you said. I mean, he hunted you down *already*."

I feel the heat of embarrassment rising in my face and know without a doubt I am blushing like a young girl talking about her first crush. Before I can come up with an answer, the air around us *changes*, vibrates with some undefined energy, and Sam pushes past the ficus plants Tara surreptitiously nudged together as a makeshift barrier between us and Xander and his group of friends.

That thought leads to another one – I don't try to interfere in her endless, bizarro mating dance with Xander, did I? And she's giving me a hard time about Sam.

I know from Tara--and tendrils of the gossip chain--that

Xander has been spotted going out to eat with Sam, and I know Xander visited Hidden Haven. I just didn't want to take a chance that Xander would see me and talk to me about Sam… who is currently staring at me like I lost my mind or something. Maybe I have, because instead of figuring out how to handle the situation, I'm staring at the way his shirt clings to his shoulders, and how strong and long his legs look in his dark wash jeans.

"Sweetheart, I didn't realize you were coming here with your friend or we could have driven here together." Sam puts one hand on the table by my glass of wine and with the other he cups my cheek, then leans down and kisses me—directly in front of Tara, and in front of anyone else who might be able to see through the ficus quasi-hedge. The kiss is soft, gentle, not ravenous and hungry, but it still sends butterflies flying and swooping inside me.

He lifts his head and keeps talking, "Although *I* didn't know I was coming here until a little while ago when Xander reached out."

I fall back on good manners and wiggle over as far as I can, patting the bench seat next to me. "Come, sit with us."

"Thanks." Sam slides in, the left side of his body pressing against mine enough to make me think of things I shouldn't be thinking about in public.

Sam drapes an arm across my shoulders, careful to not press down too heavily. "I don't want to interrupt your time together, ladies." He toys with the beer he'd set down the on the table and make polite conversation like I should have done. "Tara, Rebecca tells me you own Village Candles?"

It's Tara's turn to blush. I watch my friend brighten under the force of his attention. "Yes, I do. Come in some time if you want candles or anything to set a romantic atmosphere."

That brat.

Tara rushes to add, "We've got candles for every possible reason, and other things as well." She looks from Sam to me and back again. "You two are the talk of the town, you know."

I roll my eyes, even though I know it's true. "Don't exaggerate."

"I'm not!" Tara protests. "Well, you guys plus Ms. Richards' dog, Shelby Carpenter's lips, and Tommy Walker's broken leg."

Sam looks back and forth between Tara and me. "I can understand people talking about a runaway dog, but why is a broken leg and somebody's lips local newsworthy?"

Tara is only too happy to enlighten him. "Brutus, Ms. Richards' dog, has developed a fondness for picking up his own leash and taking himself on walks."

Sam turns his head to me, "I'm not understanding this, am I?"

"Probably not," I laugh. "Brutus is a cocker spaniel. Mrs. Richards has a doggy door that leads into her yard. Brutus picks up the leash in the house, takes it out through the doggy door, and figured out how to get out of the yard. Now he takes himself for a walk with the leash in his teeth."

Tara snickers. "Public safety can't ticket Brutus because, well, he's a dog, and they can't ticket Ms. Richards because he's not violating the leash law because he's got one!"

I shake my head. "It's ridiculous."

Sam approaches the Brutus conundrum with logic. "Why doesn't she keep the leash where Brutus can't reach it, or lock the doggy door, or secure her yard better?"

"All excellent ideas," Tara says. "But then her clever dog wouldn't be the center of attention anymore, would he?"

I toy with my wine, trying to ignore the heat of Sam's thigh pressed against mine. "Sam, it's really okay if you want to get back to Xander now. I'm sure he's wondering where you got to."

"Chrissy, the bartender, told me you were here, and somehow I'm sure somebody told Xander where I am by now." Sam drops one hand on my leg, the warmth of it comforting. I didn't even know comfort was something I needed at the moment, until his touch made me feel better.

Sam asks Tara, "Why do people care so much about Tommy's leg? Sounds like it's more than basic kindness."

"Well, there's that part of it, but it's also because of *how* he broke it," Tara says.

I sigh and take over explaining. "I don't think it's *funny* because Tommy broke his leg. Bear that in mind. Tommy *likes* Antonella. He got the bright idea that if he figured out what she likes, he could use that information to figure out how to get her interested in him. He wanted to see how she decorates her room and if she collects anything."

Tara chimes in. "Her room is on the second floor so Tommy climbed up a tree while carrying binoculars to get a good look."

I finish. "He got into position, then when he tried to use the binoculars, he fumbled them and fell out of the tree trying to stop them from smashing on the ground."

"He was more worried about the binoculars than himself? More importantly, he thought being a creeper was a good idea?" Sam is clearly disgusted.

"I think we left out a key part of the story." Tara pops several peanuts in her mouth. "The McIntosh Ridge Peeping Tom – or peeping Tommy – is six years old. The binoculars belong to his father."

"He really did want to see what toys she liked or collected. It was totally innocent," I add.

It's Sam's turn to look at me and Tara quizzically. "Besides wondering how this kid got the binoculars and access to where he didn't belong, I'm wondering how he came up with the idea to spy on her? That doesn't sound like something he'd learn in the schoolyard."

"Tommy is the youngest of six brothers, an 'oops baby'

because he's a lot younger than the brother nearest to his age."

Tara adds helpfully, "His three oldest brothers all have girlfriends."

Sam sips his beer again. "Enough said. Does the other person's lips fall into the category of funny or intrusive?"

"Possibly both." I try to be quick and tactful. "It involves possible Botox, possibly questionable cosmetic fillers, and what can happen if you overdo it and your lips get numb."

"Numb like when you have a popsicle?"

Tara answers him but I tune it out.

I angle myself more toward Sam, and after she stops talking, I say, "Tara and I are leaving, so maybe you want to spend some time with the people you came here to meet."

Since we are both here, I'd like to talk to Sam now, but this isn't really the right time or place. After helping me through the aftermath of Josiah, Tara has been wonderfully supportive of my goings on with Sam. I talked to her multiple times about him, and it's not fair for me to suddenly become someone who ditches a friend because of a guy. Tara deserves so much more than that. She has always been there for me when life sucks. Regardless of anything else, this is a girls' night.

Either Sam and I will part ways this week if he doesn't accept my apology and explanation, or it will end when it meets its scheduled demise. Either way, I will be fine with it. And either way, Tara is my dearest friend, and I owe her the rest of my attention tonight.

I don't know if Sam intuits my need to finish my night out with Tara, or if he is actually in need of male bonding time, but either way is fine by me when he says, "Absolutely. Want to let me know where and when tomorrow?"

"Sounds good." He stands up, and I slide out of the booth. Sam's hand finds the small of my back, it's gentle weight there a silent statement as the three of us headed for the door.

Tara looks less than happy about leaving when I coax her toward the door of the Tavern.

As the door, he curls his hand firmly around my waist, warm and solid, and quietly says, "I'm going to kiss you. Tell me if you don't want me to."

His words are loud and clear to me, but before I can decide how to react, his lips are on mine. . I forget everything else when his mouth claims my thoughts in a searing-hot kiss that steals my breath and replaces it with the desire to pull him down on top of the table right there in the Tavern.

Sam's lips are soft at first, not forcing, giving me opportunity to push back against him, but I don't. Shivers ripple across my skin, my traitorous body screaming "Oh, yes!" while my cowardly brain yells "Let me think about this!". The noise of the Tavern fades away as Sam deepens the kiss , the angle of his head changing slightly, his tongue brushing mine, reigniting visceral memories of all that's already passed between us.

The ground tilts beneath me, my legs unsteady. I reach out to grab onto him and find I'm already clutching his shirt with desperate fingers. I feel his grip on my waist tighten as his tongue strokes mine again, slowly and deliberately, like he's savoring every second. I can't stop the moan that escapes into his mouth and Sam answers it with a low growl of his own.

Our kiss gradually slows, and we pull part. His warm breath mingles with my own for a suspended moment, and then I halfheartedly push him back, trying to regain a little bit of control over a situation that's completely gotten away from me.

With a wicked smile on his handsome face, Sam steps past me and holds the door open for me and Tara to leave. Because my car is parked on the street a few doors down, he's willing to visually see us off and remains standing on the sidewalk outside the Tavern.

I busy myself with my seatbelt and checking the mirrors

while Tara remains strangely silent. I press the starter, and I it's like I pressed the starter for her mouth. "That man is way hotter than I expected. Fire hot!" I can't get a word in edgewise before she continues, "Was that kiss even half as hot as it looked?" "Did we fall into a time warp and we are 16 again?"

"Ha ha, very funny." Tara reaches over and pretends to punch me on the shoulder. "I can't hit you because you might be pregnant, you know."

I briefly tear my gaze from the road to pin her with a fast but furious glare. "What the hell are you talking about? I'm not pregnant."

"From that kiss, girl, you could be."

Head shaking, I have to laugh. She's right that it was a heck of a kiss.

Tara isn't done. "No more complaining about dealing with men hitting on you in the hardware store. Yes, you have had to deal with a lot of duds, but this time you found a *stud*!" She laughs at her own play on words.

This is serious, so it's not hard to make my voice sound like it is. "You remember that it's all pretend, right? Sam and I aren't really together, Tara."

I keep my eyes on the road and emotion out of my voice. "This thing between Sam and me is simple, really. It's a variation of the whole friends with benefits thing. He gets my guidance on his restoration project, and I get a shield from guys who want my business. End of story."

"And the face-sucking, bumping uglies parts?" Out of the corner of my eye, I see her doing intense chair dancing gyrations in my front seat.

I don't comment on her theatrics. "Like I said, friends with benefits."

"Since when are you a friends with benefits sort of person?"

"What's that supposed to mean?" She's not wrong, but I feel deeply offended. "I'm a modern woman, you know."

"You know that friends with benefits has been a thing for a long time, like since hippies and free love in the 1960s. It's not some mid-2020s thing."

"I didn't know you're an expert on sexuality and relationship trends throughout history."

"Not claiming to be that, but apparently I know more than you do about both. I've got more experience with them, too, and you don't realize –"

I completely take my eyes off the road at that revelation. "Whoa, whoa, whoa, when have you had a friends with benefits situation going on?"

"We're not talking about me, we're talking about your love story."

"I don't have a love story, T." I flip on my turn signal. "I'm just trying to live my life."

"It does sound like a story though," Tara says way too enthusiastically. "A classic love story. A fake relationship turns into a real relationship story. It's Hallmark Channel gold."

"Except it's me, Rebecca Spencer, and I'm not the queen of romance." I turn onto the road leading out of town. "Besides, Sam isn't looking for a love story, either. So even if I was, theoretically, because I am not, I can't have a love story by myself."

She crosses her arms defensively. "For the modern woman, I think that's debatable."

"You are a riot tonight, you know that" I don't mean it as a compliment. I also don't mean it as saying she's funny, because she isn't.

"It's a gift."

We both get quiet. I know she's looking at me again.

"You didn't have enough to drink to be this ridiculous." I brake at the stoplight out of town and flip on my turn signal again.

She leans into me enough to nudge my shoulder with her own.

I pull up in front of the small building where Tara has a one-bedroom apartment. "I can walk you in," I offer.

"And then I'll want to walk you out," Tara snickers. "We'd be walking back and forth all night until we collapsed from sheer exhaustion."

"You're ridiculous."

"That's what friends are for."

"I think you're right."

"The conversation about your new boyfriend isn't over, missy."

"I told you plenty," I protest.

Tara pops open the car door. "You did share some juicy details, and I thank you for that. But I have other questions, you know." She swings one leg out of the car and then twists her torso slightly to face me again. "Thanks for listening about my brother. You already have a lot to deal with, and I appreciate that you find time to deal with my crap too."

"Stop." I wave a hand at Tara in a shooing motion. "Go on, get inside so I can go home. It's been a long day."

Tara stands up and spins back around, a hand poised to shut the door. "What you really need is to get home and sext Sam. Instead of that, maybe you could have him come by for a booty call." She wiggles her eyebrows comically (exactly the way Natalie did at Tony's Pizzeria!) slams the door.

Yes, Tara is ridiculous sometimes, but she does have some great ideas.

CHAPTER 32
SAM

"SO, YOU AND REBECCA, HUH?" Luke raises his open hands in a non-combative gesture. "Nothing derogatory, man, I'm just impressed is all."

Ryan slowly turns his beer glass around and around in the condensation it left on the wooden table. "She doesn't date much. Not at all, really."

"That's not true," Donovan scoffs. He looks around at the others. "Is it?"

Xander shrugs. "Rebecca is a busy woman. She's got a boatload of responsibilities." One corner of his mouth turns up in a half smile. "She doesn't have time for the likes of you all, that's for sure." He raises his glass and tips it toward me. "Certain present company excepted, of course."

"I heard she's stuck-up." Carson stretches his legs out into the nearest aisle. "Maybe locals aren't good enough for her." His voice has an edge I don't like.

"Maybe she needs to check out a guy's balance sheet before she dates him." Donovan offers, apparently thinking he's funny. "See a bank balance and tax returns."

I'm not going to stay silent and by doing so give tacit

approval for them to say shit about Rebecca. I damn well wouldn't do that if she *really* was my girlfriend, and it doesn't matter that she isn't. If a woman went out with guys (or girls) as much as possible, or didn't do it at all, that is her business, nobody else's. It doesn't give anyone the right to be an asshole about it. They aren't being crude or nasty, but it's a slippery slope to get from what they are doing down to verbal abuse like Parker heaped on my mother. I'm not going to ignore it.

The way these guys are talking about Rebecca is wrong.

"Rebecca is a good, intelligent woman with a lot of demands on her time," I say firmly, my tone calm but being forced to be that way. "I'm a lucky man that she is doing her best to make time for me in her life." Now, I make meaningful eye contact with each of the other men clustered around the pushed-together tables.

Xander speaks up. "On that note. Sam, I haven't had a chance to tell you some of what this motley crew are into. Luke has a construction business, Ryan is a paramedic, Donovan does freelance computer stuff, and Carson is part of a search and rescue team. You haven't had a chance to talk with Beckett at all yet, but he is the owner of this place and works here sometimes – as you can see. All of us are veterans."

Donovan chimes in, "We joke around, but we've all worked with women who were hella smart, badass, and capable as fuck." He runs a hand over his jaw. "Sorry if we came off otherwise."

The admission is unexpected, especially from a guy who looks like he could bench press a small car. "Thanks for that."

Conversation around the table meanders from a concert coming to the venue nearest the Ridge, to the stupidity of both New York pro-football teams being based in New Jersey, and a recent big money boxing match between a long-retired heavyweight champion and an MMA fighter/boxer/social media influencer. None of which were the kind of touchy-feely, examine your soul subjects I expected. Truth be told, though, I hadn't expected a veterans' support meeting in a Tavern, either.

Luke finally pushes to his feet. "I gotta call it a night, guys. Early morning tomorrow."

I take the opportunity to make my exit as well. "Same here."

It's the truth. It isn't a professional construction worksite, but my mother's land is a construction site anyway.

After handshakes all around, I beat a hasty retreat and don't slow my pace until I'm in the front seat of my truck and the sound of the door slamming has faded away. The silence in the vehicle washed over me and sweeps away the remnants of the loud music and voices inside the Tavern.

Before I manage to make my exit without further interaction, Xander makes sure to mention that he'll be in touch, and that I can let him know anytime I need anything at all – including help on the property. The guy's sincerity is obvious. In the Teams there were plenty of guys I could count on to have my six no matter what. If I reach out to any of them now, whoever could would be here to have my back. Xander was a Marine, but the sense of Brotherhood is the same.

I start my truck.

Parker is gone and never coming back. I'm not a child anymore. I can handle what needs to be done and be friends with Rebecca. Maybe *not* friends with benefits because the aftermath of that hadn't gone well. Not for me, at least.

The rest of my plans will fall into place. Finish the renovations, rent or offer lease to buy arrangements for the entire property and everything but the cottage, so I'll have a place to stay on my required visits back to the Ridge. I'll also keep seeking ways to circumvent Parker's outlandish conditions.

Once the renovations are done, I'll take that job downstate

and find out where life will lead me. This plan accomplishes everything I need it to. It lets me honor the good memories I have of Mom and simultaneously helps Rebecca steer her own ship on the course she chose for herself.

We'll both have smooth sailing and blue skies ahead, bound for our different destinations.

CHAPTER 33
REBECCA

THE SPENCER HARDWARE truck is fairly new and
has good springs, but the long driveway into Hidden Haven
has me repeatedly bouncing in the driver's seat. It isn't
uncommon for people to leave driveway restoration to the
end of a project, but it's still frustrating to have my teeth
clacking and my bottom wishing there was another way to
drive onto the property. My long ponytail sways back and
forth with the motion of the ride and tickles my neck.

The nights have been colder for more than a week already,
and the days are catching up and catching on to the calendar's demands. Over the past few days, , the daytime temper-
atures have dipped noticeably. It's still beautiful weather, but
summer is becoming a memory already.

After work I swapped my T-shirt for a more stylish blouse
in burgundy and cream, but didn't change my dark jeans and
Timberland boots –today with the wine -colored laces. They
aren't a perfect match, but sometimes, in some things, close is
good enough.

I navigate around the big bump I know is directly before
the main house and pull over to the side of the cleared area
where the pathway runs between the main house and the

barn. The pathway also winds around to the cottage and other outbuildings.

I open my door and swing my knees out to jump down.

Sam calls out, "Wait one second, and I'll give you a hand."

Looking up, I see he's almost to me already, wiping his hands on a rag that he then tucks into a pocket of his jeans. Despite whatever he was cleaning off his hands, Sam is wearing a button-up shirt that looks clean. His stone washed jeans have no visible tears or holes, although they'd obviously been well broken in. The boots look new if I'm not mistaken, black of course, with a composite toe. Does the man ever look less than hot? It's both awesome and infuriating. Since I can't exactly berate him for that, I stick with my original plan.

"Are you ready to go?" I ask, injecting my tone with as much enthusiasm as I can.

"Go where?" Sam counters. "You said you wanted to talk."

"I do."

He crosses his arms. "I didn't think you'd want to take a chance on being overheard."

"That doesn't mean we have to talk inside, does it? The weather is still good."

"It is," he says slowly. "Where do you want to go?"

"Not far," I assure him. "Hop in."

I slide back into the driver's seat and close my door. Sam stays where he is for maybe ten seconds that feel like much longer and then walks around the front of the truck to get to the passenger door. I watch him open it, then I start the engine. When he snaps his seatbelt in place this sound is unexpectedly loud, as is the whirr of his window being lowered .

Sam's own silence drags on while I make a tight U-turn and head back to the driveway. I focus on avoiding the biggest bumps and dips wherever possible, but don't curse at any of them the way I did on the way in.

As I near the end and can see the road stretched perpendicular to us, I finally dart a glance at Sam. With his right elbow on the door frame and his legs sprawled in front of him as best the truck cab will allow, Sam looks way more relaxed than I am.

I order myself to relax.

It only makes me tense up more.

The clacking of the turn signal echoes the thumping of my heart.

There isn't much traffic passing in either direction. I wouldn't mind if there was; maybe it would distract me from my thoughts.

I gave up looking for roses and romance after Josiah showed me how foolish it was to believe in them. Things like that are better left to the pages of fiction books. Novels aren't "real life", but all good fiction contains at least a kernel of truth. It's hard to accept that usually it's the painful part of romance novels that's based in truth and the happy ending part that's fiction, but there you are.

I glance at Sam again. What about the old saying that sailors have a woman at every port? It's probably survived through the years because there is truth in it. I have no problem believing a man as infuriatingly attractive as Sam could make that happen.

Books and social media are full of accounts about how Navy SEALs have to be ready to up and leave on a moment's notice – is that a lifestyle, a habit, easily broken after twenty plus years? Not likely, unless the guy wanted it enough to make it happen.

Like Sam already told me more than once, he isn't a guy who will stay. He's not going to be

I ease my foot off the gas pedal to go around the next blind curve, one that also has a deer crossing sign. It isn't baby deer season, but you can't be too careful about deer crossing the road. Hitting one can kill the driver and the deer.

Awareness of natural road hazards is part of living in McIntosh Ridge and the surrounding areas.

There are multiple ski resorts, beautiful valleys, and scenic drives, plus fantastic farms and orchards. There are also lots of deer, too many skunks, and other wildlife, along with plenty of tourists and day-trippers too busy taking in the sights to pay attention to the dangers.

Back on a straight stretch of road, my mind veered right back to Sam, my silent passenger. Right now the silence isn't comfortable and I'm not sure how to break it.

He might be annoyed with me because he thought it was rude the way I snuck out on him, but it's not like he is a sentimental sort; he wouldn't be planning to get rid of his mother's ancestral property if he was sentimental. And it's not like I broke his heart. To have a broken heart, his heart would have to be involved, and we haven't known each another anywhere near long enough for that.

Time is such an important factor in everything, isn't it?

In my case, time taught me that Josiah was a spoiled, cold-hearted guy, not the sensitive intellectual my barely 21-year-old, naïve brain believed him to be. Things are different for girls than they are for guys, at least when it came to sex and heartbreak and relationships.

With Sam, that night, I protected myself by behaving like a guy, and Sam apparently wasn't prepared for that. I didn't mean to make him mad or hurt his feelings or anything like that. Honesty will set the record straight and we can go forward with our plan without any more messy misunderstandings.

This is going to be an awkward conversation. But like with a construction project, I prepped a plan, and I'll make it work.

First step, pick him up. Done!

Second step, food.

I let music fill the slightly awkward quiet that Sam hasn't

broken. If he doesn't recognize where I pulled off the road, he gives no indication of it. It's a narrow, unpaved road, more of a well-worn dirt track that's even bumpier than the Hidden Haven driveway. Some of the overhanging trees brush and scrape the roof of my truck. I'm hoping no other vehicles are at this scenic overlook because it's not something advertised anywhere or marked. Unless you grew up here or someone showed you, you not only wouldn't know about it, but you'd a hard time locating it.

We emerge on the other side and we are in a wide clearing. I don't know if it was originally cleared for some purpose, or who keeps the grass relatively low, because it's obvious that someone does. It's one of those things I only think about when I come here, which isn't very often anymore. Luck is with us today, and the clearing is empty except for my truck.

"Here we are," I announce unnecessarily. I open the rear door of the truck cab. I have to climb halfway into the backseat to grab the picnic basket and the folded blanket next to it. I scoot backward until my feet are on the ground and drag both items across the seat and out the door. I clamp the blanket under my right arm and heft the basket in both hands. Using one hip, I close the door with a snap.

I smile at Sam. "Would you rather picnic on the back of the truck or on the ground?"

He plucks the basket out of my hands. "Ladies' choice."

I visually survey the ground around us. Three days ago I scoped out the area when I came up with this plan but hadn't counted on there being so much rain in the past 24 hours. The ground isn't visibly muddy or soggy, but underneath the topsoil it's probably at least damp.

"The truck, if you won't feel too cramped," I decide. "The risk of soggy pants would put a damper on everything."

Sam nods, "Hoped you'd say that." For a split second I think he is going to smile, but he doesn't, and I silently scold myself for being foolish. Conscious of my notoriously bad poker face I go around to the back of the truck.

I unlatched the flap that secures the tailgate and drop it down. I'm preparing to hop up into it when Sam rumbles, "I've got you" and grasps my waist in his capable hands. Quicker than I can protest, he deposits me in a seated position where I was intending to go. The blanket is still neatly tucked under my arm.

No point protesting that I could do it myself, because he knows that, and I'm embarrassed to admit that his two second man-flex felt good. I turn to crawl further back on the truck bed. I take a minute to carefully spread out the red plaid blanket I brought from home. For the briefest moment I consider jumping right into the conversation we need to have, but I just as quickly decide against it.

Instead, I plant myself cross-legged on the blanket and unlatch the lid on the picnic basket. I plan for us to eat first because it's easier to be calm, cool, and collected when you're not hungry. It's definitely dinner time or past it, and I doubt Sam stopped and took a break from working to eat.

Verifying what my intuition told me, I ask, "Are you hungry?"

Sam's eyes, a darker gray in the dappled light, flicker to the basket and back to my face. "I could eat."

Those are words I said to him before, and I think that means something, him answering like that. I don't know what, though.

"Sit?" I pat the blanket next to me. Or does he plan to stand the entire time?

Sam stands there beyond the tailgate for another minute then leverages himself up into the truck bed and positions himself beside me. That's better than I hoped and more than I expected.

I busy myself setting out containers I neatly packed into the basket a few hours ago. Some pieces of fried chicken.

Simple turkey sandwiches. A couple of cold salads. Two bottles of water, two of iced tea, and a single beer. I'm not drinking alcohol today, and I only had one beer in the house.

"I'll take out dessert when we're done with this, so it doesn't get to be too big of a mess." I hand Sam plastic cutlery rolled in paper napkins. "Sorry, I went for convenience over style with the forks."

"Sounds good, and no problem." Sam looks over the food appreciatively, sliding his gaze over in my direction. "Looks really good."

I don't miss the fact that the way he says it, the food isn't the focus of his compliment. I decided to also ignore the blush I feel warming my skin and focus on our meal. "Help yourself to whatever suits your fancy."

Anxious to fill my hands so I have something to do, I grab a drumstick for myself, half a sandwich, and a small pile of green salad with chopped walnuts and fresh diced apple. I don't bother watching exactly what Sam serves himself, although I do notice he isn't shy about it.

We eat in companionable quiet, accompanied by the random noises that go along with eating and the low-key musical background queued up by nature – leaves rustling, birds calling, bugs clicking, and the like. The closer I get to finishing, the louder my internal monologue chatters in my ear.

Finally, I lay my fork down. "Before we finish and move on to dessert, I want to say a few things." I correct myself. "I mean, I *need* to say a few things."

Sam shifts to partly rest his back against the side wall of the flatbed. I sense his eyes on me but don't check for his gaze. It is easier to talk if I keep my focus elsewhere. The clearing in front of us and the overlook beyond are perfect options.

"I'm sorry about the way I left you the other night. Embarrassed by it, actually." I blow out a hard breath. "It took me a while to figure out why I even did that. I mean, it's not like me." I shake my head slightly. "That's not a good way to put it. Just hooking up with someone isn't like me, either" Gah! I'm making such a mess of this. "I mean, it's fine for people who do that, so no offense or anything, but it's never been my thing. If you know what I mean."

Sam's continued silence isn't helping. I take a peek at him, only to find him staring at me with a studiously neutral expression on his face. Listening and waiting.

I go on, "It's been a long time since I was physically *with* someone, and I think I didn't know how to handle it. The *after*, I mean. Especially because my last serious boyfriend turned out to be a liar and a cheat. He was a king of the one-night stand with other women, and I never suspected a thing. He said the other women never meant anything to him, like that made it better. As it turned out, I didn't matter to him, either."

After all this time, it still stings to talk about this at all. "Josiah proposed to another woman he'd been seeing while we were dating, while he was carrying on his one-night stands and whatever else. At that point, I didn't care about him marrying somebody else because I was lucky to be rid of him, even if in the midst of everything it didn't feel that way. In the years since all that, I have moved on, of course."

That's another truth. I've dated a bit, had sex with a couple of different guys. I've been busy with all my obliga-tions and responsibilities, and the last thing on my mind has been trying to find a mythical good guy among all the rest. So my reaction to Sam was totally unexpected, and I was totally unprepared for it.

"I don't know why I had a flight response after the night we spent together, and in the end it doesn't even matter. What matters is that I'm sorry I ran."

And that's the truth – at least as much as I am able to share with him. No way am I confessing that my overwhelmed, sex-starved brain got overstimulated in the moment by his bedroom skills and it tricked me into thinking that I was having real *feelings* for him. Admitting that would show him I'm a ridiculous, immature woman, and would send the poor man running for the hills. Then I would miss out on all the good that could come from a relatively brief fake relationship between us.

CHAPTER 34
REBECCA

SAM IS LOOKING at me like I've been speaking another language.

My apology was sincere and true, if not 100% complete. It doesn't really need to be completely complete for it to be real. Right?

I go on, "I think of myself as somewhat courageous, at least, but I wasn't that morning, and I regret it." I tip my head back to look at the sky where the sun is descending toward the horizon. It crosses my mind that we are sharing another beautiful sunset.

"So like I said, I'm sorry." I hope Sam understands how sincere I mean those words.

My words fade away into a silence that becomes unbearably heavy. I wait for a response, a reply of any kind, some acknowledgment that he'd heard what I said.

Nothing.

The sun sinks further into the welcoming horizon, spreading its fingers of pink, orange, and purple in a grasp at daytime before embracing the night. I start to fidget, unsure if I should speak because I'm now so uncomfortable with the lingering silence.

Sam finally speaks. "Thank you for that, Rebecca."

He leans forward and takes one of my hands in his own, the warmth of it making me subtly aware that I've become chilled. He gently tugs me across the truck bed to sit at his side. I go willingly despite my surprise and begin to relax when he puts his arm around my shoulders. Without thought, I melt the smallest bit against his side, and Sam rubs my shoulder.

His voice is strong and impassioned. "I'm sorry you went through all you did with that jackass, Rebecca, but make no mistake, you are absolutely a courageous person."

"It's nice of you to say that." My mind rejects the undeserved kindness, the misplaced compliment. "I appreciate the sentiment, but that's not what I am. Not at all."

Sam resists my attempt to disengage my fingers from his, but he doesn't tighten his grip. He adjusts his hand and begins stroking the back of my hand with the pad of his thumb. It's unexpectedly soothing.

Sam's voice is steady when he says, "It takes courage to put yourself out there when somebody betrays you. It takes courage to take over and run a business that's been in your family for so long. It takes courage to deal with all the extra stressors placed on women in the workplace, especially in positions of power and authority."

As Sam talks, my body gradually relaxes against him more, and it feels natural to let my hand rise until it rests on the broad expanse of his chest. I ignore his first statement and comment on the other two.

"I'm not so sure running the family business takes courage. It's what everyone, including me, expected since I was in middle-school. I'm impressed you see there are extra pressures women have to deal with at work."

Silence cloaks us again. By now, I know it means Sam is thinking about what to say or how to say it, or something else. It doesn't mean he's checked out the conversation.

Moving with slow deliberation, he uses a bent knuckle to tip my chin up and makes sure I meet his eyes. "I'm going to tell you how I see it. Just because you grew up with knowledge of the expectations on you doesn't make the pressure any less, Rebecca. It makes it worse." This close to his face, I see a tiny muscle in his jaw flex. "A man has to be willfully ignorant to not see that women have to deal with a fuck ton of extra pressure at work because they are women."

Sam takes an extra breath, maybe two, before his next sentence. I feel the tension radiating off his body.

"My mother *worked* at home, as a traditional housewife, and was under horrific pressure. Most of it was from Parker, from his impossible to please demands and expectations. But some of it was from people in town, people she thought she had to put on a face for."

Sam closes his eyes for a second, maybe two, maintaining his composure. "She didn't think anything about that was out of the ordinary. She didn't complain or rage against it. She expected it and accepted it." Sam turns his head to look at me directly again. "Women I knew in the military operated under workplace pressures us men didn't face at all." He leaned his head back again and but kept it toward me. "Anyway I look at it, woman, you're courageous."

I haven't moved while he's been speaking. Calling me "woman" sounded sexist... until you took into account all the things he was saying. Things I know he truly means.

I ran my hand over Sam's forearm, enjoying the interplay of hard muscles beneath his skin, warm despite the cooling air. "I'll accept the complement then, and thank you for it."

He makes one of those not quite definable sounds, less than a word and more than a grunt. I hesitate.

Maybe you should leave this alone for now. Quit will while you're ahead.

No, I need to gather the courage Sam gave me credit for having. With that daunting thought fixed in my mind, I force myself to press ahead. "Are you still okay with the original plan, or are you having second thoughts?"

If he's changed his mind about the façade we agreed to put on, I have to understand and let it go. I will still help with the restoration and decide to tell him so.

"If you changed your mind about that, I absolutely understand. No matter what, I'll help you out with the restoration." I hope he understands how sincere I am. "Please don't let it be a factor in your decision about this."

Sam answers without hesitation. "I'm good to continue mission, if we still agree about mission goals. One, by being each other's "significant other" as it were, we preemptively avoid aggressive tactics by third parties. Second, you boost your local rep as knowledgeable in the restoration, and I benefit from skilled guidance on restoring the house I inherited third, we both get to mutually benefit from and enjoy our time together. If you want to change those goals, speak up."

The way Sam delivers that concise summary thrills my list-loving soul. The way he habitually stands with hands on hips and feet firmly planted – or sits, like now, with legacy sprawled and ankles casually crossed – or relaxes with knees bent, forearms braced on his long legs – well, those moments thrill entirely different parts of me. "Nothing has changed," I say with confidence I don't feel, because I'm self-aware enough to know that the *feelings* I'm feeling about him are changing. "We spend enough time together to be believable, which we'll be doing anyway to get your project to the finish line. And when you're ready to leave Macintosh Ridge, we break up." I force a smile. "I can ride the wave of heartbreak as long as I want."

"Yes," Sam responds easily. "And I get the benefit of women and their eligible relatives being scared off from approaching me because I have a girlfriend."

"Then we both win." I hope I sound appropriately enthusiastic, but my words are hollow. At least I feel hollow when I say them.

Those dangerously intoxicating feelings I experienced after *that* night in his bed were real enough that I vividly remember them and how they made me imagine champagne bubbles were fizzing and popping merrily under my skin. Like some unfamiliar form of giddiness had taken over my body and was looking for a way out.

I have read way too many romances, that's for sure. Watched too many rom-com movies. Consumed too many fairytales as a child. Whatever the root cause of it was, I need to get a hold of this romanticism disease and myself.

"Then we both win." I mentally mock myself.

If those feelings arise again, I am going to lose big time, and probably end up with a broken heart compounded by a pathetic reputation.

Sam clears his throat like he has something to say and is preparing himself. "Rebecca. we agreed there is real attraction between us." He lifts the hand to the back of his own neck, and I wonder if he is stressed or uncomfortable. Maybe both. "Friends with benefits sounded perfect for us, and that night was... perfect, so we were right. Except I'm thinking that might also make it *not* such a good idea."

I think so too but stay quiet and simply nod. I know he is looking at me but I can't quite bring myself to meet his gaze again. So I keep looking out at the view over the ridge, where distant lights below highlight the Crescent Valley.

Sam takes my silence as agreement, or maybe he is taking it for what it is – willingness to hear anything he wants to say. "That's why I'm thinking we need to stay out of the bedroom going forward."

This wasn't at all what I expected to hear out of Sam today, and it makes me sit up straight and turn toward him. The moonlight is bright enough already to illuminate us, and the reflective lights along the back of the truck bed illuminate things even more. Sam's eyes are fixed on some distant point, just as mine had been.

Now he runs a hand through his already messy hair and keeps talking. "I don't want to sound like an ass, but it was damn hot between us, at least for me. But I understand it wasn't the same for you so I think we should keep things uncomplicated now."

"Uncomplicated," I repeat.

"Yes." Sam slipped away from me and pushed the picnic basket aside. "Uncomplicated."

CHAPTER 35

SAM

"UNCOMPLICATED." I repeat for Rebecca, making sure to keep my expression impassive despite the fact that what she was saying is completely ridiculous.

No way in hell anything between me and this woman is *uncomplicated*. It's already complicated as fuck and is only going to get more complicated in the coming weeks. The days when she doesn't come to Hidden Haven suck . I've had to exert way too much self-control to not keep showing up at the hardware store with flimsy excuses.

I have already bought more than enough supplies to repair every wall and roof on the property, even the ones that don't need any repair at all.

No matter how many hours I spend working on the property, sometimes alone, sometimes with a few guys I hired, or Xander's friends when they volunteer, my mind invariably shifts over to her.

When Rebecca is not around, I can't get her out of my head.

I want her, yes. I also wonder about her. And I worry about her.

God, I'm pathetic.

Like today, I can't stop stealing glances at her, trying to not look like I'm looking. Technically, I barely know Rebecca, so I need to get a handle on this thing that sizzles between us. Between her leaving the other night, and her calm resolve today, I have to admit she's got a stronger handle than I do on this thing between us.

Her hand on my arm sent electric pulses through my body, like she's some kind of secret weapon. Does she even know the effect her simple touch has on me?

Good God, she's so fucking sexy. Honest to God, I don't think she has a clue.

With the number of times I think the word God, it's like she's turning me into a holy man or something, and with the life I've led, I couldn't be further from it.

I squared my shoulders, drag a hand through my hair again, and force down the need I feel to take Rebecca in my arms. It's a good thing I didn't drink even that one beer she brought. The least little hint of anything that could potentially lower my inhibitions, lesson my self-control, and I might give in, that resolve collapsing like a house of cards in a hurricane.

I sneak another peak and find Rebecca's golden- brown eyes are bright and shiny in the dim light, and unnaturally wide. Is she trying not to cry? She says, "I don't understand what you mean by that?"

The words would have been a statement, but her voice curled up at the end, the inflection declaring it a question although her word choice did not.

A wave of panic crashes through me. *What the hell is she talking about?* I was so lost in my own thoughts I can't remember what I said… Uncomplicated. That's what I last said.

One thing that made me good at my career is that I'm good in a crisis. Good at thinking fast, at going with the flow. Rolling with the punches.

I give her a small smile and explain my comment. "Sex,

especially good sex, releases natural chemicals in the bloodstream."

Idiot. What are you, some kind of sex doctor or something?

I ignore my own derision and forge ahead. "Sex can cloud judgment, muddle your thoughts, distort a person's feelings." I feign an indifference I don't feel with Rebecca. "If someone isn't used to casual … encounters, it could get messy."

"I understand." Rebecca's knees are drawn up to her chest, her arms wrapped around them in a casual pose that screams "defense" –whether she realizes it or not. "Hit it and quit it takes practice to perfect?"

It takes strength I didn't know I had to smother my internal cringe at that ugly expression and maintain my relaxed posture. "For some people."

"For some people," she echoes, not really hiding the fact that she's mocking me. "And others are born with that … talent?"

"Never thought about it that way, but maybe." I scratch a thumbnail against my stubbled chin. "Not for me to judge. That's got nothing to do with this anyway." I need to keep this conversation on its intended path. "We stick to the plan and don't tack on those kind of benefits."

"Let me get this straight. You think we can be friends," Rebecca *said* it like she'd sooner be friends with a rattlesnake.

I don't get involved with women past the superficial stages, but I never felt as awkward as I do right now. "We don't know each other well enough to be *close* friends, but I suppose that's a fair description."

Rebecca's tension was something I could feel when she showed up this evening, and now it's so heavy it's damn near visible to the naked eye.

I give myself a direct order: *Don't think about naked anything around this woman.*

My automatic response to the order is total insubordination, because an image of Rebecca languishing naked and gorgeous across my mattress springs to mind, and flat-out refuses to leave. Memories are like that.

Like she knows the degenerate turn my thoughts have taken, Rebecca is staring at me with her head cocked to the side, like she's trying to figure me out. I'm pinned in her gaze like a bug pinned to a tray in a science lab.

"So how do you see this plan we had proceeding?" Rebecca asks me. "How are we supposed to sell the story of us being involved if we don't even touch each other at all?"

"I wasn't suggesting we go to that extreme." I adjust my legs a bit, trying to get more comfortable. I've spent extended ridiculous lengths of time crouched in heat, sand, mud, human jungles, being gnawed on by bugs, being on guard for all types of predators – including humans. But sitting here with a half-hard situation in my pants, on a blanket in a clean truck bed having this conversation is near the top of my new "most uncomfortable" situations list.

"I gotta stretch my legs," I mutter and move to the tail-gate. Ithrow my legs over it, feel the smooth edge of the heavy plastic liner under the heels of my hands, the cold metal of the surface brushing my fingers before I stand up. Registering the tactile touch-points grounds me.

The small distance from Rebecca lets me breathe more easily. The last of today's late summer heat has all but dissi-pated, and the clear air plus the quiet of the ridge overlook, cool me down and off enough for me to notice how star-studded the ink black sky is tonight. It's not like the endless sky over a desert, but it's awe-inspiring all the same.

I stare up at it for too long. I compel my breathing to slow, even out, regulate my heart rate like I would in a combat situ-ation. Fierce and focused. Calm and controlled.

I master myself, like I always do.

When I turn back around, Rebecca is staring at me. I can't

read her expression, despite the bright moonlight and the lights in the truck bed. Her plush lips are pressed tightly together and her delicate eyebrows are knitted together in confusion.

Is she confused about my behavior? About the words I said, or those I didn't say?

I can't help her figure it out because I can't figure it out for myself Not entirely, or not yet. Not ever if I know what's good for us both.

I tuck my thumb through one of my belt loops to have something to do with my hands that can't be misconstrued as defensive or belligerent or weak.

"Enough people saw us being very familiar with each other, so dialing it down shouldn't matter." I can't imagine she'll disagree with that. From what I learned about the blazing speed of town gossip, people knew about our public kisses practically before our mouths moved apart.

Rebecca releases her grip on her knees and hip-walks forward to the tailgate. She twists to the side like when we arrived and pulled the picnic basket forward.

"I agree," she says.

But My instinct is to grasp her waist, her hips, and lift her from the truck. Maybe encourage her to wrap both legs around my own hips and rub herself against the ridge that was once again making itself known behind my zipper. If that thing could talk, man, would it be groaning.

After the conversation just now, would Rebecca do that? Would she join me in forgetting every stupid thing I said in the last few minutes and revel in the unique fire that spirals out of control when we give it the least bit of free reign?

Calm and controlled, I remind myself. *Calm and controlled.*

"I'll drop you off," Rebecca informs me coolly, making a military-worthy about-face and heading for the driver's side door.

I stand there for too long, temporarily shocked by her

abruptness. It's as if she couldn't hear my thoughts. *Fucking idiot. You honestly expect her to read your mind?*

She opens the door, and it slams shut barely a moment later.

I hurry to fold the blanket and secure the tailgate. When I open the passenger side rear door to put it there, Rebecca's head is turned and she is looking out the window at the perimeter tree line.

I join her in the front row of seats and am putting on the seatbelt when she threw the truck into gear and beats a hasty exit from the overlook area. I can see the pulse in the side of her neck beating rapidly, keeping pace with her quickened breath. I want to lick that sweet spot, then nip it with my teeth to make it sting, and then kiss the sting away.

Yes, this could get way too complicated if I let it, so there was no way I can let it.

For her sake.

CHAPTER 36
REBECCA

I KNOW I'M SMART, the same way I know my eyes are more golden- brown than regular or dark brown, and that hot fudge is infinitely better than chocolate syrup because, well, it just is. And in the same way, I know that pretending we are dating benefits me way more than it benefited Sam. Yes, it saves him some time and awkward interruptions, but he doesn't have more at stake than me.

Even helping him with his renovations benefits me more than him. He could certainly find another company to help him. I haven't even done a great job of it.

Days ago I texted him to set up a place and time to go over next steps in his renovation project, and he responded that it'd be most efficient to email him the list. Of course I had a list of recommendations and a suggested supply list already in a Word document. I added a few notes to it and sent it. Beyond that I haven't done anything.

I know Sam ordered some of the items we carry through our online store, but I don't know if he ordered the specialty supplies from the sources I suggested in my email. He never told me, and I didn't happen to ask.

I should grow the heck up and deal with things.

You have been dealing with things... the store, the lumber-yard, the little questions about your new boyfriend. I growl at my own inner voice, who is being more annoying than necessary today, and finish signing off on the payment authorizations that were stacked in my inbox when I got here this morning. That task doesn't take long and I remain seated, tap- tap- tapping the ends of my pen back and forth like a seesaw, tapping both ends in turn on the desk.I'm still thinking about my arrangement with Sam. It's giving me more than a temporary reprieve from unwanted attention while Sam is in McIntosh Ridge. My feigned heartbreak after our breakup will buy me another long stretch of being left out of the crosshairs of guys looking for a date, girlfriend, or wife, and give me another defense against men looking to latch on to a stable business via marriage.

That marrying formoney, or *perceived* money, isn't only the stuff of historical novels.

Then there are the guys who can't comprehend that a woman is able to go forward 64 run a hardware/lumber business without testosterone– or a husband.

I glance at the old school style clock on the wall next to the office door. Mike will be unlocking the doors in 15 minutes, no one called in sick, and it's the middle of the week, when the fewest emergencies take place.

I owe Tara a call, but she might be sleeping. Village Candles opens hours after Spencer Hardware does.

I want to call Sam. I know he is awake; he's probably been working since sunrise.

Before I can talk myself out of it, I grab my phone off the corner of the desk. It's amazing that Face ID technology works even when the user's face is twisted up by a scowl.

Sam's voice is gruff. "Miller."

I get right to the point. "Can you have dinner with metomorrow ?"

His answer isn't an answer. "Any particular reason?"

Is he kidding me right now? I try not to sigh, and remind myself he doesn't know what I'm thinking. "We have to be seen together to be believable, right?"

"I wasn't aware you decided to continue this."

"Well, I have." Once again, I waited longer than I should have to reach out to him. "I didn't mean to leave you hanging," I say. A bad thought occurs to me. "Did you say anything to anyone about the truth?"

I know he's not comfortable with lying in general, the man made that clear. Did he somehow blow up our story in the few days since I last saw him?

She *had* meant to leave him without an answer, at least for a day. I wanted him to decide he wanted this thing between us, too, so I wouldn't be taking advantage of him somehow. That the one day turned into three isn't really my fault.

Two delayed shipments caused problems with two commercial customers and one residential customer, none of whom was willing to understand that Spencer Hardware couldn't control other companies or their logistics.

Thankfully, Sam doesn't comment on my lack of communication.

"Dinner tomorrow is fine." Sam says, and I hear what I think is a small sigh. Is sharing a meal with me some kind of burden now? "What time is good for you?"

He's trying to make our plans more concrete, and I am probably imagining things to be upset about. But I have an idea where we could grab dinner, if it's going to be open. "Would you be able to meet me here at the store at say, 6:00 ? I know a place we can go."

Sam doesn't hesitate. "I'll be there."

"Thank you." If I could rewind those two words and stuff them back in my mouth, I would. It sounded silly, right? I should have just said, "good", or "great", or "see you then", or anything that maybe sounded less like a weirdo.

At least Sam doesn't make any comments about my weird response. He says, "Have a good day, Rebecca." Then he disconnects the call.

Less than five minutes later one of the stock guys is looking for me because there is a problem with a shipment that came in at closing time yesterday. Then a residential customer showing up in a panic because she had 4 gallons of inexpensive paint mixed in the wrong color for her project. And on, and on, and on until I was grateful to go home and spend time researching some key issues concerning the restoration act Sam's property.

The morning of my dinner date with Sam, I am determined to have a good day. I arrange to go in to the store at 12, and to spend my morning doing errands I've been putting off for one reason or another. I also squeeze in a visit to Beth's bakery. I'm pretty sure her new café is open until 8:30 PM, but I want to be totally sure. She's only been offering dinners for a couple of months, and I think it'll be a low-key way for Sam and I to be out.

Beth herself is behind the bakery counter when I duck into her shop, full of questions.

"The café is open tonight until 8:30, absolutely," she promises, tugging clear plastic gloves off her hands after filling up a box with cookies I ordered to bring back to my store. Right now, there are at least a dozen people in Sweet & Savory Café. Someone has a double seated stroller in there, another patron is in a motorized chair, and yet another table is filled with a group of teenagers who probably have the earliest lunch break from school.

"I'm kind of wondering if the nighttime Café menu is the same as the one during the day?"

"You mean you don't want your dinner companion needing to decide between quiche and a Caesar salad or garden omelet?" Beth teases me. "He might not mind. From what I've heard, that man takes good care of his body."

I want to say "You don't know the half of it!" or "More than you could imagine!" but I don't. It must be written all over my face, though, because Beth's poker face isn't any better than mine.

"Don't worry, Rebecca. We have a Monte Cristo sandwich, a French dip, and a few other things that should satisfy even the heartiest, manliest appetite."

The items might be filling, but I can't quite picture Sam spreading raspberry preserves on his Monte Cristo or dunking his French dip sandwich into a little cup of *au jus*.

Beth's dark brown eyes sparkle at me as she gives an exaggerated wink and screws up her mouth to try and blow an errant strand of hair away from her cheek, where it landed after escaping her neat bun.

"That's your job, though, right? Satisfying his manly appetite?"

The tinkling bell above the door saves me from needing to reply. A mother rushes in, holding the hand of a little boy who can't be more than five or six years old. The woman is mid-sentence when they burst into the bakery. ".The cupcakes are for your sister's birthday party. I'll get you something else if you don't try to swipe a cupcake when we get home."

I pay for my cookiesand make my escape into the sunny afternoon.

I'm glad that Beth believes Sam and I are a real thing, because if she believes it, so do other people. Again, I feel the twinge of regret for deceiving friends, but I do think she'd understand if she knew.

I'm looking forward to enjoying a cookie; I especially love the rainbow squares and the chocolate filled crescent drops. I'm looking forward to trying dinner in Beth's café. What I'm looking forward to most is spending time with Sam.

I don't need to dwell on the fact, though.

CHAPTER 37
SAM

I LISTEN to Rebecca's phone ring four times and mentally prepare to leave a message. I don't like leaving messages, bbut I've tried unsuccessfully to reach her several times already.

When Rebecca picks up, she sounds aggravated. "What is it, Sam?"

I know herwell enough at this point to know she doesn't talk that way on the phone at work, but that's probably where she is right now. .

"We can talk later, Rebecca. You sound busy."

From the noise clues in the background, she's on the move. "No, now is fine. One second."

The line goes dead silent, and it's obvious she muted me. That's a novel experience. I put my own phone on speaker and set it down on the old kitchen counter in the main house. Most of the kitchen is already demolished, but I took a break because it's been more difficult than I expected.

Attached I needed to think about something else for a few minutes before I rip out the rest and that meant Rebecca went from the back of my mind to front and center. It's been a bunch of days since dinner at the café, and I want to see her.

I mean, I *need* to see her so we can keep up the pretense of their being a romance between us.

Plus, I simply want to see her. We have established a friendship of sorts. Admittedly, she's the only friend I ever want to strip naked and do dirty things to with my fingers, my mouth, my dick. When we kissed outside the bakery, it was so anybody watching could see we are romantically involved. When I got home, Rebecca was again the only friend I've ever pictured while I jerked off in the shower. And in the bed the next morning.

"Sam! I'm so sorry, are you still there?" Rebecca asks apologetically.

"I'm here, no problem." I hate being put on hold, alone on mute. "Everything okay?"

"Yes, or it will be. What's a day without headaches and problems, right?" She forces a laugh, but it's obviously fake. "How about you? How are you?" Before I can answer she adds, "I'm sorry I haven't been by. Did you get the other materials I emailed?"

"Yes, and things are moving right along. You don't need to worry about that." The woman has enough worries and stressors to deal with. She damn well doesn't need me to be one of them. "Look, I want to take you out. Because we are friends, and it sounds like you could use a break from thinking about work. F. What's the soonest night I can give you that?"

I'm not going to set the day for our outing, she can do that. I'm trying to get done with my project here as soon as possible, but I'm not answering to other people the way she has to. I know every business has its burdens, but it seems to me that hers is chock-full of them. I know she has employees, but I wonder if she has enough of them. Do they pull their weight? Would they take advantage of her? Is the business too much for her? Should she sell or find a partner?

I can't grill her on it though, no matter how nicely I'd try to do it. She's a smart and capable woman running a business she knows better than anyone else does, except maybe her father. She doesn't need some guy (including me) sticking my nose in and acting like I can magically make things better.

"What were you thinking?" Rebecca asks, and she sounds genuinely interested. "I could use a night out."

I can hear the rhythmic beeping sound of a truck backing up. She must be near the loading dock. "I'm sure it's a place you've been before, but I'm not going to tell you. I'll just say you can dress casually and be relaxed."

"Well, I dress casually every day at work. But I definitely don't get to relax, that's for sure." She makes a couple of low sounds, familiar sounds, and I feel my brows pulled together while I try to figure out what she's doing.

REBECCA BLOWS OUT A DEEP BREATH AND TELLS ME THE ANSWER TO MY UNSPOKEN QUESTION. "SORRY, JUST STRETCHING A LITTLE. IT'S A GOOD WAY TO RELEASE TENSION."

The words are in my mouth to make a joke about other ways to release tension. But I don't say it. It

We are keeping this uncomplicated. My stupid words, and she agreed. It was said for Rebecca's sake, and that's exactly why I am going to stick with the bargain.

Therefore, I say, "Back to my question, what night is best for you?"

When she tells me any night is fine, I decide tomorrow is the better choice. It'll give me time to finish demolishing this room, for the two guys working with me to help me clear it out, and for me to get my head in a slightly better space. More importantly, it might give Rebecca something to look forward to.

I tell her, "Okay, then, let's go tomorrow. I've got my hands full right now."

"I can come over and help out if you want," Rebecca offers. "We are closing in an hour."

My response is quick. "Not necessary." I hesitate, looking around at the wreckage of what was, long ago, my mother's beautiful kitchen. "I've been doing demolition today, and it's been a tough one." I straighten up. "I've got to go."

And I do just that.

It only takes six more swings of the sledgehammer to bring down the last of the old cabinets. They were made of mismatched wood, but they weren't original to the house and weren't worth keeping. Parker had literally sold the original cabinetry to someone who was renovating another old Victorian house. I'm sure the selfish miser made a pretty penny on them. He had the original ones replaced with cheap cabinets someone was getting rid of for.

I was only nine or ten years old at the time, but I remember that Mom cried about the cabinets, although she told me they were tears of happiness. Even then, I knew they weren't. Then she spent a lot of time painting them a very pale green with sunny yellow trim. I thought that was weird, but it made her happy, so weird was fine.

I stand in the rubble for another few minutes. I brought Mom a huge pile of those little yellow flowers that grew wild in the grass where the all the farming rows were before Parker stopped using them.

"These are for you, Mommy." I can hear my own little kid's voice in my head. *"They match the yellow paint, right?"* I was proud that I noticed that right away when I saw the flowers.

Our*"They match perfectly, Samuel. They are exactly the finishing touch I needed to make this kitchen perfect!"* She hugged me so tight until I had to wiggle free. Then she found a glass jar to put them in, and positioned it on the counter next to the sink. *"Maybe you can come with me to the store soon to find the right yellow fabric to make curtains for the windows in here. You* *did so well finding the right flowers, I'm sure you can help me with that, too."*

That never happened. Even I, just an innocent kid, knew that the curtains were something she really wanted. There's no way Parker didn't know that. But every time I asked about getting the fabric, there was some reason it needed to wait. It wasn't until a long time later that I figured out the real reason; she could never put together money for fabric for what she would've seen as an unnecessary thing like kitchen curtains, not when she had to feed me, and clothe me, and cover sports fees and other expenses that all focused on me.

The alarm on my watch beeps and it's a good thing, because I totally lost track of time. Memory Lane will do that to you.

———

The next night after I pick up Rebecca for our "friends" night out, the miniature golf course is more crowded than I thought it would be. It's tucked behind a housing development on the main road between McIntosh Ridge and Eagle's Landing, and I only knew about it because I saw the roadside sign when I was driving us to the bowling alley.

The name of the place, Happy Holes Miniature Golf, is bizarre. If the sign didn't include a rendering of a miniature golf scene, I don't know what I would've thought it was.

As I turn onto the narrow, two-lane driveway that leads to the parking field, I still can't believe it. Rebecca echoes my thoughts.

"The name of this place is so—" she seems to be reaching for the right adjective. "Wrong. It's just wrong."

Rebecca is focused on looking out the window at the little signs marking the driveway. Each one is suggestive, especially the way she reads them out loud in a breathy, sultry voice.

Can you get it in on the first stroke?
Treat every hole with respect!
Do you have a favorite hole?
We take good care of our holes.
You'll love our holes!!

I'm mostly paying attention to what's in front of me, but out of the corner of my eye I see Rebecca looking at me now. "They have to understand how it all sounds. They have to."

"Agreed. Definitely a joke."

"Miniature golf is a family activity," she points out. "It doesn't seem like the right thing to make those kinds of jokes about."

"Maybe it's totally innocent, and you have a dirty mind."

I follow the car in front of us into a gravel topped parking field. Facing the lot is a long building with signs identifying where to purchase tickets, where to get food, restaurant locations, and a gift shop.

"If I have a dirty mind, so do you," Rebecca says, laughing. "You totally agreed with me." She lowers her voice in what is obviously supposed an imitation of me. "Agreed. Definitely a joke."

"If that's supposed to be what I sound like, it's a terrible impersonation."

"Since I'm a regular-sized human, my voice is also regular sized."

I shut the engine off. "What the heck does that even mean?"

She takes off her seatbelt and it retracts noisily. "I don't even know."

It's great that she's laughing. Even better than she's laughing at nothing in particular. Yes, the goal today is to reinforce to the world –to this little corner of it, at least – that she and I are a "we". But in my opinion, the more important goal is to take her mind off the things that are stressing her out. I know it's a temporary break at best, but everyone needs some R & R.

I can't whisk Rebecca away to a tropical paradise or European escape, but I can give her a couple of hours of simple entertainment at a miniature golf course. I hadn't initially thought much about the name of the place because it said Miniature Golf right on the sign.

It turns out, the facility is larger than I thought, with two 18-hole mini golf courses, not one. I ask Rebecca to choose which we are going to play, and she selects the Gold course rather than the Silver one. By the time we get to the third hole, it's obvious that she's been holding out on me.

"Rebecca, are you an undercover golf pro?"

"Who, me?" She bats her eyelashes in mock innocence. "Whatever do you mean, sir?"

"Nice try." "All that about the name of this place, that was fake?" If that's the case, she can be an actress. A very successful one.

"This place used to be called Pirate's Cove, so they changed the name along with the theme." Rebecca looks around us again, the way I've seen her do multiple times since our arrival.

There are heart shapes scattered around and shadowy things that look like they belong in bad dreams. Glittery things appear here and there, like the box of coins that appear as part of a rotating obstacle on this hole. With this new information about the history of the place, the box of coins makes more sense.

I point to it. "A treasure chest."

"You are totally right." Rebecca twirls her pink golf club, then swings it slightly from left to right. "I think they saved a bunch of the old course decorations."

We approach the next hole, where a small pirate ship is perched on a trio of rocks. "You think?"

CHAPTER 38
REBECCA

FOUR DAYS LATER, sitting at a table in The Witch's Brew, I'm taking sips of my peppermint hot chocolate with mini marshmallows. The crowd on the second floor of the place is loude r than usual for a weeknight.

Instead of popular music streaming through the hidden speakers, the vocal stylings of a local songstress fill the air along with her acoustic guitar, which is a nice change of pace. The Witch's Brew is an eclectic coffee house, restaurant, and late-night spot located in a Victorian-style house at one end of Main Street in McIntosh Ridge. The comfortable vibe appeals to everyone, it seems, which is not an easy task.

I'm not appreciating the live performance as much as I should be because I'm preoccupied listening to a couple of young women at the table who are giggling and chattering about their friend who is dating a "real catch" at college.

"Sorry I'm late." Sam puts a hand on my back and kisses my cheek, then sits in the chair across from me at the table.

I had been so preoccupied with my eavesdropping that I hadn't noticed his arrival, something that rarely happened. "It's okay." I pause to enjoy the sight of him in his black cargo pants and long-sleeved, cream -colored shirt. "I've just been enjoying my hot chocolate."

"I hope you haven't been bored." Sam glances at the people whose conversation I was listening to and he smirks at me.

Busted.

I'm not someone who intentionally listens in on other people's private conversations, but they were talking so loud, and this is a public place. I couldn't help but pay attention to them –especially when I caught a little of what they were saying.

"Was everything okay with the work on the main house today?" I know he was particularly on edge about the work he and a couple of guys he met through Xander were starting on in the main house kitchen today.

"It's fine," Sam says and picks up the menu at his place setting. He doesn't elaborate at all. It doesn't take a genius to read that as a sign he doesn't want to talk about it.

The college girls at the next table stand up to leave, pocket-books and shopping bags in hand. I don't miss how they both stare at Sam as they pass our table on their way to the stairs that go down to the first floor. I track their progress until the back of the second girl's royal blue coat vanishes from sight.

"What's wrong?" Sam wants to know.

"What do you mean?"

"Something about them or their conversation bothered you." He says it as a statement of fact, not a question.

Maybe that's why I give him and honest answer – that and our agreement to have truth between us. "Something in their conversation made me think of Josiah."

"The cheater."

"Yes."

I don't feel the usual upset and embarrassment when I think about that time in my life. And, for the first time in all these years, I really am thinking of Josiah as something from a different time in my life – not part of my reality.

"Yes," I repeat. "He tried to break me, but he didn't succeed."

A server materializes at Sam's elbow. "Can I get you a coffee, hot chocolate, or anything else, sir?" The young woman isn't much older than the two customers who just departed, and she bats her eyelashes at Sam like she is trying to take flight.

He never takes his eyes off me when as he tells her, "Coffee, please."

Her eyes flicker to me and then back to Sam. "Okay, well, I'm Sally, if you need anything else." Now she looks directly at me and touched a finger to the tented card on the table. "I know you had one hot chocolate, but remember there's a table minimum tonight because of the live music."

Sally spins on her heel and heads for another table.

Sam hasn't forgotten what we were talking about. "How did he try to break you, Rebecca?" His jaw looks tight, but his voice is quiet.

I take another sip from my mug, the drink not hot anymore. I inhale the aroma of it anyway, and exhale slowly. "I mentioned that Josiah was a cheater. We dated for two years in college, and I thought it was forever. He talked about us getting married, getting engaged at graduation. That he wasn't much of a small-town guy, but if my parents needed help with the business, of course he'd be there for me and for them."

The disgust I feel now is for myself more than for Josiah. "He met my parents a couple of times when they visited me at school, but he was never able to get to McIntosh Ridge when I went home to visit. Something always came up, some kind of emergency."

Server Sally swoops by our table, barely stopping long

enough to deliver Sam's coffee. Aside from a thank you from Sam, neither of us speaks until she's hurried away.

"Where did his family live?" Sam picks up where he left off.

"Rhode Island. At least that's what he said. I never met them or was invited home with him. Both of those things should have been bright red flags, but there was always a reason for everything."

When I think about it all, I want to shake my younger self.

"Seems to me you didn't think he'd have a reason to be a lying lowlife, so why would you think anything of it? That's not your fault."

Sally reappears again. "Can I get either of you anything else yet?"

Sam frowns at the interruption but directs his question to me. "Would you like another of the same, Becca, or something else instead?"

"Sally, I'll have a hot tea, please," I tell her.

She scribbles a note on her pad and then something else when Sam requests she bring cookies for us both. Sally grants him another flirtatious smile before she flounces away again.

"Her mother owns this place," I say by way of explanation for her behavior. "The cookies are usually very good."

Sam nods at me, and empties a packet of sweetener into his coffee. "As I was saying Rebecca, you not suspecting him of lying was certainly not your fault."

"The same way I never picked up on a single clue that he was cheating on me?" I try to not sound bitter, but it's difficult because maybe, just maybe, sometimes I'm still a little bitter. "He had a girlfriend the *whole* time. She was a student at the University of Virginia. Relatively close, but far enough away that she wouldn't show up on our campus looking for him."Sam reaches across the table and takes one of my hands in his own. His touch grounds me and comforts me at the same time. He encourages me to continue. "How did you find out?"

I can't help but cringe. To this day, the memory of it makes me queasy. "A week before graduation, I was walking back to my dorm from one of the dining halls. I heard a woman calling out his name. In my years there, I never ran into anyone else named Josiah, so it got my attention. I was curious."

I look toward the ceiling, blinking rapidly in an attempt to forestall tears. "I followed the path three steps around in the direction I'd heard the voice, and there they were. Josiah and a gorgeous redhead, kissing and clutching at each other."

In my mind's eye, I see it unfold like it's scene in a horror movie unfolding on a screen in front of me.

"What happened next?" Sam prompts. His hand tightens on mine in quiet support, like he understands this is tough, but he's here to help me get through it.

"I was horrified but so shocked that I rushed up to them and said, 'Josiah, what's going on?' The redhead couldn't stop smiling while she told me he'd just proposed and showed me the huge diamond on her hand."

Sam winces. "Ouch."

Isn't that the truth? I flex my fingers in his and feel compelled to tell him so. "It doesn't hurt anymore. It took me a long time to get over it, not because we shared a great love or anything like that, but because it was such a shock to me. I never, not even once, thought he was cheating on me." The sound that escapes me is a derisive one, aimed entirely at myself. "Although in reality, he was cheating on *her*, and I was the other woman. It felt like a real kick to my stomach when I figured that one out."

"Hey!" Sam tightens his hand around mine and gives it a little shake, like he wants to be sure he has my full attention. "You were an innocent party, and maybe so was she. Who knows? None of it was your fault. Please tell me you know that."

"I do. *Now*. But it did take me a long time to get over the betrayal and my anger at myself for being so easily fooled and for ignoring all the red flags I saw in hindsight." I consciously fight the urge to sigh. "You know the rest, we talked about it. I decided not to date. I hadn't made good choices about boyfriends in high school, or early in my time at college. Then Josiah came along." I make a face. "In the aftermath of that, it was easier to steer clear of men."

"This whole time?" Sam looks like he doesn't quite believe me.

"I'm not *that* old, you know, so it hasn't been all that long." I joke. Sort of. "I worked in the hardware store full-time for a couple of years, then spent a couple of years getting my master's degree, and that kept me too busy to date."

Sam drinks more of his coffee. I think he's considering what to say, so I keep talking. "Our arrangement is already helping me so much."

"The harassment has stopped?

"It wasn't always actual harassment," I say. "Sometimes it was, other times it mostly felt that way because I wasn't interested."

He's frowning again. "When it's unwanted and uninvited, but it continues, that's harassment."

I don't see the usefulness of debating the fine points of what's harassment or not, so I don't.

"The coming *heartbreak* will be a perfect excuse for not getting involved with anyone." I attempt to sound sincere, even though I'm having serious doubts about that part of the plan. It feels like the pretend heartbreak I'm planning could feel too real when it happens.

Sam remains focused on his own questions. "You don't miss being involved in a relationship?"

"Yes and no." I have to look away from him again. "I miss

little things like holding hands and sharing a joke, cooking for someone special and having someone to talk to about everyday things *Like I do with you.* I add, "And I *have* dated. I just haven't been interested enough to pursue something more."

Sam makes a noncommittal sort of sound in his throat, and I don't like it. This may all be uncomplicated for him, but it's getting more and more complicated for me.

"I know you understand, Mr. Uncomplicated. I'm figuring you figured out how to keep things casual because something difficult got you there."

I can't identify the expression that moves swiftly across Sam's face. I don't get the chance to raise the point again right away because Sally reappears to ask if we want anything else, and then Lilac and her sister Chrysanthemum are shown to the table next to us.

"Rebecca, it's great to run into you! And is this Sam?" Lilac coos the second half of her greeting. She knows darn well who I'm sitting with.

Displaying his good manners, Sam places his hand on the table and stands up. From my seated position, I watch Lilac scrutinize his hand with great interest. Chrissy mostly looks bored, like usual.

"Hi, guys." I try to sound friendly. We want people to see us together. No, we need people to see us together. "Chrissy, I know you met Sam the other night. Lilac, I think I told you all about him?"

There is a solid two minutes of polite conversation, then my friends move to their table. I can still see that their heads are bent toward one another across their table.

Sam picks up his coffee mug, takes a tentative sip, and makes a face. He puts it back on the table with an accusatory look, like it betrayed him.

"Cold?"

"Yeah."

"I'm sure Sally would be happy to warm you up – whoops, I mean warm *it* up." The expression on his face when I tease him is memorable. He looks like he inhaled a combination of boiled cabbage and high school gym sneakers. Added bonus? I think he's *blushing!*

"We can leave."

I gesture toward the little plate of cookies, still right where Sally left them. "You didn't touch the cookies." "I don't like cookies."

"Everyone like cookies."

"Not me."

"Maybe you just haven't found the type of cookies you like." I lean into the innuendo when I say that, and I'm not sure why. Wait, that's not true. I do it because it feels fun, and brave, and freeing.

"What are you talking about?" Sam is picking up what I'm putting down, those intense eyes of his sparkle at me even in the dim light of this place.

I run a fingertip around the rim of my empty mug. "Cookies. Right?"

He runs his thumb in a circle over the palm of my other hand, his voice rough when he says again, "I don't like cookies."

"You said that already. I still think you're wrong."

CHAPTER 39
SAM

MY WORK BOOTS echo in the mostly empty house as I make another circuit through it, looking for who knows what. Nothing else on this cursed property needs demolition. Unbelievable. Smashing something or tearing something apart would feel good right now.

And I have only myself to blame.

Uncomplicated. *Brilliant, you moron.* Your noble bullshit made your own life more difficult and a lot *more* complicated. I should've acted like a lot of other men would: fuck her and move on.

Rebecca isn't looking for strings of any kind, so she's the perfect bed partner for screwing around with no regrets. Damn, she even spared us the awkward morning after goodbye when she vanished like a puff of smoke into the air.

On my way up to the second floor I turn around mid-ascent and cast a critical eye over all I can see. Walls are patched and primed, new light fixtures are installed, ceilings arefinished. Work on the floors starts tomorrow. Some areas will be sanded and refinished, others will be replaced. With Rebecca's professional guidance, the overall project has been moving right along with less difficulty than I'd expected.

Keeping my hands off Rebecca is getting more and more difficult.

I have to touch her in public in furtherance of our "relationship", but then when there is no need for it, I have to keep throwing myself back into the friend zone. It is self-inflicted torture, and my blue balls might never forgive for me it.

I can't even get annoyed at Rebecca about it. Nope. I'm the one who decided it would be better to do things this way. That it would make it less uncomfortable.

You're a dumb fuck, Miller.

When my phone rings, I cringe, hoping it isn't Rebecca with something she thinks we should do together. Spending time with her is a damned double-edged sword. It calms me but excites me at the same time. Soothes me and seduces me, all without her even being aware. When she's near me, the heat builds in my gut, and lower, until it's so uncomfortable I can hardly think.

Much to my disappointment and relief the caller isn't Rebecca. It's Xander. I swipe to answer, welcoming the diversion despite the disappointment I'll never admit to.

"Miller."

"We are having a somewhat impromptu meeting tomorrow evening because Diana, the therapist, is unexpectedly available. You said you've been meaning to come check out a meeting. Interested?"

I take off my baseball cap and push a hand through my hair. He's invited me to a couple of the veterans' meetings in the last month or two, but they weren't a priority for me. For all the crap I experienced during deployments and everything else, the in-service sessions and my brothers-in-arms have been enough to get me through. Ironically, growing up the way I did also probably made me harder than I should have been by the time I enlisted.

"I don't know, man, I'm busy getting things ready for the next stage." I keep walking up the stairs, sort of lying to my new friend but not completely. I *am* getting things ready, it just isn't necessitating that I do much.

Xander answers me. "When I was there a couple of days ago, things were already in good shape for the floors to be done."

I start moving through the second floor the same way I did the first.

I hate the second floor of this house, and I hate that Xander is right.

"Sam? You still there?"

"Yeah." I lean against the doorframe of the primary bedroom. "I have to take care of something here. Talk later."

I hang up before Xander can reply.

This room is big, and so were the arguments that took place within it. The ones I heard, that is. Sometimes, somehow, I didn't hear the arguments but in the morning when Mom had a new bruise or other visible evidence of the previous day's argument with Parker, I knew there'd been one. Sometimes the proof was in a little limp, or the careful way she moved, or the way she flinched when she forgot to move carefully.

I can see enough of the room from the hallway ; I don't need to go in there.

There are a total of five bedrooms on this floor. I looked in the other three already. Those memories revolving around the primary suite are the toughest. Looking at my own former bedroom didn't bother me at all. The only good memories from that room were of my mother reading me books at night when I was little, but she read to me in different places in the house and on the property, so it wasn't a good memory tied only to that room.

The final bedroom, that gives me pause. My mother converted one of them into a sewing room. Looking back, I'm surprised Parker let her do that.

Maybe it's not so surprising, after all, I think as I open the door to that space. After all, Mom earned some money sewing things for people; that's one of the ways she paid for sports gear and school supplies for me. She also made clothes to supplement what little she could buy with the money Parker allotted her. What an abomination. Parker living in Mom's ancestral home, on her family's land, and doling out scraps for his wife and child to live on.

Even though I've been in McIntosh Ridge for months at this point, this is the first time I've stepped foot in this room. I couldn't face it before. I have to rip the Band-Aid off and stick my head inside, then they can have at it tomorrow. Hopefully the walls don't need much work, because I didn't let them do anything in here yet.

I've got no patience for myself. *"Grow the fuck up. It's fine."*

But I am wrong. Abso-fuckin-lutely wrong. The light streams through the eastern-facing windows as best it can get past the grime on them. It highlights the spiders and their cobwebs, both in abundance. They are a silvery counterpoint to the two long tables piled high with stuff that's hidden under blue cloths.

I know what is under those cloths, because the dark fabric hints at the size and shape of the piles it protects. I rub my hands on my pants, not to clean them because the fabric is covered in dust, but to steady them. I can't fling off the table cover in some dramatic reveal. This isn't a cinematic moment of drama and pathos.

I use both hands to flip back the edge of the blue cloth. Stacks of fabric await me, so many colors and patterns and finishes. Now that I feel like I've broken the seal, I spend several minutes carefully revealing the rest of what's hidden on this table and the other one perpendicular to it.

I stalk over to Mom's sewing machine table and uncover that, then the small filing cabinet that contains the clothing patterns Mom bought and the ones she created. The measuring tapes and straight pins and safety pins and scissors are all where I remembered.

Where is Mom's chair? She sat for hours on a folding chair that she made cushions for. They were bright cushions, and she had two sets of them so they could be washed. Hands on hips, I look around the room again. No chair.

The closet. It's got to be in the closet.

I pull open the door to the closet on the far wall and there it is. Not exactly difficult to find, but I feel like I accomplished something special, which is ludicrous because it's just a chair.

.

I pick it up and bring it over to her sewing table. The chair is stiff. The cushions that are stuck in place with Velcro are holding tight, their colors as bright as if Mom made them yesterday.

I wonder where the other cushions are, the ones with the animal prints, and I look back at the open closet. They are probably in there, where I can see a bunch of finished clothing hanging on a clothing bar. I need to close the closet anyway, so I decide to do that. Tomorrow, I'll bring boxes to pack up the fabric and Mom's supplies. Maybe I'll find something I want to keep because all I have of her are a couple of old photos and a silver charm bracelet. I'll find the other cushions then, if they are still here. Right now, I had enough memories for one day and I need to get out of this house.

My eyes rove the closet once more before I close the door. On the top storage light reflects off an old-fashioned bicycle lock on a silver box. It's incongruous with Mom's other things in here. I don't think about it before I'm reaching up to pull the box down off the shelf.

It's one of those fireproof security boxes, and it's heavier than it looks. Is it Mom's? What would be in this that it would have been in here? Important family papers and stuff like that were always kept in Parker's home office room. Before I took off years ago, that's where I grabbed my birth certificate and medical record file from.

I put the metal box on the edge of one of the fabric tables and take a closer look at the lock. Like I thought at first, it's one of those standard types I had for my locker in junior high and high school. It takes a minute to try and remember how to break into a lock like this without physically breaking it. I pull up on the blue dial and turn it clockwise until I hear an audible click. I check the number the dial is on, mentally add five to it, and kept on with the sequence of steps to find all three numbers I need to open the lock. When it parts in my hands, I freeze.

I try to put my head in operator space – calm, steady, continue mission.

I trace my fingers over the lip of the metal box that overlaps the bottom part. It's hard and cool and grounds me to the moment.

I slow my breathing. I exhale. I open the box.

A stuffed animal stares up at me from the confines of the box. He's a lion, proudly named Leo by a little boy who thought that was the perfect name for a lion. Leo's mane and tail are perfectly brushed, his coat is loose, his eyes are polished and catch the light. I touch his head with one finger, momentarily surprised by how much of it my finger covers. My hands are a lot bigger now than they were back then, but my skin remembers the feel of Leo's fur. It feels like safety and comfort and good things. Like happy times playing with him and my mom, and us reading books to him, and playing hide and seek with him even though all he could do was hide (with Mom's help).

Parker took him because it was amusing to watch me cry.

I gently set the small toy aside and check out what else is in the box. Small silver earrings I mowed lawns and shoveled snow to earn money to buy Mom for her birthday. An envelope with two tickets from a kids' movie she took me to when

I was 11. A few recipe cards for favorite dishes of mine that she made whenever she could work the ingredients into her grocery budget. And at the bottom of the box, a small envelope with its flap tucked in. Carefully, so carefully, I ease it open to find it full of dried flowers that must have been pressed for a while in the book first. An equally careful sniff tells me they have no fragrance. There's nothing written on the envelope, either, so I don't know where or when they are from. But they mattered enough to mom that she kept them with other things she obviously wanted to keep safe and protected.

Lion in one hand, I think about it for maybe another twenty seconds and I know. They are dandelions from the fields behind the house. Flowers I gave her because I thought they were beautiful. Flowers Mom kept because she did, too.

Would Parker be happy I'm crying now?

CHAPTER 40
REBECCA

MY HOME OFFICE is cozy at its best, cramped at its worst. Today it's somewhere in between. In that respect, it's just like the office at the hardware store. At least here at home, I'm not sharing the space with anyone. The glorious disaster is all mine.

I'm curled up on the armchair in the corner. With my legs bent to the side and partly under me, and the laptop balanced precariously on the padded arm of the chair, I really have some nerve trying to also juggle a cup of hot tea.

What can I say? I guess I like to live dangerously. I blow across the surface of my tea. No, I wish that was true. If I liked to live dangerously, I would tell Sam how I feel about him. Confess that I don't even know exactly what it is I'm feeling, but that it's something good. Something special, maybe that it's something with the potential to be something *more*.

The tea is soothing and I swallow another generous mouthful. Excellent hot tea is refreshing even on the hottest days of summer. During the bright days of early fall, a mug of hot tea is rejuvenating, like warm possibilities presented in a ceramic cocoon. Don't even get me started about how wonderful it is in wintertime.

No, if I was brave I would not only live dangerously, I would do it loudly and clearly so there could be no mistake about it in anyone's eyes, no room for misunderstandings. I wouldn't look for ways to stay in the background, avoid notice and attention, and scurry from one task to another day in and day out.

I reach out and carefully slide the nearly empty mug onto the table, letting my hand hover over it for an extra moment, making extra sure it won't spill. Hiding in here and guzzling tea probably isn't the best way to spend my time today. The lumberyard portion of the business is busy today, as is the store. I should be there. I should be bustling back and forth between the two sides of the business, handling things.

I reposition the laptop more comfortably, balancing it partially on my lap and partially on the arm of the chair. This is business, too. At least that's what I keep telling myself.

I'm not selfishly indulging myself by all this plotting and planning for Sam's restoration of the main house at Hidden Haven. It's no secret, really, that restoration is a big interest of mine. For heaven sake, I spent an entire year working on that, exclusively. I'm doing the right thing by the family legacy and all that, but it doesn't change what my personal interests are.

Why can't I do projects like this on the side occasionally? This time, I'm not earning much money for it, because I refuse to accept the going rate, even though Sam wanted to pay it. He is getting the supplies through the family businesses, so we are earning off it that way. I'm also getting valuable local experience, and pictures to add to my project portfolio.

The personal benefits, the ones related to men and relationships and all that, well those are worth a fortune to me. Not everything of value has a dollar sign in front of it.

A couple of hours later I am deep into researching door

knockers from 100 years ago when someone knocks on my door. Embarrassingly, it takes me a full minute or more to realize what I'm hearing, that it's not coming from my computer but from the front of my house.

I'm not expecting company, but that doesn't mean anything around here. It could be kids selling stuff for scouts or for school. It could be someone who wants info or advice about a home improvement project – although I think most people know to find me at the store for that stuff, not here. Before I swing the door open, I check my reflection in the mirror.

Yes, I'm decent. There's nothing showing that shouldn't be showing, no catsup on my face from the chicken nuggets I ate for lunch. *(Don't judge me.)*

As I open the door, I remember that I forgot to check the peepholes to identify my visitor. Sam reminds me. "Did you bother to look and see who knocked before you opened the door?"

I can tell from his tone that he thinks I didn't. Which is true. But I don't have to tell him that; he's not the boss of me.

I don't go with that childish comment, or any version of it. I go another direction entirely and ask a question of my own. "Hi Sam. What's going on?"

He crosses his arms and levels me with a look that might be amusement or might beirritation – I'm not sure which. "Your nonanswer is duly noted."

A frisson of awareness tickles along my spine when he uses that commanding tone with me. I don't need him bossing me around. I wouldn't stand for that. He looks good today, but that's nothing new. He smells like soap, and a touch of sandalwood, and Sam, altogether a potent blow to my senses no matter how many times I experience it. It's arousing and makes me nervous and shy, even though I am normally none of those things.

"Are you going to invite me in?" Sam asks, and this time his amusement is unmistakable. How long have I been standing here and staring at him like a nitwit?

"Oh, of course." I step back to give him space to come in. "I'm sorry, I've been working and have to shift gears."He moves past me and I close the door. My pulse is skittering strangely, even though I have been alone with Sam many times already. Having this reaction every time makes no sense.

I brace myself and turn to face him. Sam flashes me a lopsided grin, something rare and wonderful from him. A fine layer of stubble already shadows his strong jaw, and I wonder how early today he shaved. Combined with his workmen's uniform of black cargo pants, a blue T-shirt, and boots, he's unfairly handsome. A streak of something glorious blazes in my core.

This entryway to my house is average in size, but with Sam in it, everything is dwarfed. Yes, he's big, but it's not about his physical size – it's his aura, his vibe, his energy that fills the space until I can't think clearly about anything else.

I want to kiss him. Am I brave enough to do that? All this effort I've been expending to not fall into feelings with him, am I going to trample right over that? I don't trust myself to stop at a kiss and not yearn for more.

I'm so focused on Sam's space, his sensual lips, that I barely notice when I close the small distance between us and lift my open palms to his chest. I hear him, feel him, when he takes a deep breath and says, "Becca?"

The way he rasps my name is a question and a plea.

I matched his single word with one of my own. "Yes."

I don't know if I'm simply acknowledging my name, or maybe telling him I want to take off his clothes, or take off my clothes, or do anything he wants to do with me. Or all of the above.

Yes, to all of that.

Sam leans his forehead against mine. "Tell me that yes means you'll stay the night with me until breakfast in the morning, or yes, you're not being swept away by hormones and heat so much that you aren't thinking this through." He lifts his head to pierce me with serious eyes. "If those yeses aren't what you mean, I can wait until they are."

"You can?"

"Absolutely." Sam punctuates the emphatic word with a slow, but close-mouthed kiss. "I would rather wait than be a regret for you."

His gray eyes glow with unmistakable desire for me, but I can't let that distract me from his serious words. I want to tell him not to worry, that I am a thousand percent sure of everything between us, limitations and all. But the words don't come immediately and I blink at him, hesitation making me mute.

Sam doesn't let my silence linger or pollute the moments beyond this one. He cups my cheek and brings his lips to mine again. It's a deeper kiss this time, his tongue gliding against mine, teasing and caressing until I am breathless once more.

"Am I interrupting anything right now?" he asks at last. "Are you expected at the store, or have an appointment anywhere?"

"No." My eyes and my brain feel hazy with lust. "I decided to stay home today and do some research, some more detailed planning for your project."

"Ah." Sam touches my upper arms lightly then loosely drags his warm hands down to my wrists and up again. Fine goosebumps follow in the wake of his touch.

"One of the reasons I'm here is that I wanted to talk to you about a couple of changes."

The rather abrupt change of subject throws me. The teasing, sexy expressions he's worn since I opened the door have totally disappeared. Whatever is on his mind, he doesn't look happy.

"Come on into my home office," I invite, trying to shake off all the passionate feelings of a minutes ago . It's not easy.

I lead the way, and Sam silently follows me.

I try to pretend this is a professional meeting with a client, but it's difficult with a man whose tongue was just in my mouth and whose hand was just on my breast.

Sam has no such problem, apparently, because he gets right down to business. "I want to preserve my mother's sewing room on the second floor."

"Okay," I say slowly, trying to wrap my head around that. It's the first time he's mentioned anything about his mother or a sewing room. "I'm sorry if I'm overstepping, but what made you decide that?"

Sam is back to crossing his arms over his chest, putting up a figurative wall between us. But he does answer me. "I was doing a walk-through of the house before the floor work got underway. On the second floor, I found her sewing room still intact, in one of the additional bedrooms. I never thought Parker would keep that untouched after she died."

"Wow." It's not a brilliant statement by any stretch of the imagination, but it's my first thought. Old gossip and what little Sam has told me about Parker, about his family life growing up, definitely wouldn't indicate his father would be sentimental like that. Keeping the woman's hobby room intact for more than 20 years had to of been a shock for Sam.

"You want to keep it exactly where it is?" I'm thinking about the floor plans of the house. If everything in that bedroom was shifted to one of the unspecified spaces on the first floor, it would maintain a five bedroom upstairs, which is good for renting or selling the house.

Did he think about the fact that buyers won't keep the room that way? I want to point out that they will clear it out and toss everything. Renters might even be put off by having a sort of tribute or memorial to a dead woman in the house. Sam is picking up and putting down random items on a bookshelf, on a tabletop. "I intend for it to stay where it is." He gives me another look I can't decipher. "My mother died when I was 16, Becca. To me, it was sudden, but she knew she was sick. She knew what was coming for her. That all room is like a strange… gift or something. I don't know. I do know that I'm not letting it go."

I shift my weight from one foot to the other and back again. I am supposed to be guiding him in this restoration project, but I am also personally involved with him. Technically, Sam isn't even a client, so do the guidelines for dealing with a client truly apply to my feelings with him? Dealing with a client or customer can have personal undertones or overtones or however you want to describe an amicable working relationship. It doesn't involve kissing and fondling and time together between the sheets.

This is uncharted territory for me and I don't know what to do.

Sam crisscrosses the room again. Something is definitely amiss with him, and I hate not knowing what it is or what I can do to help. Can it be that discovering his late mother's sewing room still exists distressed him this much? For a man with his background, it's hard to imagine that would shake him up for more than a very short while.

It's not for me to judge, though. I'm fortunate my parents are both alive and well. Sam is older than me, and his parents had him later in life, so maybe it's not surprising they are both gone, although from what he's said, her passing was a shock.

I know about grieving a relationship, and betrayal, and friendship, and those types of things. I don't have much experience with the deaths of people I love, so who am I to think or say Sam is handling this wrong? It's his house. But still…

"Sam, maybe you should just give yourself time to think it through. It had to be a shock."

I extend a hand towards my laptop. "Do you want to see what I've been working on regarding your property?"

Sam doesn't answer for long enough that I think he's not going to. Then he nods and says, "I'd like that."

CHAPTER 41
SAM

ON THE DAY, but not at the time Xander told me the meeting was supposed to start, I drive into the parking lot of a one-story building forty-five minutes from Hidden Haven. After running into a problem with the work at the main house, I had to shower and change into clothing that wasn't covered in construction dust and debris. I texted Xander I wasn't going to make it after all, and he texted back a request that I come anyway – even though I'd be late.

I count at least eight other vehicles in the parking area, in an assortment of sizes and types. Among them is the sleek vehicle I've seen Xander driving.

Xander is a good guy, but I grimace when I get out of my truck. Being last to arrive at something is a blessing and a curse. Everyone stares at you when you walk in because you're a rude asshole, but you also don't have to make pointless conversation before whatever you're late for begins. It doesn't matter if it's a debriefing, a planning meeting, or any kind of group session, there's always pointless conversation beforehand.

I don't do *chit chat*.

Arriving late to a group therapy thing – a support group –

though, feels particularly awkward. Bailing on this and taking off isn't an option. I said I'd be here. Breaking my word would be worse than being late.

A handwritten sign taped to the front door of the building announces the space is in use. Xander told me to come in whenever I arrived, so I can't play dumb and say I didn't know. I stop anyway to send him a heads up via text. I wait a second, once again fight the urge to bail, then put a hand to the doorknob and push forward.

The door swings open to reveal all a large, generic, space, with wood-paneled walls from some previous decade and wall-to-wall industrial carpet in shades of brown. The carpet muffles my footsteps as I walk toward the group of people seated in a semicircle of folding chairs. I recognize Xander, Ryan, Luke, and Donovan from that evening at Braeburn Tavern. There are others present who I don't recognize, including a few women.

It doesn't take much brainpower to deduce that the oldest of the women, with a clipboard on her lap and a lanyard around her neck, is Diane, the professional Xander told me leads the group.

Not wanting to create more of an interruption than I already have, I slip onto an open chair next to Xander. No doubt he left it open for me.

"I'm Diane Hughes, the group facilitator," clipboard woman greets me with direct eye contact and a friendly but professional smile. "Welcome and thanks for joining us…" Her voice trails off, inviting me to introduce myself, even though Xander probably told her I was going to be here today.

"Sam Miller," I say.

Xander volunteers. "I told him he should just walk in."

"I remember you said someone new might be joining us." Diane gives me another professionally polished smile.

"Would you like to tell us a little bit about yourself, Mr. Miller?"

This is very much *not* something I want to do. Unlike forced situations like this during my military career, I am here voluntarily. *When did you become a masochist?*

With everyone watching, I try to get more comfortable in the metal folding chair. They really could use cushions like the ones Mom made for hers.

"Call me Sam. Please."

With my thumb, I scratch below my lower lip. I don't want to be a standoffish prick and say nothing more. "I retired from the Navy about seven months ago. Maybe eight." How did I lose track of the weeks? "Was based out of Coronado for most of my 20 years in."

"You must have enlisted young," Diane comments.

"Yes." I've been here mere minutes and I'm already uncomfortable. Mostly because of the chair, but not entirely. I guess it's not really fair to blame the meeting or the facilitator, because I was uncomfortable before I got in the truck to come here.

The group leader tries to engage me further, and I almost get drawn into her kind approach, but no. I'm not going to spill my guts about issues with my dead parents and childhood trauma in some group therapy with strangers.

She tries one more time. "Are you living in McIntosh Ridge or the surrounding area?"

"The Ridge. I'm not staying here long." I don't volunteer anything else. I'm here at this meeting because Xander invited me (multiple times), and as courteous gesture to the other guys I met at the Tavern. I am not there for counseling.

Diane nods agreeably. "That's fine, Sam. For however long you are in the area, you're welcome to join us. There are some blank notecards on the table against the wall behind you. You can leave your mobile number or email address and I can send you a list of meeting dates and reminders the day before each one if you like."

She moves on to Ryan, who was evidently talking about something or getting ready to when I arrived on the scene. I figure Diane knows what she's doing, but wonder why she'd cut to me if he was in the middle of something, but what do I know? Ryan talks about a younger brother who is getting into trouble with reckless behavior, and his worries about the kid.

It's obvious Diane is already familiar with Ryan's family situation, which sounds complicated. The suggestions and resources she offers are practical and would probably be helpful if Ryan follows through on them.

Diane moves on to a question from Luke, who shares that a young man he hired for his construction crew is working out well. I'm not sure how that connects to this group here, but I guess it does.

Diane occasionally makes notes on her clipboard during conversations, but always seems attentive to whatever is being discussed. She finishes writing something that she tells us is a reminder to herself about another resource she thought of that could possibly help Ryan's mother, and that she'll look into it more. Then she flips the clipboard over on her lap.

"Later today, I'll be emailing a revised meeting schedule for the next two months," Diane says. "If you get notifications by text, I'll send it to you that way."

Her stiff body language makes it obvious to me that she's stressed about whatever else she needs to say, and I only met the woman an hour ago.

"The company that owns this building is going to be renovating it. There are only a couple of days we can use it next month. I was already able to get a short-term space for us in Eagle's Landing that we can meet in a few times." Her grip on the clipboard betrays her tension. "Between now and the end of those dates, I'll figure out a plan for a more permanent solution, for this group and a couple of others I meet with here."

She makes eye contact with us one by one, including me. "I believe we have something valuable with this group, and I'll do everything I can to preserve it. It matters, and you all matter."

I'm not a big fan of talk therapy, but her sincerity rings true. I stand with the others as the meeting breaks up. Diane shakes my hand, and I fill out the contact form she hands me. I probably won't show up to every meeting while I'm in McIntosh Ridge, but no harm in stopping in sometimes . Even if I don't need help with anything, it's good to support fellow veterans.

Xander leads me toward a table that has a display of brochures about therapists and treatments for mental and physical traumas, information about state and federal resources, and a bunch of other subjects.

Two disposable boxes of coffee are on the next table over, surrounded by upside down stacks of paper cups, brown stir sticks, miniature cups of creamer, and sweetener packets. An already empty box of mini doughnuts and a few individually packaged coffee cakes remain for whoever wants to partake.

I accept a cup of coffee from Xander and add a creamer to it. Next to me, Xander preps his own cup. "I'm glad you made it."

"I told you I would."

"You did," he agrees. "I'm still pleasantly surprised."

"Sorry I was late," I say. "I was in the middle of things I couldn't ignore and lost track of time."

Xander shrugs. "People come in late, leave early. Some never miss a meeting, others only show up once in a while. All Diane expects is that when somebody is here, they try to be respectful and cool to everyone else." He smirks. "Sounds simple enough, but it isn't always."

A guy I haven't met comes up to us and extends a hand to me. "Good to meet you. I'm Grant Angrisani."

I accept the handshake. "Sam Miller."

"I'm former Navy, too," the man says. His hair is just a little long, his beard bordering on unkempt. "If we meet again, maybe we'll talk."

It's vague, but that's fine with me. "Sounds good."

Angrisani fist bumps Xander. "Good to see you," he says then turns to go.

Xander and I silently watch the guy take his leave and see him stop to have a quick word with Donovan on his way out. Angrisani has a limp, but I don't comment or ask Xander about it.

"Always good to meet a fellow Navy veteran, right?" Xander remarks. "I think all Navy vets around here wonder how they ended up so far from the water."

I try to smile to be polite.

I'm not wondering anything about water; I'm wondering if Rebecca has reached out to me since the last time I checked my phone. I swore to myself I wasn't going to check compulsively like a lovesick teenager, but trying to not let her distract me is also distracting me.

Unbelievable.

Maybe I stumbled into a time warp around here and somehow I'm a teenager again.

CHAPTER 42
REBECCA

I CAN THINK of at least a dozen things I'd rather be doing instead of sitting in an already too long meeting in the McIntosh Ridge library. I've got nothing against the library. In fact, I know we are lucky to have one in our town at all. Not all small towns are as fortunate.

Claire, one of the librarians, has been a friend since high school. More than once over the years I've heard her explain how the public library system works when library locations are chosen. I'm ashamed to admit I zoned out each time. I like to read, but I only have so much attention bandwidth, and there wasn't space for all the info she was sharing.

We are sitting in the biggest open area for people who want to read or study here. It looks like extra chairs have been distributed among the glossy tables. A podium is positioned at the front of the room.

Claire separates from the group of people she's been talking with and goes to stand behind the podium. The light above it makes her nearly black hair gleam and catches on the little crystals that accent the corners of her eyeglasses. She fiddles with a couple of things up there and clicks on the microphone. Claire's voice is confident when she says, "Testing, testing, one, two, three."

"Thank you all for coming," Claire continues, welcoming us. With her ivory -colored cardigan set and black pencil skirt, she looks more like a sexy secretary than prim librarian. At least that's what I think, but what do I know? It's not like I've met many librarians in my life. Claire pushes her eyeglasses up the bridge of her nose. "I'll turn this over to the chairwoman for the McIntosh Ridge AppleFest events, Mrs. Patricia Mulvaney."

A polite smattering of applause welcomes Dragon Mulvaney. She was my ninth grade social studies teacher, and she scared the hell out of us students. That was 16 years ago, and her rigid demeanor hasn't gotten any softer or more approachable since then. While she drones on and on in her nasal voice about the history of AppleFest and McIntosh Ridge, I work on lists I maintain in the notes app on my phone.

I update the one for the store, add a few questions for my division manager on the lumberyard one, and jot down a couple of ideas for Sam's renovation. I am typing some questions I have about the sewing room situation when I hear my name being said in a decidedly shrill and annoyed tone.

"Rebecca Spencer? Are you listening?"

Mulvaney's accusatory tone is an ugly reminder of ninth grade. How that woman managed to make such an interesting subject so incredibly boring is still beyond me. From her icy voice and stony facial expression, and the way everyone else is looking at me, it's not hard to figure out she's waiting for me to say something.

There's no way to bluff my way out of this, so I have to own the fact that I wasn't paying attention. I try to smile ruefully but doubt I accomplish it .

"I apologize, I've been dealing with an urgent business matter and didn't catch everything you said." She can't really argue with that. She glares at me. "It would have been better to excuse yourself from the room and deal with your emergency outside."

Is she serious right now? I don't have a second to decide what to say because Dragon Mulvaney is already on to her next order of business. Or rather, back to her last point, the one I wasn't paying attention for.

"Pay attention to this, Ms. Spencer, because it specifically involves you. This year, the town wants a new bandstand and gazebo created for Orchard Park, something in the spirit of the original one." Her already narrow eyes narrow even more behind her eyeglasses. "It makes sense for you and your business to handle the project from start to finish, but it must be completed before the opening day of AppleFest."

Are you kidding me?

I stand up and choose my words carefully. "Everybody knows my family and my business support AppleFest, but opening day is in ... eight weeks or so. That's an impossible timeframe for me to research authentic turn-of-the-century designs and reinterpret them into something more modern for those structures, *and* also make them a reality." My head is already shaking no because there's no way. "I'll be happy to work on it starting now, and we can create it and debut it for next year."

Mrs. Mulvaney acts like I didn't even speak. "It must be completed for the start of AppleFest this year." She clasps her hands together in front of her. "If you can't do it, that's fine. There is a big box home improvement store in Middletown that is willing and able to make it happen."

Holy crap. What the heck is going on here?

I look around at the two dozen or more people in the room with us. Most of them look shocked, and aren't meeting my eyes. Tara and Beth are the two exceptions; Beth appears confused, and Tara looks furious.

I need to break down this problem, which is first and foremost the timeframe. "Mrs. Mulvaney, why does this project need to be done so quickly?"

Look at me, being all calm and rational about this crazy idea.

"It is needed this year because the executive committee decided so," she says pompously. "The structures currently there have problematic issues." Mrs. Mulvaney says that ominously, like the bandstand and gazebo are in danger of imminent collapse. She leans toward me a little bit like she really wants to get her message across. "I wouldn't think it's so difficult for you to do the necessary research because you're already working on the restoration of Ron Parker's house. Aren't you?"

she says triumphantly, she's sharing a big secret rubbing my nose in it.

"By now, that's common knowledge. It's also not relevant because the structures of the house and what you're talking about are very different."

"A lot of things are *common* knowledge," Mrs. Mulvaney declares in a way that makes me feel like she just insulted me again. "Individuals in McIntosh Ridge and the wider business community are all aware."

Anger washes over me so quickly I actually see red. The pieces of this strange challenge begin to click into place.

Mrs. Mulvaney is Kyle's mother. I don't know if she's doing this of her own accord because she thinks I insulted her son somehow, or if he came up with the plan and put her up to it, but messing with me and my business is an outrageous abuse of power.

If the town brings in a home improvement conglomerate to handle a project like this in our town's main park, there will be all kinds of ads and promotions tied to it. Area residents are going to wonder why Spencer Hardware wasn't put in charge of the project, and on top of that, they will be hit with inducements to shop at my competitor's stores.

Mrs. Mulvaney– and Kyle – are screwing around with my

business and everyone I employ, because if my business goes under, they lose their jobs. She and her son are messing with my family legacy and insulting all the good we've always done and continue to do for local residents. Shock and anger combine to make me nauseous.

Mrs. Mulvaney throws in another patronizing dig at me. "I hope trying to run the business on your own isn't too difficult for you."

Censoring myself is what's too difficult – so much so that I nearly swallow my tongue along with the words I want to say. "Oh no, my business is wonderful. Better than ever."

She doesn't bother answering that, simply gives me a look that can only be described as pitying and moves on to her next order of business.

There is no way I'm leaving this room right now, but I'm also not listening to anything else that's said. I don't have time for that. I'm too busy seething… and writing of things I know I'll need to do to create and replace the bandshell and gazebo in Orchard Park.

CHAPTER 43

SAM

I'M IN THE GARAGE, deciding if I want to keep it sized for two cars or enlarge it enough to handle three, when I hear someone approaching. I stand up from my crouched position in the rear corner of the garage . It's got to be one of the guys who are working on the floors in the main house, or one of those painting the barn.

Who I don't expect to see is Rebecca.

She looks beautiful, no shock there, but also tired and stressed beyond what I've seen before. I'm by her side as quickly as I can move.

With a knuckle bent under her chin, I lift her face so I can study it more closely. "Becca, what's going on?" She doesn't look physically injured, but something is definitely wrong.

"It's that obvious?" Rebecca closes her eyes in an extended blink. When she opens them, her head drops forward against my chest.

I want to demand she tell me what the hell is going on, but I clamp down on that urge. Whatever is wrong, she came to me, so she's going to tell me – right?

"Mrs. Mulvaney, the chairperson of the AppleFest

committee, informed me at the event planning meeting that they want the bandshell and gazebo in Orchard Park redesigned and reconstructed. She offered me the job."

"Okay." I am clearly missing something here, because that sounds like a good thing and she's acting like it definitely isn't. "Is that bad?"

"Sam, they want the project completed in time for the opening of the festival."

That makes no sense. "This year's festival? Isn't that in –" My brain pictures the calendar. "Nine weeks?"

"Eight," Rebecca corrects me. "Eight weeks. Two months to coordinate removal of the existing structures, come up with the appropriate plans, get the approvals fast-tracked somehow, build both structures and get occupancy approvals." Her laugh is as far from amused as it could possibly be. "The permitting alone would normally take longer than that."

"You told her it's a no go, right?" I'm sure she feels bad about refusing this project, but it sounds like she'd be setting herself up for eight weeks of massive stress and frustration.

"I wanted to." She's still not looking at me. "I wanted to laugh in her face because it's so insane." Rebecca takes a breath, still standing so close to me that I feel her chest rise. She steps back and finally looks me in the eye. "I was informed that if the project and its deadline are too much for me to handle, the nearest Home Depot or Lowe's is ready to take it on."

"You're telling me this timeframe is so damn important to them that they would undercut in McIntosh Ridge business because of it?"

I haven't been back here for long, but I know for a fact that this town, like many other relatively small towns, avoid big, commercial businesses whenever possible. The Spencer family has operated a successful business here for at least three generations, but the town would rather bring in a big corporation instead?

"Oh, yes, that's exactly what she told me." Rebecca steps back and wraps her arms around her middle. "She said the 'big box' corporation already agreed to do it."

Even more shocking. "Wait a minute, they – this woman– already spoke with one of these bigger companies? Before she or anyone else approached you about it?"

"Yes. Apparently, they were making sure somebody could do it," she confirms. "They expected me to say I couldn't or wouldn't do it."

"Back up a second. Why the urgency?" I haven't been to Orchard Park since I was there with Rebecca months ago, and that was in the dark. "Are the bandstand and the gazebo falling down or something? If they are, no way it's a sudden deterioration, they had to have known about the problem, right?" Another thought occurs to me. "And where are they getting the money for this? Doesn't it have to be approved? Was the money raised, or donated, or something like that?" I have another question. "Are they offering a fair contract for your work?"

Even with small town bullshit, money is a reality no one can avoid.

Rebecca sounds angrier the more she talks. "I asked about all that after the meeting, and was told a private donor is giving the town an interest-free or low-interest loan because the project is so important." She starts pacing back-and-forth in front of me. "As far as compensation for me, of course it isn't fair. But I'm between a rock and a hard place. If I tell her to stick it, I'm handing the job to a competitor who will then have a free ad continually running in Orchard Park. They'll probably also market directly to McIntosh Ridge locals. I *can't* say no."

Since Rebecca pulled away from me, I'm not sure how she'll react, but I can't *not* reach out anyway and lightly grasp her upper arms when she passes in front of me again. She doesn't flinch or pull away this time. I stroke the soft skin with my thumbs in what I hope is a soothing and supportive gesture. Even when she's agitated like this, I'm drawn to her like a doomed moth to his fiery death.

I need to stay focused if I'm going to try and help her. "Becca, I feel like I'm missing something about all this. Something's not right." I know that's putting it mildly.

"You think?" That spirited flash of attitude doesn't. "Sorry, did I mention that the chairwoman of the committee is Patricia Mulvaney,

"Kyle's mother," she adds.

Who the fuck is Kyle? The name is familiar, but I don't know – and then I do. "That asshole who –"

It's Rebecca's turn to interrupt. "Yes. I was polite to him because his business does a good amount of business with my store. I should have kicked him in the balls."

"You think the fact that you don't want to date her son put you in the crosshairs of this woman? That's fucked up." I'm sure it's also illegal, but I don't mention that right now.

"You know that, and I know that but that's still the way it is."

I hate the way Rebecca sounds so defeated, even though she's mad. One of the things I like so much about this woman is her fearless, never give up attitude. She runs the Spencer family businesses like a dynamo. I hear the way people talk about her with respect and admiration. Xander and several of his friends have been helping out around here, and they all have good things to say about Rebecca. Yeah, they think she's my girlfriend, so they're not exactly going to be disrespectful. But I can tell that the nice things they say about her are sincere.

The way she looks right now, simultaneously troubled and angry, possibly a little afraid, is making me crazy on her behalf. *You're crazy for her, too*, my conscience chirps, always a pain in the ass.

My mouth knows what to say, even if my brain isn't sure.

"I gotta tell you, Becca, I'm here for you, whatever you need. You might not need me to slay dragons for you, but I can guard your six while you kick their asses."

Rebecca surprises me when instead of backing up, she moves closer. "That's a hot thing to say," she murmurs. In the quiet space, the words are loud and clear.

"Fair warning, I want to kiss you right now," I say. I don't know if she's going to agree or walk out the door, but no way am I inviting regrets.

"So do it," she challenges me.

Game on.

I am damn skilled at multitasking. I grip the back of her head with one hand and bring my lips to hers without hesitation. I growl into Becca's mouth and she growls right back, my sounds seeming to excite her, which is only fair because hers set my body on fire.

She pulls me closer. We kiss deeper, then deeper still, our connection white-hot, full of tongues and teeth and moans. Like a double shot of tequila, Becca goes straight to my head and I only know that I want more. More of this, of her, of us.

I slide my fingers into her hair, the soft strands caressing my skin as if by intention. Her fingers are exploring my biceps, then my shoulders, and inching their way across my chest. We kiss deeper, hotter. Hungrier. Breath coming fast, I break the kiss and coast my lips down the soft, fragrant skin of her throat.

I feel lost in the haze Becca puts me in. High on knowing this thing between us, this connection, is different. I've shared more of myself with this unique woman then I ever shared with anyone before. I don't know if it's that epiphany or amendment of logic but an alarm sounds in my brain.

You need to stop this.

I need to stop this. Right now. There are men working in

the main house, more men working on the property. Any or all of them could walk right in here looking for me. The sounds Becca is making, and her thoroughly kissed mouth are for me, alone.

"Becca. Sweetheart." My voice is thick with arousal and reluctance. "We have to stop. Too many guys here working today. We have to stop."

"No, no, no, no." She has both hands on my face now, trying to guide my mouth back to hers. "I closed the door behind me."

"It's not locked," I remind her. "I don't want to stop, either." I drop a fast kiss to her lips, more of a brush of my mouth against hers then a true kiss. "I *don't*," I repeat.

Rebecca's hands slide down my chest. "You're right. I know you're right." She takes several steps back from me. "I should go."

"I'm glad you came by." I mean that sincerely, and I hope she knows it.

This isn't the time to try to put my confusion into words. I don't understand these feelings that are swimming to the surface inside me. There are too many to identify, let alone wrestle into submission.

"I don't know why I did," she admits. "I was upset and I didn't think, I just drove here."

Be practical, I order myself. Practical is safe. "I hope you know that I'll help you get the town project completed. Whatever you need, I'll help you."

"You have your own renovation and restoration to finish here."

I am adamant. "That doesn't matter, you can always come to me. Remember that." I want to be the one she can turn to.

Rebecca looks at me strangely. "But I can't, Sam. Remember? You're leaving."

I freeze. What a stupid thing for me to say.

She's right. I *am* leaving. As soon as I can, I am out of here, and I will only be back when I absolutely have to be to abide by the terms of the well.

"Bye, Sam."

And she's gone.

CHAPTER 44

REBECCA

BETH SHOVES a cup of coffee at me across the bakery prep table where we've set up our quasi--war council. I fortify the black elixir with cream and sugar before daring to take a sip. Beth gets up early because her business requires it and likes to stay up late, so when she drinks coffee it's strong – like industrial-strength strong.

Tara studies a spreadsheet she populated from lists that she demanded I share with her. "Rebecca, are you absolutely sure you want to do this? It's… a lot."

I drop my coffee-stirring spoon on the table so I can throw up my hands. "I know it's a lot. In one way I *do* want to do it, because it's great to think of Spencer Hardware being credited with creating this new centerpiece for Orchard Park."

"But you don't want to do it under this time constraint." Beth correctly identifies what I haven't said yet tonight.

"Exactly." I bypass my coffee and grab a chocolate chip cookie off the plate of treats Beth set out for us. "I can't believe Kyle is so butt-hurt over me refusing to have dinner with him that he cooked up this whole thing to get back at me."

Tara practically growls. "His fragile baby-man ego can't take a woman telling him no."

Beth leans back against the counter behind her and sips her own coffee. "I can't believe he got his mommy to go along with this." She shakes her head, her chestnut brown braid swishing side to side behind her back. "Aren't there any ethics rules or things like that for the town council, or the committees?"

"You think the mayor wants to go up against the Dragon?" I scoff at the remark. "I think the mayor and the head of the council both had her as a teacher in high school. They are probably still afraid of her."

Tara laughs at that. "You do realize she's only maybe four or five years older than that guy who's chairman of the council? She couldn't have been his teacher."

"You do realize that she's probably immortal, right?" Beth counters. "I bet the Dragon Lady lives in one of those caves down over the Ridge."

I held up a hand to stop them before they get into a deep debate about where the Dragon rests her fire-breathing head. "Regardless of the ethics, lack of ethics, ridiculousness, and everything else, I have to make this project happen. Otherwise, whichever big box store she was talking about will get a lot of publicity out of this, and it'll make my business look like shit."

Loyal no matter what, Tara protests. "Another company doing the project doesn't make yours look bad."

"Please, T." I bring my cup of coffee to my mouth, pausing to try and appreciate the aroma. Spoiler alert: It smells like stress and desperation. I set the cup down without drinking. "Everyone will wonder why I didn't do it. Am I going to have to try and tell everyone over and over that I was given less than two months to design and install two turn-of-the-century, but also modern style structures?"

Tara eyes me over the half-eaten cookie in her hand.

"What was that weird comment she made about the restoration work you're doing for Sam? How does she know about that? I mean, I didn't think it was common knowledge that you are consulting about that."

Beth finally sits down on a stool she pulls out from under the prep table. "Yeah, I want to know about that, too."

I should've known the two of them picked up on that nasty little comment of Mulvaney's. "It was just another indication Kyle is behind this."

Tara gives me a rolling hand gesture demanding I continue. I make a face but go on. "Basically, she said if I have time to work on the restoration at Sam's place, I should be able to find the time to do this for the town."

"That little bitch! I can't believe the audacity!" Tara shouts and crams the rest of her cookie into her mouth, chewing furiously.

Beth hushes her. "She was always a piece of work, even when we were in high school."

"I wasn't talking about *her*, Beth. I'm talking about that little bitch, Kyle. And you know what, she's one, too, and I don't mind saying so." Tara is a picture of indignant fury despite the cookie crumbs clinging to her shirt.

"Look guys, I appreciate your support, but the bottom line is that I need to figure out a way to get it done. If I don't, Spencer Hardware's constant struggle against the big box style home improvement stores is going to slam into a whole bunch of new obstacles."

And those could be enough to tip us over, finally. I share with them the terrible thought that's been plaguing me. "What if the town puts up some kind of signage on the new structures thanking whichever store handled it, and it's not Spencer Hardware? I'd have to deal with that crap however long I'm in business."

I see my friends exchanging meaningful looks, then Tara

says, "We all have to deal with big corporations nosing in on our businesses. Screw them."

Beth agrees. "Every supermarket has a whole bakery department with cheap baked goods, and you can use your phone to order cakes and cookies and everything else delivered right to your door, now. It stinks, but we got this, Rebecca. *You've* got this."

"Same for candles, my friend." Tara is finally brushing crumbs off her shirt. "Yankee Candles, Party Litre candles, Adirondack Candles, candles here and candles there, candles freaking everywhere."

Beth interrupts Tara's growing rant. "Even Baxter's Department Store practically across the street from you, Tara, has that big candle department now!"

"Thanks for the reminder." Tara says sarcastically.

Before that exchange can derail into a spat, I voluntarily speak up. "Anyway, so I have to do this project and do it damn well."

Tara refocuses on me. "The same way you do everything else, my friend. Damn well."

Beth lifts her cup in solidarity. "Damn right."

"How can we help?" Tara asks. "Give us your commands."

Beth has a different question. "How is Sam helping with this?"

I don't know why I wasn't expecting that question, but I wasn't. I drink more coffee to stall and decide what to say.

Tara has no patience for that. "Don't stall. What did he say about all this?"

My eyes flicker to Beth then back to Tara. Tara knows that Beth *doesn't* know about my fake relationship thing with Sam or anything else about what's really gone on between us. The whole thing is confusing to *me*, and I'm the one who orchestrated it. There's no way I'm trying to explain all of that here, this evening. Not happening.

"We are not asking about your sex life, you know," Tara makes a face like she doesn't always want to hear about my sex life, even when I don't have one. Even when I tell her to butt out. "You told Sam about this situation, didn't you?" She frowns at me again. "Or did you not tell him, or edit the story because it involves another guy?"

I frown right back. "Yes, I told him." I point a finger at her. "And it doesn't involve another guy, not the way that sounds at least. I never went out with Kyle, never considered it for a single second."

"Hey," Beth says in the way people do when she's remembering something. "I sort of remember hearing something about Kyle and Sam having words at your store…"

Tara jumps on that thread and unravels it more. "That must've been quite the wake-up call for Kyle to get over his delusion that you would ever date him."

I try to steer the conversation back on course. "Look, guys, none of this has anything to do with my problem."

"It absolutely does," Beth insists. "That's probably one of the reasons Kyle is so butt-hurt, to use your words, and one of the things that got his mother on his side with this."

"That plus you refusing to help with his restoration project must've been too much for his little ego to handle," Tara says derisively. "Pathetic loser. Sam won you, got you to share your restoration skills with him, and won the dick measuring contest."

Beth sputters, "Wait a minute, there was a dick measuring contest? How did I not hear about this?" She pauses. "Sam won, huh?"

I bury my face in my hands. Tara answers her, "I'm not being literal, Beth, but of course Sam won. From what Rebecca tells me, no one could beat Sam in that department."

CHAPTER 45
SAM

WHEN REBECCA ASKED if I could go with her to the site of the bandshell and gazebo, I was in my truck and driving her way before she finished asking.

Now, I notice (again) that Rebecca's hand in mine is incredibly soft and smooth, especially since she works with those small hands at every kind of task, without hesitation. She keeps her fingernails relatively short, but immaculately filed and polished in different colors every time I see her. At least it seems that way.

Those fingernails were a luminous shade of lavender when Rebecca's hands were exploring me in my bed. When they were braced against the white wall in my bedroom. When she was on her knees, and her hands were clutching the beige pillow in front of her while she pleaded with me not to stop. Despite the fact that she snuck out on me after that first time we were together, that lavender color is burned into my memory. Truth be told, in my mind I revisit those scenes more often than I care to admit.

Today the color on her nails is a bright pink. It's unexpected and shines brilliantly, just like she does.

With everything she's dealing with right now, I'm

surprised Rebecca found time to change her nail color. I probably shouldn't be. She's the embodiment of *Expect the Unexpected*.

Rebecca walks down Main Street with me, explaining her basic plan for the Orchard Park project. She's already made lists, made phone calls, roughed out a schedule, and is putting extra people on shifts at the store to cover for her. This morning, she's going to be photographing the bandshell, gazebo, and surrounding areas.

When she invited me along and suggested we get breakfast afterward, I was all for it. I don't know if Rebecca thinks it's only to further our dating story, but for me, it's because I'll take any time I can with her.

When we get to the light from the street crossing, she lets go of my hand to push the button on the post since her other hand is holding the strap of a heavy bag she refuses to let me carry. I move my hand to her lower back. While we wait for the light to change, I run my fingers over Rebecca's back, my eyes moving from her profile to the passing traffic, and back again.

Her phone rings in her purse and she taps the Bluetooth device in her ear to answer it. From her first couple words I can tell it's one of her employees. I don't mind her inattention because it makes it easier for me to stare at her profile too long.

Damn. This woman.

How did she slip into my cold, closed heart and make a place for herself there? And when did it happen? I haven't been back here all that long.

The traffic light changes and as we cross the street, she ends her call.

"Do you remember AppleFest from when you were a kid?" she asks me.

"A little." That's a lie. I don't want to lie to her, so I amend my answer. "That's not quite true. I remember bits and pieces of things when I was elementary school age. After that, I mostly avoided it." I know she's going to ask why, so I head off the question. "I didn't have money to spare. Whatever I earned, I gave to Mom for things."

I don't bother telling Rebecca that those things were mostly utility bills and groceries. I don't need her sympathies for some of what sucked about those years, when those were the minor things.

Rebecca must pick up on that, because she keeps the conversation going as we move toward the entrance to Orchard Park, passing other people here and there despite the early hour. She tells me how Spencer Hardware always shows support for AppleFest despite not being the kind of business that tourists and daytrippers care about.

"Our support benefits McIntosh Ridge and area residents, and that's what's important to business."

We stop at the next corner to wait for the last light before we'll enter the park.

I don't like that she's carrying that heavy bag and I'm not. I try again. "Rebecca, let me take those things from you." I point out the obvious. "You're going to need your hands free to take your pictures, aren't you?"

"Yes, but I can leave it on a bench." Her sunglasses aren't too dark, so I can see her eyes on me. "I don't want you thinking I can't handle it myself."

"That's what this one-woman juggling act has been about?" It's funny, but it isn't. "Becca, I don't think I've seen *anything* you can't handle yourself. You don't need to prove anything to me."

"Maybe I'm not trying to prove things to you as much as to myself."

We are both quiet walking through the open gates to Orchard Park. A woman pushing a baby stroller passes us on the path, her focus on her child.

I want to reassure Rebecca that physically burdening

herself unnecessarily isn't proving anything to anyone… but that's not for me to say, is it? I'm more concerned with *her* thinking that accepting help with a trivial thing shows weakness. It's tough, but I bite back the words because I know this isn't the time or place to dissect that with her.

"I'm not forgetting about your restoration, you know." Rebecca looks over at me but keeps walking. "I checked in with the last suppliers to check delivery dates are on track."

"Don't worry about any of that," I tell her, maybe more sharply than I should. "Hidden Haven is the last thing you need to worry about."

I hear the change in her footsteps on the paved path; now she's borderline stomping. A guy on a blue bicycle passes us cautiously, conscientiously keeping to his side of the wide path. She doesn't speak until he's out of earshot.

"I'll thank you to let me handle my own schedule and responsibilities." Rebecca's tone is decidedly frosty, and damn if that isn't hot, too.

You're definitely messed up, man.

I'm okay at being civil, but I'm no diplomat. Navigating this conversation is like defusing a bomb. "That's not what I'm trying to do, Rebecca. I'm just recognizing that you've got a lot of big things to deal with, and my project is progressing well , so you don't have to give it as much attention." When have I ever let a woman make me so nervous about a conversation? This is ridiculous. "That's all."

Like every time we've walked together, I'm trying to shorten my stride to keep pace with hers, instead of her needing to keep pace with me. I'm distracted by our conversation and forget, then get ahead of her so I abruptly modify my steps again, and stumble. Geez, I must look like I forgot how to walk. In my defense, my attention is also being waylaid by the way Rebecca's hair captures the sunlight.

It's embarrassing how shallow you can be.

The stubborn woman insists on holding onto that heavy

bag until we get to the bandshell, and the nearby gazebo. She puts her bag on a bench like the one we shared after that first dinner at Tony's Pizzeria.

Rebecca spends the next half hour taking pictures of the bandshell, and then the gazebo, from every possible angle. She climbs up on a couple of different benches, and then passes me her phone so I can take a few photos, too.

"Do you need measurements?" I ask. She probably has a tape measure in the bag.

"I have the schematics for the existing structures, and for the area they are built on." She studies the scene in front of us. "There are a couple of measurements I'd like to take, if you wouldn't mind giving me a hand."

I don't bother pointing out that I've been repeatedly offering her any kind of help I can possibly give her. "No problem."

CHAPTER 46

SAM

NEARLY A WEEK after I helped Rebecca take measurements in the park, I sit across from Xander in a booth near the bar in Braeburn Tavern. It's late for lunch but early for dinner and the crowd is thin. The burgers are thick and juicy. I add ketchup to mine and re-settle the top bun over the lettuce, tomato, and cheese that dress the char-grilled patty.

Xander finishes making final touches to his own food and prepares to take his first bite. "When I was in the Navy, I thought about these burgers anytime the chow hall sucked more than usual or I was somewhere surviving on MREs." He takes that bite and when he's done enjoying it adds, "Man, I don't miss those things."

"Heard and agreed." I don't miss military rations, either. They were "meals ready to eat", all right, but some of them were tough to get down. "They were reliable calories. Necessary fuel." I eat a couple of French fries.

"Don't get me wrong, when we needed them I was grateful to have them." Xander swipes one of his own thick cut fries through a pile of ketchup he'd squirted on his plate. "A couple of the varieties were even pretty good."

"Chili -Mac," we say simultaneously.

"You owe me a beer," Xander laughs, first to invoke the time-honored claim made when two people say the same thing at the same time.

I lift my beer in acknowledgment. "I'll pay for that beer today and you can consider the debt settled immediately."

I know he's watching me while I continue eating, but I focus on my food.

He finally speaks. "You're still planning on leaving the Ridge?"

"I am."

I don't elaborate. We both keep eating, and the tension at the table grows. When I finish the last bite of my burger, he doesn't waste any more time.

"What about Rebecca?"

"What about her? She's well aware that I'll be leaving." I wipe my mouth with the napkin from my lap. "You know that."

He waves a hand at me dismissively. "I know a lot of things, Sam, including the fact that it makes no sense for you to leave."

"And how do you know that?" I challenge him. "You hardly know me. You didn't know me when I was a kid and I lived here, or when I served." It's true. He's a few years younger than me, which is a big deal when you're a kid. I knew his family name, because everybody around here knows of the Baxter family, but nothing more than that. My hand is tight around my glass of iced tea.

I'm not a man who is ruled by my temper, but I suddenly have the urge to hit someone. I don't know if it's Kyle, Xander, or myself that's my target. Probably all of the above.

Xander doesn't back down. "Things change. You and I both know that."

Yes, even on the most carefully planned op things could sometimes change, and usually not for the better. It would be fucking great if things with Rebecca could change for the better. But my head is still screwed up from my childhood and teenage years and then all the shit the Navy SEALs "blessed" me with.

Don't get me wrong, I'm proud of my service and of those I served with. But the way to get through it, the mental compartments you have to develop and the separation of emotion from what you have to see and…, well that's not conducive to being a good family man, is it? The sum total of my whole life makes me so far removed from everything Rebecca deserves that it's laughable.

Then throw in the all-important fact that Rebecca isn't looking for a man to have a relationship with, and it's all a non-starter for a happily ever after. I'm giving her what she asked me for –a pretend relationship, and a planned breakup that gives her justification for how she chooses to live her life. Restoration of the main house on my mother's property gives Rebecca practice and proof of her talents with that. Hell, this bullshit with the town's AppleFest is going to prove it to everyone for a long time.

It's not Rebecca's fault I screwed up the mission and lost sight of the critically important *fake* part. But that's my problem, not hers.

Xander pulls in a breath and leans forward. "Rebecca and I have been friends for a long time. I think you're a good guy, Sam, and it'd be great if you two ended up together. But in the past she's been burned badly, and if you really aren't staying here –"

I don't let him finish his sentence. "I'm not. We're having a good time and that's it. We both know this isn't a long-term thing."

I like Rebecca, way more than I should, and the sex was more than incredible. But I'm going, she's staying, so even from a purely logistical perspective, we don't work.

Xander presses. "And you're sure she knows that? That she agrees?"

"I am. I'm not making any promises that I can't keep."

"I'm not saying you would." Xander scrubs a hand through his hair. "Believe me, this isn't a comfortable conversation for me. But I'd hate it if there was a misunderstanding between you about this. Rebecca's a great person." He grimaces. "Plus, Tara asked me to make sure."

I thought I was picking up on something between Xander and Tara, and brushed it off as none of my business. Especially since they don't act like they are together.

Time to change the subject.

"I'm going to make damn sure Rebecca kicks ass on this project in the park." I punctuate my words with several sharp raps on the table. "That's the main reason I asked you to meet me today."

Xander shifts gears right along with me. "What do you both need?"

"The way some of your friends have been helping out at my property has been tremendous. You know how much I appreciate it."

"I hope you understand how much they enjoy it."

"I do." I take another swig of my iced tea. "Rebecca got the permits for the demolition today. I was thinking if any of you guys can assist with that, the process will go faster. She's narrowed down the field of demo professionals who might be available to help."

Xander is already taking notes on his phone. "I know a couple of demolition guys through the veterans' groups. I can reach out to them."

"I appreciate the offer, but apparently she has to use someone off the town's 'approved' list," I tell him.

"Because of course they have to make things more complicated." Xander toys with the straw in his glass, then pushes the glass away. "Rebecca got all the specs about what she'll need from whoever she hires? Insurance and all?"

"She's definitely on top of all that." Rebecca is a force to be reckoned with when she's working on something, especially something that matters to her as much as this does. "She and I were talking, and it's bound to be helpful if there are extra hands who could help out whichever contractor she uses."

"I can promise there will be multiple volunteers. I'm sure of it." Xander starts looking around for something, then signals our server for drink refills. He settles back against the padded booth seat. "What about the construction phase? Is there a plan for that, or is it too soon?"

"She had ideas about how it should look within hours of hearing about the project." I can't not smile at the memory of Rebecca sketching like a maniac and muttering to herself the whole time. "She already reached out to a local architect she knows because architectural renderings have to be presented to the town and approved before construction can begin."

"How the hell is it all going to happen fast enough?" Xander shakes his head as our drinks arrive at the table. "The timeline is brutal, man." He smiles at the woman who sets the glasses on the table. "Thanks, Mindy."

"You're very welcome!" She pressed her round tray against her body, arms crossed over it and pins me with a serious look. "You're Sam, right? Rebecca Spencer's friend?"

I don't know why she's asking, but I make sure to look her straight in the eye. "Yes, I am, ma'am."

"That young lady is a special one, you know. All her life, she's been a friend to everyone in this town. She's not one to ask us for help, but if you know anything we can do to help her with that Orchard Park business, don't be shy about it."

I shoot a look at Xander. Mindy's words are unexpected but a welcome surprise. "I won't be. Don't be surprised if I get in touch with you."

She gives me a big smile, a sharp nod, and a real laugh. I swear I get a glimpse of how she must've looked three decades ago, maybe as a customer in this same tavern. Mindy claps a hand on my shoulder. "I can't tell you how glad I am she found a quality man like you."

Mindy collects our empty plates along with the empty glasses, turns, and walks away. I have to fight the urge to stop her and confess that I'm not a quality man at all. I'm a guy who's passing through, albeit slowly, and getting to take advantage of Rebecca's scarred heart and frustrated dreams.

Fuck me.

When I think of it that way, I want to kick the shit out of myself. The sooner I help get Rebecca's burdens sorted, mine in order, and McIntosh Ridge in my rearview mirror, the better off she'll be.

Xander doesn't say anything for a couple of minutes after Mindy leaves the table. He's an intuitive son of a bitch, and I wonder if he is purposely letting me stew in my own miserable thoughts. I glare at the fresh iced tea Mindy left in front of me. *Why didn't you get something stronger this time?*

Xander decides to break his silence. "I'm not one of the town gossips, but I do have a question about your property. Are you planning to find a buyer or a renter before you go?"

I take my time to think before I answer. I've spent enough time with Xander over these past months that I know the guy must have a reason for asking.

"It's a complicated situation right now. But yes, I'm looking to rent it out. Everything but the small cottage on the property that I've been using."

I'll need Mom's cottage for when I'm in town because of that ridiculous Trust requirement. Even if my legal efforts manage to get those demands tossed out, then I'll decide if I want to keep the property or sell it and be completely done with it all.

Selling it would mean cutting ties with the land owned by my mother's family for more than a century. More than that, I would be giving up her cottage retreat where she carved out a little happiness in the shadow of the big house. And I would be walking away from her sewing room where she hid the little lion she rescued for me. I'll never know why she didn't tell me before she died. *Stupid thought.* She didn't know she was going to die when she did.

That bit of enlightenment hits me like a thunderbolt. I always thought she knew how sick she was and was trying to spare me that reality. But maybe she *didn't* know. Maybe she thought she'd get better. Get better and then – what?

Maybe she had some plan for us to escape Parker's clutches? Some plan for us to evict him from the property? Tell me the story of why my missing lion was in a lockbox in her sewing room closet? So many things she could have told me.

Like I could tell Rebecca how I feel about her. And help her with what she's going through. And have her help me with what I'm going through.

Good Lord, I'm losing my mind.

If I dump all that on her, she'll probably go along with it because she won't want to hurt my feelings. Until that level of faking isn't enough anymore. Until *I* am not enough anymore.

The silence swirling around my thoughts gets very loud and I'm suddenly aware I've been lost in there too long. Xander is politely waiting for my attention to come back to earth.

My brain snaps back to attention. He asked about my plans for Hidden Haven. I ask a question of my own. "Why?"

Xander displays one of the traits I most appreciate about him; he gets right to the point. "The Vets group needs a new meeting place. Last year I set up a nonprofit to apply for grants to set up a place for veterans looking for or needing support who understand them. Not a hospital or anything like that, but a place to maybe learn a few skills, brush up on a few skills."

Xander glances down at his glass and gathers his thoughts before he continues. "Maybe take a breather, you know? Or have a chance to appreciate different things in their lives."

I could absolutely understand. "What do you see people doing there on the property?"

Xander half shrugs. "Deal with animals? Grow shit? Be around other people they might have stuff in common with?" He reaches for the glass he pushed away a few minutes ago and drinks. "It's been a work in progress while I try to find a place to set up and orchestrate funding."

Xander's description wasn't full of specifics, but it's enough that it gives me an understanding of what the guy wants to achieve. I like it.

"The rent will have to cover taxes and insurance on the property," I say. "Aside from that, it'll be relatively inexpensive. At least, if it's for that purpose." I stop for a moment, still thinking. "You'd be responsible for all the costs of running whatever it ultimately is."

"Absolutely." Xander agrees without hesitation, but I see the surprise on his face. "Don't you want to see a proposal first? The written plan?"

I shake my head. "To be honest, no. I sat in with the group a few times, enough to know that it's worthwhile." I cross my forearms in front of me on the table. "I've lost enough brothers-and sisters-in-arms to know the struggles are real and deeper than we give them credit for."

I don't mention my mother's battle with her struggles. The image of her lifeless body floods my memory, softened a little by time, but still a gut punch. I push it away.

"The property is held in Trust as part of the legal structure of it all." No reason to give the guy a detailed explanation of Parker's machinations. "Some stuff is being sorted out still, but I'll keep you in the loop. Meanwhile, I give you my word you'll get first dibs on it."

Xander doesn't try to hide the fact that he's pleased. "Your word is good enough for me."

The vote of confidence isn't something I take for granted; in the grand scheme of things, Xander barely knows me. But sometimes you make a friend and it is just… right.

Like with Rebecca. The situation with her is getting more and more complicated, no matter how much I want to deny it.

Uncomplicated my ass.

CHAPTER 47
REBECCA

I LEAVE McIntosh Ridge Town Hall with a spring in my step and the tube of architectural plans clutched like a baby in my arms. Stephen Daventry, the guy who's in charge of these things here went over everything carefully while I waited. I know he didn't have to do that, but when I called to let them know I was on my way over, he told me he'd clear the next few hours so he could focus on what I needed done.

Turns out using Darnell Richards as my architect was a great decision, because in just a few short days he managed to translate all my notes and sketches into the magical blueprint I was carrying like the golden child. He's worked with McIntosh Ridge powers that be before, and they with him, and no doubt that worked in my favor, too.

I'm not discounting the value of my having helped Darnell with selecting all the paint for the inside and outside of the fixer-upper he and his wife purchased in town last year. Or the fact that I've helped Stephen and his wife, Grace, more times than I can remember while they dealt with endless interior and exterior home projects over the years since I returned to McIntosh Ridge.

I think it also helped that they both low-key indicated that the Town Council – Dragon Mulvaney's coven – are being outrageous with this timeframe.

I put the tube of rolled plans on the rear seat before I clamber up into my Spencer Hardware truck. I refuse to admit, even to myself, that I was tempted to strap in the fat cardboard tube like it's a baby or something. That would be crazy, right?

By the time I slam the truck into gear, the call I placed is ringing through my speaker.

He answers on the second ring. "Luke Sheppard, Sheppard Construction." A momentary pause, then "Rebecca, is that you?"

"It sure is. The plans are duly authorized! Stephen Daventry kept one set of originals and gave me the other. He says I'll get a formal letter in the next few days, but that we are good to go as of right now. I have the work permit number for you."

I hear Luke moving around on the other end of the call, and what sounds like drawers opening and closing, things being banged around.

"That is freaking phenomenal."

His excitement makes me even more excited. Luke is one of Xander's friends, which was probably the main reason Xander recommended him to Sam and then me. He's part of the veterans' group to which several of them belong. It was a huge break when it turned out Luke is on the approved contractor list for McIntosh Ridge.

The sound on Luke's end of the call has changed; I think he's outdoors now. He says, "We are going to get demolition started today. I have a crew on standby."

He spends another several minutes giving me a few particulars I don't really need but I let him talk. Normally, I would want to be as involved as possible in every step of a project, but there's no time. It's terrible that something that could've been a dream come true and an honor, have instead been perverted into a bizarre attempt at petty revenge for me refusing a dinner date. In what world does something like this happen?

I know the answer to that. It happens in a small town world where a big dick with a little one can't deal with a woman rejecting his smarmy invitation. And shame on his mommy for enabling this crap.

"I'll text you pictures of our progress," Luke promises. "We've got your back, Rebecca."

"Thanks, I know you do."

I push the button on my steering wheel to disconnect the call. I am already halfway to Sam's property and debate with myself about whether I should call to let him know. I want to see him, to update him in person, but even if he isn't there I need to stop there anyway.

I have to make sure Sam's restoration efforts are on track. I know the electricians were in to update the panel, and plumbers to make a few overdue improvements. I can't abandon that project because of the town one. No matter what Sam says, that wouldn't be right. It doesn't matter that I've gone way past what we originally agreed I would do for his project; I am invested in it--and in him.

My tires spin away the miles along the asphalt county road that separates me from him. At some point in the not-too-distant future that separation is going to be way bigger. We'll be separated by towns, states, oceans, and who knows what else. It's important that I keep reminding myself about that.

My phone rings and saves me from my thoughts, but when I see who it is, I think I'd rather not be saved at all right now. I really don't want to deal with this right now, but I also really don't have a choice, do I?

"Hi, Mom." I make myself smile so hopefully the gesture will carry through to my voice. Isn't that what they say happens? "How are you doing today?"

"We'd be better if you toldus anything that goes on with you Rebecca." Oh my God, she's using the *I'm disappointed in you* voice with me. I was so sure I finally outgrew that voice and the guilt it brought with it.

I can't pretend I don't know what she's talking about. Truth be told, I'm surprised I didn't hear from them about this already.

"I wanted us to call you two days ago, but your father convinced me to wait. I waited. Now I can't wait anymore. Rebecca, what is going on?"

Mom sounds confused, agitated, and exasperated all at once. That can't be easy, even for her. I'm trying to figure out how to best explain this to her when my father speaks. (I should have known he was on the line, too.)

"Rebecca-girl, is what we are hearing accurate? They want you to renovate both the bandshell and the gazebo in time for this year's festival?" He sounds as disbelieving as I was when Mulvaney dumped this on me.

I begin, "Okay, I'm going to try to explain this as simply as I can because it's complicated."

"You don't have to simplify things for me. I'm not stupid." Now my mother sounds offended. Great. She adds, "And neither is your father."

I merge into the next lane as I drive further out of town and pray for patience.

"I don't mean that at all." I try to get to the point quickly now, before I get to my destination. "Do you remember Kyle Mulvaney? And his mother, Patricia?"

Both my parents make sounds that effectively convey less than flattering opinions of both Kyle and Patricia. Excellent. "Well, Kyle has been hounding me to go out to dinner or some other kind of date with him, and I always say no."

"Good," Dad mutters. Simultaneously, Mom asks, "What does that have to do with this? I'm confused."

Dad speaks up again. "Give her a chance, Jean."

I jump in again before they can start going back and forth between them. "Kyle isn't too pleased I'm dating Sam, and he got angry that I'm helping Sam with a house restoration when I told Kyle I wouldn't help him with a possible apartment building restoration."

"You can date whoever you want, Rebecca, and you can consult on any restoration you want to do. Neither of those things have anything to do with Kyle." Dad sounds angry on my behalf. "You never dated him, did you? Not that it would matter if you did in the past. I'm just trying to figure out what he's thinking."

"He's thinking he wants to have all Rebecca's attention," Mom declares, "and he needs to get over himself. But what does any of that have to do with the project for the town?"

How to explain what makes very little sense to me? "At the last planning meeting, Patricia Mulvaney told me they want new, turn-of-the-century inspired bandshell and gazebo structures both put in place of the existing ones, in time for this year's AppleFest."

Dad sputters, "That's impossible. I hope you told her no!"

I slow down because the cars in front of me are driving so slowly. Probably visitors or tourists looking for the deer after seeing the Deer Crossing sign. "I started to, but then she told me if I can't do it, one of the big box home improvement stores in Middletown will handle it."

Again in tandem, both of my parents loudly gasp in outrage, then Mom says, "How dare she!" and Dad shouts, "That witch!"

Mom rebukes him gently, "I agree, but we don't need to resort to name-calling."

Dad is unrepentant. "She'd be inviting one of those megastores to poach our customers, our business, in our own town! It's an outrage!"

Mom has reconsidered. "I take it back. She is a witch!"

I am almost at Sam's place so I have to wrap this up.

"Exactly. So I told her Spencer Hardware can handle it." It feels good to tell them what I have managed to accomplish so far. "I met with Darnell Richards who met with me in person and on zoom, and got the architectural plans finished in record time. I filed it all with Stephen Daventry, who gave me the approval and permit numbers this morning."

Dad is listening closely. "No one else needed to review it?"

"He handled it all, and if that included getting it in front of other people, he handled that within 24 hours of when I gave him the plans. I think it was easier than it might have been because neither structure is a residence or has a kitchen, or anything like that."

Dad makes a noise of agreement or understanding then asks, "What about demolition and construction? It's a really tight timeframe to get it all done…"

"I just got off the phone with the construction company who's doing the project with me, and it's all under control." I hope they can be satisfied with that reassurance, at least for now. "Right now I have to go."

Mom cries, "But I have more questions!"

Dad tells her, "Rebecca has it under control, but she has a lot to get done so she can't spend time on the phone with us right now."

I jump on that. "As soon as I can, I promise to update you both. I love you!"

After I disconnect the call, the silence is a blessing reprieve. I love my parents, and I know they love me, but sometimes – especially when life is overwhelming – it's a lot. It's a relief to know they have my back with all this. Not that I thought they wouldn't, but somehow I thought it would be harder to make them understand what went on that put me in this position.

That conversation took up the rest of the drive, so when I

drive under the metal arch with the intertwined H's, not for the first time I wonder if Sam will eventually take that down.

There are several vehicles parked in the area in front of the big house. After I get out of my truck, I spend a few minutes visually surveying the exterior. The last few times I was here, it was entering the evening hours or full dark, and I couldn't appreciate all the outdoor work that I can clearly see now. The work on the porch appears mostly complete, and protective material covers the steps and entrance to the house, obviously to shield the new material underneath from the ongoing construction work.

The exterior paint is a dark gold balanced by warm brown and ivory trim. New windows gleam, and I can imagine how they'll look with lights peeping through them. I hear noise coming from inside the house, and men's voices laughing from somewhere outside. Wouldn't it be great if Sam was among those laughing? The few smiles I've wrung from him felt like rare treasures.

A peep in the front door reveals scuffed paper runners covering big sections of gleaming wood floors. The voices I heard in the house are coming from upstairs, so I take several minutes to wander around the first floor. Room after room reveals more of the same – beautiful floors, lovely crown moldings, paint colors that are modern takes on what were traditional color schemes dating back to when the house was built. When I get to the kitchen, it quite literally takes my breath away. I guided Sam on appropriate alternatives to choose from for building materials and interior design components. I gave him feedback for all his questions, and made the executive decisions when he didn't know what to choose.

I've been here to the site many times during the work phases. But seeing so much of it having been completed is almost overwhelming. The kitchen in particular is a show-stopper.

The appliances aren't in place, but the cabinetry is stunning. There is an open U-shaped design, with a freestanding kitchen island for additional workspace. The window overlooking the yard is larger now, and there's two more on the outer east-facing wall. It feels homey and elegant at the same time, and it's not even anywhere near finished.

"What do you think?" Sam asks from somewhere over my shoulder, prompting me to turn around. He sounds uncertain I'm going to approve, which is crazy.

"About the kitchen, or about everything I've seen so far?"

He gestures at nothing in particular. "About everything but start with updating me about Orchard Park."

I smile despite my stress about that subject, because so far so good. "Plans are approved and filed with the clerk. I notified Luke right away. He's going to pick up the permits and get started on demolition today."

"The part about Luke and the demolition I knew," Sam admits. "He called me when he got off the phone with you." Before I can say anything to that, he continues, "He wanted to find out who's working here today so he didn't waste time trying to track them down if they were on his list."

"That makes sense," I agree. "Was there much overlap?"

Sam reaches up and adjusts the angle of a pendant light that hangs over the kitchen island. "Not at all. Everyone working here today is cleaning up and heading over there."

"Everyone?" I repeat. "That can't happen, Sam. Your job is important, too."

"In some ways, yeah, but nowhere near as important as the Park."

A protest is on the tip of my tongue but he cuts me off before I begin. "Don't even start, Becca. You know better than I do all the reasons that project needs to get done right and be finished on time. There is no set in stone finish date here."

Sam isn't holding my gaze, like he's not telling me something, or isn't being entirely truthful. Maybe he isn't in a hurry to get finished because he's not in a rush to leave McIntosh Ridge? Maybe he's deciding he wants more time with me? Or am I reading too much into this?

I am. I am absolutely reading way too much into this conversation.

The man knows how important this Orchard Park project is because if I mess it up, Patricia Mulvaney will bring in that big store to do it, even if it's after the deadline they gave me. Sam is being self-sacrificing, the same way he had to be in his military career. That's all.

CHAPTER 48
SAM

TWO WEEKS LATER, I'm looking over the worksite in Orchard Park and can feel how hard Xander is trying to not speak. In the months we've known each other, we've gotten to be pretty good friends, and I'm sure what he wants to say has nothing to do with the bandshell or the gazebo.

He doesn't wait too long before he can't stop himself. "Spill."

"Spill what?" I don't bother looking at him.

"You know what."

If he wasn't so annoying, I might laugh. "You fit right in here, you know. I can't believe you're such a gossip hound."

"It's not like that." He squares up with me. "I consider Rebecca a friend. Not best friends, but good friends for a lot of years. I'm also good friends with Rebecca's best friend." Now he's meandering right off a cliff. "I know she's been through some difficult times, and for some reason, she looks happy when she's with you."

Xander's eyes are assessing me, and I wonder if I'm coming up short. He says, "When we met, you told me when you're done renovating, you're out of here. Has that changed?"

He doesn't give me any indication – not even an eyelash flicker – about whether he thinks my answer will be yes or no. I've got no reason to lie.

I keep my voice quiet and my answers short. "No."

Xander also keeps his voice down "No?" The way he says the one word, he sounds surprised. "You guys are together a lot. But you're just going to take off?"

I stand closer to him. "We're together a lot because she consulted on my restoration project, runs the hardware store where I get all my supplies, and I'm helping out with this project she's doing." Xander knows about the true relationship between Rebecca and me, but I have to be careful anyway.

"Things can change," he says. "Plans can change."

"Not mine."

"Word is that you two went to play darts at Braeburn Tavern and had pizza at Tony's. You made some other outings, too."

"What are you, a stalker?" I'm only partially kidding.

"The gossip train chugs directly through my family's store."

It's easy to forget Xander's family owns the local department store because the guy isn't flashy or full of himself. His one indulgence appears to be that sports car he drives, but that's about it.

"Do you chat with the older ladies in the housecoat department, or while they are picking out sensible shoes?" I'm busting his chops, but I'm also curious about his role in the company.

"You're a regular riot," he informs me, with no shortage of sarcasm. "And FYI, there's no housecoat department."

"You *do* sell sensible shoes, then?"

"You need a new pair, Miller?"

"Nah." I look down at my steel toed boots. "These are fine."

Xander glances around, checking to see if anyone has moved within earshot. "I would never gossip about you guys, except to help whatever you need to put out there. You know that?"

"I do." I clap him on the shoulder. "Thanks."

He's still serious when he asks, "How is Rebecca holding up?"

I let my eyes wander the area in front of us again. The signs for Luke and Rebecca's respective businesses are prominently displayed. If she hadn't taken this on, I cringe to think that there would've been a huge sign for one of her nationwide competitors right here in the heart of Orchard Park. It would have damaged her business, yes, but it also would've been a huge personal insult to Rebecca and her family's legacy.

"She's stressed." That's not telling him anything he doesn't know. "But she's handling everything like the boss she is."

Xander kicks at a cluster of small rocks with his expensive looking loafer. Leave it to him to wear those shoes to a construction site. He says, "I know she's tough, and strong, and all those things." He looks up and spears me with a more intense stare then I expect from him. "Even the toughest, strongest people sometimes need a secure space to let their guard down."

He's talking about Rebecca, but I know there's a message in there aimed at me. I can't unpack it here and now. I settle for saying, "Heard and understood."

Xander and I part ways at the park exit gate. He says he's got to go to his office, and I make some inane remark about having things to do because I would sound like an idiot saying I'm going to hunt down Rebecca.

Not that it's going to be much of a hunt. She's not here at the park, and she's not at my property. So odds are she's at her store or her house. Since the store is so close to the park, that's my first stop.

I'm formulating my plan of attack when I head through the door of Spencer Hardware, the now familiar bell announcing my arrival. The guy who works for her, who she says is her friend, lifts a hand to acknowledge me from where he's helping a customer in plumbing supplies.

"She's in her office," he calls out and I signal my thanks with a lift of my chin. With that intel, I adjust course and I'm soon lifting my hand to rap on the office door.

"Come!" Rebecca invites, and with the mind of a pubescent teenager, I formulate a half-dozen responses, all of them dirty. I shake that off and open the door.

Rebecca is seated behind her desk, which is piled high with folders, papers, and miscellaneous items including what looks like a metal pipe fitting and a wiring kit. It's a relief to see her smile when she sees it's me. It's also gratifying, but I'm not about to unpack that.

She pushes to her feet. "Sam! I didn't expect you here today."

There are two other women in the small space, each seated at a desk of their own. Eileen and Sondra, if memory serves. I give them a polite nod. "Ladies."

Rebecca has arisen and is walking around her desk to me. "Do you need to pick up something?"

I certainly don't have to fake my smile. "Yes, actually, I do." Before I'm done with those few words, I have her in my arms. "You."

If my kiss surprises her, she sure doesn't show it. Nope. She kisses me right back with as much enthusiasm as if I spent hours teasing her and building up the anticipation. When I gradually release her, the bemused expression on her face is everything.

"Rebecca, why don't you cut out early today?" suggests the older woman, breaking the spell.

The younger woman bobs her head in agreement and looks like she's trying not to laugh. She adds, "You should definitely do that." Her eyes under the electric blue eyeshadow and spiky false eyelashes she bears are busily examining me from head to toe. "Go out with your boyfriend and have a good time."

At this point, Rebecca is blushing instead of simply flushed with passion. "I can't, not really. I've got so much to do, and only barely five weeks before AppleFest."

The older woman... I think she's Eileen ... hushes her. "Nonsense. Rebecca, I know everything is hectic for you right now, but knowing *you*, I'm sure you're on top of everything."

At that, Sondra loses her battle to not laugh. "Eileen is right. Go with your boyfriend, Rebecca." She has the sass to wink at me when she says, "I'm sure he can help you figure out anything else you can get on top of."

Eileen doesn't try to hide her own snicker, which is even funnier because she looks like a very proper woman who doesn't snicker often. "I'll call you if we have any emergencies, which I can't imagine we will."

Since the ladies have effectively pled my case, probably better than I ever could, I keep my mouth shut; I can't put my foot in it if it's closed. I have held onto Rebecca's hand the entire time since that kiss.

I squeeze her fingers now and give her a look I hope is encouraging. "You know she's right, and they'll call you if they need to."

Rebecca takes a deep breath and blows it out slowly, lips slightly pursed. "Okay. I'll go with you, for a little while at least."

Sondra goes behind Rebecca's desk, opens a drawer, and is quick to press Rebecca's bag into her hands. "Don't forget this. Anything else you need to take with you?"

Rebecca laughs at the young woman's enthusiasm. "All right, I'm going, I'm going." She herself keeps hold of my hand and leans over her own desk to pick up a couple of files on top of it. "I think I'll be good with these."

"Excellent," I say and tug Rebecca toward the door before she can reconsider. "Ladies, good to see you both again, and thanks for everything."

I don't want to say "thanks for helping me get this woman's stubborn but sexy ass out the door", so I figure I'll be nonspecific. I can be smart that way.

Hustling out the front door of the building is no easy task, but I figure trying to take her out the loading dock will take even longer. I suspect Eileen or Sondra somehow gave Mike a heads up on my mission because he's right there to run interference for me the whole way out, and he's got another worker positioned to intercept anyone else who interferes. When I open the door for Rebecca, I convey my thanks with a meaningful look at him over my shoulder.

When Rebecca and I are buckled up in the front seat of my truck, she turns to me as much as the restraint system will allow. "Okay, you've got me here. Where are we going?"

It's a damn good question.

I better come up with a damn good answer.

CHAPTER 49

REBECCA

THE WEATHER IS perfect for an outing. At least I'm hoping that Sam is taking me somewhere outside that's not a job site. It's sunny, but not in the kind of glaring way that makes your eyes tear, but in the sparkling sort of way that makes the world gleam with possibilities.

It also highlights the darkest strands in Sam's hair and the silvery ones that peek out from just above his ears. In his gray-and-white, long-sleeved baseball style T-shirt, gray eyes shrewd as they assess the road in front of us, the autumn leaves of the roadside trees behind him, Sam looks like someone out of a fall catalog.

"What's your plan, Sam?" I ask in a singsong way, determined to be as lighthearted as possible. I feel guilty taking even a few hours off, but I *have* been working at least 16-hour days, seven days a week since the Orchard Park project was strapped to my back. I'm not afraid of hard work, but even I can see the wisdom of a mental break. A *short* break.

Too bad we went apple picking last month because this is a beautiful day for it. I indulge in some thinking about that day among the apple trees. How right Sam looked amidst the scenery, how deftly he handled the apple picking apparatus.

My gaze wanders to his hands on the steering wheel. In those capable hands, the big bushel basket didn't look so big at all.

I want to see those capable hands on my body again. Feel them on all my skin again, not just my hands. Holding his hand in the store made me remember very clearly how the slightly roughened tips of his fingers felt when they traced my curves and teased my valleys.

"I'll confess, I'm still coming up with a plan," Sam says. "I wasn't completely sure you'd agree to leave the store today."

I think I'm as surprised as he is that I saw the wisdom in it, but I don't say that. "I'm not a stick in the mud, you know. I can have a good time."

"I don't think you're a *stick in the mud* at all, Becca." Although I can only see his profile right now, I can see his frown. "You're a hard-working person with a lot of responsibilities that you take seriously. That doesn't mean you need to put yourself down."

I look out my own window at the passing scenery. I know he's right about that, too. But that's a phrase Josiah used when he dumped me, and it's one another boyfriend once used, and one a female friend of mine used. She at least didn't mean to be hurtful, she was joking around, but it stung.

Sam clears his throat and tries to leave that subject behind. "Is there something you'd like to do today? It's such a good fall day."

I'm glad he's asking because I do have an idea. If he likes it, that is.

"Well, since you asked, I was thinking it's a good day for the apple orchards, but I know we did that."

"There's so many orchards around here," he says dryly, "we can go to a different one if you don't want to visit the same one again."

"I appreciate that idea, and it's definitely a possibility. But I was thinking it's a good day for pumpkin picking."

Sam swings his head toward me and repeats, "Pumpkin picking."

"Yes." I'm warming up to the idea more and more. "I know it's technically still September, but pumpkins are out there and ready to go. Some of them, at least."

"If you get one today, is it going to last until Halloween?"

"It should, but does it matter?" Suddenly, I'm a thousand percent sure pumpkin picking is what I want to do. "When a pumpkin starts to rot, you just let the squirrels and the birds have at it. Everybody wins."

"I never thought about that."

"What would you do with yours, just toss them in the garbage?" As soon as the words leave my mouth I regret them. It's not like he would have been buying pumpkins when he was in the military all those years. "That was a silly thing for me to ask. I'm sorry."

Sam looks at me again and this time he's full-on smiling. "No reason to be. About your idea, Rebecca, I like it. Where should we go? Are there multiple options?"

That easy smile of his is powerful stuff.

I force my focus back to his question. "Yes, there are a couple of farms that have pumpkins patches. At least one also has some apple trees."

I'm on my phone already, finding the address for Waverly Farms. "Do you want me to put the address into your GPS or run it on my phone?"

"That's your call, Navigator."

It's simple enough to punch it into his system so I can leave my phone more easily answerable in case someone needs to reach me. Fortunately, we've been driving in the right direction to get to where we are now going, so we haven't wasted any time at all.

"Their website says Waverly has gala apples, which is great because I can make a pie or some tartlets with them."

"You bake?" Sam sounds so surprised, I think I should be offended "You can bake an apple pie?"

"I don't bake as well as my friend Beth, who owns the bakery in town, but a basic apple pie is not that big a deal to make, especially when you grow up in apple country. I baked my first one in first grade. Tartlets are like mini pies," I inform him. "Simple."

I don't want to look at him and that dangerous smile of his again, but I hear the laughter he's trying to smother. Sam stops at one of the few traffic lights on this road, and I can't stop myself.

It surprises me when he apologizes. "I'm sorry. I just never *pictured* you in the kitchen baking."

The way he says "pictured" makes me think he's *picturing* a heck of a lot more than me baking anything right now.

And the way his eyes burn with gray fire makes me sure of it.

The traffic light changes and it breaks the spell. Sam puts the car in gear and I busy myself on my phone, doing a whole bunch of nothing. The miles click by. I feel like I should say something but my mind refuses to give my mouth any guidance. At least, not any good guidance. Telling the man "I want to sniff you" or "You look lickable" don't seem like good options.

I know he looks at me more than once, but I don't say anything, just keep app hopping and adding random items to lists in my notes. When a glance at the GPS shows me we are almost at our destination, I break the silence.

"Looks like we are almost there."

"Looks that way," Sam agrees.

Silence returns but this time it's less charged with tension. I don't know why that is, but I'll take it.

We roll up to the Waverly Farms entrance and join a line of maybe a dozen vehicles waiting to be allowed entrance to the parking field. The sides of the entrance are decorated with decorative, stacked hay bales with small scarecrows and other autumn decorations atop them. A sign staked into the ground tells us to be sure and check out their gift shop before we leave today.

Sounds good to me.

By the time we are through the entrance and meandering into the right section of the property, I am already in a better mood than I was all morning. The air is fresh and sharp, a precious blend of waning summertime and early autumn that invigorates the soul. There is no chill to it, only pure delight.

There are wide boxes of pre-picked pumpkins set on wooden pallets, for anyone who doesn't have the time or desire to traipse among the vines in the fields. Sam looks at me, one eyebrow raised in question. "I suppose this won't do?"

"What are you Sam, a desk jockey who doesn't want to get dirt on your shoes?" His boots already dusted up from whatever he was doing today before he showed up at my store, which enhances my joke.

"No, I'm perfectly willing to battle weevils and whatever other critters are protecting the pumpkins from you." He holds one arm out in a sweeping gesture. "After you."

It's still early enough in the pumpkin season that I think we won't need to go far into the depths of the field to find good stuff. Sam walks behind me. "I have to say, you are dressed perfectly for this, aren't you?"

I have to laugh, because he's right. Denim jeans, and a floral shirt, paired with my favorite Timberland boots (dark pink laces today, thank you). I'm comfortable and not afraid of getting dirty, but I still feel like a woman.

Sam has that look in his eyes again, so I know he at least agrees with that part.

I pick out three pumpkins, one after the other, all in record time. The bright gourds are heavy. Like apples, they can also be contained in a basket or other container.

"Are you sure these are big enough?" Sam asks, those gray eyes twinkling at me, though his expression is serious. "Maybe you want a bigger one?"

"No, these are good." Hands on hips, I scrutinize my selections again. "I'm going to also grab a few of the small ones from the bins at the front when we leave."

He's turning and looking around in a 365° circle, taking in the signage we can see posted and various decorations the owners have displayed here and there.

"Craft barn?" Sam reads it like it's a question.

"Handmade and machine made that look handmade decorations and things like that. I don't think I'm in the mood today. How about you?"

Sam gives me a look that shouts, "Are you kidding me?" and announces another option. "Petting zoo?"

I'd love to see him dodging goats looking to chew his clothing, and holding those big baby bottles for the animals, but as I tell him, "By this time of day the little ones won't be that hungry, plus I don't know that I am ready for a bunch of kids right now."

"I'm figuring you don't mean four-legged kids?"

"Definitely not. I like children, but a bunch of cranky ones? No thanks."

"Understood." Sam nodded and his head tilted as he tried to make out a sign further away and at an awkward angle from where we stood. "Vegetable patch?"

"Waverly has vegetable fields, which are great. But if you do the U-pick, it can be hard to figure out what you're trying to harvest because the signs are so low and tend to be buried under vines and greenery and stuff."

Sam smirks at me. "Stuff? Is that a technical term?"

"It is." I smirk at him. "And the way the bins are set up, it can also be hard to find what you want."

Sam tries again. "You mentioned apples." He indicates our

pumpkin collection. "Do we take these with us to find your apples?"

"Would you really do that for me?"

"Do you really think I wouldn't?"

I hold my hands up, palms toward him in the universal gesture of surrender. "Forgive me. I know you would, and thank you for it. But no, we can just bring them to that hut over there," I point over his shoulder toward where we came from. "They will hold onto them for us until we are done."

"Roger that." Instead of picking up any of the pumpkins, he grabs me around the waist and pulls me close to him. "Is anybody around who might know you?"

"What? Why?" I sound breathless.

"So I have an excuse to kiss you." He looks into my eyes like I'm a succulent something he wants to devour.

"You don't need an excuse."

His mouth steals the second half of thatword and the shreds of my resolve with it. I can't remember why I've been avoiding physical contact with this man as much as possible.

My lips part under the gentle pressure of his, and my heart zings. *Now,* I remember why. I don't want to get hurt when he leaves.

He spreads his hand wider on my back, the heat of it burning through my shirt, adding another layer to the intensity of our connection. My own hands aren't innocent, either; I'm trying to pull him down, pull myself up, climb this man like a monkey climbs a tree.

The inevitable need for new air drives us apart. I open my eyes to see his are still shut, and I wish I could decipher his expression right now. Sam drops his hands to his sides and opens his eyes.

"Okay, then." His voice is a little rough, and it makes me happy that he's clearly not unaffected. "I'll get these."

"I'll take one," I say, angling past him. I'm not some helpless female.

I know I didn't say that out loud but he still tells me, "It's not because you're a woman, Rebecca. It's because you're my woman."

The second comment leaves me frozen and open-mouthed, brain scrambling. What does that mean? What is he trying to say? What *did* he say? Did I hear him right?

"Well look at that, I figured out a way to stop you from overthinking."

Sam is in front of me, arms full of pumpkins, and stealing the air in my lungs all over again. He's everything I want but never knew I needed, and he's driving me crazy.

He's everything except uncomplicated, So how is whatever this is between us supposed to be that way?

CHAPTER 50
SAM

REBECCA IS A WALKING, talking, contradiction that keeps me endlessly fascinated. None of it is intentional on her part. She's too guileless to play games like that. She is who she is, who she chooses to be – look at how she's chosen not to date, to deliberately remain single. She's an independent woman who handles stress from all sides of her life and is determined to emerge from it shining like a diamond.

With her pumpkin haul delivered into the hands of the teenager working in the checkout building, here I am wandering among apple trees again. Rebecca isn't wearing a dress this time, but she's still hot as hell in her jeans, a shirt with those little flowers on it, and those work boots that light me up like they are stilettos or something.

Rebecca shoots me a look over her shoulder. "Waverly has a much smaller orchard than most of the other growers, but that's because they specialize in pumpkins and other things."

She brings the little map card up to her face and then pivots sharply at a break between the trees. The whole place is laid out in something of a grid pattern, including the apple part. Sure, it smells good, but I would've just grabbed whatever number of apples she needed from the first couple of trees we came across and been done with it.

Except I brought her out to get her mind off the pressure she's under, and it looks like it's working, so if I have to stop through fruit trees until midnight, that's what I'll do.

"Jackpot!" Rebecca points at the row in front of her. "I still think we should have gotten a picking pole."

No, I put thumbs down on that. She said she wants to bake a pie or two, or some little things. That amount of apples I can carry in my shirt, or snag one of the little baskets they have scattered around like the other orchard did. We'll grab low hanging fruit. I can get my hands on her and lift her up to reach more.

Damn. I'm supposed to be keeping things uncomplicated, and all I could think about are things that would definitely make it all more complicated. I never should have kissed Becca in the pumpkin patch – another thing that sounds like a freaking Hallmark movie – but I lost my mind then lost control.

It's embarrassing to admit, but I can't truthfully say I'm sorry about it.

"How about we grab the apples you want and start there."

She gives me a strange look but says, "Fine."

I start plucking apples from as high in the tree as I can reach. Rebecca is circling the tree and a couple of others, twisting the fruit off lower branches. There are even a few on the ground that I see her collect. The pile of our combined bounty is already a lot bigger than I expected her to want, so I stop.

"Isn't that more than enough?"

Rebecca looks from me to the apples on the ground and back to me again. "No."

"Seriously?" She's got to be messing with me. "How big is this pie going to be? Or how many little tart thingies are you planning to make?"

Her hands snap back to her curvy hips again. "Good sizes, Sam, with plenty of filling." She tilts her head, too. "What did you do with the apples we got last time? Not the batch of them I took after, but the rest."

I grip the back of my neck. Now I'm thinking again about that last night we spent together, and I just promised myself that I would stop. *Knock it off, jackass.*

"I ate a bunch of them. Gave some to Xander and the rest of the guys working on the property. You think these people would be sick of apples, but that's definitely not the case."

"They go fast, don't they? Well, when you put them in a pie, you have to slice them thin, and pile them high because they cook down to a fraction of their original size." She takes a few steps toward me. "Do you like apple pie, Sam?"

I do, but even if I didn't, that's one thing I definitely wouldn't be truthful about right now. Not when she's promised to make one for me. "Yes, ma'am."

She gives me a look that's way too sultry for this conversation. "Do you prefer a scrawny apple pie, or a voluptuous one, Sam?"

"Seriously, Becca?" Who describes apple pie that way?

She rolls her eyes at me, like I'm the one who asked a ridiculous question. "Answer the question, please."

"Voluptuous." Come on, *scrawny* doesn't sound good as a description of anything.

"Of course." Rebecca nods, her hands on those hips again. "That requires a lot of apples, you know."

At this point, I couldn't care less about this conversation. My feral brain is trying to figure out how I can get her naked and under me in world record time, all with her enthusiastic participation..

Rebecca turns away from me and moves quickly to the

baskets stacked underneath the first tree in the row. She snatches one up and carries it back, where she drops it directly in front of me. Upside down. With one booted foot she taps it firmly into the ground. Then she steps up, bringing her up enough to look me almost in the eye.

Her eyes are fierce, sparking and sparkling in the sunlight. The fullness of the apple tree branches make the sunlight dapple and play, and surround us with an intricate basket of sun and shade.

Rebecca reaches out to put her hands on my shoulders. "Sam Miller, you make me crazy."

I curve my own hands around those hips of hers to make sure she's steady. "It's your own fault. I can't think straight when I'm with you."

"What do you need to think about?" Rebecca asks, a question that's also a challenge.

"You make me forget sometimes."

"Forget what?" Her body sways further into mine.

I can't answer.

No one is around.

No one is watching.

We don't need to touch each other. Or hold each another. Or breathe each other's air.

But we do all those things.

She winds her arms around my neck, her short nails still long enough to lightly scratch my skin in a way that sets my nerve endings on fire. The sunlight is caressing her light brown lashes. It's also highlighting that they are lighter at the tips, something I never noticed before. Her pale golden freckles are sprinkled across her nose, perfect in their symmetry, like they were painted on by a divine artist.

The breeze kicks up and catches Rebecca's ponytail, making it dance in the air behind her. She laughs. The sound is light and happy, and it lights me up inside.

I need to kiss her again more than I need to talk, or to

breathe, and from the way she kisses me back, Rebecca feels exactly the same way.

This is definitely complicated, and I don't give a damn.

CHAPTER 51

REBECCA

IT MADE sense to head for my place when we made a hasty exit from Waverley Farms, simply because it was closer. I'm sure everyone who saw us knew we were in a hurry to leave the family-friendly place because we were desperate to do X-rated things to each other.

At least, that's what I was feeling, and still am. I'm hoping Sam is, too.

I drop my shoulder bag and keys on the half-moon console table under the mirror in the front hall. Automatically, I lift my eyes to the mirror and am startled to see Sam's watching me. I don't need visual confirmation of the blush I feel rising in my face, but the mirror makes sure I have it. Nervous excitement makes my mouth dry.

"Would you like something to drink?" Falling back on good manners is always smart, and usually safe.

"Sure, if I can drink it from between your legs." His strong hand on my hip gently turns me around to face him. Ready for this moment since the kiss at the farm ended, my lips part for a desperate breath before his touch mine. It's both a blessing and a mistake.

This kiss is no gentle prelude to more, no smooth introduction to a seduction scene. It's instantly explosive, a devastating biochemical reaction I didn't expect, even knowing how powerful our physical connection can be.

Sam groans, the pads of his fingers trailing down my neck, cupping my nape to draw me closer. The taste of his mouth, tinged ever so slightly with rich apple cider, lights me up inside even more as his tongue draws mine into play. My house is quiet, but even had there been a marching band or full orchestra in the next room, I know there would be only him filling my senses.

Without thought, I lift my hands to clutch at his shirt, and now I slide them up, up, up, to plunge my fingers into his thick hair. My body pulses with desire, so intense I cannot think of anything but how to get closer to him.

Sam is clearly sharing my thoughts, because he flattens me against the wall across from the mirror, molding his body to mine, talented hands roaming everywhere at once. One of his big palms gently cradles my breast, his thumb strumming my hardened nipple. His other hand curves over my hip and then drops behind my thigh where he tugs my leg up and around his own. I feel his rigid length against me and tried to grind against him to ease the frenzied need in my core.

I seek out Sam's mouth again, drowning in want that only he can satisfy. It's a wet and sloppy kiss, full of passion and little finesse, but when our mouths separate, I'm incredibly gratified to see his vacant gaze and kiss swollen lips, proof positive I'm not the only one so powerfully affected – as if the hard length I still feel against me isn't more than proof enough.

I allow my forehead to drop against his chest where I feel the movement of his deep breathing while he gets himself under control. His breath skims over my hair.

"Better every time," Sam mutters. "Incredible."

He's definitely not wrong. I move in to him again and he stands his ground, our bodies bumping then flowing into each other like we two are meant to be one. He cradles my face in his hands, looking at me in a way that makes me feel seen and cherished. This time when he claims my lips I feel his passion, his *greed* for me, all of it.

"Where am I taking you?" Sam rumbles, and I wonder if the double entendre was intentional or not, but then the thrumming of my blood reminds me that doesn't matter. All that matters is what's between us in these precious moments. Even though it's not the first time, it feels reckless, and I can't stop.

I grab for his hand and start leading him down the hall to my bedroom.

My room welcomes me with its peaceful vibe, and I welcome Sam with his intensely masculine energy and impassioned focus on me. The combination is intoxicating.

Clothing disappears and with it any lingering inhibitions are also discarded. The crazy heat that invariably flows between us burns it all away. I'm dizzy with the scent of his skin. I'm high with the need for more, more, more.

The comedown in the wake of this will probably flatten me, but I can't manage to care.

This encounter is all heated skin and burning kisses, reverent touches and animalistic instinct to taste and mark and stake ownership. My cries, Sam's groans, and our mutual shouts of completion linger in the air along with the scent of sex and the faint tang of sweet sweat. The aroma makes the taste of him reignite on my tongue, even though my mouth is closed.

All after the haze of those exertions and the necessary cleanup is complete, I curl into Sam's side and he wraps an arm around me to anchor me close. His steady heartbeat is a quiet comfort. Course chest hair tickles my fingertips when I smooth them over the carved lines of muscle and sinew protecting the source of that beat.

The curtains are pulled together across my bedroom

windows so only the barest hint of newly gone daylight filters through them. That, combined with the soft glow from the light on my nightstand, is enough to outline the angles of his face.

My body wants to sleep but my mind wants to indulge in conversation, in pillow talk. I'm trying to decide where to start, but Sam beats me to it. "When I came back to McIntosh Ridge, I never expected anything like this. I want you to know that, Becca."

"I've been back here a good long while, and I never imagined finding anything like this here, either."

Or finding it anywhere at all, but I don't say that part to him.

Sam starts to stroke his hand up and down my arm. It's a soothing motion that adds to my relaxed state. His audible sigh makes me wonder if it's soothing to him, too. My eyes drift closed. My mind starts to follow. I'm adrift in that twilight consciousness before sleep takes me when Sam speaks again.

"I haven't found myself in a lot of situations where I didn't know what to do, at least instinctively if not from training." He gives a short, sharp exhale, the noise of exasperation, maybe. "I don't talk about feelings, don't think much about them, either. Since I met you, seems I'm doing both." His hand stops moving and his fingers tighten briefly, then relax. The slow gliding begins again and so do his words. "I've been thinking about why that is as much as what it is."

I want to say something, ask a question, make a comment. Something to encourage Sam to keep talking. But I'm also afraid to interrupt because maybe he'll *stop* talking, and I definitely don't want to take a chance on causing that.

Without permission, my fingers start moving more firmly against his skin, like I'm trying to push the words out of him or something. I've almost convinced myself that he's actually done talking when he speaks again.

Sam's voice is even lower when he says, "I came up with a couple of reasons, but I'm thinking the biggest one is that you make me feel safe." He shakes his head like he can't believe what he said. "Sounds crazy, right? I don't mean safe physically, you know? I mean…" His voice trails off into silence. I think he's trying to process what he just shared, and I'm trying to do that, too.

Safe? That's good, right? I mean, it must be because he's saying it's what makes him willing and able to talk to me. Even though he doesn't do it much, it's apparently more than he does with other people.

But safe is kind of boring. Pretty much the opposite of exciting or passionate or intense or any of the things that would make for a real relationship. You don't battle dragons or tilt at windmills or… or… or whatever the hell heroes do for love because of *safe*.

Sam's been quiet now and I think he might be waiting for me to say something in response to all that. My stomach feels hollow and twisted with disappointment, but I try to find a positive side to latch on to so I'll sound sincere.

"I'm really glad about that, Sam." I slide my arm a little further across his broad chest and give him a little hug. "I really am."

I'd be happier if *safe* was the kind of emotion that made a person want to change course, change their mind, change their plans. Making Sam feel emotionally *safe* is a massive compliment, and I'm truly honored by his admission.

I just wish it gave him a reason to stay.

Since that's not happening, I need to focus more on protecting myself from our rapidly approaching end date.

That's what I'm going to do, starting tomorrow.

For now, though, I'm going to enjoy these moments in his arms, pretend I'm also in his heart, and pretend it's enough.

CHAPTER 52
SAM

A FEW DAYS after I had a post-sex meltdown in Rebecca's bed like a blubbering fool, I'm kicking myself in the ass for it. I'm sure I sounded like an idiot, and the way Rebecca has been avoiding me proves I'm right. I'm in a bad mood, and I'm not doing a good job hiding it.

The front door closes sharply behind Ryan when the men troop out in a cluster, heading for Orchard Park to meet up with Luke. They'll be working on the build at the Orchard Park bandshell. I didn't want them here today at all. Not only is Rebecca's project way more important than mine, but at this point, there also isn't a hell of a lot to do here now. Between the crews of workers I hired, the specialized tradesmen, and them, Hidden Haven is at the decorating stage – and I'm not doing that.

I've got no business being snappy with guys who put time and effort into this restoration/renovation project of mine and wouldn't even let me pay them, but here I am, being a dick. There's no justification for it. I'm acting like a toddler lashing out because he didn't get the treat he wanted.

Only if Rebecca is the treat – which she certainly is – I got her. Had her, multiple times. And then I backed away like a coward and hurt her.

Like I knew I would. Which somehow makes it worse.

Xander walks across the sunroom or morning room or breakfast room or whatever the fuck it's supposed to be called and stands an arm's length away from me. I don't know if he's standing outside range for me to punch him or protecting me from him throwing a punch of his own. Regardless of which it is, I appreciate it.

"What's up with you?" he wants to know.

I continue examining the white wainscot panels on the wall with the breakfast table. It's perfect, so there's nothing to study here, but I do it anyway.

"Nothing."

"Bullshit." Xander says with more anger than I ever heard from him *before*. "You want to lie to yourself, that's your business, but don't lie to me."

I straighten up and face him.

His eyes bore into mine. "You want to tell me to mind my own fucking business, that's fine, but don't disrespect me and lie to my face."

"You ever think that my life is none of your business?"

"You're right. Your life is none of my business. But *Rebecca* is my friend. It doesn't matter that we're not *best friends* or some shit like that. We're friends and have friends in common." Now Xander looks like he really does want to punch me. "I'm one of the people who's going to be here with her after you fuck it up and disappear."

He's right. That truth feels like he did punch me right in the gut.

"I already did. The fuck it up part."

Xander blows out a short, sharp press and shakes his head. "If you're like this, how's Rebecca?"

"I don't know. She's not answering my calls."

"You didn't think you might want to call me or call Tara to give us a heads up?"

Damn, this is awkward. "She wants space."

"What does that mean?"

"What you think it means?" I am not in the mood for this.

Xander speaks slowly, like I can't comprehend what he says "What did she say to you? What words did she use?"

This is ridiculous. "You seriously want me to recite our conversations to you?"

"You know I'm talking about the one where she said she wants space away from you."

"She didn't exactly use those words."

"Okay, how did she say whatever it was she said about that?"

"It's not what she said. It's what she's been doing. Avoiding me like I'm the plague."

Xander stabs a hand through his hair. "Man, you really are stupid, aren't you?" I scowl.

He tries to use a more reasonable tone. "Look, I've been giving your attitude leeway because you *are* a friend of Rebecca's, but enough already."

I might be the one to punch something – not Xander – out of sheer frustration with myself over how I bungled everything. I don't need his *you're a dumbass* lecture.

I'm not a *relationship* guy. I've got no experience with relationships. No training in what to do or not to do. Hell, you don't send an untrained man into a war zone.

I warned Rebecca about that from the beginning.

I made it clear again the other night. That's when things went completely off the rails between us, didn't it? Her sneaking out of my place that first time was nothing by comparison.

Not that I'm about to tell this jackass any of that. Just like I'm not going to point out that he can't get out of his own way with his own love life, either.

Our situations are totally different, anyway, because I don't have a *love life*. Not here or anywhere else, and I'm not going to. By choice. To protect Rebecca. To safeguard her future heart, I needed to bruise her heart now.

That I obliterated the heart I didn't know I had didn't even factor into the equation.

This conversation with my new friend isn't going to lead anywhere but to cuts and bruises, so I change course to a different but slightly related topic I need to broach with him.

"Moving on." That's what I'm doing with this conversation, and that's what I'm doing in my life. I scowl so he knows he needs to yield on this. "The guys seem to like how this place turned out." Hopefully, he understands how sincere I am about this. "I couldn't have done it without them. And you."

A Navy-man, Xander goes with the flow. "We were all glad to do it."

"Like I mentioned to you, I want to lease the property to you, or to that LLC you spoke about. If you want it."

He doesn't try to hide his surprise.

I elaborate: "When I said that, I wasn't just talking for the sake of hearing my voice, you know. I was there when Diane spoke about needing to find a new meeting place. Before you mentioned it, I already knew some vets benefit from working with animals or the land or different things you could have here."

"I didn't think you were fucking around, but I guess I didn't entirely believe you were serious. Or if you were, that it would come about so fast."

I do understand what he means. When something seems too good to be true, it usually is precisely that.

I plant my feet more solidly. "I was definitely serious."

"Yeah, of course. You've gotta know, Sam, none of us ever thought about something like that when we volunteered to help you. We weren't trying –"

I cut him off. "I know that. I didn't think that either, until I saw that although the place doesn't bring me peace, it seems to have a good effect on some of the guys." G

I'm not going to specify details like what I saw and heard that led me to that conclusion. I'm not gonna act like I'm some kind of therapist wannabe. Christ, wouldn't that be a joke? I'm sure my daddy issues and mommy issues could keep a therapist busy for years.

Xander nods slowly, no doubt thinking it through from business angles. "Have you thought about rent amounts yet?"

"Some." I shrug. "I've got a pension and some savings, and I'm going to get a job somewhere. I want the rent from this place to cover the taxes and expenses that can't be put into the renter's name."

I redirect my gaze out the window. This view is of the rear of the property, toward where the fields once produced vegetables, and where I picked those yellow dandelions for Mom. This isn't the time to get pulled into those memories, but they are clamoring for my attention.

"If a percentage of the property gets used for farming, there is a cheaper tax rate, and I'm thinking it's possible there could be a veteran's or charitable use deduction. Something to make it cheaper." I shove the tape measure I'm holding into one of my pants pockets. "Xander, I'm spit balling here. If you're definitely interested, we can let the lawyers hammer out the details." "Damn right, I'm interested." He extends a hand for me to shake. "I can't believe you've got me wanting to hate you and hug you all within two minutes."

I'm glad to shake his hand. "How about you don't do either? For God's sake, you make it sound like we're the ones dating."

Chapter– Rebecca

. . .

I dig the heels of my hands into my eyes, trying to ease the headache brewing from too many hours spent studying computerized spreadsheets and pondering my non-relationship relationship with Sam. The spreadsheets are boring, but I can deal with them just fine. This thing with Sam, though, that's never been boring, but I can't figure it out no matter how much I try. At this point, why am I even bothering?

Sam makes me feel beautiful and brilliant, sexy and capable, like I can do anything.

I make him feel safe.

That's a good thing, and a compliment. I get that – I do.

But still…So many times during these past months, I have turned my head and caught him watching me, sometimes with an expression of longing that made my breath catch in my throat. Maybe that's just been me seeing what I wanted to see.

Sam is determined to leave, to put McIntosh Ridge and his traumatic memories here in his rearview mirror. He hasn't talked about it all that much, but I know he hired a second lawyer to try and break the conditions of the trust that requires him to periodically come back to Hidden Haven.

"I have these three I think you should start with," Lilac says, ducking past the curtain that shields my fitting room. "One a pastel color, one in a mid-tone, and one a jewel tone."

She hangs each on the wall that's fitted with slots for that purpose. "With your coloring, you can wear just about anything."

I eye the clothing skeptically. "These look very attention-getting."

Lilac laughs at me. "You do realize you're going to get plenty of attention no matter what, right? Successful business owner, the designer and builder of the gorgeous new features in Orchard Park, the girlfriend of one very sexy new McIntosh Ridge resident... "She lets her voice trailed along suggestively. "*Everyone* is going to be looking at you."

The knot of dread in my stomach grows. "Way to make me not want to go."

"Stop." She shakes her head at me and gestures toward the dresses like a game show hostess. "What do you want to try first? Or do you want me to bring in three other choices?"

"These are fine." They are beautiful, fancy dresses, but I'm not a beautiful, fancy person. Sometimes I kind of wish I was, but I never feel comfortable getting dressed up. Not that I've had many chances, but when I have, I felt like a country bumpkin in someone else's clothes.

Lilac apparently gives up on waiting for me to choose where to start. She tugs down the hidden zipper on a pale yellow creation. "We can go palest to darkest."

"I can get dressed myself, you know."

"I figured that." She gives me a side eye. "You know this is what I do for a living, right?"

"I know. But you're also my friend and I don't typically get undressed in front of my friends." This is so awkward.

"If you're that uncomfortable, no worries. You can yell for me when you're ready, or if you need me to help with the zipper." Her smile is encouraging. "Try to relax and have fun with this, Rebecca."

The yellow dress is lovely, but way too sweet looking. It has ruffles around the tiered hemline and I feel like I should be standing with one of those doll braces cinched around my waist.

"Are you sure you don't want to try on a formal gown?" Lilac suggests, not for the first time since I showed up for my appointment. "I have a couple that would look stellar on you."

"Since I don't have to wear formal, I'm not going to," I repeat my earlier answer to the question. "But did any of the people who got dresses from you for the gala choose a formal gown?" I really should have asked that before.

"Some." She busies herself hanging up the yellow and then prepping the next one, a rich blue option. "It always strikes me as strange that they let it be a stylistic free-for-all instead of specifying formalwear or whatnot. I take it Sam's not wearing a tux?"

I freeze. How did I not ask him that? Or why did he not ask me if he should? It's not hard for Lilac to read the truth on my not-poker face.

"It's not surprising you haven't thought about it yet, Rebecca. You've been busy!"

I am already digging through my belongings for my phone. "Thanks for not making me feel dumber than I already do."

"Take your time," Lilac says, slipping out of the fitting room.

Thankfully, Sam answers on only the second ring. "Rebecca. How are you doing?"

"Not good," I hiss, keeping my voice as low as possible. The salon is a good size, but sound carries in a weird way and I don't need anyone overhearing my conversation with my erstwhile boyfriend. "We never talked about clothing for the gala."

"Well, I figured we wouldn't go naked."

"Not the time for jokes, Sam." Men. "Are you wearing a tuxedo? Do I need a long gown or can I get a party dress?"

There is a beat of silence before Sam answers cautiously. "Isn't that your decision to make? I mean, a tuxedo is just a fancy suit. Or I can wear my dress uniform, since it's a formal event. It's all up to you."

I was so sure I wanted to be as low-key as possible, but now I'm reconsidering. But am I reconsidering just because I want to see Sam in a tuxedo or in his military finery? Am I that shallow?

Yes. Yes, I am. That's an easier decision than many of the others I've had to make in the last few weeks.

"Okay. Plan on your dress uniform if you're comfortable with that, or a tuxedo if you prefer." I reassure him, "Either one is fine with me."

I hang up before he can answer or say anything about when we are going to get together. I frown at the remaining dresses in the fitting room with me and call out for Lilac.

She quickly appears. "Ready to continue?"

"I am, but with a change of plans. We are going to go more formal, after all."

Her cornflower-blue eyes light up like I just gave her a gift. "I have some terrific options I set aside for you, then. Or do you want to look on the racks with me?"

"No, thank you. It'll stress me out." I take a few steps to my right and plop down on one of the pink and white spindly chairs along the wall. "I think I'm going to check my emails and stuff like that while you do your magic, if that's all right?"

"Absolutely." She busies herself gathering up the dresses that are no longer suitable. "Anything you particularly like or don't like in a formal gown?"

"No?" Lilac faces me with the dresses piled over her arms. "Rebecca, when was the last time you wore a formal gown?"

"Senior prom."

"Senior prom?" she repeats like she's not sure she heard me correctly.

"Senior prom. So I have no idea what is stylish or going to look good on me." I know I've been a less than enthusiastic customer today, and that's not Lilac's fault. I stand up from the chair and to lighten the mood, gesture at my camisole shirt, Lycra exercise shorts, and bare feet, I give her my best *Bridgerton* curtsy. "I gladly put myself in your hands, milady."

Lilac gives me a gratifying giggle. "If I was a lady, I don't think I would be working in a dress shop, but thanks for the curtsy."

Instead of sitting down again, I start pacing, even more agitated now than when I arrived. Sam's words last night threw me for a loop. They shouldn't have. He didn't say anything I shouldn't have expected. I expected it so much, that's why I ran after the first night we spent together. I knew there was a risk of developing feelings for him; those feelings already started rearing their ugly little heads by that point.

Then instead of sticking to my guns, and protecting my heart, I threw it right into Sam's war zone. I told my stupid self all kinds of stupid things to justify and excuse spending too much time with him, sharing too many kisses and other things I shouldn't have.

He told me things. I told him things. We got closer.

Closer obviously isn't close enough to give him sufficient reason to stay in McIntosh Ridge.

He'll find a tenant or a buyer for his property as soon as he can and come back as little as he can until that high-priced lawyer figures out a way to get him out of even those visits.

And I'll be left faking a real broken heart that I'll have to hide from Tara and from Sam, if I ever see him again. The breakup hasn't even happened yet and it already hurts worse than what happened with Josiah.

Tears well in my eyes, and I blink as fast as I can. I'm desperately trying to beat them back, will them back to the devastated place they came from. The headache I had earlier has blossomed beyond belief. I have to get out of here. I've got two weeks to the Gala – if I come back in a week, won't that be enough time to find the gown in stock and have it altered to fit me?

A sharp knock on the door and her cheerful greeting announce Lilac's return. "Wait till you see what I pulled for you!"

I press the heels of my hands against my eyes again,

hoping to blot the wetness and shove back the tears trying to emerge. Theoretically, at least.

"I can't wait." I say as brightly as I can. I turn to face her and she's hanging up the gowns in a row on the same display board where she'd put the other dresses. Her face is serious, and so are her words.

"If something's wrong, Rebecca, you can tell me. The dressing room is like its own little confessional. I never tell anyone what is said or what happens in here. I promise you."

I know she means it, and my gratitude is as real as her promise. "It's okay, Lilac, but thank you." I don't try to hide wiping my fingers under my eyes. "There's been so much pressure what with my regular work and the project in Orchard Park. It all kind of caught up to me for a second."

"I totally understand," she assures me. "You want to take a few minutes? I can leave the closed for lunch sign up a little longer today it's no problem."

"Believe me, I appreciate that, but it's okay. *I'm* okay." I make myself focus on the dresses now in front of me. "Wow, I can't believe all the options you have here. Really amazing."

I'm not even kidding or being overly enthusiastic.

"Thanks, Rebecca." Lilac looks at her own selections with a smile. "Not everyone in the area who wants a gown is looking for something like you'd wear to the Oscars, you know?"

I touch a tentative finger to a gown crafted in shades of chocolate brown and amber. "They are all so beautiful."

"Let's get you into one, then," she says enthusiastically, and I rally myself for the experience.

———

Getting into the Spencer Hardware delivery truck after more than an hour spent trying on luxurious, super feminine gowns is jarring. Back to reality.

Orchard Park is only a couple blocks away from the Main Street shopping district, so close I don't need to move my vehicle, but I also don't want to leave the truck right outside the Gala Bridal and Evening Wear store. Parking on Main Street is always hard to find.

Despite that scarcity, I manage to score a parking place relatively close to the entrance by the bandshell and gazebo. My work boots feel heavy after the delicate shoes Lilac had me wear to try on options.

Before I see the construction site, I hear it. Because work on the project is winding down, it's nowhere near as loud as it's been. There's no heavy equipment being used, and the sounds of drills, saws, and the like no longer fill the air.

Men are working here today, though, on quieter things. Some are clearing the overall site of trash, tools, and equipment. Others are busy painting. Luke is standing on the far side of the new bandshell, working on a handheld device. Nearer to me, Xander is speaking quietly on his phone. He catches my eye and lifts a hand to indicate I should wait, that he's going to be off the phone soon. I don't need to speak with him, but I smile politely.

I move closer to the bandshell I designed, with its graceful lines and turn-of-the-century flourishes. It's a huge difference from the modernist structure that was here before it. Beyond the bandshell is the similarly elegant gazebo, also very different from the squared off style of what came before. The previous bandshell and gazebo didn't even have anything in common with each other. Now, they are cohesive. Both also complement the style of street signs and light posts installed on Main Street a couple of years ago.

I wander over to where a tiny sign bears a placard crediting my company with the design and creation of these

Orchard Park features. It makes me feel good. The fact that Kyle Mulvaney and his mother didn't win their petty, unfair attack against me makes it even better.

"Definitely a job well done, Rebecca." Xander speaks from close behind me. "Both structures are beautifully designed and executed."

Facing him, I reply, "Hopefully they don't decide they want to change it again too soon."

He snorts at that. "Not likely. I'm kind of shocked they dug deep enough to do it now."

"It's not like they're paying me much," I tell him. "Not even close to what they would if it was a bid out job."

"What, you mean after they basically forced you to do it, at a ridiculous rush, they didn't want to pay you fairly?" Xander's sarcasm game is strong. "What a shock."

It's a sore subject for me, so I don't bother telling him how Dragon Mulvaney tried to make it sound like it was my choice, and a civic responsibility, all at once. We stand quietly for several beats and watch the activity around us. I try to be objective about it, but I honestly think everything looks terrific. "You should be truly proud of yourself," he says with sincerity. "I know you got forced into this project, but you knocked it out of the park. Just like with Sam's project, and you clobbered that one, too. Two in the win column for you."

"It's ironic," I admit. "I didn't want to do restoration work because even though I love it, I knew it would take too much time away from the store. But somehow life made it happen."

"Life has a way of changing our plans, doesn't it? Sometimes in unexpected ways."

I resume watching the crew paint, but I know Xander is looking at me when he says, "That's what I was thinking when Sam offered me a lease for Hidden Haven. Well, me and the veterans group. It's a perfect property for us, and I never would've expected it. Like you said, life made it happen."

My heart stutters and so do my words. "He did – I didn't

– when did – that's . . . great." I slam my mouth shut because I sound like a fool who can't string more than two words together. I swallow and try again. The words pain me. "I didn't know Sam made a decision."

Xander tunnels a hand through his hair and messes with the top strands. "Yeah, I don't know when he decided or if it was a spur of the moment thing."

I bite down on my lip so I don't say something about that. By now, Xander knows as well as I do that Sam doesn't do things without thinking. He's methodical and deliberate. If he offered Xander a lease, he had to have…

"A plan."

"What?"

I clear my throat around the lump that has materialized in it. No, I hadn't meant to say that at all. But now, here I am. "I'm just wondering if he finally decided on a plan."

Obviously, he has, and it doesn't include me. We are supposed to be a couple. A person who's part of a couple doesn't make big plans and not bother informing the other person about it. That's the exact opposite of couple-dom. Isn't it?

I know we are not a *real* couple, but I thought we are at least real friends at this point. Not telling me about this, letting me be caught unawares and uninformed, that undermines everything. It's mean.

Xander swipes a hand over his mouth and looks like he'd shove his words back into it if he could. "Well, like I said it might have been a spur of the moment thing."

Again, neither of us has known Sam all that long, but we both know that's not true.

"He is probably finalizing things now." That doesn't make sense, either. "Things in his plan, I mean."

"Yes!" Xander jumps on that lifeboat. Or maybe a land-mine. "I think he was on the phone with that job he has waiting for him on Long Island."

Score another hit to my already bruised heart. "The job he has waiting for him?"

Xander's tanned face pales right there in front of me. "You know, Rebecca, I'm supposed to be at the office this afternoon. You know how it is, family business stuff." He backs up a few steps while he's talking. "This is looking terrific. A bang-up job. See you soon."

Then the big coward with the big mouth takes off so quick he's practically running.

CHAPTER 53
SAM

I HAVEN'T REPLACED the gravel driveway for a few reasons. First, it's a helluva lot of gravel and it would be pricey to replace it with anything, let alone anything that looks good. Second, there is an argument to be made that gravel is the most appropriate for the restoration of the property; there weren't a ton of materials a homeowner could have used early in the century. Most important, that gravel works as an early warning system that someone is here. Good luck sneaking in here over that stuff.

Right now, I hear tires on the gravel and shove my phone back into my pocket. No point returning Rebecca's calls now, when that's probably her.

Just my luck, or rather, the lack of it, that I was on the phone with Xander when Rebecca called the first and second times. Then I was talking to the New York City lawyer I hired when she called the third time, and with Parker's lawyer the time after that. I feel bad about not being able to take her calls, but it was unavoidable.

The Spencer Hardware truck pulls up to within three feet of me. Rebecca slams it into park. As if her driving didn't give me a clue, through the windshield I see her flushed cheeks and messy hair – signs that she's agitated. Her voice carries through the open window, and then is louder when the door pops open.

Before she's out of the truck, she's demanding, "What's going on, Sam?"

And before I think better of touching her when she's obviously aggravated, (at least partly because of what Xander told me), I do exactly that. A gentle touch to her arm and she jerks away from me, then I receive the dirty look I should have expected. It's not a *good* kind of dirty look, either, but one that hovers between anger and upset. I step back with my hands up and open slightly in the universal sign of surrender.

God, she's beautiful when she's like this. Not surprising, because she's always beautiful. Thoughts of the passion that's so quick to flare between us already has heat growing into molten lava in my gut. I'm thickening in my pants and growing more desperate for her, straining against the confines of my jeans. My shameless dick iswillfully ignoring the fact that the vibes Rebecca's sending are as far from welcoming as they could be.

My lizard brain continues its inappropriate barrage of mental images. Rebecca's leg wrapped around me, her desperation a mirror of my own. Her sounds as she rubbed herself against the hard ridge ready and waiting behind my zipper. My intentions about keeping things between us uncomplicated after what we shared, after how we burned up the sheets, were nothing short of idiotic.

Rebecca squares up to me, shoulders straight and back. Xander's warning rings in my head. "She's upset, man, probably pissed off. Can you blame her? How the hell did you not tell her you're leaving?"

He was right, and I know it.

I also know better than to act like a moron, but I did it anyway. I should have told Rebecca during the days since I decided for sure to lease to Xander and the veterans group. I know that decision signals that I'm leaving, which I am. Rebecca has known that from day one. It's not unexpected. But that's no excuse for my thoughtlessness.

I should have called her or better yet, found her in person and told her. I should have – at the very least – texted her. Sent a carrier pigeon or fired off a flare. But once again, I took leave of my senses and my good judgment and was an idiot.

I mentally slap myself for my own stupidity; hadn't I learned anything at all since the first night Rebecca and I shared? The woman is dealing with dark shadows from her own past. It didn't matter then that Rebecca hadn't called me after she ran. Well, it mattered to my pathetically sensitive feelings, but that was my own fault and my own problem.

I dealt with my strange feelings. Mostly. Rebecca handled her issues. We moved past those complications, like adults.

As Rebecca faces me in the dappled autumn sunlight that filters through the trees in front of this place, tension continues to radiate from her. It's visible in the way she stands, like she's facing down the enemy's forward line.

I try to make a preemptive move before Rebecca can lay into me, if that's her intent. "What's wrong?"

I mentally pat myself on the back for not saying "Calm down", though I hope that's what she'll do. My resolve might not be strong enough to avoid crumbling in the face of her distress.

"You were too busy to answer your phone, so I'm saving you the trouble."

Wait a minute. She's here because I couldn't pick up her call immediately? Maybe I'm wrong about why she was calling. Maybe Xander misinterpreted something in his conversation with her at the park.

"What's so hellfire urgent?" I ask, more brusquely than I intend.

Rebecca narrows her beautiful eyes at me. She replies with an exaggerated politeness that makes it clear she isn't being polite at all. "That's useful, we can use your terminology. What's so hellfire urgent about you leaving the Ridge? I get it that your father was a terrible person. You know what, Sam, lots of people have terrible parents. Little kids run away because they are desperate and don't have the tools to cope. Adults deal with things, they don't ignore problems and pretend they don't exist." She gives me a look that screams pity. "You can't be a coward when something makes you *feel* things you might not be used to feeling."

I recoil. She thinks I'm acting like a *little kid?* She thinks I'm a *coward*? That's what this confrontation is about? I fight the irrational urge to laugh at this ridiculous situation, except nothing about it is funny. Trying to approach this logically, I know that feeling is my discomfort looking for an out.

Unfortunately, I can't stick with logic when I'm feeling too many ways I'm not prepared to handle right now.

The other night when I told Rebecca that she makes me feel safe, it was an ill-advised confession made in a moment of weakness. Safe isn't something I'm used to. I only experienced it in rare moments as a child, and even less during my military career. I don't have many pleasures in life, and I've always kept them close to the vest. I've had a lot of hurts, and I keep them even closer.

In all the time I've spent with Rebecca during these months, it's always been easy. No uncomfortable lulls in conversation, no awkwardness, no boredom. Sexual tension, yes, but that makes time spent together even better.

I've let Rebecca *in* more than I've ever let anyone else, and when I think about that, it's scary as hell. We've become real friends, and I also want to touch her in all kinds of ways, all the time. I want to fuck her, yeah, but I also want to hold her, comfort her, laugh with her, let her know I'm here for her and feel her here for me.

It's got to stop.

I've got to stick with facts and truth, like the professional operator I am. That part of my life is over now, but those characteristics are a permanent part of me now, and always will be.

"We haven't talked much about my military career, but I spent decades dealing with problems in whatever way necessary to resolve them. Head-on, covertly, as part of a team, and sometimes solo. Whatever it took to deal with the problem facing me."

The more I talk, the more aggravated I get. What right does Rebecca have to judge me? She has no clue about anything I haven't yet shared. But she's passing judgment on my character and finding it lacking.

Maybe she's recognizing that as well, because Rebecca reaches out to put her hand on my arm. "You know I'm not talking about your military career, Sam. Not at all."

"So I'm just cowardly about my personal life, is that what you're saying?"

She drops her hand to her side. "You're putting words in my mouth. You're twisting what I said, or deliberately misunderstanding."

Maybe I am, and maybe I'm simply reading between the lines like any reasonably intelligent person would do. I hadn't judged Rebecca at all for what she told me about that cheating scumbag, Josiah. Thinking about that again makes my anger rise, fresh and hot. It would've been nice to lean into it, vent the outrage I feel on her behalf, maybe punch a speed bag or heavy bag to release tension. Or put my fist through one of the walls I so recently fixed.

Instead, I stay calm and in control of myself. "I'm not dealing with this right now."

"Of course you aren't." Rebecca presses her lips together so tightly it must hurt. "Do the stars have to align just right? The constellations need to be in some special formation?"

She's lost me now. "What are you talking about?"

Hands on hips again, she says, "About when you'll be ready to talk to me, Sam."

"You don't understand…" "Exactly!" Rebecca seizes on that. "I don't understand because you don't want to tell me anything. I told you about Josiah and the long, ugly aftermath of that. I shared with you about the pressure I feel upholding the family business legacy. I told you about Kyle, and why his mother did what she did, and my fears about what would happen if I refused the Orchard Park restoration project." Her voice is strong but also trembles with emotion. "This isn't about some military exercise where you have to keep me on a need to know basis." She scoffs at me. "You're not even doing that, because you're not telling me things I need to know, are you?"

If I was in a better frame of mind, I might have recognized how close I was to saying things I didn't mean. But I wasn't. And I don't.

"Parker wasn't some run -of-the-mill bad parent, Rebecca." I sneer. "You probably think a bad parent withholds allowance and takes your car away when you're bad. You can't imagine one who kicks you up the stairs or throws you down them for the smallest reasons, or for no reason at all. Just because he feels like it."

Not like I ever had an allowance or a car when I lived here. I hear the derisive edge in my own voice and hate myself for it. What does a Spencer know of a parent like Ronald Parker? I didn't intend to start spouting off a list of his violent and cruel acts, so I clamp my mouth shut.

From what I casually learned, her parents are as nice and normal as a kid could hope for. I'm sure they have flaws, like anyone else, but I doubt either of them ever kicked Rebecca with filthy work boots. Or locked her in a room for three days with no food and just a single cup of water. Thank God for that, because the thought of those things ever happening to her makes me want to throw up.

If it wasn't for the bits of food my mother snuck me every time I was punished, and that she managed to grow some vegetables to supplement us, I probably would have been sick more than I was. When I had infections, Mom managed to make sure I received treatment, and managed to get me care when I had broken bones or things she couldn't treat.

The fact that I was too young to make her get care for *herself* is something I'll always have to live with. The same way I have to live with knowing, in my dark heart, that my mother's accidental overdose was no accident.

The moment I found Mom under the tree behind her cottage, a week after my 16th birthday, it was obvious that her death wasn't even peaceful. That her body had fought the effects of the pills and deprived her of whatever illusion she might have held about falling into a gentle, permanent sleep. One final, tragic disappointment in her life.

I still wonder why she did it in the same spot she'd given me the birthday cake she baked for my 16th birthday week earlier. And why she had my missing lion in that lockbox in her sewing room. Too many questions I'll never have answersfor .

I jam my thumbs through my belt loops, an old trick to force myself into a more relaxed stance, hoping the change in physiology would have an effect on my psyche. Sometimes it works. Today it doesn't.

"I don't think you want me to give you a chronological list of the abuses Parker doled out, do you? Because that's not happening."

Rebecca looks horrified. "Of course not! How could you think that?"

"I don't know." I shake my head. "It seems lately I don't know a lot of things until it's too late."

Like the fact that convincing myself that our fake relationship could work was a good idea, or that we could move forward as a non-physical friendship after the first night we shared. Like imagining that genie of sensuality could be shoved back into the bottle and forever buried in the sand. Like we could discover something powerful and rare and just... forget about it?

I am more than old enough to know better.

Rebecca looks at me, something akin to hope in her eyes. "It doesn't have to be too late."

It's on the tip of my tongue to ask what she's talking about, but in that instant I know. She's telling me it isn't too late to change my mind about leaving. To change my mind about the possibility of an *us*.

Except she still doesn't understand that I can't live in this town again. Not where no one cared enough about my mother to help her at all. Where no one noticed anything that prompted **them** to act.

But I'm sure they gossiped about her. About Parker.

About me.

The few times I thought about this place over the years, I vowed that I'd never come back. Being here at all is a violation of that solemn pledge, but I've been justifying it to myself as what I had to do to make sure Mom's ancestral property is handled properly. That's why I've decided to keep it (now at least) and restore it the way I'm confident she would've loved. Plus, it'll be serving a great purpose by helping veterans. I think she'd have liked that.

But how much more am I going to tweak that vow before it's completely broken?

"Rebecca, I'm not bailing on our agreement. I'm honoring it, the way we made it."

I say it like it's reasonable. Like she and I don't *fit* in so many ways it boggles the mind. In kisses and rowdy pursuits, obviously, but also in quiet conversation and discussions about the world, in mundane moments and recreational silliness. We fit.

Even if I figure out how to sort my own baggage a better

way, *really* being with me is not what Rebecca wants. I am not who or what she wants.

I'm the one breaking us apart.

This whole thing feels wrong, but it's what we plan to pretend happens in front of everyone. Me saying this now might make it easier for her at the gala.

Right?

CHAPTER 54

REBECCA

A WEEK after our painful conversation at Hidden Haven, Sam and I haven't spoken again, and that's causing a dull ache in my chest. How did everything go so wrong? I shift in my desk chair, trying to get comfortable. How the heck have I dealt with these uncomfortable cushions strapped onto this uncomfortable chair and tried to convince myself it's comfortable? All to save a couple hundred dollars on a chair I use at least six days a week. Business Is Fine, it's a legitimate expense, so what is my problem?

You could ask yourself that about a lot more than this chair, couldn't you?

Well, I can't deal with everything so easily as I can deal with this. I use the shortcut saved on my laptop to sign into my Amazon account. No point deluding myself that I'll go to a furniture store or office supply place and sit my butt in various options to see what feels best. I might as well cut to the chase, order something online, and save myself another six-month delay in getting what I need.

I'm in the checkout part of my transaction when my phone rings. I can't ignore a ringing phone, especially that ringtone. I leave it on the desk and tell Siri to answer it on speakerphone.

"Hi Mom," I say because it's usually either her, or her and Dad together.

"Rebecca, you haven't sent pictures since the new gazebo has been finished," Dad says. "Your mother received pictures from Tara's mom." His tone shifts from slightly annoyed to very proud. "Both structures look fantastic. I can't tell from the pictures, was it double coated yet?"

I'm smiling by the time the order is placed and I answer my father, "Double coat of paint and a double coat of sealant."

"Excellent, excellent. Maybe you can get them to contract with you for maintenance work, that kind of thing."

Mom chimes in, because of course she's on the call. "Doesn't Macintosh Ridge maintenance department or public works or something handle that sort of thing?"

"They would take care of more general maintenance," Dad tells her, "but they wouldn't necessarily be able to handle things having to do with the design and maintenance of the new structures. You don't want them screwing things up."

As usual, I picture them in the same room together, each leaning toward the phone when they speak. They are no doubt communicating with each other at the same time in silent conversation that they have mastered after so many years together.

Is it terrible to be jealous that my own parents share a long -term, incredibly committed relationship, the likes of which I'll probably never know? Because there are days I feel so jealous of that, of them, that it's embarrassing.

I have to hurry this up because I can't get distracted from the things I need to do to get through this week. "I'm sorry I didn't send photos, and I'll get a bunch over to you soon. I promise. Is anything else going on with you guys?"

There is as full minute of silence, and I imagine them

signaling to each other in their silent language. Finally, Mom says, "Your father and I are thinking about coming to McIntosh Ridge for AppleFest. We would be there for the opening dance and a couple of days after that."

My stomach twists. This is not good, not good at all. I already don't know how I'm going to keep it together when Sam and I "break up" at the gala. How am I to fall apart for public consumption but not crumble inside?

Oblivious to my distress, Mom continues, "We'll finally get to meet Sam! I've heard so many good things about him from people in the Ridge, and even a few in Eagle's Landing. Can you believe that, Rebecca?" She lowers her voice, like she's confiding in me, not on a three -way conversation that includes my father. "I've heard over and over again how handsome and enigmatic he is. I can't wait to meet him."

Oh. My. God. Please help me. I'll get to church more. I'll pray more. Donate more to worthy causes. Just make her change her mind about coming here now.

Inspiration strikes – maybe I can get Dad to help convince Mom to wait until after the opening gala. I'll talk to him separately, and explain that I'm so busy catching up on work that I've had to push aside to make time for the restorations, and so I won't have time to spend with them.

Dad chooses that moment to speak up. "I'm also looking forward to meeting your young man, Rebecca. When *I* was a young man, I wanted to join the Navy. Sail the seven seas, experience the oceans, see the world, you know."

What? No, I absolutely did *not* know that. Dad and I have always been close, how did I not know that? I find my voice. "No Dad, I had no idea. Why didn't you, then?"

He doesn't answer and Mom steps in. "Your dad was the only one who was willing to learn the family business."

I'm so surprised I don't know what to say. Some things become very clear with that revelation, like how much Dad encouraged me to pursue my interest in restoration. How he enthusiastically listened to me talk about different subjects that piqued my interest in college.

My parents are coming and both of them are eager to meet Sam, who will then shoulder the blame when we end our arrangement. Both my parents will be even more worried about me, and so disappointed in the man they've been looking forward to meeting. Heck, they are probably hoping he'll be joining our family.

CHAPTER 55
SAM

SINCE I DECIDED against wearing my dress uniform, I've got to pick up my rented tuxedo from the shop in Eagle's Landing and return a couple of calls. Nothing big or burdensome, but it feels like a lot.

The distance between the McIntosh Ridge outer limits and the start of Eagle's Landing isn't all that far, and at this point I've made the drive more times than I can recall. The visits there with Rebecca were all the best ones, but I'm determined to not think about her today. I take advantage of my ability to split my focus and lose myself in the sights outside my truck windows as I maneuver through consistent traffic. It's not only consistent; it's considerably more than there was a week ago. In fact, traffic has been steadily increasing over the last month. People come up here in the summer, sure, but boy do they love the autumn leaves and all that shit. There's some good skiing around here, too.

A sign for the County Highway catches my eye, and without thinking about it, I make the turn. I'm soon driving past farms and housing developments. It's not far at all before I exit the highway where a small sign is posted on thin metal legs. Rosemount Gardens Cemetery.

The exit leads to large gates that stand open to allow vehicles in and out. My heart squeezes in my chest, and I rub my thumb over it while I try to get my bearings. I checked out the cemetery website multiple times over the years, looking for I don't know what, really.

I know the gravesite number by heart. I haven't been here since Mom's burial, but I send flowers, in addition to the "perpetual care" package I got that regularly provides flowers for her.

There are aged monuments here, dating back beyond Mom's ancestors, and all kinds of statuary. In every direction there are softly rolling hills that break up the clusters of headstones. Weeping willow trees and other evergreens are line the sides of the long cemetery roads.

It's a somber place, but so different from military cemeteries. Here, there are no neat rows of perfectly coordinated headstones. There is a beauty in that type of precision, but there's also beauty in this place with its headstone variety of sizes and shapes and styles. On its surprisingly high-tech website, I've explored more about this place that I care to admit.

I drive slowly, paying attention to the guide markers. I haven't been here in decades, but technology has allowed me to memorize the path.

Mom's final resting place is at the top of a graceful rise. Objectively, the view is probably beautiful, but it's horrific to me because she's been here for too long.

I can't stop my whispered, shameful confession. "I don't want to be here."

That irritating voice of conscience is stern with me. *Yeah, but you need to be.*

I pull over as far as I can and grab the flowers off the other side of the front seat. They feel small and flimsy in my hand, and I curse myself for not buying a better tribute to her.

Maybe I can use my military service as an excuse for all

the years I avoided coming here. But for all the months I've been back? Yeah, pure cowardice.

Another flaw Rebecca correctly identified in you.

I hear the distant sound of someone's car engine. The breeze carries a couple of low voice to me, but the words are indistinct.

My eyes are scanning the terrain, looking for anything I've seen in the images I've studied of this place. And suddenly she's almost directly in front of me. I take the couple of steps to the side required to face her headstone.

It's not the original, plain marker some kind people from her church put together money to buy. When I was ready to truly understand those things, I wrote a letter to thank the parish for their kindness, and explained I was replacing it because I wanted to give Mom something from *me*. I enclosed what I hoped was a generous donation to pay their kindness forward. Months later a compassionate reply caught up with me, and I was able to set aside my worries that they would think me ungrateful. I'm not a religious man, but it was also good to know they were praying for me.

I crouch in the manicured grass in front of Mom's head-stone and do what a lot of people probably do in cemeteries – I trace her name etched perfectly on the marble slab. *Beloved Mother* is shadow-scripted underneath.

The words and the marble are cold. Shockingly cold. Which makes me remember how Parker kept the house cold all the time, and how Mom wore so many layers in winter to try and chase the chill away. In those cold months, she kept me wearing so much clothingI couldn't wait for spring.

For a long time, I had nightmares that she was cold in the ground and forever would be.

The song of some bird grounds me to the moment, and I remember the flowers still clutched in my hand. I lay the pile of dandelions at the base of the stone, trying to fluff them up or something. They are only weeds, though, too scrawny to amount to anything.

Scrawny immediately makes me think of Rebecca's question about apple pie and I shut that down quick. I can only handle so much regret and sadness right now.

"I couldn't protect you, Mom. I'll always be so damn sorry for that." *Geez, am I really cursing at her gravesite?* "I know, Mom, language. The Navy kind of brought it out in me."

I ease back into a seated position there on the ground. "Aside from the language and having to do certain things you wouldn't approve of as part of my job, I hope I've made you at least a little proud all these years."

In the back of my mind through all the tough work was my mom encouraging me and telling me "You can do it, Sam." She never could've imagined all the dark deeds I'd be called upon to do for our country, but I like to think she'd be proud that I never gave up and never gave less then I could.

"There's this woman, Mom." I stare at the three-dimensional angel carved into part of the stone. "Her name is Rebecca, and I'm sure you would like her. She's smart and funny, independent and so capable. You might have known of her, she's the daughter of the people who own Spencer Hardware. She's a few years younger than me." I scrub my hand over the side of my jaw. "Well, technically, she owns the hardware store now." I pause. "I was 16 when you had to go, so she would have been nine, I guess."

I lean back on my hands, feel the grass under my palms, connecting me to the earth. Connecting me to Mom.

"She's got a talent for authentic house restorations, and I got her to help me restore your house. I honestly think you'd like it." I shift to free one hand and push it through my hair. "I don't know what's true about someone who isn't here anymore. Maybe you can see the house. Or if you can, but haven't looked, you might want to check it out."

I sound at least a little crazy, don't I?

I force myself to my feet, tears burning my eyes. "So I don't know if you know Ron died. I had him buried somewhere else. I thought long and hard about that, but you weren't happy with him at all, and I know how he treated you, and how he treated me. He didn't deserve to be in this place with you for eternity."

My first step backward is a small one. I brush my hands against the legs of my jeans. Clear my throat.

"Oh, I found Leo in the box in the closet in your sewing room. I guess I'll never know where you found him after Ron threw him away, or why you didn't give to me then, but that doesn't matter." I'm feeling embarrassed again. "I was going to bring him to you because you saved him. And then I was thinking you must've saved him for me, to give him to me at some point, right?" I wait a second, like she's going to answer me. "Anyway, so that's why I didn't bring him. But I want to show you something."

I take a quick look around but I don't see anybody close to me; the nearest person is several rows away and facing a different direction. I turn so my back is facing the headstone like it's some kind of camera that's going to transmit a photo to my mother. I pull at my shirt enough to reveal my arm where a tattoo of my lion roars. I also show her where her name is emblazoned on a yellow memorial banner, a dandelion next to it.

My voice is rough because I'm thirsty, not because there's a lump in my throat.

"I haven't been here enough, but I always have you with me."

CHAPTER 56

REBECCA

"MOM, if I go to Tara's place, it'll be easier for all of us to get ready."

I drop a *goodbye, see you later*, kiss on her cheek and rush back into the hallway where I've already assembled everything I need to bring with me.

Mom follows me. "I don't think it would be difficult, Rebecca. We shared a house your whole life, except when you went away to school. And the last couple of years, since we moved. Oh, and the 18 months after you finished college, before you came back home."

"Yes, and the last few years before you guys moved, I got ready for going out lots of times at Tara's," I remind her. Then I add, "She and I don't get ready together anymore, so this is going to be fun for us, too." (It's a little bit of a lie, but nothing nefarious.)

That makes her smile, at least. "I didn't think of that. Go, go."

I drape the glossy black garment bag over one arm and swing my stuffed backpack over my other shoulder. Mom's smile slips away. "Are you sure you have everything? Your accessories, beauty products, jewelry, shoes…" She trails off like the list is endless.

"Yes," I reassure her, trying to sound cheerful. "Shoes and anything related to my outfit are in the garment bag." With a flex of my shoulder I draw her attention to the kid's backpack. "Anything and everything else is in here. And if I somehow forgot anything, I can always borrow from Tara."

"She's fine," my father chimes in from the kitchen doorway. He gestures toward the front door with his coffee cup. "See you there, Rebecca."

I can see my mother wants to worry at me some more, but she doesn't. "See you there."

I quickly make my escape from my own home, rushing to my car like my shoes are on fire. Today I'm not using the truck; I really am using my car. I texted Sam that I would meet him at the venue because I had to take care of some things.

Let him wonder what *things* I mean. *As if he cares.*

There is actually nothing I have to take care of before tonight. I can't believe he even believed me about that. Would I really leave the store with a problem? Besides that, I had Mike close up early today for the start of AppleFest. If anybody has a crazy emergency, they'll certainly be able to find me.

Does Sam think my parents have me running errands for them? Or that I'm setting up the venue for a party I don't want to attend? Or that I am drinking in the Tavern to brace myself for dancing with him this evening? *Dream on, buddy. Don't flatter yourself.*

I secure my garment bag on the rear seat, my backpack on the floor in front of it. Seatbelt on, mirrors checked, I link my phone to the car audio and tell it to call Tara. I barely put the car in gear before she's shrieking at me.

"My mom and grandma left already for their club meeting. Why isn't your ass here with a margarita in your hand?"

"You're the one who likes margaritas," I remind her. "Not me."

"You should give them another try. It's not the margarita's fault you got sick that time."

"I'm not going to the Gala drunk."

That's all I need to do, show up drunk and give people that as a reason to gossip about me. I can't risk that. Not when I'm already planning to be the subject of their talk, but for reason of my own choosing , to suit my own purposes.

———

I'm not nervous anymore.

Not about the Gala, at least.

I remember the framed print on the wall in the dressing room where I was trying on gowns: *Style is a way to say who you are without having to speak.*

My evening gown definitely says something about me. I think. At least it speaks to me. The fit is body contoured but not overly tight, the bodice shaped and fitted to hint at more than it actually shows, so I don't have to worry about nip slips or anything like that. There is a high slit for my right leg that gives me ease of movement. All the wonderful design elements are there, but it's the color – the *colors* – that speak to my soul.

The fine fabric is a dark amber at first, where it cradles my assets, then as it floats down the lane of my body gradually becomes darker and richer until it gets to the hem. Along the way, it's decorated with some kind of glistening crystals or something that glisten in the light.

The Gala is being held at a country club in Bellwood Terrace, which shares a border with McIntosh Ridge on its northern edge. It's been the venue for the event since I went away to college, and since there's nothing else large enough within the McIntosh Ridge, I'm sure it's going to stay that way.

When Tara and I exit the back of our Uber, I'm surprised to see Sam standing outside the vehicle door, wearing a black tux that looks like it was made for him. He opens his hand to me to offer me his support, and I automatically take it. His grasp is firm and steadying.

I can't stop myself from asking, "How did you know when we'd be getting here?"

Sam is giving Tara the same assistance he gave me exiting the car in her gown, which is much snugger than my own. She busies herself fussing with the jeweled details of her dramatic sapphire blue attire, but he isn't paying any attention to her gyrations. Sam's focus is on me.

"Your parents were kind enough to tell me you were planning to arrive here early."

He escorts both Tara and I to the front doors under the portico. The uniformed doorman murmurs a welcome and opens one of the carved white doors. Sam hesitates ever so slightly when we step into the cool, scented interior of the vestibule. Tara looks back and forth between him and me.

"I'm going to duck into the ladies room and get myself straightened out. See you inside."

Before I can decide what to do or say, she's vanished into the lobby. Sam tucks my hand into the crook of his arm and escorts me inside. Tara is nowhere in sight. Cocktail lounge music is providing a backdrop to the scene of uniformed waitstaff bustling about in every direction. There are people who I don't recognize and who, based on their clothing, are guests..

I keep my voice low. "When did you speak to my parents? You haven't even met them."

"You haven't called me back in days," Sam says, like I don't know that. "Didn't you think we had things to talk about before this party today?"

Yes, we did, and he's right, but I couldn't deal with it. "I think what we already talked about was enough," I say instead.

"We never went over potential scenarios, never reviewed things that could happen and how to respond." Sam's jaw is set, and he's walking a little faster.

"This isn't a mission from your career, and you made the important things very clear to me at my house." I'm not saying more than that about it.

The wide main corridor takes us past a coat room, restrooms, a pair of elevators, and a sort of spiral staircase. At the far end of the long corridor, there are huge double doors, one of which is open a few inches. I imagine management is allowing fresh air to circulate before it gets too cold.

"We can step outside for privacy or find somewhere inside." Sam stops walking and waits for me to decide. I don't want to decide. I don't want to deal with this tonight. I don't want to have us break up tonight. I don't want to find the look of him – the *smell* of him – so insanely appealing. I also don't want to beg him to think through again, to think about how maybe we can change our plan and not break up at all. And I'm worried that I'm too weak to resist that urge.

He's waiting for my reply, so I huff at him. "Outside."

Sam acts as doorman and pushes the open one out further. He signals that I should wait and steps outside on his own first. He can't see me, but I grimace. Does the man really think there's danger on a country club terrace?

Before I can get myself riled up about that, Sam is back and opening the door to invite me outside. "The outdoor heaters are running, but let me know if you're cold."

I scan the view from the wide patio with its gleaming white stone. Gardens surround the patio itself, and the expansive golf course seems to stretch in all directions. Even though it's dusk, the recessed lighting and opulent fixtures on the patio and in the gardens reflect off the pristine marble, to create excellent ambience. I have been here before, attending previous events, but it's still impactful and impressive.

I turn around, determined to resume our conversation, and Sam is looking at me like he wants to bend me over a railing and ravish me. I can't say I don't feel the same about him. I don't ask why Sam isn't in his Navy dress uniform, but in a tuxedo that looks bespoke – though it can't be because he didn't have time for something custom-made.I don't mention anything about his clothingbecause I'm hung up on something else. "I can't believe you met my parents without me. I'm sorry."

He doesn't comment on that specifically. "I liked them both," Sam admits. "It was easy to see how much they love you." He swallows hard enough that I see his throat move. "When I commented about them, Rebecca, I was jealous because it was clear you grew up with good people as parents, and I was being disgustingly immature about my envy."

I am speechless.

But not for long.

Trying to choose my words carefully, I also force myself to keep my voice calm and my eyes on Sam's face, even though it's not easy. I'm not sure how calm I sound, but I'm trying.

"I appreciate that. Truly. Before they got to town, and since they've been back here, they've told me they were looking forward to meeting you. I was planning to introduce you, so I guess I'm surprised you met without me being thereIt must've been awkward."

I'm more than surprised. I'm kind of freaked out, but I'm not going to say that.

One side of Sam's mouth kicks up in a half- smile. He slips his hands in the pockets of his tuxedo pants as if he's wearing blue jeans. I recognize the move as one of the things he does when he's thinking or uncomfortable, and I wonder which he is right now.

"I went to your house looking for you, and your father answered the door. He knew who I was before I said anything."

"It probably wasn't hard to figure out."

It's not like there's a lot of big men my father never met before showing up and ringing my doorbell. For all I know, one of the town gossips sent him a picture of Sam. Maybe more than one of them did that.

"I suppose."

Sam rubs the side of his jaw with his thumb, an ordinary sort of movement that anyone might make, and it's aggravating how sexy it is when *he* does it. Oblivious to the effect he has on me, he continues, "Before we get interrupted, I've been trying to reach you because –"

CHAPTER 57
SAM

"THERE YOU ARE!"

A woman's voice interrupts me. Rebecca and I both looked toward the doorway, where a middle-aged woman in a shockingly bright green evening suit is holding a clipboard and looking harried. "Rebecca,Mayor Hawkins needs to speak with you."

Hawkins? The name isn't familiar to me.

My attention shifts to Rebecca. "Do you know him ? Hawkins?"

She starts retracing our steps back to the door as she rolls her eyes and answers me. "Yes. The mayor."

For the next nearly two hours, Rebecca is pulled in one direction then another, over and over again. I am at her elbow or a half step behind her for most of it. She introduces me to several people, but it appears that everyone already knows exactly who I am.

Our ruse these past months has been successful.

When we were on the patio prior to the official start of this party, I wanted to speak to her about maybe delaying our breakup. About making sure she knew how sorry I am for behaving the way I did the other night, and being inconsistent with her instead of being a steady presence in her life.

I'm conscious of all those things. Now, I make sure to touch her frequently, my hand on her lower back or around her waist. Offer to get her a drink, ask if she wants hors d'oeuvres.

The couple with whom she's speaking move on to socialize with someone else and Rebecca leans closer to me. I'm immediately attentive, looking forward to what she has to say.

"Sam, it would be better if you act bored or disinterested. Maybe even annoyed. What is coming later is not going to be convincing if you've been all caring and attentive tonight."

Her eyes flicker around our immediate vicinity. "We haven't been seen out together in days. Let's capitalize on that."

"What exactly does that mean?"

"It means we might already be perceived as cooling things off between us, and we can maintain that here tonight."

"You honestly think people are paying close attention to where we go and what we do together? I get that there's a gossip network alive and well around here, but don't they have anything better to do than monitor our activities? Are there cameras in our bedrooms? If someone is selling a video of our encounters, where do I buy a copy? Do I get a discount for being a co-star in the show?"

"You don't have to be overdramatic about it." She sounds flustered. "I'm trying to say that people might have noticed. If they did, us breaking up tonight will be good timing."

My body goes completely still. None of that was what I expected Rebecca to say. Here I thought she might be having second thoughts about the original plan, the way I am. No, the way I was.

Well, that's okay. She's saving me from embarrassing myself, and also giving me a much needed reality check.

I let that visit to the cemetery fuck with my head.

I let it make me melancholy or some shit like that. Whatever happened, it's probably being compounded by ending my career and being unsure about the future.

I can fix this. I won't let so long pass before visiting my mother's grave again. I'll visit there every time I have to visit Hidden Haven. And if I get that stipulation in Parker's will overturned, I'll still come visit Xander and the guys living there a couple times ayear and visit Mom then.

See? I have this handled.

Problem identified, action plan developed, problem solved. All in less than two minutes.

"Heard and agreed." I fight the urge to snap a salute before I turn and walk away. Rebecca said what she said, yes, but I'm the one who gives myself the order.

The room is crowded. There are more people mingling in two other celebration spaces, and outside.

Since the event is also a fundraiser for a couple of local causes, there is a cash bar. I drove here tonight, but I'll still allow myself one vodka tonic before I switch to something else.

"Sam, were you able to catch up to Rebecca before she got here?" Rebecca's father asks from behind me.

I drop a tip into a brandy snifter clearly set out for that purpose. "No, but I was here when she arrived. Thank you for the assist, though."

We shake hands and I'm once again struck by how *nice* the guy is. Sure, anyone can be nice and polite in a social setting. But just like Parker gave off a bad vibe, Paul Spencer is very much the opposite.

"Least I can do." He lowers his voice. "Can you spare a minute?"

I've got nowhere to be tonight, except dumping your daughter for the world to witness. *Because she wants me to.*

"Of course," I say, because what else can I say?

Mr. Spencer stands closer to me, facing outward toward most of the ballroom. "I know I don't have to tell you what an amazing person Rebecca is. You probably already noticed my daughter is a good businesswoman. She can handle an awful lot."

He turns his head to pierce me with as fierce a look as any I have received from her. "But she's also a talented restoration person, able to look at messed up, run down, damaged structures and see what they could be, and what they were in their heyday. I haven't seen it yet, but I'm told that's what she's done at your place. And I've seen for myself what she created for Orchard Park."

He takes a sip of his own drink, which looks like club soda. "After college, she worked for an excellent company in that field and I encouraged her to follow that path." Paul shakes his head ruefully. "Rebecca refused to even consider it."

I feel like I need to tread cautiously here, but I don't want to. How many times am I going to get to talk to this man again, especially like this? After tonight, he'll probably want to punch me in mouth, not hear what comes out of it.

"Why?" I ask the question even though I know the answer. "Why wouldn't she want to do that if she had the opportunity?" I'm wondering if Mr. Spencer knows the real answer. And if he does, will he cop to it?

The man looks grim. "Because she has this idea in her head that she has to carry on the Spencer family legacy and run the hardware business. Oh, and the lumberyard." His eyes shift down to the glass in his hand, and he gently swirls the ice cubes. "I blame myself. Growing up, all she saw was my apparent devotion to it. I bet that's what she remembers about her grandfather, too."

Mr. Spencer's eyes are fierce the way Rebecca's get when she's fired up. "I thought when I retired early she'd finally decide the place was too much for her to have to run on her own, because she wouldn't take my word for it. It's got nothing to do with her being a woman, and everything to do with being able to have any kind of work-life balance."

It doesn't escape my notice how tightly he's gripping the glass. I feel like I have to say something. "I know she can be stubborn sometimes, but she's smart enough to decide, isn't she?"

"When I heard through the grapevine that she agreed to guide the restoration out at your place, that gave me hope that when she got her feet back into it, she'd reconsider her path." His eyes scan the room. "Then she got hit with the Orchard Park thing. Talk about pressure."

"Rebecca rose to the occasion, sir." I know I sound proud of her, because I am.

"I never doubted she would. It's just outrageous the way that came about." His eyes are back on me again. "I told you I checked out the site. But it was the very first place we went when we got back here, her mother and me, because we were so excited to see what she did there. Absolutely amazing, especially in barely two months."

I want to say more about that, but I hold my words, acutely aware of what's coming later tonight. If I am extremely complementary right now, how is that going to fly with a breakup in a couple of hours? It won't. So I have to content myself with, "Maybe Rebecca's restoration successes will get her to reconsider what she wants to do with her life."

Mr. Spencer exhales heavily. "That's what her mother and I are hoping, Sam. Rebecca can sell the business, keep it and hire a full-time manager, or do whatever she chooses. Her mom and I are set, so she doesn't have to worry about us." He eyes me differently now. "I don't know how serious things are between the two of you, but you should know that there are legal and financial protections in place for my daughter's future."

I smother a smile. I'm not sure if he's saying that I can take a hike if I'm a gold digger, or that I don't have to worry about financially supporting her if I'm one of the many veterans out there hurting for money. Either way, I'm glad he's protective of her.

"As it should be, sir." My own eyes straight back to where Rebecca is now standing with yet another group of people. "She's an amazing person, and she deserves all good things in her life. It's great to know she has freedom to follow her heart."

———

When Mayor Hawkins gives Rebecca a plaque from the town commemorating her work on the Orchard Park restoration, she says, "Thank you so much, it was an honor and privilege", or something along those lines. She also gives a shout out to Luke's construction company and the veterans who volunteered their time and talent to help make it happen. Rebecca is too nice to say, "You people blackmailed me into it, gave me a ridiculously small budget, and barely paid me anything for my time and all that work."

Have I mentioned that she's an amazing human being?

She's also a smart businessperson and no doubt decided that badmouthing the town where her store is located isn't a good strategy.

In the time since my conversation with Paul Spencer wrapped up, I've spoken with a couple of other people – mostly Xander and a few of the guys I know because of him.

Xander is standing next to me at the back of the ballroom, from where we watched the speeches and thank you's and miscellaneous stuff promoting the town. I'd much rather have been right by the elevated platform that was wheeled in and positioned at the center of the floor.

Tara has joined us, her normally outgoing personality

completely subdued. She and Xander look at each other, and it's not like any of the other looks I've seen them exchange. There's no teasing, no needling, no lust being kept tightly leashed.

They are the two people, aside from me and Rebecca, who know what's really going on between us. Since they know the whole deal, they know tonight's the night it ends.

"Tonight, really?" Xander's voice is so low it's barely audible, even to me, and I'm standing right next to him. "Why ruin a good night?"

Staying focused on the people milling about the room is a challenge because the only one I'm interested in is Becca. "It's what she wants." I pull my gaze away from the room to pin it on Tara. "You know it is. I'm sure you do."

Tara's glaring at me the same way Xander has been. "What I know doesn't matter, does it? What matters is what you two idiots decide."

Xander looks as confused as I feel. I stay silent, but he asks her, "What does that mean?"

She throws her arm out sideways and thwack, hits him in the stomach. The big oaf grunts "Oof!" and responds like a grown man just punched him full out.

Another moment passes in tense silence. Xander can't help himself. "And you two really talked about it?" He sounds skeptical. "That doesn't compute with what I saw, man."

I can't make him understand what I don't quite understand, and he's starting to piss me off. "Whatever you think you know is bad intel." I glare at him to reinforce my point. "Stop."

Tara folds her arms across her middle and also hisses at Xander, "Stop."

I'm sure Tara doesn't realize that her change in position pushed her breasts up to where they look like they could escape her gown at any moment. Xander sure as hell notices. He gives me a dirty look when he notices that I notice.

Then he mimes zipping his lip, locking them, and throwing away the imaginary key, like he's some prepubescent girl. And again, just like the aforementioned prepubescent girl, he immediately breaks the seal.

"I want to go on record saying I think you're both making a major mistake."

REBECCA/SAM

REBECCA

AFTER I ACCEPT the engraved plaque from Mayor Hawkins, and handshakes from Patricia Mulvaney and the rest of the Town Council, the official event photographer needs pictures of me with them all. Then it's hugs and photos with my parents. All the women are wearing long gowns, and I made a mental note to sincerely thank Lilac for her guidance with that.

The whole time I'm accepting congratulations from people, I'm looking for Sam. He wasn't near the platform, and I still can't find him. But I know he's here. I can sense it.

At least fifteen minutes pass before the crowd shifts enough for me to spot him standing with Xander and Tara against the furthest wall from where the platform is positioned. Xander looks unhappy, Tara looks unhappy, and Sam looks stoic.

So this is definitely it, then.

Sam isn't having second thoughts about ending this, whatever this is.

"Congratulations, Rebecca," Xander says with a smile so forced I'm sure it hurts.

Tara is already examining the plaque I received from the

mayor. She's overly enthusiastic. "This is beautiful! They actually got a nice one for you."

Sam hasn't said anything

We all know why.

I can't stand dragging this out any more than we've had to, so I take control over the situation. "Sam, shall we get some fresh air?"

Tara clenches the plaque to her chest like it's a protective shield. As Sam and I start to leave the ballroom, she and Xander are huddled together, whispering.

Outside, the lights and the heaters are still on, and a three-quarter moon gives everything a more luminescent glow than before. Tall speakers play upbeat instrumental music, different from what's in the main ballroom. A lovey-dovey couple is making out in one corner. Four people are standing in their own little circle just outside the doors and none of them look up when we walk by. There are maybe a dozen other people scattered around the patio. Uniformed staff members move about, collecting and plates at the tables.

When we are as far away from prying eyes as we can be, I back myself into the corner, acutely aware that is exactly what I've done with my life; I backed myself into a corner, and now it's time to start digging myself out.

I face Sam head on. Why does he have to look so good tonight? No, to be fair, he looks so good all the time. It's not fair to other men who can't compete, or to my heart.

When we were out here earlier, Sam started to say something that was interrupted by the mayor's assistant. All night since, I waited for him to pull me aside so he could continue whatever it was he was going to say.

I kept stupidly hoping he was having second thoughts about leaving, second thoughts about not staying. That he was having thoughts that would lead him to choose me over the ghosts of his past.

But maybe it's not the darkness of the past pushing him

away as much as it's the pull of an exciting future. How can ordinary me in this ordinary town possibly compete with the wide world Sam is used to experiencing?

I can't.

I knew all that when I got into this arrangement. I promised myself I wasn't going to get attached to this man. With the effect he's had on me since we first met, I should have known I wouldn't be able to do it.

I need to stay in my lane, in business and in my personal life. It's the smart thing to do.

It's the only thing to do.

Sam

Rebecca faces me stiffly, like she'd rather be anywhere but here with me.

"I think this is a good spot for our breakup scene. No one can hear us, so I don't think we need to say much of anything," she tells me.

"No?" Wow, she's figured out a way to make this as short and sweet as possible.

"Is there something you want to say?" She tilts her head quizzically. "I'm not trying to keep you from speaking if you want to. I'm just pointing out that we don't need to."

"So you figure we can stand here for a minute or two and then stomp out and go our separate ways?" I don't know if she's picking up on my sarcasm, but I'm damn sure not trying to hide it.

"Yes. I guess?" Rebecca turns to look out toward the golf course. It doesn't take a genius to know she's not looking *at* the golf course so much as she's not looking at *me*. "That's what you wanted, right? Uncomplicated?"

I really hate that word already. "There's been nothing *uncomplicated* about this, about us, from the moment we met. I was a first-class fool to think it could ever be that way."

"What's that supposed to mean?" She looks over her shoulder, and her eyes zero in on my face. I swear, the mood lighting and the accursed moon deliberately reflect off the pale amber highlights within them. "Sam, what are you trying to say?"

What does she want me to do right now, when she's made her decision crystal clear? Am I supposed to beg her to give us a real chance when she's so eager to end our connection?

Does she expect me to say it's all been no big deal? Wish her well and tip my imaginary hat? Make some lame Navy-adjacent joke about us being ships passing in the sea of life?

Fuck that.

"Absolutely nothing." I retreat a step. Then another one. "This whole thing was grounded in bullshit and lies. I appreciate all you did for me, and I don't want to end this on another lie."

The need to touch her is making my fingertips burn. "Instead, I'll give you a truth. I can honestly tell you, Rebecca, that my best memories in McIntosh Ridge were spent with you."

I give her a minute to think about what I said. To formulate a response. Maybe a question. Maybe tell me to wait, or to stop. To tell me if she ever saw us as more than fuck buddies or friends with benefits. To give me some reason to stay.

Rebecca quietly says, "Goodbye, Sam."

Then she turns around and lets me go.

Chapter60 – Sam

I leave Rebecca on the country club patio because what else am I supposed to do with people watching after she told me goodbye and turned her back on me?

This all feels wrong.

Inside the country club, the main corridor isn't any emptier than it was when Rebecca and I walked through it a few minutes ago. I stay focused on my destination as I stride toward the men's restroom. I'm gonna calm the fuck down, give her a minute to do the same, then somehow get her to listen to me.

There is one other guy in the overly elaborate bathroom. Amidst the dark green striped wallpaper and fancy trims, he and I do the universal nod to acknowledge each other's presence then studiously ignore each other, a routine practiced by men almost everywhere.

I do my business, wash my hands, and have a stare-down with my reflection in the gilt-edged mirror above the sink. I may not be a guy who chatters about feelings, and I may be guilty of avoiding them whenever possible, but I'm not stupid, either.

There's no ignoring the fact that I've shared much more of myself with Rebecca than with any other woman, ever.

I've been trying to avoid analyzing this thing between us, because almost from the very beginning I knew it wasn't going to go into a neat compartment in my mind or in my life. It's messy. For all Rebecca's lists and clipboards, she's chaos. Beautiful, brilliant chaos.

The bathroom door slams open and Xander barrels in, bowtie askew. When he sees me, he stops in his tracks. "So you are still here. We weren't sure."

"Since when are you supposed to be my keeper?"

I accept a paper towel from the uniformed restroom attendant and decline his offer of the various toiletries displayed on the little table near the sinks.

"I'm not. Not officially," Xander replies.

I drop a gratuity in the tip jar on the table and approach Xander. "Then unofficially, you are? That's fucked up." I open the door for both of us. "I don't need a keeper, so knock it off."

"Don't be weird about it. Think of it as having a concerned friend."

"Yeah, no." He's following me and I don't need an audience. "I have to talk to Rebecca, and I don't need your help. Take a hike."

"Then where are you going?"

"I just told you."

I'm almost at the doors to the rear patio when Xander tells me, "Rebecca isn't out there."

I stop and focus on him more closely. "If you know that, then where is she?"

He runs a hand through his already disheveled blonde hair. "I don't know. Tara wouldn't tell me."

"I don't care about Tara," I growl at him. "Where is Rebecca?"

"Rebecca took off for the front exit as you went into the

men's room." Xander says it slowly, like I'm dense. "Tara ran after her. She texted me they got a ride."

I reverse course towards the front door of this place and demand to know, "With who?"

"I don't know. Between Tara and Rebecca, they seem to know everyone within a three -town radius, if not more." He shrugs like it's no big deal. "Could be anyone."

Fuck me.

CHAPTER 59

REBECCA

I FOLLOW Tara out of Lilac's car when she drops us off behind Village Candles. Lilac also gets out of the car. She looks worried. "Are you sure you're okay, Rebecca? Do you have everything you guys need here, Tara?"

"We're good," Tara assured her. "I don't use the place much, but I keep some clothes and stuff here so we'll be okay."

I know exactly what Tara uses the little apartment above the candle shop for; it's her hook-up spot. From what I know, (and I know a lot), she doesn't use it all that much for that reason anymore. Sometimes, I think she wants to be able to get away from her mother and grandmother, both of whom share a house with her. It's also a convenient place for her to get some peace and quiet when she needs it.

Tara quickly unlocks the heavy security door and pulls me inside where she disengages the alarm. She flicks on a single light to illuminate the stockroom in which we are standing. Then she re-locks the door and sets the alarm again.

"I swear, I think I always hold my breath while I do that because if I screw it up the alarm is horrible," she confesses, while I breathe in the scent of so many candles all in one place. It doesn't matter that most of them are boxed and packaged within those boxes. When taken together, you can still smell *something*, and that something is great.

Despite my own jumbled nerves and the distracting scent, I try to stay focused on the conversation. "You've been doing it for years."

"Which makes it even more ridiculous that it stresses me out."

She leads the way up the stairs that hug one wall of the stockroom. When she pushes open the door at the top of the stairs, I'm not surprised it looks pretty much the same as I remember it from last time we hung out here. For all Tara encourages customers to try new things, and encourages me to try new things, she doesn't apply that advice to her own life.

We kick off our high-heeled shoes almost simultaneously. I bend a little for the second it takes to line mine up by the door. Tara kicks hers off to land wherever they land. which means one ends up in the kitchenette, and the toe of the other gets caught by a short stack of throw pillows that for some reason are against the wall on the other side of the door frame.

It's a little thing, but might be a good indicator of why we never tried being roommates.

I'm so tired, I don't want to talk about tonight. Or think about it. All I want to do is curl up into a ball and pass out.

I don't even need to say it because Tara is already digging into a small chest of drawers that divides her kitchenette from the living room area of the small one-bedroom apartment.

"I've got sweats here, shorts, T-shirts, that kind of stuff. There's underwear, socks, hoodies, nothing fancy just comfortable."

"Thanks again for offering this, T."

"Well, with your parents crashing at your place, and me

still living in the same house as my mother, I figured you might want an easy option where no one can find you."

I start carefully rummaging through clothing options. "By 'no one' you mean Sam."

"Duh. Who else?"

I choose a soft hoodie to add to the pajama pants and long T-shirt I'm clutching. "Everyone, including my parents and my other friends, and any nosy people who picked up on what went on."

"You kept this breakup awfully low-key for someone who wanted everyone to know about it." I know Tara is looking at me closely when she says that, but I'm not ready to look at her right now. Best friends see too much sometimes.

Tara sounds as confused as I am about why I did, in fact, make sure my big breakup with Sam seems so low-key. It was supposed to be dramatic and possibly tearful so everyone could understand why I'm not going to be looking to date again anytime soon. Instead, I doubt anyone even noticed. #Epic fail.

Tara takes her own little stack of clothes to the couch and flops down with it. Her bright blue gown looks incredibly out of place against the shabby brown couch. She looks none the worse for wear after the Gala. I wouldn't be surprised if she didn't even have a cocktail because she was on alert in case I needed her.

I try to focus on her. "You looked killer tonight. You should be here in the love nest right now with a hot guy, not me."

"Eh, I didn't feel like letting my inner tramp out to tromp around tonight." She winks at me. "I was busy this week and never found time to wax. Kind of ironic, right, since I'm surrounded by wax all the time."

"Well, I don't think you want to be using *Autumn Harvest* or *Apple Grove* on your legs, do you?" I remember those candle names from a big display in the window on my most recent stop in her store. "Do you still carry plain, unscented wax?"

"Yes, but maybe I want my cooch to smell like *Pumpkin Paradise* or *Cinnamon Apple Pie*." Tara winks at me. "Good enough to eat and come back for seconds."

"Oh my God, T. You probably get some kind of rash if you use that wax--" I wave my hand in the general direction of the body parts up for discussion "--there."

"Maybe, maybe not." Tara leans her cheek into her hand like she's thinking it through. "I'll have to look into that."

"I'm surprised you never have." Come to think of it, I'm surprised Tara hasn't developed a candle line specifically marketed for personal waxing. Or for BDSM wax play.

I'm not mentioning either of those things tonight, that's for sure.

She exclaims, "Me too!" She slaps her hands down on her legs. "Well, do you want to shower first? Guest's choice."

REBECCA

WHEN TARA CHECKED in with me early this morning, she offered to open her shop later than normal, claiming it would be no problem. I refuse to interrupt the flow of her business more than I already have. I hid up here Sunday, which was the day after the Gala and the final street fair of AppleFest. I heard distant sounds of music and laughter while I wallowed in my misery.

On Monday, I couldn't manage to do much more than cry and watch tearjerker, "chick flick" movies. Tuesday was Village Candles' usual day to be closed. Spencer Hardware was closed on Sunday, as planned, and Tara told Mike I had a stomach virus on Monday and would not be in. At least Tuesday I spoke to him myself. I knew that *he* knew my absence had nothing to do with being ill, but he accepted everything I said and encouraged me to take my time getting better.

Today, after pacing the confines of the studio apartment above Village Candles for what has to be the thousandth time today, I have to get out of here. I haven't been able to stomp out any of my feelings because her shop opened at 10 o'clock, and one of her employees showed up to work at 9 o'clock, so I have to be mindful of the noise I make.

Why should Tara or her business suffer because of my stupid feelings?

Why did I have to end up with a broken heart because I fell in love with Sam?

I knew better. I did.

Why couldn't I follow my own plan,? My own rules?

I set the rules because I wanted to do the thing. It's not my fault that Sam turned out to be something – someone– I never expected. It's not Sam's fault, either. He agreed to the fake dating to help me out, pulled back on the "friends with benefits" part when he sensed it could become tricky, and did his best to keep things casual. No, it's not his fault I feel hollow inside – way more than I did after everything with Josiah.

I stop my tiptoeing march around Tara's apartment when a particular truth becomes clear.

This is Kyle's fault.

It's all his fault.

If Kyle hadn't refused to take *No* for an answer, hadn't refused to accept the fact that not all women are flattered by his relentless advances, then I wouldn't have been pushed over the line into desperation mode.

I wouldn't have hatched the crazy idea of fake dating Sam, and then offer it up to him.

I wouldn't have been so persuasive about getting him to go along with it.

I wouldn't have been tempted to indulge in the whole *friends with benefits* thing, which lowered my inhibitions and weakened by resolve.

And then Kyle wouldn't have run crying to Dragon Mulvaney, and she wouldn't have tasked me with the whole Orchard Park restoration project (which she and/or Kyle definitely hatched), and which gave me so much added stress I became more irrationally desperate for Sam's affection.

Maybe my logic is a little iffy, but it all makes perfect sense to me – the pain I'm going through is Kyle's fault.

I grab my car keys and my pocketbook and leave the apartment as quietly as possible. When I jump in my personal car in the rear lot, my mind is clear and focused for the first time in days.

Phone in hand, I tell Siri what to do. "Call Kyle Mulvaney, on speaker."

I don't know if Kyle has separate phone numbers for personal and business calls, or if he uses the same one for everything. But I've only got one number for him in my contacts list, so I don't have to overthink it.

The ring tone sounds twice before Kyle's irritating voice greets me. "Rebecca Spencer, this is s the highlight of my day."

"It's sad if seeing Spencer Hardware on your caller ID is the highlight of your day."

Kyle completely ignores my sarcasm. "Are you calling to finally accept my invitation to dinner?"

"We need to talk."

I swear, I hear his smarmy smile right over the phone when he says, "Isn't that what we are doing?"

My jaw is tightly clenched. "Face to face. Where are you?"

He sounds ridiculously smug when he says, "Can't wait for dinner?"

I start the car, ready to hunt him down if I have to. "Where are you, Kyle?"

"My office, but I –"

"Don't move, I'll be there soon."

I stab my finger at the red dot to disconnect and toss the phone onto the passenger seat. I barely remember to fasten my seatbelt before I hightail it out of the parking lot, my newfound focus solely on dealing with Kyle. After I'm done with him, I'm going to track down his mother. I've got a few choice words for her, too.

I've only been to Kyle's office once, for a project presentation years ago, but I remember exactly where it is. That's good, because now that I'm focusing on Kyle and his mother, the anger and frustration I've forced myself to keep in check is eager to escape.

Kyle's business operates out of a two-story building in an area of McIntosh Ridge where a couple of landscapers, commercial businesses with multiple trucks, and small manufacturers are located. A variety of construction vehicles belonging to Kyle's company are parked in a fenced in area adjacent to the building. In the paved area in front of the building itself, three vehicles are parked. I pull into a spot and march to the front door, a woman on a mission.

When I fling that door open, the receptionist is standing behind her desk, like she's waiting for me. She's young and busty, with tons of blonde hair, big blue eyes, bright red lips, long red nails, tight white blouse struggling to do its job.

"Good morning," she greets me with a friendly smile. "Are you Ms. Spencer?"

I'm embarrassed I'm being judgmental about her appearance, and remind myself that it's probably not her fault she works for Kyle; good jobs can be hard to find. "Yes."

"Mr. Kyle is finishing up a meeting but he'll be right with you."

"An early meeting," I comment. "One of the downsides of the construction industry."

"Oh, it's not that kind of thing," she says. "She has to get to school."

Good God, Kyle's my age and he's dating a college coed?

"But I'm sure she's leaving soon. The bell is at like 8:50 I think."

I can't entirely hide my cringe; he's dating a high school student?

When the facts click into place, the adrenaline I was

running on amps up again. He's not with some girl, he's with a dragon.

I give the receptionist or secretary or whatever her role here is, a genuine smile. "I'm so glad Mrs. Mulvaney is here. I was going to go see her next."

The young woman smiles back but it slips when I head down the hall I figure leads to Kyle's office. She hurries after me. "Ms. Spencer, you can't go back until he says it's okay."

"Oh, it's okay." I reassure her, moving faster. "You know he's expecting me."

Several doors in the hallway aren't open, but the one at the end is ajar. A framed photo of Kyle shaking hands with some other guy is displayed on the wall directly facing me. I hurry through the would-be doorway, and there is Mrs. Mulvaney standing next to Kyle's desk. She's got one finger raised and pointing at him like she's in full lecture mode, just like in high school.

When Kyle sees me he jumps out of his chair. "Mother, my appointment is here, we can discuss this later." He waves off his receptionist. "Thank you, Candy, that'll be all."

Candy? Seriously?

Mrs. Mulvaney is frowning so hard it looks painful. "Kyle, you can't possibly be thinking to take this woman back after she got dumped by that vagrant." Before he answers, she says to me. "You left my son for that man, you don't get to come crawling back now that he left *you*."

I will not let her control this conversation. "Look, lady, you're either confused or Kyle -" I point at Kyle, "has been feeding you some combination of half-truths and lies."

Kyle isn't even looking at me now, he's focusing on Mrs. Mulvaney and trying to coax her from the room. "Mother, Rebecca is having a difficult day. Let me sooth her and we'll have lunch with you later in the week."

Is he kidding me?

"Are you kidding me?" I yell, giving up any attempt at

staying calm. "I'm not having lunch or anything else with either of you. We never had a single date. No drink, no cup of coffee, no anything. Nothing like that is ever going to happen. I'm polite because I'm a businesswoman and you and your business are customers of Spencer Hardware." I throw my hands up in frustration. "Why can't you understand that?"

It's a rhetorical question so I don't give Kyle to chance to answer before I turn my attention to his mother.

"And no matter why you somehow thought he," I glare at her son, "and I ever dated, that gives you no right to interfere in my life and try to ruin my business with the Orchard Park restoration."

Kyle rushes to defend her, because of course he does. "Mother wouldn't do that."

"She absolutely *did* do that," I insist.

Mrs. Mulvaney glowers at me. "What do you care? You managed to pull it off, anyway."

"That's not the point, and you know it."

"What is your point, then?" Dragon Mulvaney challenges me. "You're shopping for a new boyfriend, aren't you? Well, my Kyle is out of your league."

How can I not laugh at that? It's not possible, and I don't try to hide how funny her statement is to me. "For once that's something true, but definitely not the way you're thinking." I'm not going to bother telling her that he's peewee league and Sam is an All-Star because she'll never see anything but her own delusions about her son. Instead, I focus on the point of this conversation.

"You based your little vendetta against me on whatever nonsense Kyle told you, so here's the facts. There's never been anything between him and me. Never. You used your position with the town to force me to do the Orchard Park project on a ridiculously tight schedule, something that could have been handled after AppleFest. By threatening me with involving a corporation outside McIntosh Ridge, you crossed all kinds of ethical lines."

She's still glaring and still looking at me like I'm insect, but it doesn't concern me at all anymore.

"In addition to the ethical violations, it's misuse of town funds. The timeframe you demanded to try and make things impossible for me meant increased costs for obtaining rushed materials, and securing necessary subcontractors to work evenings, over time, and weekends at time and ½ and double-time rates."

"If you overcharged the town –" Mrs. Mulvaney starts to say, belligerently of course, but I cut her off.

"The contracts specifically state that those costs are completely out of my control, because that's the truth. You set the deadline. You set the terms. You made the threats. All I did was make sure the project was completed in time to avoid your penalties, while maintaining all quality and safety standards, and passing town inspections."

I focus on Kyle again. "You know about quality and safety standards, and the need to pass inspection, don't you Kyle?" I'm certain he cuts corners wherever he can and does whatever he can to get the approvals he needs for his projects. I've never tried to cause trouble for him before, but I'm ready to do it now.

I am so ready. In fact...

"Even if you didn't put your mother up to it, specifically, you knew what was going on, didn't you? That means you knew it was wrong. Unethical. Outrageous. When this all gets out, don't you think your behavior will make people talk more about your questionable deals and arrangements?"

Mrs. Mulvaney sneers at me. "If they take a break from talking about you, you mean. You and that shiftless, no-good ruffian."

"Are you talking about the man who spent 20 years serving this country in the Navy, most of that as a highly decorated member of the special forces?" I'm so angry, I'm vibrating with it. "The hero who returned home to renovate and restore his late mother's property to its former glory? If you're so concerned about preserving the history of this town, you should be glad and grateful he's brought it back to its original grandeur."

Kyle looks ill. I don't know if it's because of what I said to him or to his mother, and I don't care.

"Last chance, Kyle. If you continue doing business with Spencer Hardware and Lumber, Mike will be assigned as your account manager, or you can deal with a different company. It's up to you. But if I find out you're bad mouthing me or my company, or Sam Miller, or anything involving him, I swear I'm going to make you regret it."

I don't care what Kyle thinks or says about any of that. His words are meaningless anyway; action counts, like my actions now.

Without sparing either of them another look, I deliberately take my time walking to the door. "I hope both of you have the day you deserve. I already have."

CHAPTER 61
SAM

FOR THE FIRST TIME, walking through the main house doesn't cause me pain because of my memories of the distant past. No, all the emotional upheaval, aggravation, and agitation which are weighing on me are from the past week.

I need to break something. Smash something. Use up some of the frustration that's pulling me down like I'm marching through quicksand. My footsteps echo loudly as I stomp through the rooms. When I stride through the kitchen to the back door, I'm focused on getting outside to do… something. No clue what.

It's quiet behind the house, like when I first arrived back in McIntosh Ridge. Then, the quiet was welcome. Now I hate it. The quiet allows my thoughts to get too loud, and those thoughts are busy telling me I really screwed up with Rebecca.

My gut knew the *friends with benefits* thing wasn't going to work with her. No way. From the moment I saw her, my reaction to Rebecca wasn't typical. It's not simply that she's beautiful, or sexy, or smart, or funny, or clever, or talented, or any of the other adjectives I could use about her. None of that alone explains it.

It's just *her*.

I circle the house twice. Circle the cottage more than that. Assess the barn, inside and out. Everything looks too good to mess with.

When I walk a bit further south of the cottage, my eyes zero in on the two large storage sheds that sit parallel to one another. Those haven't been worked on yet, because I haven't decided what to do with them, if anything.

The first is full of old gardening implements and small farming equipment. The other is full of old car parts, rusted machinery, and other miscellaneous crap. I'm not sure what these spaces should ultimately become, but they both need to be emptied first.

It doesn't take long to grab heavy-duty work gloves and get started. I've got a system established for sorting everything I'm removing from the sheds and I'm focused on the task at hand when the interruption comes. "Want a hand?"

I know Xander's voice well enough I don't need to even turn my head. I ask, "You got nothing better to do?"

"Nah. I've got time and a current tetanus shot, so I'm good to go."

I drop an ancient gasket in the area where I've been putting machinery parts. "And you want to spend your free time sorting junk with me?" I cast an eye over what I've hauled out of the small structures so far. "No work to do? No good deeds to do? No women to wine and dine?"

"I'm taking a break from work, wining, and dining today. Thought I'd do a good deed instead."

"And I'm the lucky recipient? Wouldn't you rather do your good deed for some lucky lady?" At least that might get Xander a happy return, instead of wasting his time on a foul-tempered fellow veteran.

He completely ignores my questions and asks one of his own. "You decided what to do with both these sheds?"

"Not entirely, but I can't do anything with them until they are empty so here I am."

It's not until hour later that Xander brings up the real subject of the day. "You still haven't spoken to Rebecca, have you?"

"I'm busy."

"You're making yourself busy," he says mildly.

I'm not letting Xander draw me into conversation right now. "That's exactly what I said."

"Finding some bullshit to do is not the same as being busy."

"Leave it alone," I warn.

"I did." Xander pauses. "Rebecca hasn't been back to work since the Gala."

That makes me look at him. "What? You've got to be wrong. The Gala was five days ago." No way she would be away from her business that long. "Maybe she went away somewhere."

"Nope. I have it on good authority that she's around."

On good authority? That's got to mean he's either lying and did talk to Rebecca, or maybe to Tara? "You spoke to Rebecca? How did she sound?"

"I haven't spoken to her at all; she didn't answer my two phone calls, or my text." Xander narrows his eyes. "Did she answer you at all?"

"I haven't called," I say, then admit, "I didn't text."

His eyes get wide with surprise, then narrow. "What the fuck is wrong with you, man?"

"What the hell is that supposed to mean?" I'm immediately on the defensive because he of all people knows the situation. "You know the whole thing was fake, with a planned expiration date and everything. Rebecca pulled the trigger on it because she wanted to. Why the fuck would I call her?"

"Is your brain waterlogged from all that time in the Navy, or are you just stupid?"

"Back off," I warn him again. "I get that you mean well, but you're out of line."

"Too bad. You acting like a dumb fuck isn't helping her. Or you." He shakes his head at me like I'm pathetic."

My hands clench into fists at my sides. Hitting Xander might be more satisfying than hitting a wall would have been. "For the last time, mind your own damn business."

Unlike me, Xander is the picture of calm. "No, I'm looking out for my friends."

It's a simple answer, delivered with absolute sincerity, and it freezes me in place. I force my hands to relax and shift my tight shoulders. I know he's been Rebecca's friend for a long time, and he's quickly become a close friend of mine, as well. Being included in his statement hits hard – maybe as hard as he would have. Well, not likely, but it rocks me all the same.

"Low blow, Xander. I've got enough I don't know what to do with and you adding uncomfortable conversation isn't making it any easier.

"Hey now, don't go getting all mixed up in there about your feelings." He wiggles his fingers in the general direction of my chest, and I'm figuring he means my heart. "I'm your friend, I'm not part of the love life you need to sort out."

"There's nothing to sort out."

"Oh, great. Sorry my bad." He brushes his gloved hands together like he's dusting them off. "I didn't realize you told Rebecca how you really feel about her, instead of assuming she can read your mind, and that you promised to no longer be a dick, and you'd be there for her no matter what, and that she still told you to fuck off." Xander turns his head enough for me to see him roll his eyes at me. "Yeah, I didn't realize any of that."

I strip off my work gloves and jam them into a back pocket. "I thought I made it all clear enough."

"Sure you did." Xander picks something up from the pile of objects yet to be sorted. "That's why she's here with you right now, or you're getting ready to go wherever she is. Or you're satisfied you guys talked it out and there's no way forward for you together, so it sucks, but you can move on with no regrets." He tosses the rusted out gearbox into a different pile where it lands with a harsh clatter. "Stupid me."

Xander goes back into the shed. I hear him muttering loudly and moving shit around.

Maybe he's right. Maybe I didn't make things clear enough for Rebecca to really understand. She always gets me so well, was I counting on her to understand too much of what I didn't actually verbalize? And then am I letting it all go – letting *her* go –without making sure?

"Stupid me," I echo Xander's words and head back toward the cottage. Talking about feelings is uncomfortable, but being without Rebecca is unbearable.

CHAPTER 62

REBECCA

LOUD BANGING JOLTS ME AWAKE. The obnoxious noise again rips through the apartment above the candle shop. My mind is scrambling to identify the sound when Tara staggers out of the bedroom. The staggering becomes barefoot stomping until she gets to the black box next to the apartment door.

She slams her open palm against it. "What?"

"I need to see Rebecca," Sam demands. His voice is slightly distorted by the speaker, but there's no mistaking it's him.

My jaw drops. Tara is staring at me now, one hand on the box and the other on her hip. "You know it's 3 o'clock in the morning, right?"

Sam answers casually as if it was 3 o'clock in the afternoon. "Yes, I know."

Suddenly she's practically nonchalant about this insane visit. "One second," she says and presses something, probably some kind of mute button. "Do you want to go down or have him come up?"

"Neither!" I hiss, like Sam can hear me. "Tell him to go away."

"He wants to talk to you." She says it like I'm stupid or something and don't understand.

It's my turn to state what should be obvious. "I don't want to talk to him."

"He tracked you down," Tara points out, like that matters.

"Not that hard to do."

Really, how many places could I have gone? He could have found out from my parents, her mother, or a dozen people at the Gala that Tara has this apartment. He most likely found out from Xander.

A loud thumping echoes up from downstairs.

Tara's eyes widen like it's a shock. "He's knocking."

"More like banging on the door."

"Why don't you talk to him?" Tara presses the button again and tells him, "Hold on a minute!"

I clutch the pillow I was laying on and pull it against my chest like it's a shield. "No, I don't need a minute. There's nothing for he and I to say to each other. We've got nothing to talk about."

As if he can hear me, Sam shouts through the speaker. "Tell her I'm not leaving."

Tara roots around in the basket next to the door and tosses me a pair of tennis sneakers. "Woman up and talk to the man, Rebecca. He managed to find you, he deserves at least that." She gestures impatiently at the shoes, which landed near my feet.

"Like I said, it couldn't have been that difficult in this town." I'm determined to hold onto the pillow, but Tara is even more determined to get it away from me.

I open my arms to let it go and fling it at her and get the juvenile satisfaction of seeing her stumble back several steps and almost lose her balance. "Fine, you big bully. I'll talk to him." I lean over to pick up the shoes, muttering, "Hope you're happy."

Tara doesn't bother answering me because she's answering Sam through the intercom.

"Give her a minute, she's putting shoes on."

CHAPTER 63
SAM

REBECCA LOOKS GLORIOUSLY RUMPLED and infinitely holdable when she comes out the rear door of Village Candles. She couldn't look more different from the last time I saw her days ago at the AppleFest Gala at the country club, but she looks every bit as good.

Better than good, but I'm not going to focus on that now. Not if I can help it, because I tracked her down a reason – one that doesn't include getting her naked and panting my name. Not yet, at least.

It's not easy, but I manage to keep my hands off her when I say, "Do you want to do this right here, or in my truck, or somewhere else?"

She crosses her arms over her chest and glares at me. "Do what, exactly? Try being more specific if you want an answer."

"You want to end this thing between us, well, I'm going to say my piece."

"All I did was save us the trouble of putting on a whole big act when we both knew what the plan was. I cut to the chase."

I'm not accepting that from her. "Plans can change. Sometimes the end result might stay the same, but things are still not exactly what was planned. You don't get to decide that on your own, for both of us."

Rebecca looks so frustrated, I wouldn't be surprised if she actually stomps her foot. "You're talking in riddles. It's after 3 o'clock in the morning, it's too late or too early for riddles."

I'm trying to be patient. "I asked you where you wanted to have this conversation."

"And I told you I didn't understand what conversation you're talking about."

"Okay, do you understand now?"

She throws her hands up in the air. "Geez. I don't know. Maybe."

Now I'm trying to not smile. "Then I guess I'm back to my first question. Are we doing this right here, in my truck, or somewhere else?"

"Your truck is fine," Rebecca huffs as she shoulders past me on her way to where I parked in the small lot behind this strip of stores. "This is ridiculous."

At this late hour, and so close to Village Candles' entrance, there hadn't been a reason to lock my truck, so we were inside quickly. I start the engine to run the heat; I don't intend to rush this conversation because of the chilly temperature.

Rebecca doesn't give me a chance to start the conversation before she does. She's facing forward, eyes fixed and focused out the front window, like we are going somewhere, although neither of our seatbelts are on. "No more cryptic crap, Sam. You're not making sense tonight."

"Or you don't want to admit you understand exactly what I've been saying."

Rebecca looks away from me and makes a sniffling noise – like she's hiding tears, or maybe trying not to cry?.

She mutters, "Yeah, right."

"I know the original plan was for each of us to find a

shield in the other, and maybe indulge in our mutual attraction along the way."

Rebecca's head turns further toward the window on her right. "Is this really necessary?"

I ignore the interruption, and the way I desperately want to hold her. "And then at a mutually convenient time, we'd make sure everyone knew our connection was ended. You'd be able to move on from faking a relationship with me to faking heartbreak or something like it and have a perfect excuse to not date anyone for as many years as you wanted."

"And you get to go on your merry way. Thanks for the handy recap," she says, her words smothered in sarcasm. "Are we done here?"

It's my turn to ignore the interruption. "But somewhere along the way things changed."

Rebecca doesn't say anything right away, but she stills. The little irritated motions she's been making with her hands, her head, her shoulders, even her legs stop. One minute drags into another, and then another. I'm typically the one who can be sparing with words. Tonight – well, this morning – Becca is giving me some real competition.

Finally she says, "Changed how?"

"I don't know. I just know that they did. I stopped thinking about all the things I'm going to do when I get out of this town, and started thinking about things I want to do with you while I'm living here, and that extend way past when I planned to be gone. Instead of remembering places I've been and things I've seen, I'm thinking of places I've been where I want to take you, and things I've seen that I want to show you. Want to share with you."

Her voice is quiet now. "I can't imagine they send people with your… skills to picturesque towns and resorts."

I can't not smile at that. "Not usually, no." I lean my head back against the seat and turn it to face her. "More than all that, I keep thinking about places I've never been that I hope to go, and things I never did that I want to do. The only person I can imagine by my side is you."

"Oh." She's killing me here. I don't know if that's an awed "oh" or a horrified one coated in politeness.

Becca clears her throat. "So basically, you want to be my travel guide?"

That is *not* something I expected her to say.

I fucked it up. Even after going over it in my head a ridiculous number of times, I still somehow fucked it up.

It was a mistake to let her pick where we had this conversation. She didn't know what I wanted to talk about, so how could she pick appropriately? I pride myself on being in control, on my self-control, and what do I do about choosing a battle location? I left it up to the other party instead of setting myself up for victory.

"Look, Becca, I know I'm not handling this well."

"Yes, and I also know that 3:00 in the morning is not a great time for a serious discussion. Maybe it would've been a good idea to wait a few hours." She shakes her head at me.

"3 o'clock in the morning was when you showed up on my doorstep that morning," I point out. The words rush out of me faster than I can stop them. "So it seemed right that I showed up then."

I see the corner of her mouth twitching, and I know she's trying not to smile. At least she's not outright laughing at me, though even that would be better than silence or shouting. Or storming away.

Her words confirm she gets it. "Because my judgment is sometimes lacking, somehow 3 AM is our time? "

"I thought so." That's my weak-ass response when her expression tells me she's waiting for one. "Okay. Got it." Becca hikes up one knee onto the seat so she can turn her whole body in my direction. "Keep talking."

I try to mirror her position but my stupidly long legs and

the damned steering wheel both get in my way. I force my body into compliance as much as I can.

I was planning to choose my words carefully. Get my points across efficiently.

But looking at Becca right now demolishes that plan. The pale glow of moonlight and even the security lights in the small parking area highlight her delicate features in a way that shouldn't be romantic, but damn, it is.

In her work clothes with Timberland boots she somehow makes sexy, in killer heels and an evening gown, or in her apple picking attire, Rebecca overwhelms me in all the best ways. It's not what she wears, it's who she *is* that lights me up, body and soul.

If I leave McIntosh Ridge, I'll be leaving Rebecca, and I'm not foolish enough to do that.

Rebecca's hands are clasped together in her lap, fingers restlessly displaying her nerves, her agitation. I reach out to take one of her hands into my own, hoping to settle us both.

"Thinking about what you just said , Becca, I *do* want to be your travel guide, and I want you to be mine. I want to be your safe place and your biggest supporter, your sounding board and your crying towel. I want to encourage you to try new things, big things you never imagined you could do , and little things you want to do just for the hell of it." Her eyes are wide, her fingers actively holding onto mine, and I can tell she's listening intently to everything I say. "I hope you'll be those things for me, too. If not now, maybe someday."

Becca leans toward me more, close enough so I can see where her pulse flutters the skin at the base of her throat. I desperately want to press my lips to that spot, but there is more I need to say.

"I was wrong to think avoiding this town, avoiding that property, would eventually erase the ugly parts of my past." With my thumb, I caress her fingers. "I'm sorry I didn't really figure that out before I hurt you. I was scared to let go of what I was hiding behind."

"It takes a lot of courage to figure all that out about yourself, Sam," Rebecca says so quietly I barely hear her. "I'm trying to move beyond mine, too."

"I'm sure you will," I tell her with complete confidence. "I'm not going anywhere, so like I said, I'm here for you, no matter what you need."

Rebecca makes a statement that's really a question. "You promised the property to new tenants."

"I did, and the deal includes everything except the cottage. I'll be sleeping in there." It's another easy answer, because I tried to think through everything already.

Her eyes stop focusing on our hands and sweep upward to meet mine. "You will?"

I wonder if she can see *my* pulse because it's pounding at least as fast as hers. "Yes."

Becca swallows hard before she says whatever is on her mind now . "What about the job on Long Island?"

Simple question. Simple answer. "I already called and told the owner I'm not taking it."

At that, her eyes widen again and her jaw drops. If the moment wasn't so serious, her reaction might be funny. "Really? You did?"

I confirm, "Yes, I did."

"Then what is your plan when you finally leave?"

"Becca, I told you, I'm not leaving."

"You're not leaving," she repeats. Her eyes meet mine again. "For how long?"

"I'm starting to get the impression you actually want me to go." I shake my head ruefully.

. "I'm sorry, Sam. I think I'm just so shocked."

"And it's almost 4 o'clock in the morning." Maybe my clever idea about when to have this controversy wasn't so clever after all.

"That, too," she agrees. She opens her mouth to say something more, then closes it again.

"Ask what you want to ask, Becca, say what you want to say," I encourage her.

"This is all a *big* change." She cups my cheek in her small hand. "If it turns out to be a mistake, don't feel like you're trapped here again."

I cover her hand in mine. "I spent a long time running from a lot of bad things in my life that I couldn't control. I watched my mother suffer and lose her life because she couldn't escape."

She nods in understanding, supporting me but not interrupting.

"I don't regret my career, not at all," I continue. "But that part of my life is done. I'm at peace with my past, more than I could have ever hoped to be. I started out here with a definite plan about doing what I had to do with the property so I could leave again. Then I met you. Bit by bit, everything changed, so gradually I didn't even recognize it at first."

I continue, "If you'll let me, I want to be with you. If you want to pursue restorations in this area or anywhere in this country, hell, anywhere in this world, wherever your road leads, I will gladly follow. Dreams can change, goals can change, fears and doubts can change, too. For all the changes, I want to be there with you. For you."

Even in the dim light, I can see that Becca's eyes are glistening. This is all so far out of my wheelhouse, I'm probably not explaining well again. "Am I coming on too strong here? Coming at you with too much?"

Becca shakes her head and takes a deep breath. Then a couple more. "No, it's just... what you're saying, Sam, it sounds an awful lot like a proposal."

"God, I'm sorry! I wouldn't do that like *this*, I promise

you. You deserve something fancier than my truck for that." I'm glad it's dark, because my face is so hot I must be blushing and that's not a look that's going to be good on me.

Yet, Becca's giggle the next second makes it all totally worth it. I could never erase all her worries, but I can be here to help shoulder them. She leans closer, close enough to rest her forehead against my arm. We sit like that for a while, fingers still together, breathing each other. So close, so in tune, I feel the energy shift when she stiffens.

I encourage her, "What is it? Talk to me, Becca." She and I have done enough *not talking* and I'm determined to break that pattern.

Becca pulls back from me, but at least she doesn't withdraw her hand. "Well, if you're not taking the job you planned on, and you won't have your property to work, aren't you going to get bored?"

I finish what I'm guessing is her train of thought. "And take off in search of excitement?"

"Yes."

"It's not like I'm retiring or anything," I tell her. "I can afford to figure out what I want to do, and I'll be living rent-free on my own property. I have a lot of interests; I'll figure it out." I circle back to the important part. "I've already figured out that I want you by my side." I hold up a hand to delay her response. "I know I sort of sprung this on you, and you probably don't know what *you* want yet. That's okay, no pressure. Take all the time you need, I'll be here."

"Don't worry, I'll still make sure women aren't sniffing at your door."

"Hey!" My voice is sharper than I intend, so I try to bring it down a notch. "This has nothing to do with our original arrangements, deal, or whatever you want to call it."

"So this big change is all because you like hanging out with me?"

"Is that so hard to believe? That's part of it sure." My

focus is a thousand percent on her willing her to understand that what I'm saying is absolute truth. "I love you, Becca, so much that I never imagined anything like it." The shadows in the small parking area have shifted again, and glimmers of moonlight kiss more of her lovely face. "I've never said that to anyone before, except my Mom, I guess, which is totally different, and this is a terrible place to do it, especially for the first time, but…."

God, I feel like an idiot; I'm certainly babbling like one. Navy SEALs don't babble, so got I've got no training or experience dealing with this.

I should've set up some kind of romantic scene or something for all this. Something memorable. Instead, we are in the front seat of my truck, in the utility parking area behind the candle store, near a dumpster.

"Sam." Her voice is quiet. I know she's going to say something important, and I'm not sure I'm ready for complete rejection.

"Yeah?" My voice sounds wary, even to my own ears. It's embarrassing how this woman easily wipes away years of toughness and bravado.

Becca tightens her hand over mine. "I love you, too."

"Yeah?" I repeat, and this time I sound ridiculously hopeful. Definitely embarrassing, but who the fuck cares?

CHAPTER 64
EPILOGUE

EPILOGUE I **– Rebecca**

Approximately six months later

(Time isn't always so important when you're in love)

"Rebecca, what is that noise? Are you really home?"

Mom sounds suspicious. I don't know where she thinks I'd be instead of home at 7 AM on a Sunday morning. *Maybe you don't want to know what she's imagining* suggests that inner voice we all have inside, and I make the executive decision to listen to it.

My father interrupts the conversation and says almost exactly what I was thinking barely a moment ago. "It's 7 o'clock on Sunday morning, my dear, where else would she be?"

I move out of the living room at the front of the house and towards the kitchen, where it should be quieter. Thank God they are not bringing his boxes into the house yet; it seems like something is being offloaded into the shed and the garage.

Mom isn't willing to move off the topic so quickly. "I

know Sam is moving in today, but I don't know, it just seems
—"

Noise from some shrieking power tool interrupts my mother's voice this time, but the new sound is coming from behind my house. What the heck is Sam doing now?

"Mom, Dad, I'm sorry, but I need to go. I'll call you soon. Love you both!"

I hang up, slip the phone into my pocket, and hurry out the back door onto the small deck. "Sam, what the heck?"

He looks up from where he's attaching pieces of wood to the tops of longer pieces of wood, making what appear to be street signs – only much shorter. And made from what even from a distance looks to be quality wood; it's certainly not raw lumber. Why? I have no idea.

"Okay, so what are you doing?" I look up from the odd collection on the ground in front of him. "I'll admit, I can't figure it out."

Sam directs a smile my way, one of the easy ones I've seen more and more frequently these last months. "Give me two minutes and I'll show you, sweetheart."

I take a step closer, and he holds out both hands in a Stop signal. "Freeze!" He lays down t he power tool and jogs over to me. "You know what, turn around," he gently grasps my waist and turns me until I am facing the house. "Cover your eyes."

"All I'm looking at is the house," I protest, laughing. "Why do I need to cover my eyes?"

Sam leans his head forward and nuzzles the side of my neck, then plants several kisses on and around my ear. I shiver involuntarily.

"You're very sneaky, my Becca. Now that I think about it, maybe I should blindfold you." He runs his hands up and down my sides, then slides one and up my front from my waist to my throat, and the other down my back from the nape of my neck to the curve of my butt, which he squeezes enthusiastically. "Is there anything on you I can use as a blindfold?"

It's early, and he's got me laughing already. "My underwear maybe, how's that?"

Sam growls in my ear. "The guys are unloading my boxes and a few pieces of furniture. If any of them see your underwear or your underwear-wearing parts, I'll have to do terrible things to them, so that's not a good idea."

He's being overdramatic, but the sentiment is hot. "Let me turn around so I can kiss you."

A not so gentle slap on the ass is his reply. "Just a couple of minutes. Cover your eyes, we'll skip the blindfold."

I can be a good sport. I cup my hands over my eyes. "Should I count?"

Sam answers me while he's walking back to whatever his wooden project is. "This isn't hide and seek, Becca."

I hear the smile in his voice, and that makes me smile again. "Come on, Sam. You know I hate surprises."

"I know, you like everything neatly organized, and accounted for, and listed appropriately. That's why this is kind of fun."

I hear the power tool come to life a few more times. I stay true to my word and don't move (or peek) while he returns to me.

Sam stands in front of me, and I feel the welcome warmth of him all over me in the early morning chill.

"Put your hands down," he says and I comply, also opening my eyes to look at him. "I didn't say you should open your eyes yet."

"Is this some variation of Lieutenant Commander Sam Says?" I ask. "Because if that's the case, you didn't say Sam Says put your hands down."

The smile I get for that comment is undeniably wicked. Sam slides a possessive hand around my waist and pulls me tightly to him. "Sam says give me that mouth, woman."

His kiss is everything. I wrap my arms around his neck, dizzy from the scent of his skin, high from the feel of his body against mine. A groan rumbles through his chest, and I feel the vibration in mine. One of his hands slides up my spine and he buries it into my hair, cradling my head, positioning it to help him deepen the kiss.

There is always passion in Sam's kisses, and I also find peace. Within the riot of sensations and arousal flooding my senses, my mind goes still and focuses only on him.

A catcall pierces the morning quiet, followed by several comments in quick succession.

"Hey, get a room!"

"Take it off!" followed quickly by "Not you, Sam!"

"My eyes! My eyes!"

No matter how many times Xander and the guys tease us, I still get embarrassed. Sam takes it in stride, though.

"We have a room. We have a whole house here." He gestures over his shoulder with his thumb. "You guys finished unloading everything?"

"Yeah," Xander says.

Ryan adds, "We put the furniture where you said."

Xander has another comment. "We stayed out of all bedrooms, as requested."

"As ordered, you mean," Luke laughs.

Ignoring my embarrassment, I try to pull Sam closer to them. "Thanks for helping us out, guys. I've got bagels and muffins, fruit and stuff for breakfast laid out in the kitchen, but I can make eggs and bacon if anyone wants that, too."

Sam answers for them all. "They're fine with grab and go." He starts pulling me further into the property, where his mystery handiwork is laid out.

Behind us, a chorus of goodbyes ring out. I hear them go around to the front door again and the voices dissipate.

I could have thanked them better. "I could have at least scrambled eggs or something."

"They helped out they wanted to, not for food."

"I know that, Sam." We are close enough now to the area he asked me to stay out of that I'm starting to see what he made from the beautifully finished wood. "These are tall garden stakes!"

"Yes." Sam scrubbed a hand over his stubbled jaw. "Exactly."

"You remembered,"

I don't only mean he remembered what I said that day we went to Waverly Farms for pumpkins. It also means he listens when I say things – he doesn't just hear me like I'm noise or meaningless chatter. Sam actually *hears me*. He heard me and remembered what I said about such a little thing more than six months ago. It seems like such a little thing, but it means so much.

Epilogue II – Sam

Three Months Later

 (Definitely an accurate date!) A

"I got this," Mike assures me, making a motion with his hands. "Go, go."

"I'm going." But I pause to imitate his motion and ask, "What the hell is that supposed to mean?"

"I'm shoo-ing you," he says, like that's a real thing you do to a person.

I don't know if I should laugh or be insulted. "What am I, a fly?"

The bell over the front door of Spencer Hardware jingles when Xander opens it enough to stick his head in. "You're going to be late for your hot date."

"See you guys," I tell Mike and a couple of nearby

customers. I walk out the door and pass Xander. "Is it considered a date when it's your own girlfriend?"

"Even married people call things date night, so yeah, it fits," he says as he falls in step next to me.

I've tried to plan a night out with Becca that's at least partly different than what we'd typically do. It's been a year since the day I met her right here in the hardware store I now work in sometimes, and three months since I moved in with her. I insist on covering the bills, expenses, and maintenance costs at the house. It's been easier than I expected to have her place feel like *ours*.

"You said you will be in and out of the Cottage today, but will you be around The Haven this weekend?"

Xander's question redirects my attention. Psychologically, the simple act of taking down the Hidden Haven sign and replacing it with The Haven has been unexpectedly helpful for me. (Score one for Diane).

"I'm not sure yet. Maybe for a while Sunday." Becca and I have a lot going on, and I don't want to commit myself. I look over at him as I round the back of my truck. "Why?"

He shrugs and doesn't meet my eyes. "No particular reason."

Obviously, he's full of shit and there's a story there, but I don't have enough time or curiosity right now to pull it out of him. I asked Becca to be ready at… damn, time is passing way too fast today . I've got a lot to get done before she should be back from checking out a potential restoration project. Before I "pick her up" at our place, I have errands to run and a stop to make at the Cottage.

"Okay, then. Catch you later."

———

I thought about renting a luxury ride for our date tonight, or borrowing Xander's flashy sports car, but ultimately decided against both. My truck is pretty high-end, and Becca likes it, so it's all good.

Right now, she teases me, "You can tell me where we are headed, Sam, because you know I'm going to figure it out anyway."

"That's okay, it's not highly classified."

"All the more reason to tell me."

"I told you enough."

"You told me fancy but not too fancy, casual but not too casual, and food I'll enjoy." She moves her hand off the top of my hand and wiggles her fingers so they are underneath instead. I know what she wants and oblige by curling my hand around hers.

I nod. "All true."

"Great, and as unhelpful as possible."

We are already past Eagles Landing and on our way into another small town, Crystal Springs. When I start to slow down, Becca perks up.

"Are we going somewhere here?" She's twisting left and right, looking around. "I don't come here much, it's so small." Becca tries again, "Come on, Sam."

"You can't wait three minutes?" It's impossible to resist laughing at her impatience.

"Of course I can wait, but I don't *like* to wait."

The street I'm looking for is only a few blocks into the town, and when I make the turn Becca is practically vibrating with excitement. "Already? But you're leaving the main drag?"

This time, I don't bother answering because the property I'm looking for is just ahead. It's a restaurant on the first floor of a renovated house that was built who-knows -when. From the moment I pull into the small parking area, until we depart more than two hours later,

Becca is delighted by the venue, the food, and the experience.

"I can't believe you found a place I've never been before, and it's a restaurant within a restoration." Becca sighs, sounding content. "I wanted to plan this night, but I have to say, you did a great job."

I already thought I chose well, but hearing Becca confirm it makes me feel… proud? I didn't save a life, win a battle, or conquer an enemy.

You planned a successful mission. Take the win, Sam.

Mentally, I do, and ask her, "Why do you think that's all there is to it? The night isn't over."

Her voice goes all sexy on me when she says, "I didn't think it would be, not until we're in our bed."

My cock responds to that like a trained dog clamoring for a treat. *Romance now*, I scold. *Party with you later.* I decide the wisest thing is to ignore her last comment, for now at least.

"Nothing fancy," I admit. "I just thought we could relax and enjoy some more of the beautiful night."

"Whatever you're thinking, I'm all for it," she declares.

Miles keep ticking by, bringing us out of Crystal Springs, to and through Eagles Landing, then on to the outskirts of McIntosh Ridge. It's dark enough that I need to stay alert to find the unmarked path that leads to the overlook I'm seeking. When Becca realizes where I'm going, she strains against her seatbelt, trying to get closer to me.

"What a perfect idea to end our date."

"Glad you agree," I say, and I mean it. "No picnic dinner, but I hope you will enjoy it."

Since I planned this stop for after dinner, all I packed in the cooler was some fruit and cookies, and drinks we can enjoy while we admire the stars. It would've been a great time to propose, but don't think she's ready for me to go there yet. Between building her restoration business, which is still new, and running the hardware store/lumberyard, even with my participation in it, the woman has a hell of a lot on her plate without me adding to it.

We've been back to the overlook a couple of times since the very memorable night Becca first took me here. Something about it screams romance and passion, and it just felt like the right place to bring her.

Becca has her seatbelt off before the truck is in park. "Let's sit in the truck bed."

"You read my mind," I tell her, but I doubt she hears me because she's already jumping down through the door she opened as she spoke. I smile as I hurry to follow.

I'm surprised she isn't already in the flatbed, but she's leaning against it and looking up the seemingly endless sky. "Does it look the same wherever you see it from, Sam?" Becca asks quietly. "I know you've seen it from so many places in this world."

I tear my eyes away from her gorgeous face and look up like she is. "Some things about it are the same, but not everything, no. The feeling you get, of being a tiny speck in the huge universe, that's always the same."

When I lowered my eyes back to her, she's dropping to her knees in front of me. I'm a guy, so my mind immediately goes *there*. "Becca, you don't –"

She interrupts me, shaking her head and laughing. "That's not what I'm doing right now, but maybe later. Gah, you're such a man."

I know I'm smirking, but I can't help it. "I thought that's what you like about me."

"Actually, it's one of the many things I love about you," Becca corrects me, suddenly sounding very serious. "I also love your intelligence, your heart, your mind, and your sense of humor, and how all those things are brilliant and sharp and you never flaunt them but they are always there."

She reaches out and up a bit to grab one of my hands. Her

words render me speechless, but I crouch to get closer to her when she resists my tug to get her to stand.

"Sam, I love everything about you, even things that irritate me and make me crazy, and I never want to be without you in my life." She squeezes my hand and her voice gets more determined. "What I'm trying to say is, Sam Miller, will you marry me?"

It takes me too many seconds to process what she just asked me, and even then I have to replay the words in my mind more than once to make sure I heard her correctly.

I curl my fingers around hers. "Are you sure this won't be too stressful for you, Becca? You're so busy –"

"Are you seriously going to mansplain my life to me, Sam?" She tries to pull her hand away from mine.

"Never! You know I wouldn't do that to you." I bring her hand to my lips. "It's just that I love you so much, I never want to cause you stress or anxiety."

"I just proposed to you, and you didn't give me an answer except to question my judgment about it. *That's* causing stress and anxiety."

"Yes, I'll marry you. Damn, I'll be honored to." "Oh," Becca says, firmly pulling her hand away and digging into her pants pocket. "Wait!" Her hand emerges with a small black bag. She plucks at its strains until she gets it open, then dumps the contents into her palm.

She sounds uncharacteristically shy when she says, "I didn't want to get you a ring because I didn't know if you would wear it, or a metal bracelet for the same reason, and I know you like your military kind of watch and I didn't think you would wear a neck chain, so I got you a leather bracelet because that won't catch in things the way metal might. But you don't have to wear it, you can just keep it as a memento of tonight."

I'm already securing the bracelet around my wrist before she's halfway through her words. I use the light on my phone to illuminate the design tooled onto the face of the leather band – a design that looks like stars.

"Stars?" I look at her quizzically, wondering if I'm interpreting it wrong.

"Yes." Becca confirms. "When I was trying to decide what I wanted on the band, I was remembering us looking at the sky out of here, laying on the truck bed. How it felt so right, so easy, and I didn't understand it, and eventually I did. That you and I, we're inevitable, like the stars." Her eyes shift away from me again, that uncharacteristic embarrassment returning. "At least, that's how I see it."

"You see exactly how it is." I say confidently, because she's right, and I don't want her doubting it for even a moment. "That's exactly what we are."

And so is the kiss that blooms between us in the next heartbeat.

And the gratitude I feel for the way life dragged me back to McIntosh Ridge so I could find my future in the last place I ever would have thought to look for it.

Coming this December!

Visit McIntosh Ridge for a holiday novella!

Available Now

Chapter 1: Tia

WHY WAS HER BEAUTIFUL, successful sister living in such an ugly, disgusting place?

The brick exterior of the apartment building was old and worn. Huge chunks of mortar between the bricks were missing; what remained was so discolored it ranged from dirty shades of brown to dingy degrees of black. Calling the building and street "run-down" would be way better than they deserved.

Garbage was scattered up and down the sidewalk and the street. She'd seen more than one hypodermic needle amidst the crushed beer cans, broken liquor bottles, and random piles of trash. Despite the diluting effects the water must've had, the harsh smell of trash and rotten food hung in the cold air, along with the pungent stench of urine.

Though Tia and Rina hadn't yet met in person, from FaceTime and Zoom, Tia could see that her sister was beautiful. It was awkward to acknowledge that, because saying it was like complimenting herself. The DNA matching company flagged them as 'full siblings', but the more they video chatted, the more it seemed they could be twins, even though their birthdays were different. Tia's birthday was February 17, and Rina's was August 17, both in the same year – which was obviously impossible. Was either date actually the correct one for both of them?

Rina was well-spoken. Educated. Had a master's degree in art and museum studies. Her hair was always styled, her makeup and jewelry always in place. She always looked neat and put together. Again, Tia wondered, why was her sister living in a dump like this?

The number painted over the doorway was peeling, but enough remained that Tia was sure it was 265. Trying not to be obvious, she assessed the man who stood slouched against the concrete as if the building was holding him up. Average size, his clothes dirty and torn in places, his grimy face partly hidden by straggly brown hair that extended beyond his misshapen black-and-white striped wool hat. Even from a few feet away he smelled of sweat and beer. How could he be sweating in this cold?

He didn't speak, but she didn't move. *You've come this far, just keep going.* What if he grabs me? *Just keep going.* What if she doesn't answer the buzzer? *You won't know until you ring it.*

Sometimes Tia really hated the rational part of her brain.

The man took several steps away, scratching his arms and muttering something under his breath. Tia hurried up the steps and squinted at the names scrawled on the old-fashioned panel of buzzers. *R. Evans. 3G.*

"Buzzers're usually broke, but the door's never locked," the man mumbled loudly enough to be heard from her position at the top of the steps.

She knew she shouldn't talk to a guy who looked like he might rob her or worse, but the words slipped out before she could stop them. "Thank you."

Tia put a gloved hand on the doorknob. The slight touch had the door swinging open a couple of inches without her turning it. A firmer push made it open enough that she could get through the doorway.

Inside the lobby, the air was musty, punctuated by odors of mold and fried fish. The walls were painted a gunmetal grey like the basement in the building where she'd gone to high school. That had smelled of commercial cleaner though, something this place desperately needed. She fought the sudden urge to turn around and run back into the street.

On the far side of the small lobby was an array of narrow mailboxes with little slots for the letter carrier unlucky enough to have this part of Brooklyn on his or her route. Tia thought of checking for Rina's box, but what was the point? She'd already seen her sister's name on the buzzer panel. Running into any other residents of the building wasn't something she was anxious to do, so it was a better idea to get upstairs and find the apartment.

Tia stopped again with one booted foot on the bottom step. What if Rina wasn't home? *Then you'll leave her a note.* What if she's here but she's sick? *Then you'll take care of her or get her to a doctor.* The sound of voices on the other side of the front door startled her enough to launch her up the stairs. The voices behind her got louder as whoever it was came in the building, and then the voices faded away as the people veered off to whatever apartment was their destination. She started climbing.

At the top of the third-floor landing, Tia hesitated again. She was comfortable in libraries and archives, poring over piles of faded handwritten records and digitized files on computer screens. Visiting sketchy apartment buildings in rundown parts of unfamiliar cities was definitely not her thing. She was a researcher, not a detective.

Right now, though, she needed to be a good sister. A good sister would do anything to help a sibling who might be sick or in some kind of trouble. Tia hadn't even been aware she was a sister until recently, but that wasn't going to stop her from being a good one.

Apt 3A was immediately to her right, and 3B wasn't much further down the same side of the hallway. There was a faded welcome mat on the floor in front of apt 3C. A strong smell of garlic, or maybe it was tomato sauce, was coming from either 3D or 3E. She couldn't tell which. From behind one of the doors blasted the sound of harsh music and someone screeching in a guttural language. From behind another door, a noisy car chase added to the chaos.

Apt 3G. Finally. After taking a deep breath, Tia raised her hand and knocked sharply. Just seconds later the door was flung open.

A deep voice exclaimed, "Tia!"

She froze. Rina said she wasn't married. When Tia shared that she didn't have a boyfriend, her sister had said she also was single. So, who was this good-looking, dark-haired guy with the big smile and the bright blue eyes, and how did he know her name?

"Come on in," he stepped back and made a welcoming hand gesture, inviting her into the apartment.

The man greeting her so warmly had a sharp jawline shadowed by stubble thick enough to indicate he hadn't bothered shaving in several days. His charcoal grey button-down was tucked into black trousers, those secured with a black belt that appeared to be leather. The severe look was relaxed a bit by the buttons left open at the top of his shirt and the boots he wore instead of shoes. Not cowboy boots or hiking boots. What would you call them …?

Realizing that she was staring, Tia cleared her throat. "Not to be rude or anything but how do you know my name?"

"You look so much like her, anyone could see you've got to be closely related. Plus, Rina said you'd be coming for a visit. She didn't mention that you were coming *today.* I didn't know you guys had planned it already." He ran a hand through his hair, where the top was longer than the closely cropped sides. She wondered if it was as soft as it looked.

"I wonder why she didn't say anything," he added, but she didn't know if he was talking to her or to himself.

Rina wouldn't have mentioned it because she didn't know it. They'd spoken about getting together at some point, never pinning down a date or where they'd meet in person for the first time. Tia hadn't had a choice but to come when she couldn't reach Rina for so long. She'd only known of her sister for a relatively brief time, but they'd been in contact at least twice a week for months. It was long enough for her to recognize that Rina was nervous and agitated the last few times they spoke.

And then Rina stopped calling or answering the phone at all. Tia was positive that something was wrong. Even so, she tried to downplay the urgency of her visit.

"I thought it'd be fun to surprise her. I did try to call when I was on the way, and I couldn't reach her."

"She's been having some problems with her phone, so that's not so strange." He made another sweeping motion with his arm. "Come on in, she'll be so happy to see you."

Tia started to take a step forward and then hesitated. She was barely five foot two, and he appeared to be at least a foot taller. Muscles in his shoulders and arms were clearly pronounced beneath the shirt. *Are you seriously going to walk into an apartment with a total stranger? Yes, he's calendar worthy but he's still a stranger!*

Finally, her little voice was making some kind of sense.

She paused and asked, "Who are you?"

"Daxon. I'm a friend of Rina's. My friends call me Dax." He slid his hand into his pants pocket. "She's in the shower. Up to you if you'd rather wait in here, or in the hallway. Or you can come back later."

Tia stepped into the doorway. A subtle blend of cinnamon and vanilla made the air in the apartment much preferable to the unpleasant smells in the hallway. She tilted her head, trying to hear more clearly. Faint sounds of running water were coming from nearby within the apartment. What little she could see of the apartment from her vantage point was encouraging. Decorated in shades of blue with accents of ivory, it certainly fit her sister's personality much more than the building or the neighborhood did. Tia recognized parts of the room from some of the video calls she'd had with Rina.

Standing in a hallway of this crappy building and seeing who might appear was a scary thought. Venturing outside alone again was even less appealing. After waiting quietly while Tia debated the decision in her own mind, Daxon was evidently tired of propping open the door while she argued with herself.

"I'll tell her you came by," he said.

The door was mostly closed by the time she pulled herself out of her own thoughts and reached out a hand to stop him from shutting it all the way.

"I'll wait inside."

"Come in then." Daxon moved to his right and towards the kitchen area, walking past a small oak table with four chairs that matched the table but that each had a cushion in a different shade of blue. In the middle of the table was a small rectangular container with the word 'Thankful' etched on the long sides in dramatic script. Blue tea lights and polished stones in various colors sparkled around and between the little candles.

"Tia, would you lock the door? Rina said some guy drunk or high on something tried to walk in here the other day."

"That must have been scary for her," Tia said. Walking into the building had been scary. Doing so every day and night had to be ridiculously stressful for Rina.

"It's not the safest neighborhood. I wish I could get her to move." He opened the refrigerator. "Want a bottle of water or something? Coffee to warm you up? She's got one of the machines that uses pods to make single cups."

Tia locked the doorknob and put on the security chain. Her own apartment wasn't in a fancy neighborhood, but this place seemed so unsafe. Dangerous. *That's so obvious, even you figured it out long before Daxon said it.*

"Something hot to drink would be great if it's not too much trouble. It's colder than I expected it to be," she answered.

"Not a problem." He leaned a hip against the kitchen counter and studied her. "Can I take your coat?"

"I'll just hang it up while you make the coffee."

To the side of the door into the apartment was a coat rack, so she didn't even have to move to put her coat on it.

Dax slowly spun a silver rack on the countertop. She could see it was filled with little K-cups. The light in the kitchen reflected off the coffee display and picked up on little flecks of silver in the hair closely cropped above his ears.

"Looks like your choices are Green Mountain Bold Roast, Dunkin Decaf, Heavenly Hazelnut or French Vanilla. There's also a couple with hot chocolate." He reached up and took down three coffee mugs from the cabinet above and to the right of the small machine. "Rina probably wants hazelnut, but I'll wait till she comes out and tells me herself."

He put a pod into the machine and flipped the lever. There must have been water in the machine already because almost immediately the bubbling sound and comforting scent of coffee filled the air.

"Which do you want?" Dax asked.

"French vanilla, please."

"You got it." He glanced at her over his shoulder. His very broad shoulder. "Sugar or anything?"

Seated at the table she was facing a short hallway. There was a doorway on each side of the hall, and a closed one at the end. The sound of the shower through the door hadn't lessened at all. Rina had been in there so long.

You've been in the apartment less than 10 minutes. Maybe she went in just before you knocked on the door. With the long showers you take, who are you to judge somebody else's shower time?

"Tia?" he said it just a little firmly, as if he'd tried to get her attention already. "Do you take anything in your coffee?"

"No! I'm sorry I didn't answer the first time."

"No problem." Cup in hand, he walked around behind her to put it on the table.

Tia opened her mouth to voice her thanks. The bathroom door swung open. A flash of excitement ran through her, chased away by confusion when a huge man dressed all in black stepped out of the bathroom.

"Who –"

The strength of Daxon's arm yanked her back hard against the spindles of the wooden chair and against him. Panic surged up into her throat at the same time something sharp jabbed the right side of it. The room began to blur, then dim.

I'm going to die without ever seeing Rina in person.

Available Now

Chapter 1 – Liam

IF THE GUYS found out how he spent a rare summer day off, he'd never live it down.

Doing these things online was more convenient, but sometimes Liam wanted to see with his own eyes what he was going to purchase, not have it filtered through a camera lens. In this case, handling matters 'in-person' was unavoidable.

Head down, sunglasses still on, Liam strode under the royal blue awnings with their crisp white lettering and into the building. In addition to the lights strategically positioned everywhere inside, sunlight streamed through the huge plate glass windows that spanned the whole first floor. Although they looked like regular windows, he knew they were crafted of a protective glass to eliminate harmful rays that might damage any of the valuable antiquities inside. As best he could tell without getting close to them in a way that would arouse suspicion, the windows were impact resistant as well.

The well-dressed man who greeted him was attired to meet expectations for the ritzy Park Avenue address in Midtown Manhattan. Liam had been here many times and was familiar with the layout already, but a certain level of procedural decorum was expected in these places. Hands loosely linked in front of him, the auction house representative still managed to grip a small tablet device. In-house communications, perhaps? The man's posture managed to be both relaxed and attentive, and he was friendly in a practiced, professional way.

"Good morning, sir, and welcome. How can we help you today?"

"Good morning," Liam said. "I'm here for the rare book auction."

"Excellent. There's quite a lot of excitement for that auction today. I'm Brett. I'd be glad to be of assistance."

Liam smiled politely, knowing full well that the same exact sentences were said to everybody who was there for an auction. Nothing here was personal, and he wasn't going to let the obsequious behavior distract him from his goal.

"Do you wish to review anything about auction procedures?" Brett asked.

"No. I'm good." Liam had already had enough of the niceties. "Lower level?"

Brett checked his tablet. "The Cascadian Salon." Then he added what was obviously a customary line. "Have a winning day."

"Thanks."

On the first floor was the boutique, where a wide array of luxury goods and collectibles were available for immediate purchase. Liam had bought more than one gift for his grand-mother over the years from among the frequently rotating merchandise. On some of the upper floors were the personnel necessary to run this one location for the international opera-tion that was this auction house.

In the back of the building and in the rear of the lower level were the auction rooms. They ranged from very large to extremely small, depending upon the type of items being auctioned and the size of the group of attendees invited or expected. Liam knew from experience that today's auction was likely to be small.

After being advised of the room number he needed, Liam made his way to the elevator tucked discreetly in the south-west corner. He could deal with tiny places again but preferred not to. He hadn't suffered the type of torturous PTSD that plagued so many other veterans, but memories of being trapped on that last mission still reared up when he least expected them. No point inviting them if he could avoid it.

Liam pushed through the door beyond the elevator and moved quietly down the steps. The staircase ended two flights down and he emerged into a tastefully appointed hall-way. Elegant directional plaques affixed to the wall indicated the path to the room he sought.

He tucked his sunglasses in his pocket. The only noise in the hall was the quiet hum of the central air conditioning, so the loud metal squeal of the door hinges was startling when he pulled it open. Liam stepped through, letting the door close behind him with a dull thump.

A woman softly snickered. "No one can sneak in here, that's for sure."

He looked in her direction and it required effort to hide his reaction. Women who looked like her never showed up at events like this – at least none he'd ever attended. If they did, he'd always attend in-person when he could, even if he had no interest in what was being auctioned.

Not that he was looking for a woman. Or a relationship. What he'd gone through after Kelsey had taught him that romance hurt like hell. It was something better experienced through words in a book rather than in person.

He wasn't going to risk going through that kind of pain again.

That didn't mean he didn't still appreciate beautiful women.

And this woman had plenty of reasons to be appreciated.

At first she seemed to be about 5' 7" tall, but then he realized her shoes were making up nearly four inches of that height. A snug, knee-length, gunpowder-grey skirt appreciated her curves in a way only well-tailored fabric could. Her hair was a glossy dark brown, and he noticed glimmers of auburn within it. The abundance of her tresses were gathered up at the back of her head in a way that was ordered enough to be professional, but relaxed enough to be casually sexy. If only she'd worn glasses, she'd have fulfilled a naughty librarian fantasy he hadn't even known he had until that moment.

"You'd think they could invest a few dollars on lubricant." As he said the words, he realized how they might sound to her, and quickly clarified, "WD-40. For the hinges."

Liam didn't know who was more surprised at his slightly awkward comment, him or her. A stodgy, high-end auction wasn't the place for innuendo, accidental or otherwise.

He held her honey-eyed stare, wondering if she'd reply to his words with outrage, offense, or if she would be obtuse about the double meeting in his words. She didn't miss a beat,

"Maybe I should do a good deed and loan them some. I usually have a tube in my purse," she said. Her lips quirked upward on one side, like she was resisting a laugh. "Lubricant, not WD-40."

Well, that was unexpected.

"Generous of you," he said at last.

"I try." She gestured with her chin in the direction over his shoulder. "You'd better check in, even if you're only here to watch."

The words were said with a slight but mischievous smile on plush lips that were tinted a rich red color. It reminded him of the wine his buddy liked to drink. Next time, instead of teasing Mason about his choice, he'd be thinking about her lips.

She turned around on her impossibly high heels and walked away. Rounded hips shifted hypnotically as she moved. When she'd been facing him, he'd struggled to keep his eyes respectfully above the generous curves that strained the buttons of her white blouse. During their all too brief encounter, Liam had noted manicured fingernails kept slightly long. The color matched her lips. There were no rings on her hands, which made him give a mental fist pump. They were soft-looking hands with long, slender fingers that would feel amazing wrapped around his --

"Sir, you have to register even if you're just observing." The comment was addressed to him, and the auction house representative sounded irritated. "We start shortly. You must register or leave."

"Got it," Liam said, pulling his gaze away from the beautiful stranger.

The older man shrugged and looked at her too, "I understand. I wasn't always this age."

"Never too old to appreciate beautiful women, huh?"

"Exactly. Just too old to appreciate them the same way I used to," the older man admitted.

Because Liam was pre-registered, it only took a few minutes to get his paperwork and bidding paddle in hand.

"I'm Tom, and I'll be here for the duration of the auction." The other man told Liam. "Any problems or questions, you can come see me or talk to another representative in the salon itself."

"Thanks, Tom." Liam leaned in a bit closer. "I have a permit to carry concealed, and I am. What's the current procedure here?"

"Speak to security at the metal detector and show them your paperwork."

Tom indicated a doorway across the room and a metal detector there, flanked by two security guards. It was a smooth process to get through security after Liam gave them his identification and quietly alerted them about his weapon. He was ushered smoothly around the detector, and into the larger room on the other side.

Liam had missed the auction item viewing opportunity that had been made available to bidders, but he'd looked over what was in preview online and read the comparative reports. The way modern auction houses simultaneously coordinated live streaming bids, regular online bids, and in-person bids was always impressive.

He already knew the item he wanted to win. It was a beautifully bound edition of romantic and other poetry written by Percy Bysshe Shelly and published not long after the poet's death in 1822. There was a chance the final price would end up outside his budget, but there was an equal chance he'd walk away with the book as his own.

The room was small compared to most venues for these things, but still large enough for at least four dozen chairs neatly set in rows. Each chair was a few feet from the one next to it, the placement clearly trying to make bidders feel they had a bit of privacy. Along one wall were auction house representatives standing with their clipboards and communication devices, ready to please bids by proxy for customers who couldn't be there in person.

The air was efficiently kept cool, providing a nice respite from the sweltering world outside the doors, and optimal conditions for the items up for bid. Each item would be brought out when it was officially presented and put up for auction. The atmosphere in the room buzzed with the excitement of the thrill of the hunt, money and stress, all tastefully subdued.

Liam was focused on acquiring a single, specific item. Nothing else.

Now, as he enjoyed the sight of the alluring woman again, he realized he suddenly had two interests today. Liam headed to the vacant chair closest to her. Her attention was now focused on the auction catalog, and it didn't escape his notice that she now wore eyeglasses with black frames.

Hello, naughty librarian.

Available Now

Infinite Weekend

———

From the moment they glimpse each other behaving suspiciously at the Renaissance Festival, their paths were destined to intertwine. Now Lance and Callie are swept up in the twisted dealings of a counterfeit antiquities ring that will stop at nothing to achieve its goals.

Lance is known on the fairgrounds by his joust persona, the Dark Knight. He's a skillful horseman, and wields the tools of the joust like he was born to it. No one knows he's working undercover in pursuit of a counterfeit antiquities ring using the Renaissance Festival marketplace to conduct their dirty business – raising money to fund terrorist activities.

Callie routinely buries herself in work at Infinite Security. She reluctantly agrees to take a holiday, intending it to be nothing more than a long weekend. Callie never thought she'd stumble
upon a suspicious character in the woods, or that he'd turn out to actually be a modern knight.

Working together in an uneasy alliance, Lance and Callie must prove who's behind the black market trade and put a stop to it. But their mutual attraction is a dangerous distrac-tion that threatens their focus on the mission. If they aren't careful, their first weekend could be their last.

ABOUT THE AUTHOR

DENISE DEMARCO, a lifetime New York resident, often uses her knowledge of the tri-state area in her stories. Genealogist, researcher, history buff, and collector of information about anything and everything, she creates stories from the heart from all that—plus, lots of imagination and iced coffee!